Shadows of the Somme

Shadows of the Somme

Paul Coffey

About the author

Paul Coffey was a journalist for almost 20 years before spending 11 years working in media and communications for the police. He left to become a freelance communications consultant and devote more time to his writing.

Born and raised in Nottingham he still lives there with his wife and their two daughters.

For my beloved Posie
and our adorable girls, Grace and Ella

Foreword

When six British soldiers died in a bomb blast in Afghanistan in March 2012, it was the biggest single loss of life in the decade long war against the Taliban. The story rightly dominated the news agenda in the United Kingdom with the media focusing on the victims and their families followed by wider analysis of the war and the country's role in it.

If the decision to withdraw British forces had not already been made a few months before, it's conceivable that this one terrible incident would have become a catalyst for those wanting to end the country's involvement in the conflict.

Six lives in one day. All of them someone's son, a brother, a husband, a sweetheart.

But what if it had been sixty soldiers? Or 600? What if we woke one morning to news of six thousand British servicemen and women being killed in one day?

It's a pointless and irrelevant scenario to play out for all manner of reasons but I often wonder how we would cope today, both as individuals and as a country, if the scale of the slaughter in the First World War was played out in an age of social media and 24 hour news.

If the deaths of six men could sicken and stun the country, what if we were to learn that almost 60,000 British soldiers had been killed or wounded in one day?

It's a figure that is simply too ridiculous to contemplate and yet, it happened on the first of July 1916.

In many ways the First World War is a conflict which still remains within touching distance of us today; yet in others, it is every bit as far away as the one hundred years that have passed since it ended.

By the summer of 1916 it had been raging for almost two years. The scale of death and destruction dwarfing anything that had been seen before.

On a single day in August 1914, before the British Army had even fired a shot, 27,000 French soldiers died. By the end of that first month France was mourning more than 320,000 casualties and almost a million by the end of the year.

It is hard to argue against today's prevailing view that the Somme and the Great War in its entirety was nothing but a blood-drenched, futile conflict in which the flower of Europe's youth was flung recklessly and needlessly into a charnel house.

In the four years of the Great War what is now known as the Battle of the Somme was simply one of several enormous offensives in which the level of carnage reached unimaginable levels ... Passchendaele, Verdun, Gallipoli, Caporetto, Lutsk, the depressing list goes on.

Yet, it is the Somme which continues to have such a hold on the British psyche. It is the reason I, like so many others, first became interested in the First World War.

What happened on that fateful summer's day in the French countryside changed the country forever. The losses were so catastrophic that no one could predict how long it would take to come to terms with such an appalling tragedy.

A Century on and I don't believe that we have, or we ever will.

This novel is my own small homage to every single one of those Tommies, who fate determined should forever lie in a foreign field.

Paul Coffey
August 2015

'I say now that nothing that has been written is more than the pale image of the abomination of those battlefields, and that no pen or brush has yet achieved the picture of that Armageddon in which so many of our men perished'

Phillip Gibbs, *Now it Can be Told*

'I have many times asked myself whether there can be more potent advocates of peace upon Earth through the years to come, than this massed multitude of silent witnesses to the desolation of war'

Rudyard Kipling
(on the war cemeteries
of the Western Front)

Chapter One

Saturday 1ˢᵗ July 1916

Stooping slightly to keep his head down he made his way along the trench, the sheer weight in numbers of men and equipment making it difficult to navigate his way through.

At one point he stumbled, instinctively reaching out to grab hold of something to prevent him falling.

"Are you alright sir?" ... he grimaced slightly, looking up at the young soldier whose backpack he found himself clutching to keep his balance. Then, as the two men's eyes met, he nodded: "I'm fine, thank you."

Continuing to make his way along the line, he never spoke but occasionally patted the arm of one or two, giving others what he hoped was a comforting smile, a gesture he hoped would reassure.

And then he thought how deceitful that was to offer hope when he knew there was so little. For a second his mind drifted, his thoughts turning to home and his childhood ... maybe his self-reprimand was the trigger.

Whatever the reason, his brief dalliance with the past flickered like a candle before snuffing itself out.

He paused and looked at his watch. Again, thoughts of home appeared inside his head ... his parents, childhood memories, Emma.

Maybe it was one final attempt by his subconscious to remind him what happiness and contentment felt like.

If it was, it worked, albeit fleetingly, before reminding him how brutal and bleak life now was. Jolted back to the present he shouted to make himself heard above the incessant sound of artillery and gunfire.

"Not long now, five more minutes," he said, before carrying on through the trench, where he found himself repeating the same deceitful gestures and pats on the arm.

He tried to look at them all. He knew some of their names, had been with them for months ... these were his men. Yet he was looking through them now, lest he betray his own thoughts.

Was he making any difference? Did he really believe that a knowing look from their commanding officer would evaporate the terror on their faces?

He knew the answer of course, just as he knew that one of his duties as an officer had to be keeping them calm, reassured and ready.

He looked at his watch again ... "four minutes men, on my whistle, over the top and the best of luck to you all."

It took every ounce of his officer persona to muster the enthusiasm needed to deliver those words and he cringed inwardly when he thought how they would resonate around him.

Some were sobbing now. He heard one man reciting a soldier's prayer while others stood head bowed listening... 'Almighty and Everlasting God, by whose Grace thy servants are enabled to fight the good fight of faith and ever prove victorious.'

Others were simply whimpering ... 'Oh mother, dear mother, help me please, don't let me die mother, please.'

He could see it now, taste it even. This was fear. Raw, visceral fear; and it was consuming everyone and everything.

Perversely, he found himself envying those who'd gone over first. At least they'd been unaware; still in awe of the artillery bombardment that had finally ceased after seven days, there they went, clambering out of the trenches, weighed down by their kit, yet happy to go, relieved the waiting was finally over and with a genuine belief that nothing could be left living on the other side.

They'd set off walking, as casually as though strolling through the wheat fields of home on a summer's morning.

How far did they get? He could guess, yet what did it matter now? The last thirty minutes had shattered every last fragment of optimism he had left.

He thought of those on the other side of the fields now, waiting, watching them approach ... how could they have still been there?

How could they have endured and survived an onslaught so intense, so ferocious and unyielding in its intensity? ... to have lived through that and still be able to think, let alone act.

How could you hate men as remarkable as that? Depressingly, how could you beat men like that? Astonishingly, they had shown themselves more than able and were now desperate to make their enemy pay for every one of the million shells that had rained down upon them.

Oh, how we are paying he thought.

"Three minutes now, fix bayonets."

His voice sounded hoarse, his throat was dry and his mouth parched. Desperate to take a drink from the flask hanging from his hip, he resisted the temptation knowing he had to set the example. 'Conserve your water men,' had been the order.

Amidst the sound of the guns and the murmurings of terrified men, the noise of retching and vomiting could be heard.

The clunk of bayonets being fixed to rifles silenced voices as men focused their attention momentarily on the order.

But the moment was all too brief and voices could be heard again.

"Oh Jesus fucking Christ, please God, don't let me die'...

Others were less forgiving, 'shut up, for Christ's sake, someone make him shut the fuck up!"

"All right men, easy now, almost there ... two minutes. Remember, don't bunch and keep apart when advancing."

Looking up and down this sector of trench he thought how unreal the men appeared, all dressed identically, standing still with heads bowed; they could have been shop dummies like the kind he'd once seen in the big department stores of the West End.

He felt sick. He knew what was waiting for them the second they showed their heads above the parapet.

Suddenly, his attention was turned to two men standing next to one of the ladders that would take them over. One of them, a stocky built man with an unshaven face, was shoving a young soldier away, the boy looking petrified.

"What the hell are you doing? You're pissing yourself! Get the hell away from me!"

The officer quickly intervened, grateful for the distraction.

"What's going on here?" he asked, "you private, answer me."

The soldier who was the focus of the other man's anger and incredulity, looked up.

The officer looked him in the eye. He couldn't have been more than nineteen. His face was ashen, his eyes hollow with fear spread across his scrawny features. Tears were running down his face and he struggled to speak.

"Sir, I'm sorry, sir, I couldn't help ... I didn't ... I'm sorry," his voice tailed off and he looked down. A dark stain covered the front of the man's trousers and the officer realised what had happened.

"Ok private, come and stand next to me. You can keep an eye out for your commanding officer, make sure I don't get into any trouble now, alright?"

The young man looked surprised and nodded, replying with a quiet "Yes sir."

Another glance at the watch, it was almost time.

"One minute. Prepare yourselves, all at the ready" ... he hadn't planned to say anything else, what could he say? But somehow he couldn't leave it that so he followed his final instruction with another.

"And forget everything you've been told about walking steadily, once we go over we're not hanging about so get your running legs ready and let's get among them." Some of the men looked across at him, surprised at what they'd heard him say. Then he heard some shouts and cheers as the adrenaline kicked in during the final few seconds.

He looked up at the sky, crystal blue and cloudless ... he closed his eyes, put the whistle to his lips and blew.

October 2015

"Emma, you're doing so well my love; Baby's doing absolutely fine, but needs your help with a really big push now."

The midwife looked up from her position at the end of the bed and smiled. Her demeanour was calm, yet assertive. She wasn't how he imagined a midwife to be. Not that he'd given it much thought but he assumed she'd be a rotund, matronly figure, who wouldn't even acknowledge his existence.

He was pleased to have been wrong.

She'd first come into the delivery room more than five hours ago when he and Emma had arrived. Even then she had brought a much-needed sense of calm to proceedings. Slender in build, early 40s at a guess, his first impression was that she was friendly and experienced. His judgment turned out to be bang on.

"Hi, I'm Rachel. You must be Emma? Get yourself settled, try and get as comfortable as you can.

"I know it's difficult but I want you to try and relax as much as possible, you need to conserve your energy, you're going to need it later," she smiled.

"Now, I'm going to ask you a few questions and then we'll have a look and find out how baby's doing. Ok?"

Even her voice was soft and soothing and she illustrated every word she spoke with a warm, comforting smile. He liked that. He liked her. She reminded him of somebody but he couldn't quite figure out whom. Someone famous? Someone from work? He didn't dwell long on it; he didn't have time.

"Arrrrrrrrrgggggggggggghhhhhhhhhhhhh ..... OH .. MY... GOD!!!," Emma screamed through gritted teeth.

His heart was pumping, his stomach churning. He was frantic. On the outside he was trying to hold it together for Emma, using the midwife as his guide. If she was calm, and she appeared to be, he reckoned everything was ok.

"You're doing really well Em," he said, thinking he had to say something.

He looked at her face, a flush of red and contorted in agony. She lay with her eyes scrunched shut, her mouth open and brow glistening. Her hair was wet with sweat.

She had never looked more beautiful and he had never been more in love with her than he was now.

Her face and body tensed as she pushed again, letting out another excruciating cry.

The midwife's gentle encouragement continued. "Emma, that's fantastic. You are so close; I can see baby's head now."

He let go of her hand and moved to the bottom of the bed. The thought never occurred to him not to look ... he wanted to see and he was fascinated and awed by what he saw.

Thinking back afterwards he recalled this very thing being discussed beforehand with friends.

"Follow my golden rule and never go to the business end. Do that and things will never, I repeat never, be the same again. You'll be scarred for life."

He was never sure whether Ben had been joking or not when he had said that.

But he wasn't scarred. And things would be the same. Of that he was absolutely convinced.

He reached out and took her hand again, this time joining the midwife with more words of encouragement. He was excited now and found himself grinning as he looked at her.

"It's amazing Em, I can see the head! You're so close now, come on you can do this," he said excitedly. The pain and concentration were still etched on her face as she relaxed for a moment. She formed her mouth into an O shape and blew a series of long breaths out. Then she gripped his hand tightly, threw her head back and pushed, her screams echoing around the maternity unit.

A few minutes later she was lying back, her body completely relaxed, looking spent. The baby was nestled against her and he recalled how they had both been told how important skin to skin contact with the mother was in those first, early moments.

He couldn't take his eyes off them, they looked exquisite.

At the point of delivery he had watched as, in those final few seconds, the midwife took hold firmly, but gently, and helped pull the baby out into the world.

"Well done Emma, you've done it, fantastic job. And congratulations to you daddy ... would you like to hold your little girl?"

As she spoke the midwife wrapped a blanket around the infant and carefully handed her to him.

A girl? A daughter ... the thought had not even entered his head as to what sex the baby was. He was all over the place.

As he cradled the small bundle in his arms he broke down, the tears coming suddenly, taking him by surprise. He glanced at Emma who was looking at him, a warm, loving smile across her tired face.

He sat there soaking up every precious second as the midwife's attention turned to Emma. While she helped her through the post delivery stages of labour, he looked down at his daughter. Her eyes were closed and she lay contented in her father's arms.

The tears had stopped now and he was feeling happier

than he'd ever felt in his entire life.

"Have you got a name for her yet?" he heard the midwife ask. He looked up at Emma, they were both smiling.

"Yes, we decided on a name a long time ago," Emma replied.

"Hello Daisy," he said aloud, looking at his daughter's face. "Welcome to the world beautiful."

Chapter two

July 1916

"Sherwood Foresters, over we go," he didn't use one of the ladders, instead hoisting himself up on to the ramparts and out of the trench. The fear was there but it was tempered by the curiosity of what it would look like, mixed with the adrenaline flooding through him.

His senses were bombarded, his eyes darting everywhere; he was desperate to see the landscape around him. Fields, lush and green, it could have been England ... trees, shrubs, wild flowers, yet scores of strange looking crumpled shapes, some moving, others very still ... littering the ground.

Mounds of earth erupted in the sky before showering down; his vision was scanning so rapidly now that his brain was having difficulty processing what he saw.

His ears rang as a cacophony of noise threatened to overwhelm him. He was running now and yelling, it wasn't a conscious thing; the men around him were shouting and screaming too.

Some of them were already several yards ahead and for a split second he worried about not leading from the front. But soon they began falling, almost in sequence, one after the other.

And then he heard the screams and the tap-tap-tap of machine guns, their bullets zipping past with a bee-like buzzing noise.

He was running harder now, almost bent double, an unconscious yet futile act by his brain to protect the body that carried it.

It was then he became aware of someone near to him, on his right side. He turned and saw the fear stricken face of the private he'd told to stay with him.

"Come on boy, stay close, keep going." But as he spoke the left side of the young man's face exploded, fragments of jawbone, teeth and flesh splattering the officer's shoulder.

Instinctively stopping to help, he reached out to grab the boy as he began to fall ... but the soldier's body rocked violently backwards as his chest and guts were blown open by a spatter of machine gun bullets.

He let go and turned to face the front, his eyes desperately looking for where the deadly salvo had come from. No time to stop, he began moving forward again but had got only yards when he felt a sudden, searing red-hot sensation in his right shoulder.

It knocked him to the ground and he felt with his left hand to where the intense pain was coming from. He looked at his hand, it was bloodied, and saw a hole in his jacket, exposing a bloody, open gash in his shoulder.

He lay on his back but managed to turn over, yelling in agony as the pressure afflicted his injury. Scanning the horizon and the ground around him, all he could see were the same crumpled shapes but now there were more, many more.

He thought it strange how the noise of the guns and shells now seemed to be quieter than the cries and groans of the wounded ... and his eyes were drawn to each plaintive cry he heard.

One man was staggering around aimlessly, his left arm severed; another was in the sitting position, holding his own intestines. He saw broken body parts estranged from their owners, and then three or four human bodies fly into the air, exploding into several pieces as a shell landed.

He tried to get up but fell forwards, his face hitting the grass, and for a second he closed his eyes and just lay there.

"Sir, sir, are you all right sir, can you move?" the voice roused him and he felt hands pulling him to his feet.

He looked at his helper, a tall, lanky corporal who he remembered for always being cheerful, no matter how bad the weather or hard the training.

How different you look now he thought.

"Can you walk sir? Shall I take you back? .... stretcher bearer!" he shouted at the top of his voice.

"No, I'm alright Corporal, look out for yourself, go on, leave me."

"Are you sure sir? That looks a pretty ba ..." there was an intense flash, a huge noise and then darkness.

He felt nothing, could hear nothing, see nothing. Then light slowly penetrated and his ears were ringing … he tried to lift his head, where was he? His body was stunned and he was unsure if it was still intact.

Slowly, he managed to turn his head and found himself staring at the Corporal. The man's eyes and mouth were open and he had a look of complete shock across his face.

"Corporal," he croaked, "are you ok? can you help me get up, I can't seem to move."

Shifting his gaze downwards it took him a few seconds to realise why the Corporal's body wasn't there.

"Oh Jesus Christ," he said aloud and the shock injected another course of adrenaline through his body, enough to help him to his feet.

Standing for a moment he struggled to get his bearings. His shoulder was in agony, his right arm useless because of it.

He had no idea where his pistol was; his injury prevented him using it anyway. He looked around for signs that any of his men were still going forward, all the time bullets were whizzing past, shells exploding.

Should he try and advance? How could he turn back now? Another shell exploded perilously close, he heard more screams and watched the lives of so many end randomly and grotesquely.

But strangely he suddenly felt an inner calm, as though he had learned quickly to adapt to the carnage around him. He no longer recoiled or winced when witnessing death and injury, instead, he simply watched it trance-like, in resigned, morbid fascination.

Up ahead he glimpsed a cluster of men who had found a small gap in the barbed wire, yards from the German trenches.

It wasn't quite big enough and he watched as they struggled desperately to find a way through. A momentary surge of anticipation gripped him as he willed them to succeed ... then they were riddled remorselessly by a machine gun.

He watched as the devastating velocity lifted them off their feet. For a moment, it appeared they were dancing; it was a macabre, puppet like scene.

The left arm of one man was ripped off while another's head exploded until the gun swept slowly to their left looking for more targets, leaving their obliterated remains cruelly dangling in mid air, entangled in the barbed wire.

He slumped to the ground feeling weaker now, a combination of blood loss from his shoulder injury, shock and concussion, from exploding shells.

Groggily, he began crawling towards a shell hole a few yards in front of him. Moving painfully slowly he was only able to use his left arm to drag himself forward. Every movement was agony; not just his shoulder, but also the small of his back.

The pain was intense and he yelled out each time he summoned up the effort to move.

He was hugging the ground now, only taking the chance to look up for a sense of direction. He became fixated on reaching the hole; nothing else mattered anymore.

All sense of perspective left him. It was as though he had become separated from his brain which was now working independently with his body, battling to survive.

Then something stopped his advance, his left hand probing and feeling for whatever it was. Painfully, he lifted his head and his eyes confirmed what his touch told him.

He felt for the leather braces on the back of the soldier's jacket, grabbed hold and pulled, attempting to drag it out of his way. And then the man stirred.

The stricken soldier groaned as he began to move slightly.

"Hey ... can you hear me? ... Can you move? We can't ... stay here," he was breathless and struggling to speak.

Dragging himself closer he raised his eyes and, looking at the number on the man's jacket, saw he was a private in one of the companies that had gone over in the first wave.

Summoning every ounce of energy he could muster, he grabbed hold of his webbing and yanked hard to turn him on to his back, the effort sending another surge of agonising pain through his body, provoking a primal cry.

On being moved, the private also screamed, both men yelling involuntarily at the same time.

When it was done they lay side by side and the sensation of being still brought some momentary respite.

"Private, listen ... to me" he said, "If we stay here ... we're going .... to die. We have to move ... do you understand me?"

The wounded man turned his head to look at the officer. He opened his mouth and tried to speak but said nothing ... instead he nodded.

Both men began a painful crawl to the crater, their progress tortuously slow and hampered by machine gun fire which made them flinch and bury their faces into the ground as bullets came dangerously close.

On reaching the sunken hole, the two men slumped into it exhausted.

It was deep enough to provide cover from the raking machine guns but not from shells, which continued to explode nearby and burst overhead.

He had no idea how long they lay there but eventually the noise from the guns became more sporadic, until finally, they fell silent.

The only noises now were were the screams and moans of wounded men, some close by, others some distance away. Several were pleading for help, others screamed for their mothers.

In the distance he also heard voices speaking in English and German. Occasionally, rifle shots would ring out.

He looked down at his left arm, incredibly his watch was still working. Ten minutes, he thought ... surely they wouldn't would they?

His thoughts were interrupted by a voice ... "Sir, thank you sir... I ...," before it tailed off.

He looked across at the man lying beside him. He was clutching his stomach, his hand bloodied as it covered a dark, red stain in the centre of his gut.

The soldier noticed the officer looking.

"Gut shot sir," he grimaced as he spoke. "Not exactly the Blighty one I was hoping for," he tried to smile but winced as he did so.

Reaching down the officer felt for his water bottle. It was badly dented but intact. He unscrewed the top and drank. The water was refreshingly cool and he rolled it around the inside of his parched mouth before swallowing.

"What's your name private?," he asked.

"Atkinson, sir ... Private Harry Atkinson ...8th King's Own Yorkshires.."

"Pleasure to meet you private," he wheezed. "I'm Captain Harris, company commander, 11th Battalion Sherwood Foresters."

It was then he realised the injured private had no water bottle with him and he reached out to hand his over.

"Here, take a drink, but go steady now...," he said.

Atkinson took the bottle and drank, wincing again as he swallowed, before handing it back.

"I don't think ... I'm going to make it .. sir," he said.

"Hang in there private and keep pressure on that wound," said Harris.

"With any luck ... the orderlies will manage to get out again ... and we can get you out of here," he added.

Putting his left hand underneath the right flap of his jacket he felt for the internal pocket where his field dressing kit was kept.

Taking it out he lifted it to his mouth, using his teeth to rip open the sealed waterproof package. Inside were two identical gauze dressings. He took them out and, leaning across the injured Atkinson, put one over the wound in his stomach. The private tensed and threw his head back hissing through clenched teeth.

Harris then took the other and applied it gingerly to the wound in his shoulder. The pressure made the pain excruciating and he held his breath before gasping and laying back.

"Thank you, sir," Atkinson managed to say.

Harris fiddled awkwardly with his left breast pocket before withdrawing a small, silver cigarette case. He managed to open it with one hand, put it on his lap and withdrew a cigarette, putting it between his lips.

With the end still in his mouth, he picked up the open case and offered it to Atkinson. "Here, have a smoke," he said.

The private looked weak but managed to stretch out his arm and take a cigarette. As he put it into his mouth he saw the captain strike a match, hold the flame to the end and inhale.

He then leaned forward holding out the match so Atkinson could do the same.

Both men put their heads back, closed their eyes and drew on the cigarettes. For a moment both looked lost in their own world.

Atkinson broke the silence: "Good job there's just the two of us sir ... I wouldn't want to take my chances with three on a match."

Harris smiled at the reference to the soldier's superstition that three men lighting cigarettes from the same match would see one of them end up being killed.

"I concur private ... we don't want any more bad luck today."

It was Atkinson's turn to smile, though it was brief as he grimaced again in obvious pain.

"Tell me private," said Harris, hoping to distract him with conversation, "who's waiting for you back at home?"

"That would be my Molly sir ... she's home ... with my ... three boys. Two of 'em ... I've not seen yet ..."

He paused, Harris looked at him through his own weakening eyes, desperately trying to keep them open and stay conscious.

"What are their ... names, Atkinson? Your boys," he asked.

"George and William ... or little Bill as my Molly calls him. They're the twins ... born this April ... Spit of their dad she wrote me," Atkinson replied, before adding: "My eldest boy Jack ... he's ... he's four now."

As he spoke, his eyes closed again and his head began to slump to the right.

"Atkinson? ... you have ... to stay awake. Private? Look at me!" Harris yelled.

The desperation in his voice roused Atkinson whose head jerked up and his eyes opened once more.

He looked over at the officer before glancing down to his stomach. The blood continued to seep through his wound, saturating his clothes, the crude field dressing and his hand.

"I'm done for sir," he rasped. Tears formed in his eyes and his voice, already weak, now cracked with emotion as he said "I wish ... I could have seen my baby boys ... to have held them ... what I'd give for that sir."

Harris reached out with his good arm and put his hand on the private's shoulder. He didn't speak, how could he? Exhaustion was consuming him and no words came.

Atkinson turned his head towards him, his face had changed, his eyes appeared sunken and his complexion was now a deathly pale colour.

He began speaking again but his voice was now a whisper and Harris had to lean forward, oblivious of the pain that doing so caused him, to hear what he said.

"I'm glad ... you're here ... with me sir ... I wouldn't want to die alone ... like so many of those other ... poor ... buggers," he heard him say.

His body went limp and his hand fell away from his stomach.

Harris stared at him. How old was he? In his early 20s perhaps? Strangely, despite having witnessed the deaths of scores of men only minutes before, watching this man die, lying inches away, affected him deeply.

His eyes began to well up, tears ran down his face and seconds later he was sobbing uncontrollably.

The pain from his shoulder and lower back was worsening, he was finding it difficult to breathe and he began thinking how long it would be before he too succumbed to the inevitable death that awaited him.

And then he heard the sound of several shrill whistles.

"Oh, dear God, no ..." he thought, as the guns began firing once more.

September 2015

Turning the key of the front door quietly Tom opened it slowly. He had learned from his error of barging in excitedly after his first day back at work, desperate to see them both, and waking Daisy who had been asleep for only a matter of minutes.

Now he crept in, shut the door stealthily behind him, slipped off his coat and walked softly into the living room. He was hoping she would be awake and he had to hide his disappointment when he saw her sleeping soundly in the cot.

Emma was sitting in an armchair flicking through a magazine.

He smiled at her, mouthed 'I love you' and then tiptoed over to the cot and peered inside.

Staring at his little girl he watched her tiny chest rise up and down as she lay on her back, both arms bent at the elbow, her fists clenched.

"Don't you dare wake her up I've only just got her down," Emma whispered smiling, as she lifted her head and looked at her husband.

"I won't, I just want to look at her. Has she been ok? What's she been doing?" he asked.

"Oh, you know ... just getting more gorgeous every

minute ... like her mum," Emma replied, a wry smile on her face as she turned the page of her magazine.

Tom bent forward and kissed his wife on the top of her head. "I'm not going to argue with that babe. How was your day?" he asked.

"Sophie came over today," Emma said, making conversation.

"She says Nick's organising a trip to France next spring, something about the war? He wants to know if you're interested in going. I said you'd ring him," Emma said, as she got up and wandered into the kitchen.

"Not sure I'm that fussed but yeah ok, I'll give him a bell," Tom added, speaking softly as he stood over Daisy's cot.

He was determined to be a hands-on dad, not just out of duty but because he adored his daughter and wanted to be involved in her life as much as he could. He could sense Emma also appreciated that.

Later that evening he was checking his emails when he saw one from his friend Nick inviting him on a four day trip to France next March, visiting the Battle of the Somme battlefields.

He wasn't sure he fancied that, military history wasn't his thing. He clicked reply, thanked Nick for asking and declined.

The next day at work was tough. He had offered to do the night feed, insisting even when Emma protested, but now he regretted it.

He was attempting to look busy without really doing anything when a text message landed. It was from Nick.

"France in the spring. You're coming, no arguments. Speak later."

Driving home after work his phone rang. It was Nick.

"Hey, how you're doing? You bored of changing nappies yet?" the voice asked.

"I'm good mate, knackered though. I offered to do the night feed last night so Em could catch up on some kip," Tom replied.

"Ooh, bad move. Listen, what you need is a weekend away with the lads, drinking some beer. You're not seriously blowing us out are you?"

The traffic was slowing up ahead and he eased his foot on the brake and came to a halt behind an enormous truck.

"I'm not sure, I'm not into that war walks history stuff," Tom replied.

"Nor was I until I went to Belgium last year. But it blows your mind Tom, once you see it. Trust me. And the beer is seriously good too. Come on, what do you reckon?"

He thought about it for a moment as the traffic began moving again. "Yeah ok, you've convinced me, I'm in," he said.

"Good lad, you'll love it, trust me. I'll tell the others you're in and email you the details," Nick added, before ending the call, leaving Tom alone in the rush hour traffic.

Chapter three

July 1916

He found himself pulling his knees up, tucking his chin against his chest as the noise intensified. Exploding shells and relentless gunfire filled the air once more, along with the screams and shouts of men.

He felt sure it was louder than before and for a brief moment he wondered how he'd ever attempted to advance into it.

After a few seconds he realised the shell hole was protecting him and he raised his head, glancing at the lifeless body of Atkinson next to him. Then he looked up and glimpsed moving figures.

He turned over on to his front, grimacing painfully, and cautiously eased himself up the side of the crater. He pressed his face into the soil and took a few seconds to summon the courage to lift his head, before peering over the top.

His eyes locked on to half a dozen men advancing forward, all of them jogging with their heads down and their bodies stooped low.

To the right and left he was aware of scores more, though their posture and equipment didn't make them look human. Instead, they resembled bulky, slow moving shapes, shuffling with difficulty over the terrain.

His focus moved back on the group in front. Suddenly, one of them buckled and fell to the ground. Then a shell exploded close by, blowing two off their feet.

One attempted to get up, his helmet lost, before suddenly dropping to his knees. Moments later he fell face down into the earth.

The remaining three were now bunched together and he saw one of them turn, shout something and direct the others with a sweep of his right arm. The three then veered to the left before leaping, one after another, into a hole and disappearing from view.

Harris thought about forcing himself to his feet, clambering out of the shell hole and continuing to advance. He was an officer, how could he simply lie there while above him men were dying?

Yet, what was the alternative? He was unarmed and seriously injured. He would be dead within seconds. Maybe that's what was expected of him, to die a hero's death.

But he knew there was nothing heroic about that. It would be a futile death, like the hundreds of others that were happening around him.

His thought process was broken by the lethal spit of bullets inches away, spurting small pockets of earth into the air, some of which spattered his face.

He ducked down, dislodging his helmet as he did so. His face was again pressed hard into the earth and his mouth was open. His tongue detected the bitter, alkaline soil and he started spitting to get rid of it as he turned and slid down on his back.

Above him the carnage continued. The only face he saw was that of a young soldier who suddenly appeared at the edge of the crater and stopped, looking down.

Their eyes met and he saw the familiar look of fear and panic on the face of the man who was gripping his rifle with both hands, pointing it in front of him, its bayonet glinting in the morning sun.

The mutual look was momentary as the soldier averted his gaze, moved to his right and continued his advance. Within seconds he was out of sight.

He wasn't sure how long it took but, just as before, the shelling finally ceased and the gunfire abated. Again, the only sounds were those made by wounded and dying men.

Reaching for his water bottle he saw it was only a third full now and he became conscious of conserving its precious content to make it last longer. The thought depressed him as he realised he was now contemplating being there for a long time. He held it and took a small sip to rid his mouth of the taste of soil.

Hearing others shouting for help he considered doing the same. But occasional rifle cracks and the monotonous tap-tap of the machine guns told him it remained too perilous for anyone to expose themselves.

He thought of a medical orderly risking life and limb to

reach him.

And what then? How would they both get back to the line without being spotted? No, he thought, it would be certain death for them both.

Instead, he lay back, removed the silver case from his pocket and put another cigarette in his mouth. As he lit it he became aware of the pain in his back, it was worsening.

Lifting his body slightly he reached around with his left hand to feel where the pain was coming from, surprised when it felt wet to the touch. He brought his hand back into view and saw his fingers smeared with dark red blood.

He sighed and it was then that he resigned himself to dying here, in a shell hole, in the middle of a field in France.

Yet, whether it was the soldier in him, or simply a basic survival instinct, his mind searched for a solution. He slid to his right and leaned forward, grabbing hold of Atkinson's jacket.

The dead man was still warm to the touch and the gaping hole in his stomach was now a congealed, sticky, dark red mess.

Using his injured right arm was agony, but he had no choice and felt for the flap on the inside of Atkinson's jacket. Having found it he removed the field dressing and this time used both on the wound in his back.

Exhausted and with his eyes feeling heavier, he fought the urge to close them and sleep, lest he never wake up.

His mind began wandering now and random

snapshots popped into his head, from old friends to places he remembered as a boy.

He recalled playing with a childhood friend at the edge of a river ... what was his name? ... Samuel ... Samuel Wallace. He pictured vividly the two young boys throwing stones into the water; there was a huge willow tree nearby ... and a bridge.

He wondered whether this was his life flashing before him or his brain's way of stimulating the body so it would continue fighting.

'So be it,' he thought to himself, bringing his left hand up towards the wound in his shoulder. He opened the breast pocket retrieving an envelope. Looking down he lifted the flap, withdrawing a piece of paper from inside.

Putting the envelope on his lap he unfolded the paper that concealed a small photograph within. He lifted it nearer his face, stared at it intensely and thought that if he was to die, then his very last thought would be of Emma.

The image gazed back at him and he looked into her round, wide eyes almost believing that at any moment she would open her mouth and speak to him.

She was photographed sitting elegantly on a chair, her petite figure in evidence despite the portrait only capturing her from the waist up. Her left wrist was resting on the arm of the chair while the ends of her fingers were enclosed in her right hand.

Her body was seated at a slight angle and she had turned her head to the right to look directly at the camera.

Wearing what appeared to be a white, cotton dress with intricate embroidery around the bust and neck, it had half-length sleeves and there was an embroidered flower on the left hand side of her chest.

Her long, brunette hair was high, rounded and curved away from her head, adorned with a pretty white ribbon which seemed to match her dress. Her face was slender with delicate features, though her lips were full.

He looked at her mouth and that small, half smile he had looked at so many times before, and again was rewarded with a flood of vivid memories ... her voice, her laugh, her touch.

His attention turned to the precious piece of paper, a letter he must have read a hundred times or more and could have recited with his eyes closed. Yet, he carefully put the photograph on his lap, held the letter in his left hand and began to read it again.

My dearest Edward

Words cannot describe the joy I felt at receiving your last letter. It is a great comfort knowing you are in good health and your spirits are high. Oh, how I miss you my love.

My heart yearns for the day you return home safely and I have never prayed so hard than I have these past months.

Our adorable little girl is growing more beautiful with each passing day. She has your eyes and I see your face every time I look at her.

You are in my thoughts from the moment I wake until

I drift off to sleep. Sometimes I dream of you and my dreams are so vivid that I curse myself for waking.

We are all so worried about you but very proud that you are doing your duty for King and country.

Stay safe my love.

Devotedly yours.

Emma xxx

He closed his eyes when he finished reading, put his head back and relaxed. The noises of the wounded and the dying hung in the air but he concentrated hard and, finally, his thoughts drifted far away, to another place where he could be with her.

"Edward, stop it, don't you dare," she was giggling loudly as he scooped her up in his arms and began running towards the sea.

"Edward!!!!!!! Noooooooo!!!" she cried out, laughing hard now as he began a swinging action with his arms as if ready to throw her into the water.

"Come on, tell me," he was laughing too.

"All right, all right, I will, just put me down ..." she said, giggling.

"Not until you tell me, I can't bear the suspense."

Earlier, they had picnicked on the beach; it was one of their favourite places to come. And it was while they ate that she revealed she had a surprise for him.

Despite his probing, the suspense had proved too much and now he just wanted to know, even if it did mean a playful threat to drop her into the sea.

She stopped giggling, looked at him and smiled warmly

... "I love you," she said.

There was a pause ... he was about to tell her he knew that and, of course, he loved her too, when she said softly: "Edward, you're going to be a father."

For a brief moment he stood there speechless on the sand, holding her in his arms as a gentle tide drew back and forth. A warm breeze blew over them as the sound of rolling waves and the cries of seagulls filled the air.

As if suddenly jolted out of a trance, he carefully let her down until her feet were touching the sand.

"Oh my good God, that's, I mean ... it's incredible ... you're incredible ... how? ... erm, I mean, how long have you known?"

Then suddenly, before she could reply he was openly berating himself: "What in God's name was I thinking, you were in my arms, I could have dropped you, the baby ... oh, Em I'm so sorry."

Instinctively, his hands reached down and gently touched her stomach and he looked down as he carried on speaking.

"If anything had happened I'd never have forgiven myself..."

"Edward! Stop talking, look at me," she took hold of his hands and he lifted his eyes and looked at her.

"I'm fine my darling, perfectly fine. And so is our baby. I'm not so delicate that I can't be scooped up in my husband's arms," she was still smiling as she spoke and he couldn't help but notice how different she now looked.

Her skin seemed softer, there was a glint in her eyes

that he'd not observed before and her complexion seemed rosier.

"I've known for about four weeks now. Only my mother knows. I hope you won't be cross that I told her but I was so unsure at first and I needed to talk to her."

He sensed her apprehension and replied immediately, cutting across her.

"Em, you are simply adorable. Of course I don't mind, it is what mothers are for. Now, tell me, are you sure everything is ok? Is there anything I can do?"

She laughed again. "Edward, trust me, everything is absolutely fine."

They began walking hand in hand, along the deserted beach. As far as the eye could see, the landscape was a bay of expansive, golden sand backed by dunes.

"I have been to visit Dr McCullough and he has assured me there is nothing to be concerned about. He believes the baby will arrive sometime in the autumn," Emma said.

"I'm so happy Em," he said. "You will make a wonderful mother. And I'm sorry I forced you to tell me … it's probably not how you were going to do it."

She stopped walking, turned towards him and looked up into his eyes. "Edward, it was perfect," she said.

March 2016

"You can't get your head around it can you? It's unbelievable," said Nick.

They were walking underneath the towering red brick monument that stood out like a colossus in the middle of the French countryside.

It dominated the landscape for miles around and they'd seen it in the distance a good twenty minutes before they pulled up in the car park. They'd spent the first hour in the visitor centre which told the story of the Battle of the Somme, before walking the 100 yards or so up the gentle slope to where the Thiepval Memorial to the Missing had stood for more than 80 years.

Now, they were underneath it, this three dimensional pyramid of arches, walking among the complex, interlocking archways which supported the 140 foot high structure.

Aside from Nick's audible comment, none of them spoke.

All were too absorbed looking at the dozens of Portland stone panels in which were engraved the names of more than 70,000 men killed in the slaughter of the Somme, yet whose remains had never been found.

As they made their way around they came within earshot of a battlefield visitor guide who was telling the story of Thiepval to two portly, middle aged men carrying rucksacks.

"...gave the job to Sir Edwin Lutyens, probably the most prolific and greatest architect since Sir Christopher Wren. His design has proved controversial over the years, there were some who accused him of being a pagan for its lack of religious symbolism," said the guide, who spoke with a northern English accent.

Tom hung back a little to hear more, while at the same time staring upwards and focusing on a panel which bore the names of several men from the Middlesex Regiment.

"It took four years to build and was inaugurated in 1932 by the Prince of Wales, later to become Edward VII. The monument has foundations almost 20 feet thick and this is because of the extensive wartime tunneling beneath this area of countryside."

The guide was carrying a book with him and he opened it as he was talking.

"Everyone talks about the slaughter of that first day when the British suffered almost 60,000 casualties on 1 July. But let's not forget that the Battle of the Somme continued until November 1916 during which time the British and German armies fired 30 million shells at each other and suffered a million casualties combined in an area just seven miles square … no other battlefield in the Great War witnessed more killing per square yard."

Tom was hanging on the guide's words, as were the two men he was addressing. One was about to ask a question but the guide looked down at an open page in his book and continued speaking: "The eminent military historian John Keegan once wrote: "The Somme marked the end of an age of vital optimism in British life that has never been restored. Even as late as the 1960s, after another world war, that single word, Somme, hung like a tremendous, dark sun over my childhood."

"I think Keegan's words are accurate in their assessment and both poignant and truthful about the legacy of the Somme which still resonates today, almost a century later."

The guide began walking away with the two men

following close behind, one of them now asking a question about where the respective front lines were in this area during the battle.

"Tom, we're going to spend another half an hour here then head into Albert for lunch," said Nick, who had also been listening nearby to what the guide had been saying.

"We'll probably stop at one or two cemeteries on the way, there's that many to see," he added.

"Yeah, ok," said Tom. "This place is staggering," he added.

"Glad you came then?" Nick replied. "I told you, it's jaw dropping. The numbers involved are astonishing. Seventy two thousand ... and they're just the ones they never fucking found."

Thirty minutes later and the five of them were back in the car. The atmosphere was subdued and for a moment no one was speaking as they drove through empty roads across the rolling French countryside.

It was Ben who broke the silence. The father of three, who was also Nick's brother in law, said: "I could have spent all day wandering around there, it's a phenomenal place."

That was the prompt for them to begin dissecting what they had just seen before Ben suddenly lurched the car over to the side of the road and came to an abrupt halt.

"Hey boys, we've got to go and see this one," he was referring to a small sign on the left hand side of the road which indicated yet another Commonwealth war cemetery.

It was at the foot of a valley a few hundreds yard from

a small French village. Tom looked at the now distinctive green and white sign which indicated a Commonwealth War Graves Commission. It pointed left and read Blighty Valley Cemetery.

It couldn't be seen from the road. Instead, they had to walk along a perfectly manicured grass path which had been laid next to a freshly ploughed field. Ahead was what looked like a small wood about 500 yards away.

As the path curved to the left the Cross of Sacrifice, the white, limestone Latin cross adorned with a bronze broadsword facing blade down, which signified a Commonwealth war cemetery, came into view.

"Jesus, without the sign you'd never know this was here, it's completely hidden from view," said Nick.

"How many are in here?"

Matt had already opened the heavy metal gate and retrieved a green book which sat behind a small brass door concealing a hole in the cemetery wall.

"There are 1,027 in here," he shouted. "The majority are Somme victims."

The others had already begun wandering through row after row of identical, white headstones.

"Quite a few Sherwood Foresters in here," said Alan, "and loads of them are from July first too."

Tom was walking towards the far end of the cemetery, glancing at the graves as he went, when he suddenly stopped. He was staring at a headstone against which a small yellow daffodil was about to bloom.

Beneath the intricate carving of a regimental badge was the inscription:

CAPTAIN,
E.T HARRIS
NOTTS & DERBY REGIMENT
1ˢᵗ JULY 1916 AGE 31.

Below the writing was the familiar cross carved into the stone, underneath which were the words: *DEVOTED HUSBAND OF EMMA AND BELOVED SON OF JOHN AND LUCY HARRIS. RIP*

He read it again, and for a third and fourth time. He wasn't mistaken.

"Hey, you found anything interesting?" asked Nick, who was now walking over towards Tom.

Standing next to his friend who was still silently staring at the headstone in front of him, he looked down. "Ah, same surname as yours. Always strange when you see that."

Tom replied but didn't avert his gaze.

"Look at the inscription at the bottom ..." he said.

Nick read it again and then said: "Jesus, his wife's got the same name as ... hang on ... your mum and dad? They're John and Lucy aren't they? Fucking hell, that's weird."

He called the others over and explained what Tom had found.

"So, he shares your surname and his wife and parents' names are the same as yours? That's incredible," remarked Alan, who was the only unmarried one in the group.

"Similar age to you as well isn't he Tom?" asked Ben.

"He's a year older, I'm 30," Tom replied.

"Do you know your family history? He may be a relative," Alan said.

"Pretty common name though Harris isn't it?" said Ben, answering for him.

"Well, it's pretty freaky anyway. Come on boys, shall we make a move? I'm in need of an enormous baguette and a pint," said Matt, who began walking towards the cemetery exit.

The others followed and they walked the short distance back to the car before heading into the nearby town of Albert. There, they found a small café and sat outside eating lunch, chatting about the trip so far.

"You ok mate? You've been pretty quiet since that last stop," Nick asked.

"Yeah, I'm fine. It was just a bit weird that's all," Tom replied, before taking a bite of his sandwich.

"I wonder what his full name was? The T could be for Thomas, now that would be even more bizarre," Nick said smiling.

The others were talking amongst themselves as Tom leaned forward and spoke quietly to Nick.

"My first name's not Tom," he said.

Nick looked at him quizzically but before he could reply Tom added: "My folks named me Edward after my mum's granddad. My full name is Edward Thomas Harris."

"You're kidding me? How come I never knew that?" said Nick, clearly surprised by the revelation.

"Because I hated it, I got called teddy bear at primary

school and dickhead at secondary. I always thought it was too old fashioned, so I began using my middle name and now people just know me as Tom," he said, picking up his beer and taking a long drink.

"No wonder you looked freaked out when you saw that headstone then," laughed Nick.

Tom smiled. "Tell me about it."

"You should look him up this Captain Harris. Try and find out what his full name was? You might even be related." Nick suggested.

"Yeah, I will," Tom said, taking his mobile out of his pocket and sending a text to Emma.

That evening he was the last one to make it down to the bar and the others ribbed him for it.

"Enjoying a bit of 'me' time?" said Matt. The others laughed.

If only, he thought. Instead, he'd been on the phone to Emma. He'd never admit it to the others but he missed them already.

"So how is it? You enjoying yourself? she had asked.

"Em it's amazing, much better than I thought it would be. The number of cemeteries and memorials is astonishing. It's pretty humbling, I had no idea about some of this stuff," he said.

"Sounds depressing," Emma replied.

"No, not at all. That's the strange thing. It's sombre yes, but pretty moving really," he added.

"Hey, I did see the weirdest thing this afternoon though. We were at one cemetery and I came across a grave of a captain killed in 1916. His name was E.T

Harris and, you won't believe this, but it said his wife was called Emma and his parents were John and Lucy. How amazing is that? It freaked me out a little to be honest."

"Really? God, that is weird. Not sure I'd like to see a gravestone with my name on it," she added.

He heard Daisy crying in the background and suddenly yearned to be home.

"There we go, bang on schedule. She's hungry," Emma said.

"Give her loads of kisses from her daddy ok? I love you, take care and I'll text you later. Ok?"

"Ok, have a good night" she said before the line went dead.

He took a seat in between Matt and Nick at a table outside.

"Right geezer, you've got some catching up to do. We've already had one," said Nick.

Matt beckoned for the waiter to come over: "Cinq plus grosses bières s'il vous plait."

"D'accord," the waiter replied smiling, before walking back inside the hotel bar.

Chapter four

July 1916

He awoke with a start, unsure for a moment of where he was as a loud explosion ripped through the air. And then it began again, a symphony of slaughter he thought to himself, as men and machines met in a ghastly, murderous collision.

The letter and photo of Emma were at his side and he picked them up and blew earth away from the paper. He was about to put them back into his breast pocket when he looked down at the wound in his right shoulder.

The dressing pressed against it was now a deep, crimson red, saturating the area around it. He opened the left pocket of his jacket, carefully tucking the treasured photo and letter inside.

He sensed more movement on the open ground above and was about to attempt moving when two large shapes hurtled towards him and he instinctively turned his head away, putting his hands up to protect his face.

"Jesus Christ ... we're getting wiped out," the voice was

desperate, terrified.

"Are you hit? George, answer me!" replied a second voice.

Harris opened his eyes and turned to see two men lying face down in the shell hole beside him.

"No, I don't think so ... no, I'm ok," the first man said.

The second lifted his head, turned on his back and shuffled up against the side of the shell hole. Looking around he noticed the body of the dead Private before his eyes fixed upon Harris who was looking directly at him.

"Jesus! You're alive .. I mean, sir, sorry, I beg your pardon sir," he could only have been around 18 or 19. His face was thin and pale, smudged with dirt. He was glistening with sweat.

The second man looked equally surprised. He too had managed to manoeuver himself on to his back and was sitting alongside his companion. Of a similar age, maybe a little older, he had a more rounded face.

Harris looked at them both, at their faces and uniforms, before finally speaking: "Yes, Lance Corporal, I am alive ... for now."

As he spoke the junior officer looked at the wound in Harris' shoulder before reaching for the field dressing in his jacket pocket.

"Let me take a look at that for your sir, it looks a nasty one," he said.

Before Harris could reply the soldier shuffled closer and began carefully removing the blood soaked dressing on his tunic and applying a fresh one. The movement made him wince and he grimaced.

"I'm sorry sir, almost done," the lance corporal said.

"What's your name?" Harris asked, in an attempt to focus on something other than the searing pain in his back and shoulder.

"Dove Sir, Lance Corporal William Dove." he replied, as he finished patching up the wound.

He could see Harris was struggling so continued talking.

"We're the fourth wave sir. Were supposed to follow up and secure the enemy trenches but none of us have got very far. It's carnage sir, I'm not sure many have made it very far at all," he added.

"I saw Lynch and Swinscoe ... they were ahead of us and looked like they'd got to the line," interrupted the second man.

Harris turned his head to look at him.

"What's your name private?" he asked.

"Amos, sir. Private George Amos," the man replied.

They were all having to raise their voices to make themselves heard over the noise around them.

"George, we can't stay here. We've got to try and go forward," Dove said.

Amos looked stunned.

"What? You're kidding right? It's impossible Bill," he said. "We'll be dead the minute we climb out of this hole!"

"We've got to try damn it, I'm not going to lie here cowering in a fucking shell hole" Dove snapped back.

Amos glanced at Harris and Dove, as though realising what the private was thinking, looked at the injured captain: "Sir, I ... I didn't mean ...you're injured ... I wasn't suggesting..."

Harris was still grimacing as he arched his back to relieve the pressure on the wound in his back. Without looking at Dove he replied: "Lance corporal ... I'm in too much pain ... to take offence.

"But Amos is right ... you'll be dead ... as soon as you stand."

Dove, who was kneeling now with his head bent low, said: "What shall we do sir? We could help get you back to the line?"

As he spoke a shell fell perilously close and the sound of the explosion ripped through the air showering all three men with earth and debris.

The blast came as the artillery and gunfire steadily began to ease, signalling the end of the latest assault. Within minutes it had almost completely stopped, the warm air punctured by sporadic gunfire.

Once again, the only sounds to be heard were coming from the wounded.

Harris looked at his two new companions. Both appeared physically unharmed but Amos was staring at something with a look of horror on his face.

Shifting his gaze to where the private was looking, Harris saw a severed leg lying at Amos' feet. He stared at it thinking how ridiculous it looked. The sole of the boot was pointing upright and he noticed that the hobnails glinted in the bright sunshine.

He looked at the rest of it, the puttees wrapped around the boot from the ankle to just below the knee. The knee was there, as was most of the thigh, but that was it; the gory sight of blood and bone evidence of the violent way it had been severed.

Suddenly, Amos recoiled in horror and began kicking the leg away from him with his feet and scrambled backwards up the side of the shell hole.

"George, stay down ... you'll be seen for Christ's sake," Dove leaned over and grabbed his belt to prevent Amos from sliding too far up the side of the hole.

"I can't stay here Bill... I can't ... I've got to get out of here," Amos, his voice panicking, pulled free from Dove's grasp and turned over on to his front, before crawling up to the edge of the crater.

"George, nooo!!! Stay down you bloody idiot!" Dove said, diving towards Amos and holding on to him. He was trying not to shout but the desperation and urgency in his voice meant he couldn't help it.

Harris could only lay there and watch as Amos attempted to wriggle free from Dove's grasp, both men almost grappling now.

"Calm ... down, George ... keep still," Dove said as he tightened his grip.

Moments later Amos stopped moving and relaxed, his face pressed against the earth stifling his sobs.

"It's ok George," Dove whispered, as he relaxed his grip and rolled on to his back.

For a few minutes no one spoke. Then, Amos turned over, wiped his face with his sleeve and said: "I'm ... I'm sorry Bill. I just ... I can't do this ..."

Finally, Harris spoke, his voice was quiet yet

authoritative.

"Yes, you can private ... and you will."

Both men looked at Harris. He turned his head and looked at them both before continuing.

"I'm sorry you're here ... but you need ... to deal with it," he was speaking slowly, his energy sapping with every word.

"Sir, I think we need to try and get you back to the line; if you stay here you're not going to make it," said Dove.

"Look at me Lance Corporal," Harris replied.

"I can hardly move ... I'm losing ... feeling in my legs. I'm ... I'm not going anywhere," he added.

"But sir, we can carry you, we can..." Dove never finished his sentence.

"We'll never make it," said Harris. "You're not ... dying for me."

The three men were silent again, each lost in their own thoughts.

Then Harris said: "How far is it ... back to the line?"

"I'd say about 75 yards sir," Dove replied.

"Give me your rifle Amos," Harris said, "and yours too," he looked at Dove.

"Sir?" said Amos, looking quizzical.

"I can't make it back ... but you two can. Leave me ... your rifles. I'll cover you while you head back ... to the line."

"Sir, you can't do that. We can't leave you here," said Dove.

"It's not a request Lance Corporal ... it's an order," said Harris.

Amos and Dove looked at each other, both men struggling for something to say.

Harris filled the void.

"Leave your kits here ... dump anything you don't need," he said.

Amos didn't wait to be asked. He wriggled free of his backpack and began shedding other bits of his kit that he was carrying.

Dove seemed more uncertain.

"Sir, there has to be another way?" he said.

"Lance Corporal, there is ... no other way. Get back to the line ... tell them ... Captain Edward Harris reports ... company advanced ... into heavy, sustained enemy fire ... advance stalled ... casualties, heavy."

Dove looked him in the eye and saw a determination that told him to accept what he was being told.

He too then began removing his backpack and as he did so, spoke to Amos. "Right George, listen. Once the captain's in place we're going to make a run for it. Keep low, don't look back and traverse your run so you're not moving in a straight line."

Amos looked back at him, his face fearful. Dove attempted to lighten the mood.

"Fancy a wager? A sixpence says I'll be faster than you," he smiled.

Amos didn't smile, instead saying: "I'll give you everything I've got Bill if I make it back in one piece."

Harris was holding one of the two rifles, going through the weapon to check it was ready to fire. He removed the bayonet to make it easier to handle.

He checked the ammunition clip was inserted correctly and drew back the bolt ensuring a round was fed into the firing chamber.

"Sir, your shoulder ... are you able to fire a weapon?," asked Dove.

"Enough ... to give you time," Harris replied and he brought the weapon up, grimacing as he adopted a firing stance lying down in the shell hole.

Amos looked worried and glanced at Dove. Both men seemed uncertain of what to do next.

"Worry about yourselves," Harris said, "I'll watch ... your back."

"Right, George, get ready. On the captain's signal we go, ok?" said Dove.

Amos didn't reply but simply nodded at his lance corporal. His face was white and he looked terrified.

Both men now adopted the same runner-like position, down on their haunches and ready to leap as though waiting for a starter's pistol.

Dove turned to Harris and gave him a resigned, sympathetic smile. "Thank you sir ... it's been an honour."

He didn't have the energy to speak. Instead, he simply looked at Dove and nodded before making the agonising move on to his front and then shuffling slowly up the side of the shell hole.

He dragged both rifles alongside him and, when his head was almost at the top of the crater's edge, he slowly brought one of them up until it was lying out in the open, his right hand gripping the handle close to the trigger.

The pain in his shoulder and back were excruciating and he gritted his teeth as he peered over the top of the crater.

The sun was hot now and there was little breeze. He looked across at the ground ahead of him and saw a landscape strewn with the debris of men. He swallowed hard and had to catch his breath at the sight before him.

Everywhere he looked they lay; crumpled, uneven shapes, some clearly human, others distorted, gruesome.

Closing his eyes briefly, he took a deep breath before bringing the rifle up, gingerly pressing the butt against his collarbone to avoid it coming into contact with his shoulder wound.

The angle was all wrong and he thought about the recoil and whether his collarbone could absorb the kickback when he fired. Not that he had a choice.

Scanning the horizon in front of him he looked for signs of movement. He spotted the gap in the wire where the group of soldiers had died trying to get through and saw their broken remains still hanging there.

His finger felt for the trigger and he looked down the barrel of the Lee Enfield, slowly moving the weapon to the right and left, looking for movement in its sights.

Without turning round and loud enough to be heard by the two men, he said: "Good luck. On three, ... one ... two ... three."

He heard Dove shout 'come on George my boy, time to go' and then sensed the two men rise up behind him, heard the scrambling of their boots in the earth and then running. The moment they did he heard shots ring out and his eyes were rapidly scanning the horizon looking for where they were coming from.

Then a machine gun opened up and suddenly his eyes saw the distinctive flashes coming from the muzzle of a gun in the distance.

He closed his left eye, brought his arm over the lip of the crater and held the rifle as steady as he could. Looking down the sight he aimed directly at the flashes and squeezed the trigger.

The weapon recoiled and jabbed hard into his collarbone and he yelled in agony, wondering whether he'd broken it. He fought the pain and with his eyes almost closed pulled back the bolt to load another round in the chamber.

He steadied himself, aimed for the flashes again and fired a second time. The pain was intense now yet he continued to fire, three, four, five times ...Suddenly, the earth around him was spitting up and he heard bullets whizzing past his head, hitting the ground around him.

The urge to duck down into the relative safety of the crater was overwhelming yet he continued to resist. He could feel himself growing weaker and his reloading of the rifle was slowing.

Suddenly, a shell exploded above his head showering the ground with shrapnel and he pressed his face deep into the earth in a vain effort to protect himself.

Lifting his head he was struggling to focus now, his vision beginning to blur. He wasn't even aiming but was merely firing in the general direction of the German lines.

He lost count of how many shots he fired and with a tremendous surge of effort pulled back the bolt on the rifle and squeezed the trigger only to hear an empty clack, signalling the clip was empty.

With that Harris slumped to the ground and slid back down into the hole. His hole. That's what it was now. This was his sanctuary, his only place of refuge. The place he'd spend his last moments on Earth, he was convinced of that now.

Except the firing from the German lines continued and even intensified. They knew he was in there. Machine gun bullets were raking the area and another shell exploded nearby, showering him with earth and debris.

It was only a matter of time now, the accuracy would improve and within seconds a shell would obliterate him. He opened his eyes, lifting his head only slightly, even though he was out of sight.

He stared at Atkinson's lifeless body. And then a thought came to him. It may work, it probably won't. But poor Atkinson is beyond caring he told himself.

Reaching across he grabbed hold of the dead man's leg.

Rigor mortis was already setting in and he grimaced as his hands wrapped around the stiff limb.

He pulled the body towards him but the action caused Atkinson's corpse to fall to one side in the same, almost seated position he'd been in when he died.

For what seemed an age he began pulling and pushing the dead soldier's legs, struggling with the weight and the pain he was in. All the while the firing continued yet he persevered until Atkinson's body began to emerge over the lip of the shell hole.

The effort was proving too much and with one last surge of sapping energy he pushed the dead body over the crater before collapsing on his back, breathing heavily with his eyes closed.

It was a strange sound that made him open his eyes, a weird, repetitive thudding noise almost in time with the chatter of the machine gun. He looked up and saw Atkinson's corpse lying on its side with his back facing the enemy line.

For a moment he gasped as he watched Atkinson move until he realised the movement and the thudding noise were bullets riddling his dead body.

He couldn't help but look at Atkinson's face, his eyes and mouth were open, the lifeless face expressing a look of shock even in death, at what was happening. Harris watched as the head jerked constantly until finally the gunfire abated and then stopped.

He looked down and felt himself beginning to lose consciousness; he didn't fight it, he was too exhausted.

He thought of Dove and Amos. He had no idea if they'd made it back or not. He pictured them running for their lives literally dodging bullets intended to stop them.

Then an image flashed in his mind and he saw the two men being cut down from behind, watching them fall.

There was silence once more and he thought how much George Amos reminded him of a boy who used to live in his village; shy, quiet, he had few friends. The blacksmith's son wasn't he? What was his name? … then his eyes closed and there was nothing.

March 2016

It was as easy as searching for a holiday or online shopping. 'Find war dead', 'Find a cemetery', all he had to do was type in a surname and initial, choose which service – army, air force, navy, merchant navy, civilian war dead – and select 'First World War' from the drop down menu before clicking 'search.'

He wasn't prepared for the resulting page – '145 record(s) match your search criteria.'

"Jesus, how many?" he said aloud.

Scrolling down he scanned his namesakes, there were all manner of Harris' – privates, lance corporals, captains, sergeants – the ages ranged from 19 to 43 – Christ, he didn't realise they were dying at that age!

He looked at the regiments – Durham Light Infantry, Northumberland Fusiliers, Rifle Brigade, South Wales Borderers – they went on and on. He had no idea there were so many.

The end columns were grave/memorial reference numbers and cemetery/memorial name. He clicked through to the next page and the next ... then he skipped forward half a dozen pages thinking the 'T' in the initials would place him further towards the end.

He was right. Halfway down the page he saw it – E.T Harris, captain, service number 16847, date of death 01/07/1916, age 31, Sherwood Foresters (Notts and Derby Regiment), United Kingdom, grave reference II.I. 9, Blighty Valley Cemetery, Authuille Wood.

Clicking on the name the hyperlink took him to

another page – casualty details. Here, the information was repeated in a panel which at the bottom, under the heading additional information, read the same inscription he'd seen on the headstone – though now there was something else: "Devoted husband to Emma and beloved son of John and Lucy Harris, The Hawthornes, Thornham, Norfolk."

It had been Nick who had suggested it. He was enthralled with the coincidence and had already given recommended websites to start searching. But he wanted to do this in his own time. He'd mentioned it briefly to his parents but aside from their being stunned by the coincidence, they were unable to add anything else.

"Your granddad was an only child and he wasn't born until 1905," his dad had told him.

He couldn't put his finger on it but there was something nagging away at him that made him want to know more. He'd felt that way since standing in the cemetery staring at the headstone. What was it? He was determined to shake it off, to the extent that he was ready to forget. What the heck, coincidences are just that … coincidences.

And anyway, he didn't have time for this. Daisy was growing more adorable by the day and he and Emma were closer than ever.

Even now it never failed to surprise him how much he replayed it out in his head, the entire episode, from the moment she walked in on him watching football to tell him casually: "I think my waters have just broke." Yeah right, he'd said. Only she wasn't joking.

Oh my God, the fear, the excitement, the realisation that nothing, absolutely nothing, would ever be the same again.

He recalled the hurried gathering of bags, the drive to the hospital where it took him all his self-control not to keep looking to his left to make sure she was ok.

'Concentrate, don't mess this up now!' he vividly recalled telling himself.

He was convinced she'd give birth in the car. They laughed about it later when he retold the story. His little girl would be born in a lay by on the ring road, with the rush hour traffic completely ignorant of the miracle happening at the side of the road.

Thank God he'd been wrong about that. He'd seen too many humorous, fluffy news stories of babies who had arrived a little too quickly – the boy who popped out in a restaurant at John Lewis, the off duty firefighter delivering a baby girl at a bus stop, the poor kid born in a McDonald's toilet.

No, that was not going to be how it was for his first born. It would be a delivery room at a hospital, with a midwife ... everything just as it should be.

His memories were abruptly halted by a bell ringing in his head. Thornham, Norfolk ... that rang a bell. Hang on, he'd holidayed there with Emma two years ago. He recalled the cosy cottage with climbing roses growing up the walls, the low beam on the stairs where he kept hitting his head and that fabulous gastro pub literally across the road.

The village wasn't very big, you could drive through it

in the blink of an eye.

He bookmarked the page on the Commonwealth War Graves Commission website and opened Google again, this time searching for Thornham.

He clicked the maps tab and saw a satellite image of the Norfolk coast with a pointer identifying the village. He zoomed in; spending a few minutes seeking out the cottage he and Emma had stayed in; then did the same with the pub.

He tried searching for the Hawthornes, Thornham, but nothing obvious appeared.

Next, he typed Captain Edward T Harris, Sherwood Foresters, Thornham. The CWGC website revealed itself as did one called www.greatwar.co.uk. He scrolled down the results list and opened another, this one appearing to focus on the Sherwood Foresters.

He read quickly, learning about the regiment's formation and its battalions. He didn't realise there would be so many. He read that more than 140,000 men had joined its ranks during the war and of them, almost 11,500 were killed.

Continuing his search he found a webpage listing some of the casualties, some even had photographs alongside. He was utterly absorbed now, drawn into events that he had no knowledge of. He looked at their faces, they were all so serious, yet he saw something else in their eyes? It was a resolute, determined look. One of pride.

What was it about men of that time? They had a distinctive appearance, he couldn't put his finger on it but he didn't think they looked like the men of today.

Their faces appeared much older than their contemporaries looked now.

He peered closely at the image of Private Maurice Sawcroft. His face was round and slightly chubby and his nose looked like it had been broken at some point. He was staring at the camera almost in defiance, his shoulders back and straight.

Sawcroft had died on 28 June 1916. There was nothing to indicate how or why. His body had never been found and the website said he was remembered on the Thiepval Memorial.

Maybe he'd seen it along with the tens of thousands of others while he was visiting with Nick and the boys, but if he had he couldn't recall.

And why should he? There was nothing remarkable about Maurice Sawcroft. The only other information about him said he was from Buxton, Derbyshire , and he died aged 22.

Yet, it was the name of another of those soldiers he was interested in. 'Captain Edward Harris,' he said aloud, thinking how strange it sounded to be saying his own name like that.

Who was he? What did he look like? How did he die? He wanted to know, needed to know. The more he was finding about the conflict, the more he had to know about his namesake. But he knew the chances were slim; a million to one shot maybe.

He thought about his late Gran and how she would always, without fail, wear a poppy every November and watch the Remembrance Day service from the Cenotaph on the TV.

For a moment he felt a little shameful knowing the only reason he had ever worn one was because everyone else at work did so.

And he regretted not being remotely interested in this when she was alive so he could quiz her on whether her own father or relatives had fought in the conflict.

How could he have not known about this? They should have taught him this stuff at school, they should be teaching it to everyone. But then he counter argued with himself … why should I know this? It was a hundred years ago for fuck's sake! It has absolutely nothing to do with today.

But in the days and weeks ahead his appetite for knowledge about the Great War became voracious; he was reading anything and everything he could lay his hands on.

He couldn't explain it. It didn't even register with him that what he was doing was so unlike him. He'd never shown any interest in history yet he had now bought half a dozen books online about the conflict and was already seeking out more.

It was drawing him in, the fascination with this grim tragedy that left him reeling and open mouthed the more he read of it.

At first he was just hungry for knowledge but as he unraveled more of those four ghastly years the incredulity that people now have about the conflict began to disappear.

He formed the view that the war that began in July

1914 had also ended in 1914, though without victor or vanquished. And that what followed was simply a result of neither side knowing how to win but remaining steadfast in their determination not to lose.

Tom realised that the more he learned, the more he had to find out about Captain Harris and the lack of any further knowledge only fuelled his interest.

It was while strolling around his local park with Daisy looking wide eyed at the world around her, that he decided he had to do more.

He sat on a bench parking the pushchair next to him so Daisy could look out across the lake. Two swans were gliding across the water while a family of ducks swam past.

He glanced at his daughter to see her looking out at the lake and he smiled. And then a thought popped into his head. It was perfect and for a moment he was annoyed with himself that he hadn't thought of it sooner.

But that soon wore off because he hoped, no, he knew, that Emma would be delighted.

"A weekend away? Where are you thinking?," Emma said, as she sat in front of Daisy who was eating mashed up banana off a plastic spoon.

"I was thinking we should go back to Norfolk. The beaches are great and it will be nice to get away, Daisy's first holiday! That village we went to a couple of years back was lovely and the pub was great too," he replied, as he made them both coffee.

"Oh yeah, Thornham I think it was. That was nice, lovely cottage too. It would be great if we could go back there but you probably have to book it months in advance," she said.

"It's all sorted, I rang them today. Amazingly, it's free next weekend. I've booked it. Pack your bags girls, we're going to the seaside," he said smiling.

"Your daddy's full of surprises isn't he?" Emma said, as Daisy had her mouth open eager for another spoonful.

Chapter five

July 1916

He could hear them. They were close, whatever they were. What creatures made sounds like that? Was it the noises that had roused him, or the pain? He didn't know or care.

He opened his eyes but shut them again quickly, unable to cope with the sudden, dazzling daylight. His senses began to respond and he grimaced as his nostrils detected a foul, pungent aroma.

The noises continued but he knew what they were now. He remembered where he was. He opened his eyes again, slowly this time, and wondered how human beings could make such sounds?

As he adjusted to the daylight his vision came into focus. He turned his head slowly and glanced up at Harry Atkinson's body, half of it lying exposed in no man's land, his head and torso hanging down. It took him a moment to realise there was something different about him, his face, it looked ... black?

He kept staring and saw movement on Atkinson's head ... he shuffled closer, despite the pain in his back and shoulder. "Harry?" he said, "Harry?" and with a surge of effort he lifted his right leg, pushing his boot against Atkinson.

As he did so, a cloud of black flies rose as one revealing the dead private's face.

He recoiled in horror, turning his head away sharply, and shuffled backwards away from the corpse as fast as he could, oblivious of the pain it caused him.

The thought occurred to him that he should be dead by now, lying next to Atkinson covered in flies. The thought made his skin crawl.

His mouth was parched and he reached down for his water bottle. It was almost empty. He considered taking the smallest of sips to conserve what was left but the need to drink was too much.

Emptying the contents into his mouth he swirled it around and slowly swallowed, savouring every last drop. When he'd done he returned the empty bottle into the holder on the side of his belt.

There was little breeze, the sun was now high in the sky and it was hot and humid. He looked at his watch ... 3.20pm. Had he really been lying here for more than six hours? The thought both surprised and depressed him.

He could hardly feel his legs now and what little energy he did have was steadily sapping away. He lay back and stared up at the sky. He'd always liked doing that. He was in awe of how vast it was and he recalled as a boy imagining what clouds must feel like.

There were few clouds now. The sky remained a brilliant, solid blue, punctured only by small flecks of black as swallows soared high.

And then he was home, his father walking from the path of the vicarage leading to the churchyard. He was wearing his cassock and surplice, holding a leather bound book under his right arm.

He watched him disappear, hidden from view by the huge willow tree that loomed large at the rear of the church. The bells in the tower were ringing, the magnolia in the garden was in full bloom and there were clusters of daffodils visible among the headstones.

And then he was inside the church, sitting at the front alongside his mother, aware of several other worshippers around him. His father was in the pulpit, he could see him, hear his voice ... deep, rich, warm.

"We have come together in the name of Christ to offer our praise and thanksgiving, to hear and receive God's holy word, to pray for the needs of the world, and to seek the forgiveness of our sins, that by the power of the Holy Spirit we may give ourselves to the service of God."

He looked at his father and then glanced behind him to see the congregation hanging on his every word.

"Jesus says, 'Repent, for the Kingdom of Heaven is close at hand.' So let us turn away from our sin and turn to Christ, confessing our sins in penitence and faith."

As his father finished speaking he and the congregation said aloud: "Lord God, we have sinned against you, we have done evil in your sight. We are sorry and repent. Have mercy on us according to your love. Wash away our wrongdoing and cleanse us from our sin. Renew a right spirit within us and restore us to the joy of your salvation; through Jesus Christ our Lord. Amen."

As he spoke he saw his father look directly at him and smile, before he lifted his gaze and continued his worship: "May the Father of all mercies cleanse you from your sins and restore you in his image to the praise and glory of his name, through Jesus Christ our Lord."

"Amen," the congregation said.

"Blessed is the Lord," his father continued.

"For He has heard the voice of our prayer," they responded.

"Therefore shall our hearts dance for joy," he added.

"And in our song will we praise our God."

The church organ then began to play and he and the rest of the congregation stood to sing To God be the Glory.

"To God be the glory, great things He hath done;
So loved He the world that He gave us His Son,
Who yielded His life an atonement for sin,
And opened the life gate that all may go in.
"Praise the Lord, praise the Lord,
Let the earth hear His voice!
Praise the Lord, praise the Lord,
Let the people rejoice!
O come to the Father, through Jesus the Son,
And give Him the glory, great things He hath done."

And then he was lying on the rug by the fire, it was dark outside. His mother was sitting in an armchair crocheting. He was resting on his elbows with an open book in front of him. The warmth from the fire was comforting, the crackle and spits from the burning logs, the only sound.

He could hear his mother's voice now. She was speaking with that beautifully soft voice which had so often soothed and reassured him. He saw her face, she was smiling warmly. He felt so safe, so secure. She exuded elegance and grace and he revered her.

Christmas morning, the frost on the windows, the smells emanating from the kitchen making his mouth water, hurrying down the stairs into the sitting room, the open fire, the Christmas tree they had decorated the night before, his parents smiling broadly, the stocking under the tree, the family dog, his dog, lying lazily in front of the fire.

The long walks together, they'd been inseparable for years, he was on the beach now, throwing a stick into the foamy tide and watching him retrieve it, his black and white coat drenched. And then he saw his father standing over his companion's lifeless body; he recalled the tears, the grief and his inability to understand why.

He saw himself pick up a stone from the path, tears streaming down his face, raging against the injustice, furious that He had not intervened. Why was that? Had he not been dutiful in his worship and prayers? Had he not followed the word of God? Where was the Lord's mighty power or mercy now, when he needed it?

The stone smashed through the stained glass window and he felt an immense sense of satisfaction.

And then he'd ran; sobbing through shame and fear, terrified he'd incurred both the wrath of God and his own father.

He hid in his secret place, afraid to come out fearing the consequences of his actions, before finally emerging as the rain grew heavier, the sky darker and the sound of his father's voice, desperately searching for him.

Closing his eyes he could almost feel himself there now, could picture the spot, so peaceful, so remote. The trickling water from the stream, the smell of the grass, the birdsong.

And now he was sitting next to her and they looked at the sky and listened to the stream. It was the first time he'd ever brought anyone to this place but she was special. He hoped she knew that.

He sat up and turned his head looking down into her eyes as she lay on the grass. Her right hand was shielding her eyes from the glare of the sun, she was smiling and he had never seen anyone so beautiful.

"I'm glad you let me bring you here today Laurel," he said.

"So am I, it's such a pretty place Edward," she replied.

His heart was racing now, he'd never felt anything like this. He thought back to the very first day he set eyes on her when she'd moved into the village with her widowed father.

Ever since that day four months ago she had been almost constantly in his thoughts. He recalled the spine tingling moment he approached her following Evensong at his father's church and plucked up the courage to talk to her.

Even then it was stilted, awkward, made worse by her father standing close by and able to hear every word of their embarrassed, teenage conversation.

She was older than he was, cleverer and daring. That had surprised him.

It had been her idea to meet him secretly, telling him he simply had to find somewhere private.

And now they were here lying side by side, he was blissfully happy, his heart racing and his mind a crazy, jumbled, heady cocktail of thoughts befitting a 15 year old teenage boy.

He leaned forward, her scent was intoxicating. The last thing he saw before closing his eyes was her mouth opening to meet his.

He thought about where she was now. Was she married? Had the war widowed her as it had done so many others? And then Emma ... he saw her face. Oh my God. She would be a widow soon too. He pictured her opening the telegram, unfolding the crushing confirmation of her worst fears.

He saw her collapse, sobbing uncontrollably, and his mind raced through friends, family and acquaintances who he hoped would be there to hold and comfort her in her desolation.

And then he saw his beloved daughter, the little girl who would never know her father, remaining blissfully unaware of the pain her mother was in. Except he was unable to see her, he couldn't picture her face and his mind struggled desperately to locate the memory of what she looked like.

He had to be close now; surely death couldn't be far away. There was no way back, he had long reconciled himself to that. His life was slowly ebbing away, his wounds were beyond repair. He knew that now.

Yet, the natural instincts were to resist and he figured that was why he was still alive, a mere bystander to a battle his body continued to fight but could not win. He almost smiled at the irony.

For a moment he wished his death had been quick. But then he looked again at Atkinson and thought of the other lives he had seen ended that day. He saw again the heads of men explode, bodies obliterated by bullets and shells.

And he was grateful. Because he knew that to die so violently, so randomly, so abruptly, denied any of those men the chance to search their memories one final time.

He looked up again at the sky; there were more white clouds now. The noises of the dying were still there, along too with distant voices. He was too far away to hear what they said but he didn't need to know to be able to detect the fear and desperation in their voices.

As he listened his eyes were drawn to movement a few feet away. A small bird had landed and was pecking away at the soil, nervously lifting its head and looking around for signs of danger. A wag tail.

He looked at its distinctive black and white markings and was again reminded of his childhood days. He watched as the bird turned, all the while pecking away at the ground, its tail rhythmically bobbing up and down.

The bird lifted its head, froze and fixed its eyes directly at him. Then he watched its wings open and it flew off into the blue sky.

April 2016

Walking beneath the impressive wooden archway above the gate which led into churchyard, Tom glanced at the headstones either side of the gravel path as he headed towards the church.

It loomed large and seemed far too big for such a small village.

But then he remembered seeing other similar size churches in the surrounding area and thought it must be a peculiarity of the area.

He checked his phone for any sign of texts from Emma and was pleased to see there were none. He'd left her reading in the garden of the cottage while Daisy was sleeping and told her he was going for a walk and to explore.

Entering the porch of the church he used his right arm to push open the wooden door. Its weight surprised him and he had to use more strength than he thought to open it. He stepped inside and immediately felt a drop in temperature as a result of the thick, stone walls preventing any warmth from penetrating.

There was no one inside and he realised he'd never been inside an empty church before. Not that he frequented them often. The last time had been at Helen and Mark's wedding – Emma's friends.

He thought of that briefly, only to compare the atmosphere of that church with the one he was now standing in; then, the sunlight streamed through the stained glass, there was a mass of white flowers and smiling faces squeezed in the pews.

Here, although the sun again flooded the interior with light, it felt cool. He walked down the aisle towards the nave. At the end two shallow stone steps led up to it where the altar was draped in a blue cloth. A crucifix stood in the centre.

Beyond it were five arched, stained glass windows that together gave the appearance of giant multi coloured glass fingers.

He turned and looked back from where he'd walked. On his left there were more stained glass windows, not as tall as in the nave but wider and set high up in the wall.

He walked towards the pulpit wondering what type of wood it was made from.

Above him to the right his attention was drawn to a white stone tablet mounted on what appeared to be a black marble base.

To the Glory of God, THORNHAM dedicates this tablet in memory of her sons who fell in the Great War 1914-1919.

Below it were listed 16 names of soldiers against which their rank, regiment and where they died was listed. He read down and saw there were two private Proudfoots who had died in France. He assumed they were brothers.

And there it was again, the first name on the memorial ... Capt E. T Harris, Sherwood Foresters, France.

Seeing it again had a similar effect to standing in the cemetery in France, although he also felt ... what was it? Disappointed? Yes, he was.

Clearly, Harris was going to be on the village memorial, why wouldn't he be? But what else did he expect it say? He rebuked himself for somehow thinking there would be more to discover.

He glanced at it one final time and then turned away, walking down the right hand side of the church past row after row of wooden pews. Along the wall were other plaques and tablets; one in brass thanked the generosity of Mrs Porcher for helping restore an ancient screen.

Another was from the Incorporated Church Building Society dated 1903, which granted £40 towards repairing the church on condition that it would be for free to use by all parishioners.

Then, he saw another, in the corner near the porch door where he had walked in. Walking towards it he saw what appeared to be a framed handwritten letter and photograph hanging on the wall.

As he got nearer he saw the black and white photo was clearly old and was of a soldier standing with his right forearm resting against what looked like a tall, thin wooden table.

He looked at the photo briefly before focusing on the plaque. As he started to read he felt the hairs on the back of his arms and neck stand.

*To the Glory of God and in the faith of Jesus Christ
this plaque was erected in memory of Captain Edward
Thomas Harris, 11th Battalion Sherwood Foresters, who
fell in the Great War 1914-1919.*

*Captain Harris, who was the son of the Rev John
Harris, vicar of this parish between 1908 and 1924, and
his wife Lucy, died on the first day of the Battle of the
Somme - 1st July 1916.*

The Blood of the heroes is the seed of freedom.

He read it twice before his eyes moved to the right
where the framed photograph and letter hung. It was
typed on white paper, which had clearly been folded at
some point, and dated July 1916.

Dear Rev and Mrs Harris

*It is with real sorrow that I write this letter for it
brings you I am afraid, very grave news about your son
Captain E. Harris.*

*He played a gallant part leading his men in an attack
on the German positions on 1st July. I am deeply grieved
to say that sadly, Captain Harris was wounded and
died of his injuries.*

*I cannot tell you how sorry I am; in fact I can assure
you there is not a man in the battalion who does not feel
his loss as a personal blow. He was highly regarded by
his men and officers who admired his fine sturdy
character and his unfailing cheerfulness.*

He cared deeply about each man in his Company and

85

did so much to reassure and inspire them in the days leading up the attack.

Captain Harris was an excellent officer and a fine example to all.

I wish I could help to soften the hardness of your sorrow, though I am sure you take comfort in knowing he gave his life in a sacred cause for right and justice. It is the greatest sacrifice a man can make and follows in the footsteps of self-sacrifice and duty that Our Lord himself once trod.

Let pride then be mingled with your tears.

We laid him to rest in a small military cemetery at Authuille by the side of several of his comrades who have died that England might live, and a cross now marks his grave. His soul we commended to the loving care of our heavenly Father, who will keep him until that day when you will find him again never more to be parted.

May God comfort and console you both in your sorrow; this is the prayer of all who knew your son.

In deepest sympathy

L.M.C Roebuck, CHAPLAIN, C of E, 11th Battalion Sherwood Foresters Regt, B.E.F

Tom finished reading and looked at the photograph. The man in the image stood upright, his face passive, eyes staring into the camera.

He took a step closer, his face almost touching the glass of the frame. His eyes were scanning the photo repeatedly in an attempt to absorb every tiny detail he could of the man standing before him.

The soldier's head pointed very slightly upwards and was angled away from the camera rather than facing it head on. It meant more of the left side of his face was able to be seen than the right.

It was a symmetrical face cradled by a thin chin. The nose was slim and the man's eyes had a deep set, thoughtful look about them.

The peak of his cap came down low preventing any hair from being seen.

His left ear, the only one visible in the picture, was almost flat against the side of his head.

Harris took the iPhone out of his jeans pocket, swiped the screen to open camera mode and held it steady in front of the frame. He took pictures of the letter, the photo and plaque and was about to slip the phone back in his pocket when the door of the church opened loudly.

He was standing so close that he had no time to move into view. Instead, the door swung open, a woman walked in and, as she went to close the door, she caught sight of him and shrieked.

Spinning round to find her standing in front of him, both hands brought up to her face, Tom saw a look of shock and fear in her wide eyes.

"What the? Oh my God," she spluttered.

"I'm … I'm sorry, I …" he said, but she cut him off before he could say anything else.

"Why are you hiding behind the door? You scared the hell out of me," she said angrily.

Her hands had come down from her face now and she

was looking at him accusingly.

She swept a hand through the side of her hair and he saw that her cheeks were flushed red and she was breathing hard.

"I wasn't hiding," he protested sharply. "I was looking at this," and he turned and pointed to the plaque and photo of Captain Harris.

"I'm sorry I startled you, honestly, I had no idea you were about to walk in," he added.

She looked at him quizzically and he felt she was weighing up how genuine his explanation was. She must have believed him because her demeanour relaxed and her body language became less defensive.

"Well, you scared the life out of me," she said, smiling as she did so.

The smile lit up her face and he saw someone completely different to the woman who had screamed seconds ago. She was naturally pretty with wide round eyes and a small nose. Her complexion was fair and it didn't appear she was wearing any make up.

She had straight, brunette hair which was almost shoulder length and the right side kept falling in front of her eyes, meaning she had to keep sweeping it away with her hand.

"I'm sorry, I don't usually hide behind church doors," he said, smiling too.

"It's ok, I just wasn't expecting anyone to be here. You're not from around here are you?" she added.

"No, I'm only visiting for the weekend." He thought about telling her why he was there and what he was looking for but didn't.

He sensed she was nervous being alone in an empty church with a complete stranger and he felt awkward standing there. "It was nice to meet you and I'm sorry again," he said as he made for the door.

"Don't worry about it, and yes, nice to meet you too," she said, stepping aside so he could open the door on his way out.

Chapter six

July 1916

The light was fading as darkness approached and blackness was beginning to envelope the battlefield. For the exhausted soldiers left standing in the trenches, numb from the carnage of the day, the groans coming from the wounded, left lying where they fell, chilled the blood.

At irregular intervals the sky would suddenly illuminate from a Very light followed by sporadic gunfire and shell blasts.

It made for an eerie atmosphere, made worse by wounded men appearing from the gloom after crawling back to their lines. Scores had returned, some so badly injured that the effort killed them as they made it back across.

There was furious activity in the front line trenches with stretcher bearers and other troops struggling to cope with the numbers of injured.

They were also struggling to navigate their way back

through the communication trenches taking the wounded to the dressing stations and casualty clearings simply because too many men were lying either exhausted or injured.

"Sergeant Quigg? Sergeant Quigg? We need to get these men moved out of here," said an officer, who was speaking as he clambered over a soldier lying still on a stretcher.

The sergeant was doing likewise in the opposite direction as the two men moved towards each other.

"Yes sir, we're doing the best we can but we're not set up for these kinds of numbers," he replied.

The Lieutenant looked weary. His uniform was disheveled and caked in dirt.

There was dried blood on his face from a cut above his left eyebrow.

"I know that sergeant," he said, speaking sympathetically. "But we've got to clear these lines. We've got to be ready for a potential counter attack and we can't do that with a line full of wounded."

He lowered his voice, putting his hand on the sergeant's shoulder before adding: "We both know many of these men aren't going to make it but there are those who can. That's why we need to get them out of here if they are to have any chance."

Both men were leaning back against the side of the trench as two soldiers hobbled past, one being supported by the other.

"I've got every available able bodied man helping the orderlies Lieutenant but it's slow. And for every one we manage to get down the line more keep coming in. And there are still scores of them out there sir," the sergeant added.

He was a short, stocky man, with a weathered face and a thick, bristling moustache and he spoke with a deep, northern accent. The officer was much younger, both in years and appearance.

"Then we need to round up more of the walking wounded and get them to help too. See to it sergeant," he said. "And be careful sending men out to bring survivors back in. We can't risk losing any more today," he added, before turning round and heading back down the trench.

"Yes sir," the sergeant replied, staring at the officer as he walked away before turning to look at the men around him.

He was about to speak to those in earshot when suddenly voices ahead caught his attention.

"Hey, here's another one, give me a hand someone," a voice was heard.

"Steady now, keep your heads down," another said.

The sergeant made his way towards them and looked up to see a man being hauled into the trench from the ground above. His face was etched with pain and he cried out in agony as two pairs of arms dragged him in.

"Go easy now, he's in a bad way," one man shouted.

Another turned looking directly beyond the sergeant and shouted desperately: "Stretcher bearer, we need a stretcher bearer."

The sergeant looked down at the man who had been dragged in from the ground above. He was a private with the King's Own Yorkshires. He was conscious and lay writhing in pain and groaning on the ground.

One of the soldiers who had helped him in was kneeling over him, lifting his head to offer a water bottle.

The sergeant looked down and saw that the wounded man's left leg was soaked in blood. There was a bloody stump where his foot had once been.

He knelt down next to him too and the man looked up, his eyes wide with pain and fear.

"It's all right lad, we'll get you sorted," the sergeant said, putting a comforting hand on his shoulder.

'Excuse me sir, we'll take him from here," the sergeant turned to see two men crouching down with a stretcher.

Moving aside he watched with several others as the man was lifted on to the canvas and carried away.

Looking around he gazed into the faces of the men. All had the same exhausted, numb, vacant expression.

Wanting to say something, anything, in an effort to lift their spirits he wondered if they would even hear it, never mind listen.

Instead, he simply looked at some of them, smiled sympathetically, and said: "Right lads, I know you're tired, but there are men here who need your help. They're counting on you."

"Sergeant, what about those still out there? We're going to bring them in aren't we?" said a voice.

The sergeant turned round to see a young private sitting slumped against the side of the trench, his wrists leaning on his knees.

"It's too dangerous lad and we've got our hands full

here," he replied.

There were murmurs from the other men but it was the private who spoke again.

"But sarge, we can't leave em! They won't ... well, they'll be for it sir," he added.

The sergeant scanned their faces. He knew they were appalled at the prospect of leaving wounded comrades out there in the open. Inside, he agreed but he had to tread carefully.

"Look around you lad," he said. "Our hands are full here. We owe it to every one of these wounded men here in the line to get them treated as quickly as possible. We can't do that if we lose more going to fetch the others in."

"But sir, they'll die!" said another desperate voice.

He swivelled his head towards the man who spoke.

"There's never been a day like this private. We're not able to help everybody. That's the way it is and I don't like it any more than you do but those are the orders."

The men fell silent and the sergeant was about to walk back down the line when a young soldier stood up from his slumped position on the ground.

"Sir, I know where Captain Harris is. Let me go and bring him in please sarge, he's in a bad way. He won't make it if he stays out there." Other men overheard and again the murmurings started.

"How do you know where Captain Harris is private?" the sergeant asked.

"We saw him sarge, we had to take cover in a shell hole and he was in there. He's in a bad way sir."

The sergeant paused, he was clearly thinking. He knew

Captain Harris was well liked by the men and he liked him too. He was always fair and he wasn't a stickler for formalities such as standing to attention and saluting when he appeared. The sergeant liked that about him.

He looked at the soldier standing in front of him and said: "Who's we Private and what's your name?"

"Amos sir, private George Amos. Myself and Lance Corporal Dove was with him. He helped us sir, I owe him," he said.

"Alright, slow down Amos. What do you mean and where's Lance Corporal Dove?" the sergeant added, intrigued to know more and aware more men were listening to the conversation.

"We couldn't go on sir, we jumped in the shell hole and there was Captain Harris. He's badly wounded, he stopped one in his back and shoulder I think. He told us to get back to the line and said he'd cover us. We gave him our rifles sir and we ran for it while he fired at Fritz," Amos was speaking quickly, excitedly now.

"Bill, I mean Lance Corporal Dove, grabbed me and we made a run for it. I ran like billy ho, I could hear the guns start up, they'd seen us. I heard a rifle firing and knew that was the Captain," he said.

"I never looked back sir, I just kept on running. Bill was in front of me, told me to keep my eyes fixed on him all the time. We was nearly back when a shell landed … he just disappeared, vanished. Gone, just like that … the lance corporal I mean."

His voice tailed off and his eyes were no longer looking at the sergeant but were simply staring straight ahead.

There was another pause before the sergeant spoke.

"It's too risky private, there's no guarantee you'd find him and, well, you know how it could be," he said.

"Please sir, I can find him, I know I can. Let me try!"

"I'll go with him sarge," said a voice.

The sergeant turned to see a heavy, muscular man had stood and was facing him. He recognised the face. He was a pain in the neck out of the line but during a battle you'd do worse than to go in standing next to Private Eddie Bousefield.

Of all those who had survived the day, Bousefield looked remarkably composed and least affected. He was still holding his rifle and didn't share the same exhausted, haggard looks as the others.

The sergeant beckoned him over until the two soldiers were stood next to each other.

"Right, you've got thirty minutes. If you haven't found Captain Harris by then, you get your arses back here. And be bloody careful. Do you understand me?" he said.

The two soldiers looked at each other but it was Bousefield who spoke.

"Understood sarge. Right, let's go and bring the Captain in," he said.

April 2016

He was struggling to sleep. Again. It was a still night and the only sounds he could hear were the clock ticking in the spare room and Emma's restful breathing.

Yet his thoughts were elsewhere and he couldn't decide whether lying there replaying everything he'd found out about Harris, was the cause of his insomnia or merely something to fill the void while he waited for sleep to come.

Either way, it was hardly helping. In the darkness he could see Harris, standing tall, his impassive features staring back at him. He'd looked at it so often it was virtually imprinted on his memory now.

His thoughts again went to the Chaplain's letter, he'd read that dozens of times too. Had he seen Harris' body? Did he know how he'd died or was he passing on what he'd heard from others?

Emma murmured something before turning over and resuming her quiet sleep and he briefly lost his train of thought.

He reached over and touched his phone, the screen lighting up to reveal the time ... 2:50am. He sighed and changed position, this time lying on his back. He resumed his thinking. Where was Harris shot? Did he die immediately or did he have time to know that death was coming? He'd often wondered this.

His mind changed tack again and now he was picturing the Somme battlefields, both in their vivid colour of today and the grainy black and white moving images of a century ago.

A week before he'd discovered the original Battle of the Somme film, the historic silent documentary made at the time, which depicted the build up, the battle and its aftermath. He'd seen it referenced and then watched it online. He'd been mesmerised by what it showed.

He'd started watching it a second time, this time

looking at the faces of the men in the vain hope of spotting Harris. After a few minutes he turned it off, telling himself it was a ridiculous thing to do.

It began to rain and he lay there listening to it against the window. He could feel sleep finally approaching. As he waited for it to come he began to realise what it was he was feeling ... envy? Was that what it was? How else could he describe it? Curiosity maybe?

No, he was envious ... of Harris and the millions of Tommies who had fought in the conflict.

He would never admit it to anyone, they'd think him mad, naïve, ridiculous. Yet, he couldn't help feeling that way; he pictured himself in a trench, rifle in hand. And then sleep consumed him.

"Tom? Tom? Wake up Tom, it's eight thirty," Emma was beside him, nudging him awake.

He struggled to open his eyes, squinting at the clock radio beside his bed that he never used. He dragged himself out of bed, cursing as he did so.

"I was awake for hours in the night, couldn't sleep," he said to Emma as he hurriedly began getting dressed.

Half an hour later he was in the car on the way to work. The traffic was the usual stop start and it was still raining. The radio was on and the presenter was interviewing someone about early intervention in troubled families. But he wasn't listening.

There had been no time to shave or shower and instead he'd simply splashed hot water on his face, got dressed and was out of the door, kissing Emma and Daisy on the way.

"I'll text you later," he said, stepping out of the door into the rain.

Now, he was in stationary traffic and the monotony of the windscreen wipers was hardly helping his tired head.

He glanced out of the near side door window and watched an elderly man, walking stick in hand, shuffling slowly along the pavement in the heavy drizzle. He had his head down, chin tucked against his chest, to protect himself from the elements.

He watched as the man paused at a pedestrian crossing in front him, pressing the button which activated it. The lights changed to red but the traffic wasn't moving and a battered white van had stopped in the middle of the crossing, blocking the old man's way.

Tom's eyes followed him as he attempted to navigate his way across the road and at one point he turned his head and seemed to glance directly at him sitting behind the wheel.

But then he looked away and stopped for a moment as he was forced to turn front on to get through the narrow gap between the rear of the van and his car.

By now the lights had turned green and traffic was flowing on the other side of the road. Looking through the rain soaked windscreen he became aware of movement in his peripheral vision.

He could predict what was going to happen but felt powerless to stop it. An oncoming car came into view just as the old man stepped out beyond the van. He yelled out a warning, putting his hands out in front of him as he did so.

Then he averted his gaze, squeezing his eyes shut as he heard a screech of brakes. A split second of silence and he looked to see the old man had toppled backwards against the side of the van, narrowly escaping being hit by the car, its female driver looking shocked before she drove on.

He opened the door and got out of his car. He was only a few feet from the pensioner, who looked even more unsteady on his feet.

"Hey? Are you ok, are you hurt?" he asked.

The man turned to look at him and shook his head. He was standing right next to him now and reached out his hand to help keep him steady.

"That was close, it could have been nasty," he added. The man didn't reply.

"Look, let's get you out of the middle of the road," he said, taking him by the arm and walking him slowly to the other side of the road.

By now the traffic was beginning to move freely on both sides but his empty, stationary car was now causing problems with motorists having to pull out to get past.

He got the man to the other side, helped him sit against a low wall and said: "I've got to move my car, I'll be back in a sec," before dashing back across the road.

He pulled his car over, put the hazard lights on and returned to where the pensioner was sitting.

"Are you sure you're ok? Can I get you anything?," he asked.

The man was wheezy and sat puffing for breath. He was bent forward resting both hands on his walking stick.

He looked up and said: "I'm alright lad. It was that bloody van's fault. Good job I'm quick on my feet," he said, smiling.

Tom returned the smile before saying: "Have you got far to go? It's pretty wet to be out and about."

The old man, who he reckoned was in his late 70s or early 80s, put his weight on his stick as he stood up.

"I'm going down the Legion. They do a nice cup of a tea and I have a natter with some of the other blokes," he said.

"Thanks for stopping lad," he added, before starting to walk away.

"Hey, listen; let me give you a lift. I'm heading that way; it's on my way to work," Harris said.

The old man stopped and turned his head. "You're ok lad, you've done enough."

"No, it's fine, honestly. I'd like to. Get you out of this rain too."

He could see from the expression on his face that the man was thinking about it. He didn't take long.

"Well, if you're sure. It'd save me legs," he said.

Two minutes later they were sitting in his car as it made its way slowly through the rush hour traffic.

The two men made small talk about all manner of things from the weather to traffic, his car and the price of petrol. Fifteen minutes later the car pulled up outside the Royal British Legion building.

"Right, here we are. That's saved you getting soaked," he said.

"Much obliged to you lad, thank you," the man replied, releasing his seat belt. He opened the door and was about to climb out when he turned and said: "You can come in for a cuppa if you like, they do a lovely brew here. You might even get a biscuit if you're lucky," he added smiling.

Tom was about to politely decline; he was already late for work. Yet, something held him back. He looked at his watch.

"Thanks, I'd like that. I'm not working this morning anyway," he lied.

The man seemed surprised but pleased by his answer and, reaching out his right hand, said: "Good lad. I'm Arthur."

He shook his hand, surprised at how firm his grip was, and replied: "Nice to meet you Arthur. I'm Edward, but my friends call me Tom," he said.

From the outside the building resembled one of those working men's clubs that frequent towns up and down the country, or a community centre. Its flat roof and white painted exterior made it look pretty soulless.

Perched above its entrance was a flag pole and he looked up to see the Union flag hanging limply in the grey, breezeless sky.

He stepped ahead and opened the door for Arthur who was following a few steps behind. Inside, the low ceiling gave the interior a squashed, claustrophobic appearance, though the room was illuminated by several bright, fluorescent lights.

There was a bar at one of end of the room that had a

grill pulled down indicating the early time of day.

Around the edges was sofa style seating, in a dark, tartan style pattern, with round tables and chairs in the middle of the room.

Around half a dozen other men, all what he'd consider elderly, were inside, some sitting together chatting.

One of them he noticed was wearing an army style beret adorned with several cap badges.

As the two men entered some of the others looked up in their direction and he heard voices: "Morning young man" 'How do Arthur," and "You've brought the weather with you today Arthur."

"Morning lads," Arthur replied, making his way to a table in the middle of the room. "This here is Tom, gave me a lift in the rain so I invited him in for a brew," he added, without even turning around.

The men looked at his guest, some nodding and smiling, others saying 'good morning.'

"You're in bad books Arthur, Joan's gunning for you," said the man wearing the beret.

He was smiling and turned his head towards the end of the bar where, through a serving hatch, an elderly woman could be seen.

"Ain't that right Joan?" the man shouted, "Arthur's here," he said grinning.

Seconds later the woman appeared through a swinging door, drying her hands on a tea towel. She was small and rotund, with white permed hair and glasses. She reminded him of his grandmother.

"Arthur Roebuck," she said out loud, walking towards

him, "that's the last time I ever bake you anything. That apple pie was sitting in a bag under a table for a week!"

The old man looked apologetic. "I'm sorry Joan, I forgot it. The sight of your lovely smile distracted me," he said smiling.

"Hmph, well don't think you're getting off that lightly Arthur Roebuck. And I mean it, don't come asking again because you won't get any. I suppose you want your usual?" she asked.

"Aye, mug of tea and a couple of slices of toast please love," he said. "This here is Tom," he said, looking over at him.

"Hello, nice to meet you," Tom said. He thought he detected a hint of suspicion on the woman's face and added quickly: "I gave Arthur a lift in this morning."

She looked down at where he was sitting and said: "Known him long have you?"

"I am here you know," Arthur said. "He's a good lad Joan, helped me out this morning when some bugger almost ran me over. I've told him how good your tea is. We're both gasping."

Joan seemed to relax and she smiled before turning and heading back to the kitchen. "I suppose you want toast as well then do you?" she said glancing back at Tom.

"Err, yes, please, if it's no trouble," he added.

"Nothing's too much trouble for Joan. She's a grand lass," Arthur said.

A voice piped up: "Got his eye on our Joan has Arthur ain't you?"

Arthur didn't even turn his head but replied: "I've more chance than you'll ever have Derek. She likes my northern charm."

A few minutes later the two men were supping strong tea from Royal British Legion mugs and eating buttered toast.

When they'd finished, Arthur stood up, looking unsteady as he rose from his seat.

"Goes in one end nowadays and comes straight out the other," he muttered, "sign of age that," he said, and he shuffled off in the direction of the men's toilets.

While he was alone Tom took the phone out of his pocket and sent a text.

'Hi, feeling pretty rough after being up in the night. Not going to make it in today. Tom.'

Within a minute he was reading a reply. 'No worries, thanks for letting me know. Hope you feel better soon. Justin.'

"My neighbour's daughter keeps trying to get me to have one of those."

Tom looked up to see Arthur awkwardly sitting himself back down in his seat, his eyes fixed on his phone.

"But there's no point, I'd never use it. I struggle with the remote control for the telly," he said laughing.

"They're handy sometimes. But they do tend to take over your life," Tom replied."

And then, the two men simply sat and chatted, occasionally joining in conversations with the others. For how long he didn't know. It was an unlikely pairing. He knew that. Yet, there was something about this old man and he felt drawn to him.

He didn't know why. He thought it may have something to do with never really knowing his own grandfather who had died when he was young. But it was more than that.

He felt a strange sense of belonging. It was comfortable sitting amongst these old men.

Eventually, some of them began to get up and leave, cheerfully wishing each other all the best as they put their coats on and walked out of the door. One of them turned to Arthur as he put a heavy overcoat on.

"You should escape while you can lad, stay any longer and Arthur'll start wheeling out his war stories," he said, in a thick Glaswegian accent.

"Aye, well it wouldn't take long to tell yours would it Jock?" Arthur snapped back.

He looked at Tom adding: "Only a young whipper snapper is Jock. He missed all the big stuff."

"Night patrols in Belfast were no cake walk Arthur," the man replied. "We cannae all be war heroes."

Arthur turned to look at him. "Don't get your kilt in a fizz Jock, I'm only messing with you. We've all done our bit, no matter where or when."

The two men stared at each other before the Scotsman smiled, glanced across at Tom and said, as he turned and headed to the door, "just dinnae ask him about his medals if you wanna get home this side of Christmas."

Chapter seven

July 1916

It was muggy and the smell of cordite hung in the air, punctured by whiffs of sweat, shit and the nauseating odour of death which seem to permeate through everything.

Occasional Very lights would illuminate the battlefield, followed by bursts of shrapnel and high explosive shells which hammered into the ground throwing up earth and the shattered remains of the dead or wounded.

Amos was sweating profusely, his heartbeat so loud he felt sure it would give his position away. Lying flat, pressing himself face down into the earth, he was crawling painfully slow out into the kill zone beyond, aware of Bousefield slightly behind him.

Moments earlier the two men had found themselves surrounded by other soldiers all keen to give them advice about what to remove from their kit and uniforms, to avoid unnecessary weight and, more importantly, reduce their chances of being seen by the enemy.

Amos never spoke but Bousefield had ended the discussion abruptly. "Shut the fuck up all of ya. George, dump your rifle and anything else that rattles and let's get on with this."

And with that he'd been first up on the ladder that was leaning against the side of the trench. He took two steps up, turned to look at Amos and said: "Right, I'll go over first. Keep your fucking head down and go as flat as you can. I'll wait for you to move on because you're going to have to lead the way George my boy."

Amos looked up to see Bousefield smiling, as though he was relishing the task ahead. He simply nodded at him, his eyes betraying the terror he was feeling.

Bousefield took another step up and was about to clamber over the top when he turned his head again and, whispering this time, said: "Oh, and Amos. If you end up getting me killed I'm going to wring your scrawny fucking neck."

Amos was holding on to the ladder and looked up to see Bousefield disappear over the top of the trench. He froze for a moment, half expecting a machine gun to open up and rake the area above his head. But it never happened.

The surprise silence jolted him into action and he took more tentative steps up the ladder before his hands reached the earth at the top. Digging his fingers into the soil for grip, he hoisted his right leg over, rolling his body out into No Man's Land.

The first thing he saw was Bousefield lying still, his face now passive, concentration etched upon it. The two men looked at each other and, with a mere flicker of his eyes, Bousefield motioned him to move ahead.

Amos didn't dare raise his head so instead lifted his eyes up as far as they'd go. The sensation was slightly painful. Yet, it was nothing compared to the harrowing scene ahead of him.

He had to fight all his natural instincts to move forward. Flashes from shells illuminated the landscape giving a brief glimpse of the carnage around them. There were bodies everywhere; in the gloom he could make out shapes attempting to move. After a few yards the pathetic cries and moans of stricken men got louder.

His eyes moved to his right, his vision now becoming accustomed to the darkness, and he saw two figures moving slowly towards him. They were about fifty yards away and, as his eyes focused, he saw they were two men on their hands and knees, both still wearing their steel helmets, heading back towards the British line.

He stopped moving, fixing his eyes on them both. He couldn't see their faces, it was too dark, but he wondered if he knew them. Then he heard a thud in the distance and he felt Bousefield grab his ankle.

Amos buried his face into the soil as he heard the approaching screech of a shell. It screamed louder and closer before exploding, showering red hot fragments of shrapnel over the landscape.

He lifted his face from the earth and looked up. The two men were now lying still, the backs of their tunics ripped open.

Bousefield yanked his ankle and Amos took it as a

signal to start moving. Again, the two men continued their slow crawl, passing more and more dead. At one point a cluster of corpses blocked their way and Amos stopped.

He began to shuffle back ever so slightly, only for Bousefield to jab him in the leg. "Keep. Fucking. Moving," he heard him whisper through gritted teeth.

Scrunching his eyes shut, his skin crawling with the horror of it all, Amos began clambering over the bodies. They were still warm, though some stiffness had now set in. The smell coming from them was sickly, yet sweet.

Not being able to scramble over them quickly simply made it worse. His face brushed clothing and skin, a putrid stench flooding his nostrils, making him gag. The sensation his body felt as it inched its way over the soft, moving morass horrified him and he began crying at the grotesqueness of it all.

Eventually, his probing hands felt the hard earth and he shuffled forwards until his whole body was lying flat on the ground. He stopped and pressed his face hard into the soil, sobbing.

"Keep moving George. The quicker we find this bloody officer, the quicker we get out of this shit hole."

Bousefield was alongside him now. Amos lifted his head slightly and turned to face him. He was astonished to see him looking so composed, even now, after all this.

He looked at Amos, their faces only inches apart. Bousefield's craggy features were magnified and the smell of stale tobacco as he spoke was a welcome relief to the battlefield odours.

"Stop snivelling George, you need to focus. Now, where's the fucking captain? I don't want to be out here any longer than I need to," he said.

Amos looked around him, he was feeling disorientated. Suddenly, the landscape looked alien. Frantically, his eyes darted left and right, he didn't recognise any of it. All he saw was the dark and the dead. And then his own death, only a random, second away.

He looked at Bousefield. "I ... I don't know. I can't work out where he is ... it looks different, it's too dark, I'm sorry," he spluttered.

Bousefield grabbed his tunic and pulled himself even closer, until their faces were almost touching.

"Get a fucking grip boy and focus," he snarled.

"Think. Where was he? How far away from the line did he get? Come on!" he said, shaking Amos now.

"I don't know!"

"Was he laying out in the open? Is he on his own?" Bousefield asked.

"Shell hole, he's in a shell hole .." Amos replied.

"Right, good lad. Now think. Where is it?" Bousefield's tone had changed, it was now more encouraging.

Amos looked around him, trying to get his bearings.

"Over there, it's got to be over there," he motioned with his eyes. "Bill and me had only got seventy yards or so when we had to dive for cover.

"The machine guns were mowing us down, we couldn't go on," he said, in a tone that was almost asking for Bousefield's approval for what they'd done.

Instead, the private simply let go of Amos' collar and

said: "Well, for fuck's sake, let's get over there. Lead the way George."

The two men resumed their slow crawl, passing more bodies. Occasionally they'd have to lie still and take their chances in the artillery lottery that saw both shrapnel and high explosive shells detonate randomly around them.

Progress was painfully slow, made worse by Amos unable to recall exactly where the officer was and because of the proliferation of craters that now scarred the battlefield.

Then, as a Very light exploded in mid air, showering the landscape with light, Amos saw a shell hole ahead and what he thought were rifles lying next to a body. He knew it was the right place but his heart stopped as he feared the body was Harris'.

"There," he said, turning and whispering to Bousefield. "It's over there."

"Are you sure?" he heard Bousefield reply. "We've been crawling around here for fucking ages."

"Yes, it's got to be. That's where Captain Harris was covering us. Come on," he added.

His pace quickened only for Bousefield to grab his ankle again, "Easy, George, nice and easy," he heard him say.

Every inch forward seemed to take an age but the thought of finding Harris was all Amos could think about. His fear suddenly disappeared and adrenalin surged through him, his heart beating rapidly not from fright but excitement.

The two men were only yards away now and Amos could almost see into the crater.

Suddenly, he was distracted by movement to his left. In the excitement of hopefully finding the missing captain, the sight of another dead body hadn't even registered.

Yet, as he was drawn to the movement, he realised the man wasn't dead. He was alive and he'd seen Amos and Bousefield and was now moving towards them.

"Help ... me, please ... help me," he groaned.

Amos froze and stared at the soldier, he was dragging himself along using his right hand. Even in the dark he could see the left side of his body was a bloody mess. His left arm had been torn off at the shoulder giving him a lopsided look as he hauled himself pitifully along the ground.

He lifted his head and looked at the two men. Amos gasped, wide eyed at the sight in front of him. Still wearing his helmet, the soldier's face was a gruesome distortion.

Half of his face was virtually missing, his left eye had gone and raw, bloody flesh exposed his jaw, giving him a ghoulish, mask-like appearance.

And now, like something from a horror story, he was dragging himself closer and closer. His moaning and pleading was getting louder and Amos watched with a mixture of disgust and fascination at the distorted features coming near and nearer.

"Shhhh ... it's ok, keep your voice down," Amos whispered.

The stricken soldier's hand reached out towards him, his grubby, bloodstained fingers inches away from Amos' face. The man's mouth opened again and Amos couldn't help but stare at the exposed tissue and cheek muscle that moved as he tried to speak.

Now clearly exhausted, he was struggling to form words and instead began moaning ever more loudly.

Amos reached out his hand and took hold of the man's wrist, gently pushing it to the ground.

"It's going to be alright, we'll get you some help but you've got to stay quiet," he said.

As he spoke, Bousefield crawled up alongside him.

"He's finished George, we've got to leave him," he said.

Amos turned to face Bousefield, again his expression remained impassive as though the sight confronting him was normal.

"We can't just leave him, he needs help or he's going to die," Amos said, looking back at the man who was close enough to hear what was being said.

"Forget about him, he's not why we're here. Nobody can help him George," Bousefield responded.

Amos turned to Bousefield and snapped back angrily: "We can't just fucking leave him! He's one of us for fuck's sake."

Bousefield simply grabbed hold of Amos' webbing and began pulling him away, saying: "No time, leave him and let's go."

"Get the fuck off me," Amos said. "We're not leaving him here. We can take him back to the line and then come back for Captain Harris."

Bousefield's patience snapped: "What the fuck do you think we can do for him George huh? He's a dead man. Look at him. Half his fucking face has been blown away and he's bleeding out.

"Now, you need to leave him be. We're running out of time."

Amos looked at the man, and sensed a pleading in his one remaining eye. No words were coming out of his mouth now, only low moans and gasps.

"I can't do it. I'm not leaving him," he said, turning to Bousefield.

"Alright George," Bousefield said, before turning away. Then he began crawling towards the wounded soldier until he was lying against him. He reached down to his belt looking for something.

"His water bottle's on the other side," Amos whispered, heartened that Bousefield had listened to him.

And then he saw it and he knew what was going to happen but for a split second his mind couldn't process it and he was too stunned to speak.

"Nooooo!!!," Amos said, as he glimpsed the blade of the bayonet in Bousefield's hand. Then it disappeared from view as Bousefield thrust it into the side of the man who looked at him, his distorted face still able to express a sense of shock at what was happening.

Amos watched as the soldier's body tensed and went rigid, a last gasp coming from his mouth before blood oozed out between the closing teeth. Then he went limp and slumped face down on the ground.

Bousefield looked briefly at Amos and said: "Had to be

115

done George," before he turned his body away and motioned with his right hand for Amos to crawl ahead of him so he could follow.

Amos resumed his slow crawl over the field, his eyes red with tears, his mind addled by the bombardment of brutality it was being forced to absorb.

He was struggling to focus on the task ahead of him but another sudden screech of shells followed by explosions nearby, broke his train of thought.

After lifting his head he looked again and saw the two rifles and the hanging corpse at the lip of the shell hole ahead. His pace began to quicken and he could hear Bousefield respond behind him.

The inside of the crater was visible now and as he scrambled forwards on his belly he glimpsed again the severed leg that had so horrified him when it landed in the hole next to him, Dove and Harris.

He thought of how Bill had manage to restrain him and stop him climbing out of the shell hole and inevitable death.

His mind then wandered as he thought of the two of them spending the day travelling to Nottingham, getting lost trying to find their way to the recruiting centre.

"So, you want to be in the Sherwood Foresters eh?" the recruiting sergeant had said.

"You've made a good choice boys," he'd added smiling.

He thought of Bill's parents, how proud his father was when they'd both turned up at his house in uniform on the last day of leave before departing for France. He recalled his mother in tears, apprehensive and nervous, hugging her son for what seemed like an age.

And then he remembered Bill laughing as he prised himself away from her arms. "Don't worry ma, I won't be gone forever. We'll be back before you know it," he'd said.

Amos winced as he recalled his own comment. "Aye, that's right Mrs Dove. But not until we've given Fritz a bashing." Now, there was nothing left of Bill. Not even a body for Mrs Dove to weep over. For weep she would, for hours and days on end.

He felt his ankle being grabbed again.

"Is this it then? Where is he?" Bousefield asked.

Amos glanced behind him briefly before hauling himself forward to the edge of the shell hole. He looked down in the darkness and there he was.

Bousefield appeared next to him and peered down too. Harris was slumped against the side of the crater, his head resting on his right shoulder.

"I knew it," Bousefield said. "He's already fucking dead. Let's get out of here."

Amos stared at the officer's body.

"We said we'd bring him in and that's what we're going to do," he said.

Bousefield looked at him incredulous.

"You're kidding me right? He's fucking dead George. He can lie here with these other poor bastards. I'm not getting myself killed dragging a sodding corpse in."

Bousefield began crawling backwards and was about to turn around when Amos said: "Jesus Christ, he just moved his head. He's alive!"

"Bollocks Amos, I'm not stupid," Bousefield said without turning around.

"I'm not lying, look. He's alive for Christ's sake," and with that Amos began crawling frantically down into the shell hole.

Bousefield stopped, turned around and was about to call after Amos when he too looked across at the officer and was stunned to see him lift his head.

"Fuck me," he said out loud, as he too then crawled down into the crater below.

April 2016

"You can come in if you like." Arthur said as he opened the door, swinging his legs out of the passenger seat of Tom's car.

The pair had continued talking throughout the morning before a hurried Joan had almost shooed them out of the door. "Come on, haven't you got homes to go to?" she'd said.

"Some of us have got shopping to do yet," and then off she'd gone, leaving them standing on the steps in the drizzle.

He had offered to drive Arthur home, eager to hear more about his military service. He'd felt embarrassed knowing nothing about the Korean War when Arthur told him that's where he'd served. But the old man hadn't been offended. He'd simply said: "Sadly, few people do. It's the war no one remembers. We've always been the forgotten ones."

Now, driving through the rain, Arthur was giving

directions until the car pulled up and came to a stop in the middle of a quiet housing estate.

It was a street of semi-detached bungalows and Tom's first thought was that it may as well have had a sign announcing 'homes for the elderly.'

"This one's mine, number 16," said Arthur, as his right hand gripped the top of the car door to steady himself as he stood.

Tom followed him through a small wooden gate and down an uneven concrete path. The garden was neat and tidy and he seemed surprised that Arthur could manage to do that bearing in mind how unsteady he was on his feet.

Despite being in front of him the old man seemed to know what he was thinking as, pausing to retrieve keys from his coat pocket, he said: "Alice and her husband do me garden. They come round once a fortnight in all weathers bless 'em.

"Proper green fingered she is," he said, turning the latch on the blue wooden door.

"It's lovely Arthur, who's Alice?" Tom asked, following him inside.

"She's Len's granddaughter, he lives next door. Salt of the earth is Alice."

The bungalow had a distinctive scent; clean but slightly fusty. Looking around he noticed the furniture and ornaments were old fashioned and he wondered how long they'd been here and whether people simply get to the point where they unconsciously, or maybe deliberately, press the pause button on their surroundings.

Wiping his damp feet on the doormat, the thought occurred to him that maybe he'd be destined to do the same.

"Hang your coat up and come on in," Arthur said, slipping his shoes off and stepping into a pair of house slippers, before shuffling through a door into the lounge.

"How long have you lived here?" Tom asked, following him into the room.

"October 1994 Anne and I moved in here. She struggled with her chest and the stairs would cripple her so we sold up and came here. It's small but it did for the two of us," he said, leaning forward slowly to light the gas fire.

"Feels pretty big though now it's just me," he added.

"How long have you been on your own?" Tom asked awkwardly.

Arthur motioned for his guest to sit down and, as he sat back in an armchair, replied: "February the seventh 2004 my Anne passed away. Love of my life she was. Not a day goes by when I don't miss her," he said, his eyes betraying the thoughts of a man who, for a moment, was thinking of days past.

"I'm sorry," he said quietly.

"Aye, well that's life. The good and the bad," Arthur said.

"Enjoy every day as if it's your last," he added. "Believe me, you'll get to my age and wonder how the bloody hell it all went so fast."

He turned to leave the room and said: "Right, enough

120

of that. I think it's time we had a proper drink. I've got some ale in the kitchen."

Leaning forward in his chair Tom raised his voice as the old man left the room: "No, I'm fine Arthur, honestly. Thanks, but it's too early for me. You help yourself."

Moments later Arthur walked back into the lounge. He was clutching two bottles of pale ale in one hand and holding a pair of glasses by their handles in the other.

"Nonsense, a small one won't hurt you," he said, carefully putting the bottles and glasses down on a small side table next to his armchair.

He sat down, picked up a glass and bottle and began pouring the beer slowly, a foaming, frothy head appearing at the top.

"There you go lad, get that down ya," he said handing it over.

There was no point refusing. Tom didn't want to offend his host so he leaned forward and took the glass.

Arthur poured himself the other beer and the two men clinked glasses. "Cheers Tom, good health to you."

"Cheers, Arthur," he replied, before taking a sip.

Tom's eyes scanned the lounge as he drank. He saw a black and white photograph on the wall of a bride and groom standing in the archway of a church.

On the mantelpiece were several more framed pictures, including another of a younger, smiling Arthur, his arm around a woman of a similar age. He assumed it was Anne.

Glancing around the room he saw another framed black and a white photo of what appeared to be a group of soldiers.

Arthur noticed him looking at it. "That's me and some of the boys before we left England in October 1950. Great bunch of lads."

Tom looked at him and said: "The Scottish guy at the Legion, he said …"

"That I was a war hero?" interrupted Arthur.

"Take no notice of Jock. I'm no hero lad. I was a boy, we all were. I was scared witless though, make no mistake," he said, before adding. "No, I did my bit that's all."

There was silence as both men sipped their beer again but he was intrigued.

"Like I said earlier Arthur, I'm ashamed to say I don't really know anything about the Korean War," he said.

Arthur put his drink down and looked at him.

"Some of the older lads in our battalion were regulars who'd fought through Normandy and into Germany in '45," he replied.

"They said it was worse than anything they'd seen fighting the Germans."

Tom looked bemused but none the wiser.

Arthur continued: "We had no idea what we were going into. I couldn't have picked out Korea on a map if you'd asked me beforehand. We sailed from Southampton, big adventure for all of us it was."

"How long had you been in the army?"

"I joined up on my 18th birthday in August 1948," he replied.

"My old man wasn't too keen after his experiences but

I was desperate to join up and I didn't mind where they put me. They offered me the Northumberland Fusiliers and I thought 'that sounds alright.'

Tom found himself enjoying the beer and drained his glass while he listened.

"A lot of folk were telling us that by the time we'd sailed out there we'd end up turning around and coming straight back home again," Arthur said. "What did they know eh?"

Tom interrupted, asking a question he immediately regretted but needing to know the answer.

"So, we were fighting the Koreans?" he asked.

Arthur lifted his glass and swallowed the rest of his beer, letting out a satisfying gasp as he did so.

"North Koreans to be exact ... and the Chinese," said Arthur.

"The Yanks were already in there. It was all about stopping the spread of Communism you see.

"We never thought we'd be needed. By the time we did get there things had turned for the worse and we found ourselves in the thick of it," he added.

"What happened?" asked Tom.

"They sent us up country and stuck us next to a big river. Sounds nice doesn't it?

"But there was nothing nice about the Imjin river," he added and again, Tom detected a look on the old man's face that said his mind was elsewhere.

Chapter eight

July 1916

"Captain? Captain Harris, can you hear me?" Amos was lying against the side of the crater next to the semi-conscious officer.

Harris lifted his head slowly to face Amos. His eyes were open but his eyelids were heavy.

Amos looked at him; he was slumped against the earth with both hands together over his lap. How he was still alive, he never knew. His skin was deathly pale and he looked lifeless.

"Sir, we've come to take you in. Private Bousefield and me, we're going to get you back to the line sir," Amos said.

Bousefield had taken a water bottle from his belt and was removing the cap. He held it up to the captain's mouth and poured slowly. Much of it dribbled down his chin and on to his tunic but then Harris responded and opened his mouth wider, leaning his head forward to get a better grip of the bottle.

"Easy Captain, small sips are better. I don't want you throwing up on me," Bousefield said.

He pulled the bottle away and Harris allowed his head to fall back against the earth.

"He's in a bad way George," Bousefield said, looking up at Amos.

The two men were looking at the officer. His shoulder was a mess and his tunic was saturated in blood. The soil where he lay was also damp with blood from the wound in his back.

"Sir, can you move? We've got to get you out of here sir," Amos said.

Harris' mouth opened slowly and he tried to speak.

"What's he saying?" Bousefield asked.

Amos leaned forward, turning his face so his left ear was close to the captain's mouth.

"What is it sir?" he asked.

Harris' voice was barely more than a whisper and a croaky one at that. At first Amos struggled to understand.

"Lee sir? Captain, I'm sorry, I don't understand," he said.

"Come on George, we're wasting time, we need to do this," Bousefield said, as another shell exploded and rifle shots continued to ring out.

Amos was about to lift his head when Harris spoke again. And this time he understood.

"Leave … me … Private. That's … an or…der."

As he finished speaking he closed his eyes and his head again fell back, his body succumbing to the huge effort it took to speak.

"Sorry Captain," Amos replied. "We're taking you in. You're not done yet sir."

It was then he noticed Harris' hands were concealing something. He reached over and gently lifted his left arm. Underneath was a photograph. Amos picked it up and held it close to his face.

The dark made it difficult to see but he could just make out the features of a woman. Harris stirred and his left hand began moving. It appeared to Amos that it had a life of its own, the fingers probing for something.

Harris began mumbling, his head lifted again and Amos realised what it was. He pressed the photograph back into his palm and Harris immediately relaxed.

Bousefield had crawled up to the edge of the crater and was peering out towards the German lines.

"Looks pretty quiet George but Fritz will have his eyes peeled that's for sure," he said.

He slid back down, turned to Amos and said: "Right, let's do this." Reaching into his breast pocket he took out a small hip flask.

Unscrewing the top he put it to Harris' lips, held the back of his head steady with his hand and poured slowly.

The liquid seeped through into Harris' mouth and he stirred, spluttering as he swallowed.

"What the hell's that?" asked Amos.

"Whiskey fit for an officer. He needs all the help we can give him if we're going to get him back. And if he's in pain now George my boy, just wait until he's been dragged across a field.

"This won't do him any more harm," he added, raising the flask to his lips again and pouring more into Harris' mouth.

Again, Harris coughed but this time his swallow was stronger and he looked more alert than he had at any time since they'd found him.

"It's rude to drink alone," Bousefield added, before closing his eyes and taking a long, huge swig from the flat, silver flask.

When he'd done he handed it over to Amos. "Drink up George. You're going to need it."

Amos looked hesitant. He knew it was a court martial offence to drink in the line, even to be in possession of alcohol could see a man given a stiff sentence.

"Go on, drink lad. Being up on a charge is the least of our worries," Bousefield added.

Amos looked at Harris. His eyes were open and he thought that despite his obvious pain, he could detect a small smile on the officer's face.

"Drink up ... Private," Harris whispered.

Snatching the flask from Bousefield, Amos took a big gulp and winced as the liquid burned his throat.

"That's the spirit George. Now, let's get the fuck out of here," Bousefield said, retrieving the flask and putting it back in his pocket.

When he'd done he turned to Harris and reached out his arms to grab hold of him: "This is going to hurt Captain."

Harris looked at him through groggy eyes. He managed a small nod and then his body tensed and he clenched his teeth, as Bousefield pulled him and turned his body 180 degrees. His legs were now where his body had been against the side of the shell hole.

"Ok George," Bousefield said, lying on his stomach parallel to Harris. "Roll him over on to my back. I'll take him up and over and get as far as I can. Then it's your turn."

Harris lay there, drifting in and out of consciousness. He opened his eyes and stared up at the black, moonless sky. And he then he heard her voice, she was close.

"Rest my darling, close your eyes and rest," Emma said, her soft voice purring.

"Em … ," he muttered, and closed his eyes a split second before the earth began to move and he experienced searing pain, the like of which he'd never felt before.

"Jesus, you're heavier than you look Captain," Bousefield gasped, as Amos rolled the officer over on top of him.

"Are you ok Eddie? Can you move?" Amos whispered.

"Yep … but I can't … fucking … speak … at the same time," Bousefield replied before beginning the agonising crawl back towards the British line.

Amos crawled alongside, occasionally repositioning the stricken officer to ensure he didn't slide off.

Progress was painfully slow, not least because of the dangerous, uneven landscape they were attempting to cross.

Bousefield could only move a few yards before he would then have to stop, his breathing getting harder the further he went.

Amos felt helpless. He didn't relish having to carry the captain on his back but knew he'd have to take over at some point. So he found himself inwardly urging Bousefield on, hoping the bigger man's strength would take him further.

When they'd stopped again for the umpteenth time, he made a point of checking on Harris. He was unconscious now and his breathing had slowed right down.

Amos noticed his legs were beginning to slide to the side so he pushed them back in between Bousefield's.

The movement seemed to rouse Harris who stirred slightly before his body relaxed again. Even in the dark Amos could see the officer's face; resting on Bousefield's left shoulder his right cheek was squashed flat and it gave him a lopsided, vacant look.

Bousefield began to move again, now grunting audibly as he summoned the dwindling energy from within.

Amos had no idea how long they'd been out there but he knew it was much longer than the 30 minute deadline the sergeant had given them. As they crawled he realised his fear had dissipated somewhat.

He was no longer terrified but simply desperate to make it back. And the further the three men got, however slow their progress, the more he dared to hope.

More bodies were passed along the way and he was silently grateful none were alive. He didn't know what he'd do if confronted again by a gravely wounded man.

He couldn't do what Bousefield had done, he knew that.

Simply the thought of it made his eyes water as he replayed the moment he'd watched Bousefield kill a fellow soldier. A mercy killing? Or was it murder? Amos couldn't decide.

He tried to shut it out but his mind was intent on having the debate with itself. Don't be ridiculous, he was beyond saving, he'd have died anyway. Anyone could see that. What Bousefield did was merciful. There was no other choice.

So why did he still feel so sick and ashamed at the episode. He could never be like Bousefield. He'd never want to be. Didn't he feel anything? He had the appearance of someone who simply didn't care and almost enjoyed killing. He was nothing like that.

He glanced across at Bousefield, sinking under the dead weight of a man lying unconscious on his back.

And yet, there he is, Amos thought, risking his life to drag an officer back and the effort was killing him.

Two Very lights in quick succession illuminated the battlefield and Amos was able to look up and see they were now within a few yards of the line. Then the sky lit up with explosions as more shells landed and a machine gun began firing.

Bousefield stopped and with huge effort lifted his body slightly until Harris slid off and was on the ground. He didn't move.

"Stay … still and as flat … as you can," Bousefield gasped.

Amos didn't need telling and lay there burying his face into the earth with his hands over the back of his head as shells continued to explode and the gunfire continued.

Then, as quickly as it started, it eased off and within minutes the battlefield was plunged into a silent blackness once more.

"Right, it's your turn George. Tell me when you're ready and I'll put the captain aboard," Bousefield said.

Amos lifted his face from the ground and braced himself. Harris' weight took his breath away and he felt like he was being crushed. His entire body was being pressed into the ground and he was struggling to breathe.

"When you're ready George," Bousefield said.

With difficulty he stretched his arms out in front of him and dug his fingers into the earth for grip. Then, he began pulling himself forward. It was agony and he couldn't help but cry out through gritted teeth.

"I can't .... do this Eddie," Amos gasped.

"Come on George, put some fucking effort into it," Bousefield said dismissively.

Amos didn't reply. He couldn't move. The weight of Harris was suffocating him.

Bousefield heard him crying, his face lying in the dirt, stifling his sobs. He shuffled forward on his belly and got up close to Amos.

"George, get a fucking move on ... we get the captain home and we'll be fucking heroes. Now move it!"

Amos slowly stretched out his arms, grabbed the earth and pulled himself forward another few precious inches.

After doing it a third time, he came to a stop, breathing hard. Bousefield, who was alongside him, said: "You

Kitchener's mob can't hack it. What do they train you lot in?"

Amos was too exhausted to respond and simply lay there trying to catch his breath under the weight of a man on his back.

"Well, if we're staying put for a while we may as well make it a proper break," Bousefield said.

Out of the corner of his eye Amos saw him take the hip flask out of his pocket and unscrew the lid. Putting the bottle to his mouth Bousefield took several gulps.

"Ah, that's good stuff George my boy. Found it in the pocket of a lieutenant who got one shortly after we went over. Didn't want it going to waste," he said, before taking another drink.

He looked at Amos who was staring at him through tired eyes.

"Want some help to keep you going George?" Bousefield asked.

Amos shook his head, turned away and with another huge effort began dragging himself forward.

As he inched himself along he could feel Harris' head against his shoulders, rhythmically wobbling to and fro.

Then he heard him muttering again and he stopped moving, grateful for another respite.

"Captain," Amos gasped. "We're ... almost ... there, sir."

Harris was mumbling, causing Bousefield to say: "He's delirious George, ignore him. Keep going."

But Harris' mouth was close to Amos' left ear and he began to make out what the officer was saying.

"Em .. I'm coming ... home," he said.

"That's .. right sir," Amos panted, "we're ... going to ... get you ... sorted."

Hearing Harris' voice gave Amos a shot of adrenalin and he resumed his painful crawl.

Minutes later, and to his relief, Amos could tell they were approaching the British line.

"Halt! Who goes there," boomed a voice.

"Sherwood Foresters, bringing a wounded officer in," Bousefield replied.

"Stay put, don't come any further," the voice said.

"You're fucking kidding me!" Bousefield responded angrily. "Listen mate, we're coming in."

"Stand to" the voice said, an urgency in his voice now. Suddenly, the sound of several rifles cocking could be heard, and Amos lay there, sweat pouring down his face.

"Look mate, I don't know who the fuck you are, but Private Amos and me have been out here for hours and we have a wounded officer here, Captain Harris," Bousefield said.

For a few seconds there was an uneasy silence until Bousefield shouted: "I wouldn't want to be the idiot who shoots a British officer so why don't you take it easy and let us the fuck in!" he snapped.

There was silence for a moment until the same voice responded with: "Alright, in you come but take it nice and slowly."

"You hear that George?" Bousefield said. "No running!" and he laughed, before taking the hip flask out of his pocket and taking another swig.

A few feet further and the tops of steel helmets peered

over the parapet before arms reached out and voices could be heard.

"Here they are," "They're coming in," "Give 'em a hand someone?"

Amos was at the point of exhaustion but the relief he felt when the weight of Harris disappeared from his back flooded through him. He wanted to lie still and savour the moment but grappling hands reached out and were dragging him in.

Seconds later he was hauled into the trench and, despite a handful of men trying to keep hold of him, he slipped through their grasp and fell to the ground landing on his back.

Bousefield was already there and was quick with his rebuke.

"Watch it will ya, he's been through enough has my mate George," he said.

Amos stood up groggily and looked around him. Then, as if remembering what he'd done, he said: "Where's the captain, we need to get him to the aid post and then to the dressing station."

Soldiers standing in front of Amos and Bousefield stood back against the side of the trench and the two men saw a medical officer on his knees bending over Harris.

He could only see the officer's back and Harris' legs laying out flat ahead of him.

Amos stepped forward and knelt down. He looked down at Harris and said: "See sir, I told you we'd get you back. We're going to get you sorted out sharpish captain, ain't that right?" and he turned to the medical officer.

"I'm sorry boy," the medical officer said, turning to look at Amos, as he stood: "But Captain Harris is dead," and then he turned and strode back down the trench.

April 2016

He emptied the contents of the bottle into Arthur's glass; it was his third beer in little more than an hour. He had offered to put the kettle on but the old man had dismissed that suggestion with a flick of his wrist, saying: "Not for me lad, I'm happy with the ale."

He was grateful Arthur hadn't noticed he was no longer drinking but by then he was in full flow, recounting a story he found so extraordinary that he was having difficulty believing it.

At one point the old man must have sensed the incredulity on his guest's face because he paused, leaned forward and, looking Tom in the eye, said: "Hard to believe eh?

"Aye, well it was real enough lad, believe me."

Then he sat back, took another swig of his beer and looked lost in thought for a moment.

Earlier he'd described the first time he'd shot and killed a man at the age of 19.

"You never forget that, it stays with you ... I can still see him now. On the river bank he was, only looked about my age. He wasn't on his own mind ... no, there were dozens of them," Arthur said.

"Our orders were not to let the Chinese cross. We knew

they were coming, we'd been expecting them. But nothing prepares you for it.

"Well, he and his pals slipped into the water, he was holding his rifle above his head and was wading through. Then the cry went up 'fire!' and all hell let loose," he added, Tom by now utterly absorbed.

"I'd never killed anything in my life. But I looked down the sight of my rifle and I squeezed the trigger. Hit him clean in the chest I did, knocking him back. For a few seconds I just stared at him floating in the water," Arthur said.

"But then it really cranked up, we started shelling 'em and I did what I was expected to do. Funny really, that I only ever think of that first one ... I never think of the others, but then I can't see them anymore. That first one though ... well, I've never been able to get him out of me head."

Tom was desperate to ask questions despite feeling embarrassed at not knowing anything about the conflict.

"Arthur, forgive my ignorance but I didn't know any of this. How long were you fighting for?" he asked.

"We got there in the November of 1950. We were part of the 29th Brigade along with the Ulsters, the Irish Hussars, the tank and artillery lot and the Glosters," Arthur said.

"We spent Christmas and New Year there and then in the spring we were up on the banks of the Imjin River. April 22, 1951 ... that's when it got hot."

Tom's phone went off in his pocket. It was Emma. He cancelled the call, feeling guilty, put the phone back in his pocket and said: "Sorry Arthur, go on."

"We were feeling dandy, pretty cocky we were. Many of us had never seen any action before but we were the British Army. We had tanks, artillery, there were 4,000 of us. Best in the world we were and we didn't fear anybody," he said.

"But I'll tell you this. Four thousand doesn't sound a lot when the other chap's got thirty thousand … and that's what they hit us with. I think we all wondered whether we'd make it," he added.

"Battle of Imjin River they called it. Hell on earth for three days it was. I guess we were the lucky ones in that we got out. It was the Glosters who copped it. Wiped out they were to the last man. A whole battalion."

"Jesus," Tom said. "How many's that?"

"Near enough 800. They fought to the last bullet on that hill. The Yanks tried to get them out but they were surrounded. Them that weren't killed were captured and the poor bastards spent two years in PoW camps. Some died in there too."

Tom's phone went a second time and he reached into his pocket. Looking at the screen it was Emma again.

"Listen Arthur, I ought to be making a move," he said, cancelling the call a second time and now beginning to think what his excuse would be for not answering.

"Hey, no bother lad, you get yourself home. Someone waiting for you is there?" Arthur asked.

"Er, yeah, my wife … Emma. And my little girl, Daisy," he said, standing up now.

"Ah, lovely. Well, you don't want to be sitting here

talking to an old man when you've got two lovely lasses waiting for you at home," Arthur said, and he put his hands on the arms of his chair, pushing himself up.

"It's been great to meet you and fascinating listening to you," Tom said. "I hope you didn't mind me asking about ... well, you know.?"

"Don't be daft. Anyhow, it's all in the past now," he said, holding out his right hand as the two men shook hands.

"Grand to meet you too lad. You know where I am if you ever fancy a jar and a natter," he added.

"Thanks, I'd like that, really. Maybe I could drop by one evening next week?"

"I'll be here lad," Arthur added, as Tom retrieved his coat from the hallway, opened the front door and left. "Cheers Arthur," he said as he walked down the path.

He sat in the car, it was still drizzling, and rang Emma.

"Hi Em, everything ok?," he asked, as she answered the call.

"Where are you?" she replied tetchily.

"I'm in the car, heading home now." Something was wrong, she sounded suspicious.

"When you didn't pick up earlier I rang the office. Apparently you've been up all night throwing up," she said, sounding angry.

"Em, I'm sorry, I can explain ...," he said, but she abruptly cut him off.

"You'd better. I'll speak to you when you get home ... oh, and Helen's asked if I want to go out for a drink tonight. I'm meeting her at seven so you'll have to put

Daisy down," she added, before ending the call.

"Bollocks," he muttered as he turned the ignition key.

Twenty minutes later he was home. Walking in the front door he could hear Emma in the kitchen, she was putting glasses and plates away noisily.

He glanced into the lounge from the hall and saw Daisy in her bouncing chair fumbling with a soft toy elephant which hung down from a mobile above.

It made him smile but he changed his expression as he walked into the kitchen. She didn't stop what she was doing or acknowledge him.

"Look, I know you're angry, but there's nothing to worry about, honestly," he said.

She slammed a mug down on the shelf of a cupboard, turned to face him and said: "So where the hell have you been all day? Not at work, clearly. What are you playing at?" she demanded.

"Listen, I … it's not … I didn't plan it. On my way in this morning I helped an old guy who almost got hit by a car. We got talking and I gave him a lift, he's a lovely fella," he said.

"What's that got to do with you throwing a sickie and not going to work?," she said, sounding frustrated. "Where have you been all day?"

He looked embarrassed. "I've …. been talking to him."

"What? All day? Do you expect me to believe that?"

"Em, seriously, I have. I'm not lying. He's a widower, his name's Arthur and he lives on his own. I gave him a lift to the British Legion, had a mug of tea with him and we just got talking," he said, as Emma stared at him.

"He's such a fascinating bloke, I just really enjoyed listening to him," he added.

"So, let me get this right," she said. "You've lied to your work, taken the day off and then spent it talking to some old man?"

He thought of telling her what he'd found out but dismissed that idea straight away. Instead, he simply looked at her and said feebly: "I'm sorry, Em ... honestly."

"You have no idea how pissed off I am right now," she said, walking out of the kitchen and going upstairs.

An hour later she emerged wearing a sparkly top, skinny jeans and heels. Her hair and make-up were done and her perfume lingered long after she'd bent down to kiss Daisy, pulled back the curtain to see her lift had arrived and then left.

"I don't know what time I'll be home," was all she said, before closing the door.

Chapter nine

July 1916

"There you go lad, get that down you," the soldier said, holding out a mess tin to Amos who was sitting on the ground with his knees up, his head bowed.

There was no response so he tried again. "You'll feel better when you've eaten something. Come on lad, you must be famished."

Amos lifted his head and looked at the man's face. He was much older than he was, or appeared that way, and he had a warm, friendly face.

"Amos isn't it?" the soldier asked and he knelt down next to him, still holding the mess tin. Its contents were hot and there was the familiar aroma of Army stew.

He looked at Amos, his face smeared with dirt and tear stains. His eyes were red and he was sniffling. He wiped his nose with the sleeve of his tunic and said quietly: "I'm not hungry."

The soldier put the tin down in between them and then sat down alongside Amos. The two men were sitting in an assembly trench to the rear of the lines where Amos and several other survivors had been sent back, passing fresh, nervous looking troops heading the other way.

"I've heard what you did lad, it took real guts to go back out there," he said.

Amos didn't reply.

"I was very fond of the captain ... we all were. Such a shame," the man added.

Amos remained silent and the two men sat there for a moment before the older man said: "Look, eat up lad. I'm not sure how long it'll be before the ration party gets up here again with a hot meal."

That seemed to get through to Amos and he lifted his head from his knees, reached out and picked up the mess tin. He looked at its contents before picking through it slowly, beginning to eat.

"Not as bad as it looks is it?" the older man said, pleased to see Amos eating.

"Listen, they're having a service for the captain, one of the brass hats has asked for it. Some of the lads are going if you want to join us," he said.

Amos looked at him, finished chewing a mouthful of food, and said: "Yes, I'd like that."

"Good lad, best eat up then. It'll be up near the wood from Nab Valley, they've started digging graves up there," the soldier said, as he stood up and made to walk away.

As he did so, he turned to Amos and added: "Mr Roebuck's taking the service. He'll say all the right things. Twenty minutes then?"

Amos nodded and watched the soldier walk away before hungrily tucking into the rest of his meal.

A few minutes later he followed in the same direction. The area was a hive of activity with rows of wounded men waiting for ambulances to take them on to casualty clearing stations.

There were also more new troops moving up the line and all manner of men and horses converging.

Amos found himself among a crowd of men all heading in the opposite direction. It was hard trying to push himself through but he emerged the other side only to realise he had no idea where he was going.

It didn't help that it was pitch black in places, the darkness only occasionally punctured by flashes from artillery shells which were still randomly dropping, both at the front and towards the rear.

"Mind yerself mate," Amos turned to see two figures carrying a stretcher attempting to get past. He stepped out of the way to let them pass and looked.

A canvas sheet covered whoever it was lying underneath, now clearly beyond help.

The two stretcher bearers carried on walking, one of them seeming to struggle with the weight. Amos watched them, realised where they were going and shouted: "Hey, wait up."

The two men paused and the one at the back turned his head.

"Can't stop mate, Charlie here's already struggling. We've already dropped this fella once," he said, and the two men carried on walking.

Amos jogged to catch them up: "Where are you taking him? I need to find where out they're burying an officer."

The man at the back looked at Amos as he walked. "Best follow us then. This poor bugger's going into the ground too. Better still, take over from Charlie here, he's knackered."

Seconds later Amos found himself part of a stretcher party carrying a corpse. He walked at the front, following Charlie who was now leading the way. The dead body was heavy and Amos found himself sweating and breathing hard.

Eventually, after almost losing his footing as they walked down a slope, he could make out the shape of trees ahead and heard voices and the sound of spades digging earth.

"Lay him down there next to the others. Is all ID present and correct?" a voice said sharply.

Amos stopped and looked at the man who spoke. He was pointing to his right where, even in the dark, Amos could make out rows of dead under canvas sheets, their boots sticking out in unison.

The soldier was now speaking with Charlie and appeared to be writing on a clipboard he held. The second stretcher bearer said: "You heard the sergeant, lower him down on the end of that row."

Amos did as he was told and the stretcher was laid on the ground.

"Right, grab his ankles," said the man, as he put his hands under the sheet.

Amos took hold of the dead man's boots, thankful he

couldn't feel bare skin.

"On one, two, three, lift ..." the second soldier said, and he and Amos lifted the corpse and laid it on the ground next to another.

Both men stood.

"If you're looking for a burial you're in the right place," the soldier said. "Thanks for your help," he added, before he and Charlie, who had now finished speaking to the sergeant, headed off back towards the front carrying their empty stretcher.

Amos surveyed the landscape in front of him; clusters of dark, shadowy figures were digging. In the light of the horizon he could make out the shape of several crosses and assumed there were even more in the blackness beyond.

To his right he watched two soldiers bend down and pick up one of the numerous dead from the end of a row. They walked a few yards before stopping and dropping the corpse softly, where it disappeared from view. Both men then took spades and began piling earth on top.

They were observed by another soldier who stood with a cross in his right hand. When they'd finished he planted it in the ground and the trio moved on where they set about repeating the grim exercise.

Amos stood watching but then noticed a larger group of men huddled together a few yards away. Even in the dark he could see they were standing with heads bowed.

He walked towards them and heard a voice as he got nearer.

"I am the resurrection and the life. He who believes in

me will live, even though he dies,' says the Lord."

Amos recognised the voice as the battalion's chaplain, Lionel Roebuck.

"The Lord is my shepherd; there can I lack nothing. He makes me lie down in green pastures and leads me beside still waters."

As he spoke Amos saw the men had formed a semi-circle in the middle of which was the chaplain, standing over what was clearly a corpse underneath a sheet on a stretcher.

Next to them he could make out the pitch blackness of a freshly dug grave.

"He shall refresh my soul and guide me in the paths of righteousness for his name's sake," the chaplain continued.

As he shuffled closer the heads of two or three bowed soldiers lifted to look in his direction and he recognised their faces as men in his battalion.

Standing close to the chaplain were three or four officers.

"Though I walk through the valley of the shadow of death, I will fear no evil; for you are with me; your rod and staff, they comfort me," as the chaplain spoke his words were almost drowned out by the screech of a shell which exploded in the near distance.

Amos had ducked and raised his arms over his head as soon as he heard it. He looked up to see others had done the same but was astonished to see the chaplain and one or two others standing tall.

"You spread a table before me in the presence of those who trouble me; you have anointed my head with oil and my cup shall be full," he continued.

Again, the screech of more shells, this time two in quick succession, whistled over their heads and exploded beyond.

Some of the men had flung themselves to the ground but this time Amos stood still too, watching the chaplain continue calmly.

"Surely goodness and mercy shall follow me all the days of my life, and I will dwell in the house of the Lord forever."

In the distance the sound of machine guns could now be heard, forming a natural accompaniment to yet more artillery blasts.

The chaplain was forced to raise his voice to make himself heard.

"Psalms 73:26 reads ... my flesh and my heart may fail, but God is the strength of my heart and my portion forever.

"As we commit the body of Captain Edward Harris to the ground, let us remember the words from the book of Isaiah ... 'but now thus says the Lord, he who created you, O Jacob, he who formed you, O Israel: "Fear not, for I have redeemed you.

"I have called you by name, you are mine. When you pass through the waters, I will be with you; and through the rivers, they shall not overwhelm you; when you walk through fire you shall not be burned, and the flame shall not consume you."

As he finished speaking there was another screech and an explosion, this time close enough for them all to feel the ripple of the blast as it went through them.

Amos and the others turned to see the shell had landed in the middle of a row of graves. There was now a huge crater surrounded by makeshift wooden crosses, many of which were now leaning at awkward angles.

Some of the men were clearly uneasy now and began looking around. The chaplain must have noticed because he said: "Before we commit Captain Harris' body to the ground, let us pray together.

"Our Father ..." he began.

And Amos and the others joined him in reciting the Lord's Prayer, as the guns boomed around them.

Afterwards, one of the officers gave a signal and two men lifted Harris' unseen body from the stretcher and carefully placed it into the grave.

"We now commit his body to the ground," the chaplain said.

"Earth to earth, ashes to ashes, dust to dust, in the sure and certain hope of the resurrection to eternal life."

One of the officers then stepped forward and, almost shouting now to make himself heard above the din, said: "Captain Harris was a fine man and a first class officer in the best traditions of the British Army.

"His death is not, and will not be in vain. The Hun need to be beaten ... and they will be beaten. We will win this war," he thundered.

The officer then turned away and a soldier Amos recognised as Sergeant Quigg stepped forward and said loudly: "Alright lads, head back down the line and get yourselves some rest. We'll parade on at 6am."

April 2016

He thought about trying to stay awake, hoping a tipsy Emma would be easier to placate than a hungover one, but his eyes were too heavy and he didn't make it.

Instead, the morning after was as awkward as he had feared it would be.

"How was last night? He asked. "Did you have a good time?"

She didn't answer.

"Em, I'm sorry, really I am. What else do you want me to say?" he said, following her around the house as he put on his tie.

She ignored him and poured herself another coffee, took a couple of headache pills and then turned her attention to Daisy, sitting lively in a high chair waiting for her breakfast.

He put his suit jacket on, grabbed his keys and tried again.

"Look, how about I take Friday off and we go out somewhere? A nice walk or something?" he said.

"You going to be ill a second time in a week?" she snapped, without looking at him.

"No, of course not ... I'll book the day off. I've got leave," he added.

"Come on Em," he pleaded. "I'm really sorry."

"Just go to work Tom, you're going to be late," she said.

He bent forward, kissed the top of Daisy's head and said: "I love you," before heading out of the door.

It took a couple of days for her to forgive him completely but a three day weekend helped and he made sure to be even more hands on with Daisy than normal.

He thought about trying to talk to her about Arthur but didn't want to push his luck.

A week later, they were eating dinner, Emma was on her second glass of wine and they were looking at photos of Daisy on her phone.

"Listen, you know the old guy I met?" he said.

"I'd really like to visit him again," he added, speaking as casually as he could.

Looking quizzical, she took a sip of her wine and said: "Really? What is it about him? You've only met him once."

"Yeah, I know, but ... well, he's just a really nice, interesting fella," he replied, before adding quickly: "he's on his own, his wife died a few years ago. He must be in his eighties."

"How do I know Arthur isn't actually a pretty blonde in her mid twenties," she said.

"Ah, come on Em, it's not like that," he replied.

"I'm joking Tom!" Emma said smiling.

Leaving work the next day he sent a text reminding her where he was going. Ten minutes later he pulled up outside Arthur's bungalow.

The old man was slow to answer the door but seemed genuinely pleased to see his visitor.

"Ey up lad," he said cheerfully.

"Hi Arthur, I thought I'd drop by on my way home. I hope it's not a bad time?"

"Not at all lad, come on in," he said, opening the door fully.

"So, how have you've been?" he asked, removing his coat and sitting down on the sofa.

"Not too bad lad, my knees have been playing up again but there's nowt to be done about that," Arthur replied.

Minutes later the two men were drinking beer Arthur fetched from the kitchen.

"I've got something you might want to look at," the old man said and he reached across to a small, battered looking brown box.

Lifting the lid, he peered inside and took out a silver looking medal with a yellow and blue striped ribbon.

"This is my Korean War medal," Arthur said, lifting it out and handing over to Harris.

"They gave that to all British and Empire servicemen," he added. "And this is my United Nations Korea Service medal," he said, retrieving a bronze medallion from the box, this time with a blue and white striped ribbon.

For the next hour or so Tom listened intently as Arthur reminisced about his Army days. After a while the conversation naturally widened and the old man began talking about his family.

"My dad was a vicar, a real man of the cloth. He was dead set against me joining up but, like I said, that only made me more determined," he said.

"Yes, I can see why a vicar wouldn't want his son to be in the Army," Tom said.

"Oh no lad, it wasn't because he was religious. He believed in standing up for yourself, that sometimes you have to fight, that there's no other way. No, he was no pacifist. It was because of what he saw when he was in the Army," Arthur said.

"Your dad was in the Army? But I thought ...,"

"He was a chaplain in the First World War," Arthur said, interrupting him.

"He joined up in 1915 and spent the war in and out of the trenches. Incredible man my dad was. They all were, the chaplains," Arthur said.

"It's one thing to be on the front line and in a battle with a rifle or a pistol, but chaplains never carried a weapon. They had their faith and that was it."

Tom supped his beer before asking: "Did he ever speak to you about what it was like?"

"Not really. Even when I told him I wanted to join the Army he didn't say much, only that if I knew how cruel men could be, I wouldn't consider it in a million years. He was right as well," Arthur added. There was silence for a moment and Arthur looked in reflective mood as though his thoughts were elsewhere. Tom waited a moment before speaking.

"I visited some of the battlefields in France earlier this year. We went down to the Somme and saw some of the cemeteries. It was an amazing experience," he said.

"Aye, the Somme, that's where my old man was. One of the lucky ones he was. Some of the things he saw and heard ..." Arthur said, before he tailed off and again looked deep in thought.

"I'm sorry Arthur, I thought you said … I mean, so he did talk about his experiences?" Tom asked.

"No, like I said, hardly a word. But he wrote it down. All of it. Kept a diary during the war he did. I never knew until after he'd died. Found it in the loft along with his service medal," Arthur said.

"Blimey, how did it feel to find something like that?"

"Strange at first. But when I read it, well it was like getting my dad back again. I found out things I never knew about him. As I said, he was an incredible man."

"How old was he when he died?" Tom asked.

"Seventy nine he was. Died August the eighth 1970, almost two years after me mam. Lung cancer. All those fags I suspect," Arthur added, before rummaging around in the box on his lap.

"Here it is," he said, and he lifted out a dark, leather bound book, which looked distinctly worn.

"My dad's war diary," Arthur remarked proudly. "He wrote in it almost every day."

Putting the box to one side he sat holding the book before opening it and flicking through its pages.

"Here you go, listen to this, '*I sat comforting a young private for more than an hour today. He had been gravely injured by a shell which tore away half his face, leaving him with terrible wounds.*

"*There was nothing that could be done for him but he was given morphine and thankfully didn't appear to be in any pain. I prayed and comforted him to the end holding his hand throughout. The only time he spoke was before he passed away … 'mother' he said.'*

Arthur lifted his eyes and looked at Tom. "It's full of stuff like that and some are much worse. He describes how he gave the last rites to a group of dying men blown apart as they sat opening letters from home. Awful."

"It sounds fascinating, I'd love to read it," said Tom.

Arthur leaned forward and handed the book over to him. "Of course you can," he said, before standing up. "Got time for another ale lad?" he asked, walking into the kitchen.

"No, I'm fine with this one thanks," Tom replied as he began thumbing through the diary.

It was written in black ink and he had trouble at first deciphering the elegant handwriting. Above each entry was the date, the earliest of which was the 27th of August 1915.

He began reading: '*Arrived in France. The battalion was given a warm welcome by some of the locals who cheered us off the ship as we disembarked at Boulogne.*

'*I shall be holding my first service with the battalion on Sunday. It will be wonderful to have such a captive congregation. I feel like I'm really getting to know some of the men now, though some will be a little harder to win over I fear.*'

Flicking the pages rapidly with his thumb, Tom skipped to the last page looking for the final entry.

'*4th of September 1917. A day of mixed emotions. I said a fond farewell and wished the men all the very best as I prepared to depart back home. Some of the officers presented me with a fine bottle of cognac which was a very thoughtful gesture.*

Sadly, Corporal Taylor was killed by a sniper so I spent my final hours presiding over his burial before writing a letter of condolence to his mother.'

Tom was aware Arthur had come back in the room and he heard the fizz as he opened another bottle of beer.

"You won't want to put it down now you've started," he heard the old man say.

Tom looked up, "I could sit here all night reading this Arthur. It's amazing to think this book is more than a hundred years old."

"Aye, it is pretty special lad. You wait 'til you've read it all. Some of the stories in there ... well, you won't believe some of 'em."

As they talked Tom was still thumbing through the book, its black leather bound cover and the pages giving off a musty smell. The pages had yellowed with age and some of the ink from the handwriting had faded.

Turning to the beginning he scanned the very first page and was about to turn over when he stopped and read it again.

'Diary of L.M.C Roebuck, Chaplain, C of E, 11th Battalion Sherwood Foresters Regt, B.E.F.'

He felt the hairs on the back of his neck stand on end and the expression on his face must have changed because he heard Arthur remark: "Gets to you doesn't it lad, what have you come across?"

Tom looked up, "Your father was in the Sherwood Foresters at the Somme?"

"Aye, that was his regiment," Arthur replied.

Tom stared again at the page, not quite believing what he was seeing.

"Arthur this is really ... hang on, what? ... I mean ... so, your dad was with the 11th Battalion?"

The old man leaned forward on his chair, aware that his guest was looking puzzled but unsure why.

"Aye, that's right. He was with the Foresters all the way through. Why?"

Tom looked up: "Because, this is a very weird coincidence Arthur, but I've come across your dad's name before, only a couple of weeks ago in fact."

It was Arthur's turn to now look puzzled as he began recounting the story of his namesake, beginning with the headstone in a cemetery on the Somme battlefield and ending with the letter on display in a Norfolk village church.

As he finished he took his phone out of his trouser pocket, swiped through his photos and came across the picture he'd taken of the chaplain's letter to Captain Harris' parents.

Tom stood and held the image out in front of him. "Look, here it is ... a letter about Harris' death from L.M.C Roebuck, 11th Battalion Sherwood Foresters," he said.

The old man squinted to get a better look but Tom saved him the trouble by reading the letter out loud.

"Well I'll be blowed," Arthur exclaimed. "Would you look at that?" he added.

Tom couldn't keep still, he was too excited.

"It's amazing," he said, pacing up and down the room.

"It's a bloody big coincidence, I'll give you that," Arthur remarked as he stood up again. "Sounds like we need another ale lad, all this excitement is making me thirsty," he added, before heading into the kitchen.

Chapter ten

July 1916

What remained of the battalion had been relieved overnight, its weary survivors trudging back through the lines to a small village a few miles from the front.

There, they had stopped as officers told the men to rest before they moved on again in the morning. Most simply lay down and slept where they had stopped marching.

Amos leaned against a tree, slid his back down against the trunk and closed his eyes.

"Amos ... Private Amos ... wake up soldier."

A sharp kick on the sole of his boot roused Amos and he forced himself to open his eyes, where a figure stood over him.

In the murky gloom of a dawn which had still to show itself, Amos peered up to see Sergeant Quigg.

"The battalion major wants to see you lad, best be sharp about it," he thundered. Amos didn't move but another hard kick of his boot, followed by Quigg demanding: "Private Amos, stand up soldier," saw him rise unsteadily to his feet.

"That's more like it," Quigg said.

"Now, the Major wants to see you my lad, so go and splash some water on your face, do up your tunic and get to it."

Amos was startled. "The Major? Why … why does he want to see me sergeant?"

Quigg saw the fear on Amos' face and smiled, clearly amused by his anxiety.

"Perhaps he's realised what a slovenly soldier you are Amos, or maybe he wants your advice on how to conduct the war! I've no idea. But you'd best get a bloody move on, he's a busy man!" Quigg added.

Amos answered with another "yes sergeant," before turning and heading towards what looked like a water filled horse trough which men were using to wash and shave.

Quigg followed and watched, almost disapprovingly, as Amos made vain attempts to smarten himself up by brushing dirt and dust from his uniform using his hand.

He scooped water into his hands, rubbed them over his face before straightening his helmet and adjusting the leather webbing around his waist. Then, he turned and stood in front of Quigg, as though wanting his approval.

"That'll have to do," the sergeant said dismissively, before adding: "Right, follow me and only speak when you're asked to. Understand?"

"Yes sergeant," Amos replied, as he followed. The area behind the lines was bustling with activity and, as the sun began its ascent and the day dawned, the two men made their way through crowds of soldiers.

Some were asleep by the side of the road while reserve troops were milling about waiting to move up to the lines. Others had clearly, from the haunted looks on their faces, just returned from the front.

Around a casualty clearing station there were scores of men waiting to be seen. Many were 'walking wounded' with improvised bandages wrapped around bloody wounds, but there were also more seriously injured men lying on stretchers.

Medical orderlies were going from one to another, assessing their condition and chalking their tunics with a number which determined how quickly they'd be treated.

Others were being helped by soldiers who were giving them water or a comforting word. Amos surveyed the scene around him as he walked past, his eyes fixing upon a man lying on a stretcher who was attempting to sit up.

He was naked from the waist up except for a large bandage which had been wrapped around his torso. It was heavily bloodstained. Kneeling next to him was a soldier who was putting a cigarette into the wounded man's mouth.

Amos turned away as the soldier held the cigarette for him before taking it out of his mouth so he could blow out the smoke.

Further on the two men had to pause as a column of German prisoners filed past. Amos thought how pathetic they looked in their disheveled field grey uniforms, their faces just as gaunt and hollow as those of his comrades in khaki.

Alongside walked one or two British soldiers holding rifles with their bayonets attached, yet looking relaxed. Some even seemed to be smiling, as were some of their prisoners.

Amos assumed they knew there was little chance of revolt amongst the captured, half of whom looked disconsolate, the other half relieved.

"Push through them Amos, don't stand there waiting for this rabble," Quigg snapped.

Amos hesitated slightly but a nudge in the back from his sergeant propelled him forward and he pushed his way through the column of men.

"Get out of my way, let me through," Quigg barked as he followed.

Moments later the two men were standing near to a rise in the ground, out of which appeared to be an entrance surrounded by a wall of sandbags. The Union flag flew from a makeshift pole and at the entrance there was a sign above in which someone had scrawled 'Battalion HQ' in white chalk.

"Wait here," Quigg said as he walked inside. He emerged shortly afterwards, instructing Amos to follow him inside.

Amos walked through the entrance, stooping slightly to avoid hitting his head.

It was bigger inside than he imagined, probably because it had been cut away to create a honeycomb of rooms. The first thing he saw was a soldier sitting at a table typing while another stood over him. Both looked up as he entered.

Quigg spoke first: "Private George Amos, here to see Major Howard at his request."

The standing soldier, who Amos now saw was a lieutenant, looked down at the man on the typewriter and said: "Carry on Corporal Samuels."

He looked at Quigg and Amos before saying: "Wait here," before disappearing into another room beyond.

A minute later he emerged. "The Major will see you now." Quigg stepped into the room with Amos following closely behind.

Light from lamps illuminated the room and the Major sat at a table, pen in hand, hunched over a piece of paper.

Quigg snapped his heels together sharply, spun to his left, stood to attention and saluted: "Major Howard sir, Private 16407 Amos, D Company."

The sergeant glanced at Amos who stood rigid and saluted.

Without looking up the Major said: "Thank you sergeant," and carried on writing. A few seconds later he put down his pen, and looked up from beneath his peaked hat.

"Ah, so this is Private Amos?" he said, rising from his chair and stepping out from behind his desk.

Amos stood perfectly still, aware that a bead of sweat was trickling from his helmet down his right temple.

"Sergeant Quigg here tells me you are the man responsible for bringing in Captain Harris. Is that correct?" the Major asked.

Amos glanced at Quigg, who was smiling wryly, before turning to face the officer.

"Er, yes sir, Private Bousefield and myself, we brought the captain in sir," he said nervously.

"But it was your idea was it not Amos? And it was you who carried him in over the line I understand," the Major replied.

"Yes sir, but ..."

"Damn courageous thing to do," the Major said, interrupting him.

"Captain Harris was a fine fellow, one of the best."

Amos considered speaking again but a glance at Quigg told him it would be ill advised.

"Yesterday was a difficult day Amos," the Major said. "However, DHQ is confident we are making a breakthrough along the front and this offensive will prove decisive.

"But back home people will be jittery. What they need are heroes Private Amos, do you understand?"

Amos didn't.

"Err, yes sir ... I mean ... erm, I'm ... I'm not sure sir," he said.

The Major smiled and looked Amos in the eye.

"You, Private Amos, are what the country needs. You're a hero. It took real courage to go out there on your own, risking your own life to bring back a wounded officer," the Major said.

"You may not know but Lieutenant Colonel Watson was also injured and had to be rescued. Thankfully, he's recovering well. It is a tragedy that Captain Harris could not be saved but your actions prove why the British soldier is superior to any other in the world," he added.

Amos finally plucked up the courage to speak: "Thank you sir."

"Now," said the Major, "It has come to my attention that there are those who believe you deserve to be decorated for gallantry and, I have to say, I support that view.

"I'm having a citation sent to divisional headquarters this morning recommending you be awarded the Distinguished Conduct Medal. What do you think of that Amos?" the Major asked, smiling broadly.

Amos was stunned. He looked open mouthed at Sergeant Quigg before turning back to the officer.

"Sir, I'm ... I'm honoured sir, but I didn't ..."

"There's no shame in being modest private, it's a strong virtue to have. But as I said, the country is in need of heroes and you are one of them," the Major replied.

The officer held out his right hand and shook Amos' hand: "Delighted to meet you Amos," he said, turning away to sit back down in his chair.

The Sergeant saluted, as did Amos, before Quigg indicated that was their cue to go.

Amos was about to turn and leave but stopped and said nervously: "Sir, beg your pardon sir, but what about Private Bousefield?"

Even behind him he could sense Quigg's irritation who said sharply: "Private Amos, you have been dismissed, step this way."

But the Major intervened.

"It's ok Sergeant, the boy has earned the right to speak. Go on," he said.

Amos looked at Quigg who was having trouble hiding his anger.

"Thank you, sir. It's about Private Bousefield sir, he was with me every step of the way in going out to get Captain Harris. I couldn't have done it without him sir."

The Major stood up again and approached Amos.

"You're a fine soldier and a good man Private Amos. Unfortunately, I'm told the same can't be said for this Private .... what's his name?"

"Bousefield sir," Amos replied.

"Yes, of course. Now, Sergeant Quigg, remind me of this Private Bousefield?"

Quigg looked furious but his expression changed as he looked the Major in the eye.

"Er, yes sir, Private Eddie Bousefield was placed under arrest for being drunk on duty and for striking an officer. He was found with a bottle of alcohol on him and admitted to drinking in the field."

"Damn insolence of the man, has he no respect?" the Major said sharply.

Amos looked confused. "But Major, he ... he risked his life too, sir."

"And I'm sure that will be taken into consideration Amos, but you've no need to concern yourself in these matters. The country doesn't need soldiers like Private Bousefield, they need heroes like you," the Major added, before he again turned and sat back down.

Outside Quigg couldn't hide his anger any longer and he grabbed Amos, shoving him up against a sandbagged wall.

"What the bloody hell were you doing there Amos? Well? Don't you ever make me look a fool like that again," he bellowed into his face.

"I don't give a shit if they give you the V fucking C, you will not speak to an officer again unless asked to do so and you will certainly not question me. Do you understand me Private?"

Amos looked at Quigg, the veins in his forehead clearly visible. "Yes, sergeant," he said.

Quigg relaxed his grip slightly before adding: "And forget all about Eddie fucking Bousefield. He's not your problem. Now, I suggest you go and find something to eat before we parade on," before he let go, turned and walked away.

The roll call was hugely depressing. Those who were able lined up to represent what remained of the 11th Battalion.

Amos knew yesterday had been bad but as he took his place in the line alongside what was left of around 700 fighting men, he neither felt lucky nor blessed that he'd managed to survive unscathed.

All he felt was sick.

Quigg began reading through the names as Major Howard and a small group of other officers stood impassively.

Amos willed him to speed up, not sure he could stand the agony of hearing every name said aloud of those now gone forever.

Each time a name was called he found himself holding his breath, hoping, willing a voice to answer. Mostly, they did not.

Bacon, Bailey, Barnett ... on and on in a slow, monotonous delivery that only seemed to accentuate the agony, Quigg continued.

Amos was struggling to hold himself together and Quigg was still only on the Cs.

"Crawford?" ... silence, "Crawley?" ... silence, "Dabell?" ... silence, "Daniels?" ... "yes, sergeant," ... instinctively, Amos glanced right on hearing the voice. He was relieved; he had always liked Len Daniels.

"17459 Davies?" ... silence, "17993 Davies?" ... silence, "Doherty?" ... silence, "Dove?" ... Amos scrunched his eyes shut, he saw Bill's face and the last moments of his life. Tears ran down his face.

It took more than an hour to read through them all and by the end fewer than 200 men answered.

Major Howard addressed them afterwards, speaking about his pride and that of the injured Lieutenant Colonel Watson in the battalion's performance, but Amos wasn't listening.

In an effort to hold himself together he'd been attempting to focus his mind elsewhere, way beyond the charnel house he now found himself in. He thought of his mother and he saw her smiling. And the tears streamed down his face.

April 2016

Arthur had suggested he take the diary home, something which excited Tom but at the same time left him feeling awkward. He knew how precious it was to the old man and was surprised at the offer.

"No, I couldn't do that Arthur, you should keep it here," he'd said.

"Don't be daft," Arthur replied.

"When you get to my age you know a thing or two about judging character lad. I know you won't disappear with it," he said, smiling.

Later that night he sat up in bed and read from the beginning as Emma slept beside him.

Roebuck described how the battalion adjusted to life in France from the end of August 1915. The first dozen or so entries were simply every day accounts of wartime life behind the lines, describing the living conditions, training and preparation the Sherwood Foresters were living through.

Occasionally, however, he would talk about individuals, giving a tantalising glimpse into the past about the emotions and deeds of men who were now firmly set on a path that he suspected none of them could ever have comprehended.

'19th of September 1915. Today, I was asked to be present by Major Grierson when Private Rockley was

given the awful news that his wife had died in childbirth. Remarkably, the infant, a boy, had survived and was said to be doing well.

'The news has dented the morale of many of the poor man's friends and there was a subdued atmosphere for much of the day.'

Harris read on as Roebuck went on to describe how the battalion made an exchange with the 24th Brigade in October 1915 to give the inexperienced soldiers an opportunity to learn from those with battle experience.

He later recounted in grim detail the first fatality, a young soldier aged just 19, who was killed during a training exercise.

'26th of October 1915. My first experience of the ghastly and terrible damage instruments of war can do. Private Saunders was gravely injured when a Mills bomb exploded as he and his platoon practised capturing an enemy trench.

'It would appear the device snagged on his tunic as he went to throw it and exploded in his right hand. I was asked to sit with him and comfort him until the end, it was a terrible sight.

'His right arm was missing, much of his lower torso was ripped open, exposing the poor man's insides, while the right side of his face was a bloody, gruesome mess. It was both astonishing and cruel that he did not die instantly and I sat with him for several minutes until he passed away.'

Amidst the insight Roebuck's diary gave of the day to day life of the 11th battalion, what also emerged were the

169

feelings of a man ill-suited to the environment he now found himself in and struggling to be accepted by many of those around him.

'*2nd of November 1915. My attempts at reaching out to some who have thus far ignored my ministry have yet to bear fruit. It is apparent to me that many of the men still view me with suspicion, a fact not helped, I suspect, by carrying this ridiculous officer rank with me.*

'*I did not come here to have men salute me or follow my orders. I simply want them to know the word of God and find comfort in the hardships they bear.*'

Tom noticed that future entries also alluded to the same theme and he began forming a picture of a man who was uncomfortable in the role he was being asked to perform.

However, as he read on, Roebuck's tone seemed to change, linked in no small part he thought, to the experiences he and the battalion were going through.

'*9th of December 1915. It remains bitterly cold and there was a hard frost again overnight. The living conditions of the men have worsened and it is hard seeing them huddled together in makeshift shelters trying to keep warm.*

'*Not that the winter is affecting the ability to wage war. This evening the battalion came under artillery fire and there were a number of casualties including three deaths. The burial parties are doing sterling work but to watch them toil, digging graves in the frozen ground, was sobering.*

'In the end I joined in to help, much to their surprise, and after we'd done, and buried those poor souls, they invited me to join them for hot tea brewed in their dugout. I spent more than an hour in their company before I left to write letters to the bereaved.'

As the diary continued, Tom now noticed there were hardly any entries in which Roebuck didn't mention the deaths and injuries of soldiers.

'... Private Gamble blinded by shrapnel

'... poor Corporal Parkinson lost his leg while two of his platoon were killed by a shell

'... all rocked by the terrible news that Lieutenant Crossley was shot and killed by a sniper as he directed a working party

They occurred so often that they were now almost commonplace in Roebuck's writing and sometimes merited only a passing reference. Yet, occasionally there were things he witnessed that he clearly had to record in more detail.

'5th of January 1916. One of the worst days I've encountered thus far. Today, the battalion came under intense artillery fire. Casualties were high with several men wounded and again, we lost some very good men.

'Lance Corporal Barker along with Privates Walker and Sadler, were sheltering in their dug out when it took a direct hit from a high explosive shell.

'The damage it inflicted was appalling and the sight of men scooping whatever they could find of the remains of their friends before putting them in sandbags, was one which will stay with me until the end of my days.

'I wrestled with my conscience for some time before writing letters to their loved ones. One doesn't want to lie but it is hard knowing the truth will only add to their grief.'

Tom found the accounts both fascinating and depressing. He couldn't put it down and ploughed on.

Into 1916 now and Roebuck's entries continued as he described the battalion's movements in and out of the line before the first indications that they were to be involved in a major offensive.

'12th of April 1916. The news reaching us from Verdun is not good and there are rumours the French are on the brink of collapse. All the talk now is when, not if, we launch an offensive of our own.

'The men appear genuinely excited by the prospect. Many are chomping at the bit to have a go at the enemy, rather than sit around taking their chances against the shells and snipers. They just want to get on and finish the job.'

In the pages that followed Roebuck described the battalion being moved south, away from the front line, as part of a huge build-up of men, horses and munitions.

It was a relatively quiet period and this was reflected by the chaplain writing about the countryside, wildlife, nature and French civilians, of whom he was hugely impressed by their stoicism at coping with the war and the ever growing influx of British soldiers descending on their towns and villages.

'22nd of May 1916. I spent some time in the town of Albert today along with two of the other regimental

chaplains. What struck us all was the warmth and friendliness of the French people. They have seen their land ripped apart by two years of war and many are suffering huge hardship.

'Yet, as we walked around the shell shattered town, one could not help but draw strength from the spirit of these people who firmly believe that we shall prevail.

'I stood for a while looking at the steeple of the church of Notre Dame de Brebières. It is a most extraordinary sight looking at the statue of the Virgin Mary hanging precariously since being hit by a shell last year.

'An elderly Frenchman saw me looking at it and approached me. 'Vive le France, Vive Grand Bretagne ... le victoire sera le notre,' he said.

'28th of May 1916. We are now surely part of the worst kept secret of the war ... our plans for the Big Push. There is now such a concentration of men, horses and machines, that it is difficult to find anywhere Khaki free.

'During a pleasant walk through the countryside earlier today I was astonished to see a column of British soldiers queuing patiently beside a farm house where a mademoiselle was offering haircuts and wet shaves, along with a cup of local wine, all for one Franc.'

Tom yawned and felt his eyes getting heavy but he read on. Roebuck was into June 1916 now and his entries shed light on the build up towards the Somme offensive and then, on the 24th of June, the start of the British bombardment.

'24ᵗʰ of June 1916. I'm writing this as the tremendous noise from our guns continues unabated. They opened up this morning and have not ceased. We do not know how long it will last but we're told the intention is to obliterate the German defences, ensuring easy passage when our men go over the top.

'The mood within the battalion is one of excitement and even euphoria. I happened across one group who were cheering every shell that was fired. I walked on by. There is nothing to be gained from reminding them that men are on the receiving end of it.'

"Tom … put the light out, go to sleep," Emma murmured, sounding irritated, before turning over.

"Yeah, ok, in a minute," he replied.

'27ᵗʰ of June 1916. I was invited to dine with Lieutenant-Colonel Watson and the battalion's senior commanders. Dinner was accompanied by the noise from our bombardment which continues relentlessly. It has been three days now.

'One can only imagine how abhorrent conditions must be in the enemy's lines in the face of such an onslaught. As a Christian my heart goes out to all those who are suffering and I only pray that it is 'worth it' in the end and brings this dreadful conflict to a swift conclusion.'

'Over dinner, the Lieutenant Colonel asked me to arrange a service for the battalion before the offensive begins. I'm deeply honoured.'

He yawned again and was about to admit defeat, put the book down and turn the light out. But something made him read one more page.

'*28th of June 1916. I spent much of this afternoon selecting suitable verses and passages for my sermon. Whilst doing so, I was joined by two of the Battalion's company commanders, Major Bernell and Captain Harris, who happened across my dug out.*

'*Captain Harris is quite unlike any of the other commanding officers I've come across. He appeared genuinely interested in the task given to me and asked what verses I was considering using.*

'*I explained the problem was which ones to leave out, as there are so many which touch upon courage and strength. Captain Harris simply smiled and said: 'Padre, what the men need is hope,' and he began to recite Romans 5-2-7 before he and Major Bernell went on their way.*

'*He was entirely right. The verse is remarkably apt and I've included it in my service.*'

There it was, the first mention of the man Tom had become fascinated with. The hairs on the back of his neck stood on end and he went back and re-read the entry.

And then, for some reason he couldn't explain, he stealthily got out of bed, crept out of the bedroom and went downstairs. Flicking on the living room light he walked over to a bookcase and began scouring the rows of books he and Emma had collected over the years.

He found what he was looking for, reached up and lifted out a hardback book. Looking at the cover, he opened it and saw his mother's handwriting in the top corner of the first page ... '*to our loving son Edward, may you treasure this always, lots of love mummy and daddy, Christmas 1993 xxx'*

He couldn't recall the last time he'd looked at it and briefly wondered why he still kept it. Sentiment was the reason he guessed. Flicking through, he skimmed the New Testament until he came upon Romans. Turning the pages quickly now, his eyes scanned the verses until he found what he was looking for. Romans 5-2-7: "*By whom also we have access by faith into this grace wherein we stand, and rejoice in hope of the glory of God. And not only so, but we glory in tribulations also: knowing that tribulation worketh patience; And patience, experience; and experience, hope:*

"And hope maketh not ashamed; because the love of God is shed abroad in our hearts by the Holy Ghost which is given unto us. For when we were yet without strength, in due time Christ died for the ungodly. For scarcely for a righteous man will one die : yet peradventure for a good man some would even dare to die."

Chapter eleven

August 1916

Like others before him he was drawn to the noise. Even from a distance he could tell the place was heaving, its raucous atmosphere drawing him in.

Inside, the air was thick with the foggy haze of cigarettes, their smell masking the stench of body odour in a room densely packed with khaki.

Occasionally, shrill female voices could be heard speaking French or broken English, above the cacophony.

For several minutes he struggled to squeeze his way through a sea of bodies as he made his way over to a corner of the bar. Once there, he put a pile of coins down in front of him.

"Oui Tommy .... beer? wine?"

He looked up to see a red faced, middle aged woman looking at him, shouting to make herself heard. The room was stifling and her face was glistening with sweat.

She wasn't smiling, she looked harrassed, hurried. Her make up was crude with thick black eye liner, false eyelashes and far too much rouge on her cheeks.

"Beer ... sil vous plait," he shouted.

The woman nodded and went off before returning with a large mug of beer, its head frothing over the sides.

"Enjoy Tommy," she said, scooping up a couple of coins before turning away to serve another.

For the next two hours Amos sat and drank himself into a stupor. Surrounded by crowds of people he was occasionally jostled by some of the more boisterous.

He had never felt more alone. No one spoke to him but then he didn't want them to. He simply sat and drank. After a while the woman merely refilled his glass without speaking.

Eventually, the room began to empty until Amos was one of only a handful of men left inside. The sound of breaking glass followed by cheers and then the furious voice of the woman shouting in French, caused him to lift his head and look.

He saw her ushering four inebriated Tommies out of the door, all of them laughing as she did so.

When they'd left she slammed the door, fetched a sweeping brush and began muttering to herself as she cleaned up the debris.

"Bonsoir Tommy ... can I join you?"

He turned his head slowly to see a young woman standing beside him. In the state he was in it never occurred to him where she appeared from.

Amos stared at her with a drunken gaze, his head slowly wavering and his eyes heavy.

The woman sat on a stool and her perfumed scent wafted through his nose causing him to reel slightly.

'What's your name Tommy?" the girl asked cheerfully. She was young, in her early twenties maybe, and her mousey brown hair spiralled neatly upwards where it was kept in place by a bright red hair pin.

Her features were slight yet her eyes were large and, like the older woman who had served him, she was wearing make up, though it wasn't as crudely applied.

Amos didn't speak but continued staring. She giggled and, smiling broadly, said: "My name is Marie. You are funny ... and handsome."

Her hand reached out and rested on Amos' knee.

Leaning in towards him, she said: "You would like some company Tommy? I have somewhere ... I can make it nice."

At that point the older woman shouted in their direction and came over. She looked angry and was admonishing the younger woman, both of them now arguing.

Her berating continued as she pointed towards the door but the woman stayed put and, when she didn't move, the older woman grabbed her arm and began pulling.

It was at that point Amos got up, the confrontation enough to stir him out of his malaise. Unsteadily, he stood in between the two women attempting to calm them both down.

The older woman looked at him. "Petite pute ... she is a whore! She is not welcome here," she said angrily.

Amos turned to look at the girl who was speaking rapidly, he couldn't understand a word.

Stepping towards her he almost stumbled and she reached out to take his arm to hold him steady. The pair looked at each other before Amos put his arm around her shoulder and the two of them walked out of the bar, the older woman cursing as they left.

She helped him navigate the door and the step down into the street before saying: "Merci, Tommy."

Amos wobbled in front of her and she held on to his arm to keep him steady.

"Whoa, careful Tommy ...," she said, giggling again.

Through his drunken eyes Amos looked at her face before suddenly lurching forwards, kissing her roughly. His hands grabbed and groped and she pushed him away, laughing nervously.

"Easy Tommy, easy ... not here ok. I have somewhere, come," and she took his hand and led the way.

It wasn't far but in Amos' state the short walk took longer than it should have. Finally, they stopped in a doorway and Marie opened a door which led to a narrow staircase.

She ushered Amos inside and told him to go up first. He slowly climbed the stairs, aware of her behind him, a hand on his back to keep him steady.

Upstairs led to a small living area which was tidy but cramped. There was a kitchen area with stove and sink at one end, while at the other were two chairs and a sideboard.

"Please," she said, motioning for Amos to sit down. He slumped into the chair and, despite his state, sensed she appeared nervous.

"Wait here ... please," she said, before disappearing through a door into an adjoining room.

He felt drowsy but he wanted her and thoughts of that were enough to stop him drifting off to sleep.

He heard voices then the door opened and she reappeared, holding a small child in her arms, while a young boy stood beside her, yawning and rubbing his eyes.

She said something to him and he walked towards where Amos was sitting before reaching for a folded blanket on the back of a chair.

Laying it out on the floor the boy took two cushions and put them side by side before lying down. Marie then lay the small, sleeping child next to the boy, and covered them over with the blanket.

She kissed them both on the forehead and whispered: "Bonsoir mes beautés."

Standing up she held out her hand and Amos took it, pulling himself up from the chair.

He glanced at the two children but she gently pulled him towards the door saying: "It's ok, they are sleeping now."

Amos was first into the bedroom. Inside was a double bed but not much room for anything else.

She followed him in and closed the door.

Moving towards her she held up her hand and he paused.

"The price is two Francs Tommy," she said. "Or you can pay four, stay and I make you breakfast."

Amos fumbled in his pockets and retrieved a handful of notes. He gave them to her but while she was still counting them out he had pulled her close a second time and was kissing her neck.

He pushed her up against the wall and began fondling her roughly. "Take your time Tommy, there's no rush," she said.

But Amos was beyond listening. He was tearing at her clothes now and thrust his hand between her legs.

She cried out and pushed him away, before saying nervously: "Easy, Tommy ... don't be so rough."

There was fear in her voice now, made worse by the fact Amos hadn't spoken once since she'd approached him in the bar.

He paused and she used the opportunity to take control and began to undress him. But he grabbed her arm, pushing it away and felt for her again.

He ripped her dress open, exposing her breasts, and snatched at her under garments pulling them down.

'Ok Tommy, ok ... be gentle," she said, desperately trying to remain calm and stay in control.

Amos pushed her backwards on to the bed, fumbling with his trousers as he struggled to undo them. He clambered on the mattress and forcibly pushed her legs apart.

She was scared now and looked at him pleadingly but Amos didn't see her.

Instead, he saw Bill and Captain Harris, smashed bodies, heads with no faces, the entrails of friends ... and he felt dizzy with rage.

Moments later the room was quiet and Amos heard her sobs as he drifted in and out of sleep.

Then the bedroom door opened and he heard a child's voice ... "Mama?"

Marie hurriedly got out of bed, wiping her nose and eyes with her hand.

"Shh, ok ma chérie de maman, se rendormir," she said, hugging the little boy and taking him out of the room.

Amos woke to hear birds singing and voices coming from the other room. His head was throbbing. He sat up, looked around, groggily recalling the events of the early hours.

Dressing himself, he opened the bedroom door. As he did so the young boy saw him and ran towards his mother, grabbing hold of her leg, hugging it tight.

Marie looked down, stroked his hair and whispered something to him, smiling. On the floor the younger child, a girl he now saw, was lying on her back playing with a wooden spoon.

"You are hungry?" she said, her voice distracted him as he looked at the faces of the two children.

"Yes ... er, oui ... merci," he replied.

A few minutes later he sat at the table, across from the boy and his mother, the three of them eating omelettes in silence.

"Merci," he said, when he'd finished, before standing up. "I ... I should go now," he said.

She didn't answer.

He had to step around the little girl lying on the floor as he made his way to the door. As he did so he caught sight of a photograph on the sideboard.

He saw a tall man in a French soldier's uniform standing upright and staring out from the camera. Beside him was the woman in whose home he now stood, holding a small baby.

Reaching out he went to pick up the photo only for the woman to shout angrily: "Stop! Leave it ... that is not yours to touch."

She walked across and grabbed the photo, clutching it to her chest, as though protecting it from him.

Amos looked as uncomfortable as he felt and said quietly: "I'm ... I'm sorry. Is he?"

"Do not speak of him," she replied brusquely. "It is not your business." The raised voices startled the children and the little girl started to cry.

He looked again at the faces of the two children and then into Marie's eyes and he saw what it was to be hated.

Turning to open the door he looked back once more and said simply: "I'm so sorry ... truly I am," and he walked down the stairs into the sunshine.

May 2016

Tom was excited. He'd hardly slept after finishing the

diary and was now desperate to share what he'd found with Arthur.

Over breakfast he'd tried telling Emma but in between Daisy screaming and throwing cereal everywhere, he knew he was wasting his time.

Telling her that he'd promised to get the book back to his friend the following morning, he drove over to his bungalow, the diary in a plastic bag on his passenger seat.

As he drove, in his head he replayed the key passages he'd read in the early hours.

'1st and 2nd of July 1916. Truly, I have entered the gates of Hell. The brutality of man has no limits, I know that now and the past 48 hours have tested my faith to its very core.

'I have borne witness to senseless slaughter, the scale of which is unimaginable to any right minded person. What has happened here over the last two days will, I fear, leave deep scars for generations to come.

'My faith remains unshakeable but in the few minutes I did have time to myself, I prayed to be given the strength to cope with the enormity of the human catastrophe unfolding before me.'

He tried to imagine what the chaplain had seen and wondered where he'd been during that first, horrific day on the battlefield. He pictured a man in awe of the events unfolding in front of him, yet utterly helpless.

Frustratingly, these were only the words written about the 1st and 2nd of July. But the mere fact Roebuck had combined two days into one entry, told him a lot.

Part of him had hoped to read something about Harris' death but the colossal numbers of dead on that fateful day were always going to render that implausible.

But his disappointment had been fleeting. Because what he read in the days following the second of July was fascinating.

There was no other way to describe it.

The coincidences were more than uncanny, they were a little unnerving if he was honest. But they kept occurring. What were the chances he asked himself time and again?

He had to share his find with somebody and he wanted it to be Arthur. The drive over was uneventful and within minutes he was getting out of his car, pressing the button on his key fob to lock it and walking down Arthur's path, the diary in his other hand.

Wait until he hears this, he won't believe it Tom thought. Come to think of it, I don't believe it!

He rang the bell and stood there grinning to himself. "Come on Arthur," he muttered to himself when the door didn't open.

He rang the bell a second time. Again, there was no response. He frowned, thinking it was odd before knocking loudly on the door.

Stepping to his left he cupped a hand over his forehead and pressed his nose up against the glass of Arthur's lounge window in an attempt to peer in through the net curtains.

Maybe he's out he thought and he briefly considered walking away. But then he glanced down and saw two bottles of milk standing on the doorstep.

Arthur was the only person he knew who still had a milkman. He looked at his watch, knowing full well it was almost midday. Now he was worried.

Bending down, he lifted the letterbox cover and put his mouth in front of the opening before shouting through it: 'Arthur? Arthur, it's me Tom. Are you in?"

Next he lowered his head and looked through the opening. He saw him immediately, some of him anyway.

The old man's legs were visible, as was most of his torso and an arm. Dressed in pyjamas, he wasn't moving.

Tom froze for a second before he began banging loudly on the door and shouting: "Arthur? Arthur, can you hear me? Arthur?"

He dropped the bag containing the diary, took the phone out of his pocket and called an ambulance.

"Er, yes, I can see him through the letterbox … no, he's not moving. Send someone quickly please," he said.

Arthur's quiet street was unused to the commotion and a couple of neighbours came outside to see what was going on.

"He's on the floor, he's collapsed or something," Tom said, in reply to suspicious, quizzical looks from two people.

At that, a middle aged woman and a younger man came over from separate directions.

"Where is he?" the woman asked.

He repeated himself and for a moment the three of them bent down together and were peering through the letterbox at Arthur's body.

"How long will the ambulance be? We've got to break this door down," the younger man said.

Tom looked at him, too stunned to speak.

Suddenly, the man began shoulder barging the door, slamming into it, letting out a loud grunt as he did so. When that didn't work he took to kicking at it.

Tom joined in and the pair of them were frantically kicking the door until finally it gave way and flew open, splintering bits of wood into the hallway.

They ran inside and he knelt before Arthur who was lying on his side. "Is he breathing?" the younger man asked, as Tom noticed two other people had come into the house.

He reached out and touched Arthur's head, he felt warm and he saw he was breathing slowly. His eyes were closed but his mouth was open and he was dribbling.

"Yes, I think so," he replied.

"Get a blanket, cover him over and keep him warm," a woman's voice said.

"Check his pulse, make sure his airways are free of obstruction," another voice urged.

At that point a siren could be heard getting steadily louder. Moments later flashes of blue lights swirled around Arthur's hall as the ambulance pulled up outside.

"Stand aside please, let us through," a woman's voice said, as Tom turned to see two paramedics come into the hall.

The next few minutes were a daze as he and the others were ushered out of the hall back on to the street.

One of the paramedics emerged and returned to the ambulance coming back moments later pushing a stretcher on wheels.

Tom watched as Arthur was carefully lifted on to it, a breathing mask over his face.

He was then brought out and the two paramedics lifted him into the ambulance.

"Is he ... is he going to be ok?" Tom asked as the male paramedic closed the rear doors.

"Are you family?" the paramedic asked.

"Er, no, I'm a friend of his," Tom replied.

"Then I'm sorry, I really can't tell you anything. We've got to get him to hospital," he added, before turning and getting into the driver's seat.

Tom stood there as the blue lights began flashing again and the ambulance sped off, leaving him standing in the road.

He turned and looked at Arthur's battered front door and walked back up the path. On the step was a puddle of white where one of the milk bottles had been knocked over in the rush to get inside.

Using his foot to sweep broken glass to the side, he bent down and picked up the plastic bag, the spilt milk dripping from it. Opening it carefully, he removed the diary, relieved to find it was still dry.

After making Arthur's house secure, an hour later he was sitting in a sterile, fluorescent-lit waiting area in the hospital's emergency admissions unit. On the way he'd rung Emma to explain what had occurred. She knew from the tone of his voice how anxious she was and hadn't hesitated in suggesting he go straight there.

Inside, he'd found the staff surprisingly helpful, considering he wasn't related. Though he was embarrassed at not being able to answer whether the old man had any family or not.

Invited to sit and wait, he sat down on a hard, blue plastic chair mounted on a frame in the floor. Gazing at the myriad posters and information leaflets on the walls, he found himself reading advice to prevent the spread of germs, how to spot meningitis in babies and a number to call to help give up smoking.

He wasn't alone in the waiting area and sat across from a man who had two young children with him. Both were clearly bored and he was struggling to keep them occupied, occasionally having to raise his voice and tell them to sit still.

The time crawled, made worse by him not knowing anything about Arthur's condition. He fiddled with his phone, exchanging texts with Emma and browsing the internet, before getting up and buying a cold drink from a vending machine.

"Mr Harris?" he heard a woman's voice call.

He turned to see a slim woman wearing what he assumed was some kind of nurse's uniform.

"Hello there would you like to come with me?" she said, smiling.

He followed her into a small, windowless room, fearing the worse as he sat down in one of two soft, comfy chairs. The woman sat in the other.

"My name is Helen and I'm one of the patient liaison nurses here. I understand you are a friend of Mr Roebuck's?" she said.

"Yes, yes I am," Tom replied. "How is he? He's not ... is he?"

"Mr Roebuck is stable, he's been taken to our high dependency unit where we need to conduct more tests," she replied, gesturing with her hands as she spoke.

He sighed audibly with relief and took a deep breath.

"I'm sorry, for a minute there I thought ... well, you know, that he'd ..." his voice tailed off.

The nurse smiled at him before asking: "How long have you known Mr Roebuck?"

For the next ten minutes he described how they'd met and his unlikely friendship with a man old enough to be his own grandfather.

At the end he asked: "Is he awake? Can I go and see him?"

"As I said, he's comfortable and stable but we have had to keep him sedated. I can take you in for a couple of minutes but just bear in mind that he won't be able to hear you and he is on a ventilator to help his breathing," the nurse said.

"We like people to know that as it can be a shock to see family and friends in that condition," she added.

Tom followed her through sterile corridors until they stopped at a set of double doors, a sign saying High

191

Dependency Unit above them. She took a card hanging from a lanyard around her neck and used it to swipe through a reader which opened the door.

Inside the unit was more dimly lit and a man sitting at a computer looked up from his desk momentarily as he and the nurse walked in.

There were four doors, two each side of the desk, and at the second one on the left the nurse stopped and said: "This is Mr Roebuck's room. I can let you have a couple of minutes with him," she said, extending her arm to push open the door before stepping aside to let him enter.

Arthur lay on a bed, his face covered with a mask from which a tube led to a ventilator. A plastic tube was coming out of his nose, leading into a machine and he was attached to a drip.

Next to the bed there was a digital display giving electronic readings, which Tom couldn't help but look at in an attempt to decipher what they meant.

There was a single chair and some sort of a cabinet or table next to the bed. He considered whether he should go and sit in the chair but the nurse had said only a couple of minutes so he stood awkwardly near the door.

The only noise was an occasional bleep from the digital monitor and the rhythmic sound of the ventilator.

He stared at the old man he'd known for only a matter of days and wondered whether he'd ever hear him speak again. And then, with the slightest stroke of the old man's foot through the hospital blanket, he turned and walked away.

Chapter twelve

July 1916

Walking into the room with a soldier either side, he was aware that all eyes were focused upon him. Standing to attention he snapped a salute and was directed to a wooden chair where he sat down, his hands resting on a table.

Directly opposite him sat three men, two of whom were conferring in whispered voices.

He recognised one of them but not the other two.

Glancing to his right he saw Lieutenant Blackwood scribbling on a bundle of papers as he too sat at a table. The room, he knew, was in the town hall and on the walls he saw a French tricolour and two paintings, both portraits of old men wearing mayoral robes.

At the door stood two soldiers, both were armed. It opened and in walked another junior officer. He approached the table where the three men sat, saluted and then stepped forward and spoke.

He tried to hear what they were saying but wasn't close enough.

The junior officer stepped back, turned around and, reading from a sheet of paper, addressed the room: "On active service this day twelfth of July, 1916, I, the undersigned officer in command of 11th (Service) Battalion, Nottingham and Derbyshire Regiment, on active service, state that the persons named in the annexed schedule, and being subject to Military Law, have committed the offence in the said schedule mentioned.

"I am of the opinion that it is not practicable that such an offence should be tried by an ordinary General Court Martial and I therefore hereby convene a Field General Court Martial to try the said persons and to consist of the officers here under named.

"President, Major Howard, 11th Battalion Nottinghamshire and Derbyshire Regiment, and members Captain Larkin, 8th King's Own Light Infantry and Lieutenant Bloom, 11th Battalion Nottinghamshire and Derbyshire Regiment. Signed Brigadier General H. Gordon, commanding 70th Infantry Brigade."

The officer looked directly at the soldier seated in front of him and continued: "Army number 44278 Private Edward Bousefield, Nottinghamshire and Derbyshire Regiment, you stand accused when on Active Service that on the 1st of July, 1916 you did willfully, and in direct contravention of Army Service Regulations, consume alcohol 'in the field' on more than one occasion and strike a superior officer, namely Lieutenant Munroe, of the Nottinghamshire and Derbyshire Regiment.

"If found guilty of such an offence, the maximum penalty is death by execution. How do you plead?"

Bousefield looked up and replied: 'Not guilty sir."

"Stand up when addressing this tribunal," barked a voice from the table beyond.

Bousefield stood slowly, his chair scraping across the wooden floor and looked across to the three men, repeating his not guilty plea.

The man in the centre, who Bousefield recognised, was Major Howard. He wrote something down before glancing across to the officer who had opened proceedings and said: "Thank you Corporal Whitehead. Right, let's get on with this. Lieutenant Blackwood, are you ready to proceed?"

The Lieutenant stood up from his chair and replied swiftly. "I am Major."

"Very well then, the time is 11am and this court is now in session. Lieutenant Blackwood," the Major said.

The officer glanced down at his bundle of papers before he stood and walked into the middle of the room.

He looked around at those present and paused momentarily before speaking: "Sir, this case is extremely straight forward. The accused, Private Edward Bousefield, enlisted in April 1911 when he joined the 1st Battalion Sherwood Foresters, Nottinghamshire and Derbyshire regiment.

"At the outbreak of the war the regiment was serving in Bombay, India, where Private Bousefield had already been on a charge for insubordination. The regiment returned to England in October of 1914 before landing in France that November."

Bousefield fiddled with his hands as the lieutenant spoke, looking down at the floor. The officer continued: "The battalion took part in the 1915 offensives at Neuve Chapelle and Loos where, it should be noted, Private Bousefield was involved in the action in which Private Rivers was awarded a VC.

"However, in the December of that year he spent a period in custody for assaulting two fellow soldiers in his company and was also reprimanded for failing to salute an officer and for not ensuring his rifle was clean.

"In February of this year he was reassigned to the 11th battalion along with several other combat experienced men, with the aim of supporting the new volunteer battalion.

"On the first of July Private Bousefield was part of C Company which attacked the German lines at the Leipzig Salient in support of the 8th King's Own Light Infantry. The battalion incurred heavy casualties during the offensive.

"On the evening of the 1st of July Private Bousefield accompanied another member of his battalion in venturing out into No Man's Land to retrieve an injured officer.

The officer, Captain Edward Harris, was successfully returned to the lines by Private George Amos who carried him in on his back. Unfortunately, Captain Harris died of his wounds.

"When Private Bousefield returned to the lines it was noticeable that he had been drinking, in both his behaviour and from the smell of alcohol in his breath."

The lieutenant delivered his address without any hint of emotion in his voice and there was complete silence in the room as he spoke.

"He was aggressive in his attitude to that of his comrades and, when challenged by Lieutenant Munroe, swore at the officer before physically assaulting him in full view of other ranks. It was at that point that Private Bousefield was arrested and he has remained in custody since."

The officer ended his address and turned to face the three men sitting at the table, all of whom were scribbling notes.

Major Howard then lifted his head and said: "Thank you Lieutenant, how many witnesses are you planning to call today?"

"Four sir," the officer replied.

"Stand up Private Bousefield,"the Major said looking directly at him.

"Do you understand the charges laid against you?"

Bousefield nodded.

"Answer a commanding officer when you are spoken to Private Bousefield," Corporal Whitehead snapped from the side of the room.

Bousefield looked at the Corporal, a flash of anger in his eyes. "Yes ... Major," he said, accentuating the two words.

"Private Bousefield, you have the right to cross examine the prosecution's witnesses. Do you plan to call any witnesses in your defence?"

"No, Major," Bousefield said.

At that the three seated officers looked surprised but the Major continued: "Once the prosecution has finished outlining its case you will be given the opportunity to make representation yourself. Do you understand?"

Bousefield replied again with a short 'yes Major' before the Lieutenant was invited to call his first witness.

The door opened and a small, nervous looking man entered the room. He glanced briefly at Bousefield before looking away, standing to attention and saluting.

After being sworn in by Corporal Whitehead the man was told to take a seat.

"You are Private Reginald Hill of the 11th battalion Sherwood Foresters are you not?" asked Lieutenant Blackwood.

"Yes ... yes, sir ...I am," the private answered, speaking softly.

The prosecuting officer then invited the soldier to give an account of the moment Bousefield returned to the lines after searching for Captain Harris.

Hill began speaking, slowly at first but speeding up as he went on: "On the first of July my platoon went into the front line trenches for duty at eight o'clock that night. Wounded men were making their way back to the line all the time but we were told to be on our guard and be ready for any counter attack.

"Sometime after 10.30pm I was aware that two men had gone back out to look for an injured officer. I didn't know who they were," Hill added.

Bousefield stared impassively ahead of him as the private continued his account, looking at the Lieutenant but occasionally directing his gaze towards the three officers.

"Around 11pm my section became aware of a commotion and voices a short distance from our lines. We made to stand ready and the voices were challenged."

Lieutenant Blackwood interrupted Hill asking: "Did you recognise their voices?"

"Yes sir, it was Private Bousefield. He shouted that we were to 'let him the fuck back in.'"

All eyes were on Bousefield as Hill carried on speaking. "Some of the lads saw Private Amos crawling along with Captain Harris lying on his back. They were helped in.

"Then Private Bousefield leapt into the trench. He was laughing and when he stood next to me I could immediately smell alcohol sir, whiskey I'm sure it was," Hill added.

"Lieutenant Munroe was in the line and he came over to see what all the fuss was with the Captain being brought back and all. He came to speak to Private Bousefield and when he did he asked him out right ... 'have you been drinking Private?'

"Private Bousefield got angry and told the Lieutenant that he'd just 'risked his life to save a fucking officer' and this was the thanks he was getting. Lieutenant Munroe told him to stand to attention and warned him not to speak to an officer that way."

Blackwood walked over until he was standing almost on top of Private Hill and asked: "And what happened then Private?"

Hill looked over at Bousefield and paused before replying: "He said 'you bloody officers are all the same, get the fuck away from me' and he shoved him causing the Lieutenant to fall to the ground. At that point the officer got up and called for Sergeant Quigg who ordered Private Bousefield to be arrested."

When Hill had finished Bousefield was asked if he wanted to cross examine him. He shook his head and stayed in his chair.

He gave the same reply following Lieutenant Munroe's evidence. The young officer never even glanced at Bousefield as he entered the room before giving a brief, short account of what had happened. His version of events was identical to the Private before him.

The third witness was Quigg who seemed to relish the predicament Bousefield now found himself in.

"Private Bousefield has always been undisciplined and needs a firm hand to keep him in line," he told the court, looking intently at Bousefield as he spoke.

"He's a tough soldier, I'll give him that, and I'm sure the enemy don't fancy being up against him," Quigg said.

"But he's volatile, prone to outbursts and has no respect for authority or his fellow Soldier," he added.

"Sergeant Quigg," said a voice interrupting him. It was Captain Larkin. "You're not here to give your opinion on

Private Bousefield, you're here to give us the facts of what happened on the night of the first of July."

Quigg looked embarrassed at being chastised and glanced across to see Bousefield was smirking. He flushed with anger and struggled to keep his composure.

He apologised to the court before being prompted by Lieutenant Blackwood to describe what had happened.

"Private Bousefield accompanied Private Amos out into No Man's Land to find Captain Harris," he said.

"When they finally returned, it was Private Amos who was carrying the wounded Captain. I saw the Captain brought in and then heard Private Bousefield arguing with Lieutenant Munroe.

"As I walked over towards them I saw Private Bousefield swear at the officer before striking him, at which point he fell to the ground. I immediately had him arrested," he said, finishing his testimony.

Again, Bousefield was asked if he wanted to cross examine. Quigg stared at him venomously, hoping he would, but the Private simply shook his head.

The sergeant left the room and Lieutenant Blackwood turned towards the Major and the two officers sitting in judgement.

"The prosecution now calls its final witness, Private George Amos of the 11th battalion Sherwood Foresters, Nottinghamshire and Derbyshire regiment," the Lieutenant said.

Bousefield sat up and shuffled to the edge of his seat, leaning forward and craning his neck as the door opened. In walked Amos, looking nervous, who made eye contact with him immediately.

Lieutenant Blackwood told him why he had been called and then said: "Private Amos, could you tell the court what happened on the night of July first?"

Amos looked at the Lieutenant and then the three officers seated at the table, before his eyes again fixed upon Bousefield.

"Yes, Lieutenant," he said. "I can tell the court exactly what happened."

May 2016

The hospital visits soon became part of his regular routine and he tried to get to see Arthur at least every other day on the way home from work.

He had been in for ten days now and for the first week had remained heavily sedated in the high dependency unit.

Tom had got to know the medical staff quite well and had found out that the old man did have a niece but she lived in Australia. She had been made aware of her uncle's condition but wasn't planning on coming back to the UK.

Apart from a visit from his next door neighbour Len, a man also in his early 80s, and flowers sent by Arthur's friends at the Legion, Tom was the only regular visitor to his bedside.

At the end of that first week he took it as a good sign when he turned up to find he had been moved into a room within a normal ward. And two days later he was both surprised and thrilled to see Arthur sitting up in bed when he walked into his room.

He looked tired, weak and had already lost weight around his face, making him look even older.

"Hey, Arthur, it's good to see you," he said, "You've given us a bit of scare these last few days."

The old man's eyes were heavy and he smiled briefly.

"How are you feeling?" Tom asked him, sitting down in the chair next to his bed.

"I could do with an ale lad," he answered croakily.

It was going to be a slow road to recovery. Arthur had suffered a seizure, something to do with a lack of oxygen to his heart, and would have died if he hadn't been found.

He was now confined to hospital for at least a month and would have to be on medication for the rest of his life.

For the next three weeks Tom continued juggling his visits in between work and home life. On a couple of occasions he took Daisy along with him, predicting, rightly as it turned out, that seeing a baby girl would lift the old man's spirits.

Emma also joined him one Saturday afternoon when the three of them spent an hour at Arthur's bedside.

The old man had loved that, especially when Tom had got hold of a wheelchair and they'd taken him to the hospital's restaurant for a mug of tea.

When he was finally allowed home it was Tom who collected him. Arriving back at Arthur's bungalow he noticed, as they walked from the car, how frail the old man now looked and he had to take his arm to hold him steady as he shuffled up the path.

Before leaving hospital arrangements had been made to provide him with some ongoing care at home and, despite his protests, Arthur now received a 'meals at home' service and was persuaded to wear an alarm on his wrist which he could use to alert social services if he got into difficulty.

Tom never once felt obliged to spend time with him, instead, going to see him because he wanted to and because he enjoyed his company. The two men formed an unlikely, yet close friendship.

In the weeks that followed his health scare Tom hadn't mentioned Arthur's dad's wartime diary. It wasn't a conscious decision, simply a subject that didn't come up when he was trying to sort out his friend's long term care arrangements, ensuring he had everything he needed.

There'd already been one incident where a furious Tom had spent more than an hour on the phone complaining to social services after Arthur's daily meal didn't arrive.

He wasn't impressed at being put on hold for ages and then finally speaking to someone who, though they apologised, gave him little confidence that they would sort out the hiccup.

As a result, he made sure to visit the next day, taking with him fish and chips he collected on the way. When he got there he found Arthur tucking into a steak and kidney pie, mashed potatoes and veg.

"You've just missed Lindsey, she brought me dinner round and said sorry for yesterday," Arthur said, in between mouthfuls. "Lovely girl she is."

Tom smiled and ended up staying to eat the fish and chips himself.

Despite his frailties Arthur's mind was still as sharp as ever and, as Tom took his coat off and sat in his lounge on a visit after work one evening, he was surprised when his friend asked: "So, did you finish it?"

"Finish what?" Tom replied.

"My old man's diary, you took it home with you," Arthur said.

"Yes, I did, well I read what I needed to up to and just after the Somme stuff. I came over to see you on the day you fell ill. I put it back in your cupboard by the way," he said pointing to the sideboard in Arthur's lounge.

"I couldn't believe what was in it. Your dad talks about Captain Harris a lot," he said.

"It's been a while since I read it, I don't remember," Arthur replied.

"But the really interesting stuff comes later. I've got to read something to you," he said, getting up and opening the cupboard where the diary remained wrapped in the plastic bag he had put it in.

Sitting back down, he took the book out of the bag, thumbed through it and said: "Listen to this ..."

'*3rd of July 1916. The sheer scale of the dead and wounded from the first two days of our offensive is overwhelming. Reports are patchy but would appear to* indicate that in some places entire battalions have been completely annihilated.

I have lost count how many burials I presided over today. Though I suppose they are the 'lucky ones' as many unfortunate souls still lie where they fell despite the valiant efforts of stretcher bearers and their comrades to bring them back.

One of the 'funerals' I conducted was Captain Harris. I'm told he was dragged from a shell hole out on the battlefield by a soldier who, knowing he was injured, risked his own life going back to find him. Sadly, he'd died by the time they got him back.

I had to cut the service short as shells began landing nearby. There is no respite from this damn war even in death.

This evening I sat and wrote several letters of condolence to families of the dead. One of them was to Captain Harris' parents and another to his wife Emma. I'm sure it will be of some comfort knowing he held a photograph of her in his hand when he died.'

"See what I mean?" Tom said, "Less than six months ago I stumble across this officer's headstone in France and now, I'm reading a first-hand account of the events following to his death. What are the chances of that?"

Arthur leaned back in his armchair, looked across at Tom and said: "When you get to my age lad nothing surprises you much anymore."

"It gets better Arthur," Tom said, looking down at the diary. "Listen to this ..."

'5th of July 1916. Amidst so much suffering of the dead and wounded it is easy to forget the impact upon those who have, thus far, survived. Today, I was invited to speak with a young soldier who, since the loss of his very good friend, has hardly spoken to anyone and become very withdrawn, despite being told he is to be decorated for gallantry.

He was only a boy, as so many of them are, and it took some time for him to open up and speak with me. When he did it became clear that the death of his friend was the not the sole reason for his melancholy.

Private Amos was responsible for going back out on to the battlefield to bring back the injured Captain Harris.

He is deeply saddened by the officer's death but also terribly vexed as to why the soldier who accompanied him, putting his life at risk too, is not being decorated for his bravery.

Instead, Private Amos tells me the soldier concerned has been arrested. I assure him I will do whatever I can to find out what has occurred.'

"You've uncovered a right yarn there lad, I can't remember reading any of that, though it's been years since I went through it," Arthur said, putting his head back.

Tom was absorbed by the diary once more and continued reading extracts out loud.

"He goes on ..."

'8th of July 1916. Another day spent writing depressing letters to bereaved families. All the while our

207

offensive continues yet I'm not even sure we know all the names of the dead from the first day yet, never mind those who have been killed since.

I discovered Major Bernell and Lieutenant Russell are among the fallen. I knew both men well, such a terrible loss.

This afternoon I accompanied Major Howard and other officers visiting some of the wounded in a field hospital. It was a sobering experience. I also spoke with Private Amos again and had to tell him that, regrettably, the soldier who helped him bring Captain Harris back from the battlefield is now facing a court martial accused of assaulting an officer. If found guilty, he could be executed. Killing has suddenly become so normal, even mundane."

When he finished reading Arthur opened his eyes, saying: "A mate of mine was put on a charge once in Korea. They reckoned he'd run in the face of the enemy. Bloody nonsense it was. Terry was a good lad but they wanted to make an example of somebody.

"Thankfully, even we'd stopped shooting our own in the 1950s but Terry still got five years hard labour. It finished him that did. Drank himself to death when he got out and he died in 1963."

With some difficulty Arthur pushed himself up from his chair and shuffled into the kitchen.

"Do you want a beer lad?" he shouted.

"Not for me Arthur, I need to be heading off shortly. And should you still be drinking? Doesn't it interfere with your medication?" Tom replied.

"Bugger that lad, I'm not spending what time I've got left supping tea. If a bloke can't enjoy an ale or two what's the point?" he said, returning to the room with a glass of frothing beer.

"Now, carry on, it's getting interesting this," he said, taking a large gulp of his beer.

Chapter thirteen

July 1916

He was sweating heavily, a combination of the stifling heat in the room and the pressure he felt answering the Lieutenant's questions.

His nerves were getting the better of him, made worse by one of the senior officers chastising Amos for 'going beyond the scope of what was necessary to answer a question.'

But most of all he was frustrated because he desperately wanted to tell them about Bousefield's role in helping rescue Harris.

"When Private Bousefield was with you out looking for Captain Harris did you witness any behaviour unbecoming of a British soldier?" Lieutenant Blackwood asked.

Amos looked worried. What kind of question was that? He wanted to tell them about Bousefield volunteering to go out there, of him carrying Harris on his back for most of the way, crawling in agony through a battlefield strewn with dead and wounded as shells exploded all around.

"Answer the question please Private Amos, it's very straight forward," the Lieutenant added, pressing him to respond.

"He … well, he just … not really, I mean …"

"Not really? He either did or he didn't Private Amos," Blackwood said, deliberately exaggerating his tone.

"We were out there together … it was dark, we wanted to find Captain Harris …" Amos answered.

"Yes, we're aware of that Private, but I want you to tell us about Private Bousefield's behaviour at the time," Blackwood said.

"Did you personally witness anything unbecoming of a British solider? You are obliged to answer truthfully Private Amos."

How did he know? He couldn't surely, thought Amos, as the image of the horrifically wounded solider being killed by Bousefield flashed before him.

Amos looked at Bousefield who was staring back at him, his face impassive. "He … he helped me … I couldn't have done it without him."

The Lieutenant thought about pressing the issue but paused, looked at his papers and then asked: "Did you see Private Bousefield drink alcohol while out in the field?"

Amos felt his face flush red, his heart racing. Again, he glanced at Bousefield but Blackwood pushed him for an answer.

"Ermm ... he took a drink before he carried Captain Harris back ... we both did," Amos said, sounding embarrassed.

The Lieutenant looked delighted with the answer and responded quickly.

"So you did see Private Bousefield drinking in the field?" he asked.

"Er ... yes, but like I said, we both did."

"Did Private Bousefield force you to drink alcohol Private Amos?" Blackwood said.

"No! Not at all ... Captain Harris told me it was ok," Amos said.

"Captain Harris? Please explain."

"Eddie handed me the flask ... I wasn't sure ... but Captain Harris, he overheard and he ... he ordered me to take a drink," Amos said, suddenly beginning to realise how this looked.

Lieutenant Blackwood walked towards where Amos was sitting and, standing directly in front him, looked down and said: "Did Captain Harris give the same order to Private Bousefield?"

Amos simply wanted to help Bousefield but the pressure of the Lieutenant's questions and nerves got the better of him.

"What? Erm ... no, Eddie had a drink and then passed it to me ... that's when the Captain told me to have some," he blurted out quickly.

Blackwood smiled, thanked Amos for his evidence and turned his back to face the three officers sitting at the table.

"We now have compelling, first hand evidence that Private Bousefield consumed alcohol in the field, in the presence of a commanding officer and in direct contravention of Army regulations," he said.

"For the record I would ask this court to exonerate Private Amos, who has admitted drinking alcohol, but has testified this was done only following a direct order from an officer.

"His actions that day were above and beyond the highest standards expected of a British soldier and I know he is to be decorated for his gallantry."

Amos sat there stunned, unsure whether to get up and leave, though Blackwood didn't seem to notice as he addressed the officers.

"The same though cannot be said of Private Edward Bousefield who, this court has heard today, was in flagrant breach of those regulations by drinking in the field and assaulting an officer," Blackwood said, his voice now animated.

It was Captain Larkin who spoke next.

"Thank you Lieutenant Blackwood, does that conclude the prosecution evidence?"

"Yes, Captain, it does," Blackwood said, sitting down.

The most junior officer on the table, Lieutenant Bloom, then spoke for the first time.

"Private Amos you may leave. Stand up Private Bousefield," he said sharply.

Bousefield and Amos both stood at the same time, the accused pushing his chair back slowly, not looking as assured as he had been.

Amos had to walk right past him to leave the room and, as he did so, Bousefield glanced at him and muttered smiling: "Way to go George."

"Is it still your intention NOT to call witnesses in your defence?" asked Lieutenant Bloom.

As Amos opened the door he turned around one last time to see Bousefield standing before his accusers and just had time to hear him say: "Yes ... sir."

He closed the door behind him and walked out into the entrance hall before stepping out into the afternoon sunshine. He was relieved to be outside but the air was humid and there was little breeze.

In the distance he could hear the relentless boom of artillery guns as he crossed what he thought would once have been a busy road in the centre of town.

Now, there was little traffic - human, equine or motorised. A few civilians hurried from one place to another but those in view predominantly wore military uniform.

Walking away from the town hall he couldn't help but replay the events of the last hour, however much he tried not to. He felt dejected but most of all angry. He'd convinced himself he could help Eddie. But now, as he walked through the town, with shell damaged buildings on all sides, he feared the worst.

In the room inside the town hall, Bousefield was near the end of his cross examination by Lieutenant Blackwood. His answers had been all too brief, his demeanour bordering on aggressive. Crucially, he made no attempt to mitigate his actions.

Blackwood was almost smiling, unable to believe how easy Bousefield was making it for him.

"One final question Private," he said. "Is there anything you want to say to explain your actions on the first of July?"

Bousefield stared ahead at the three officers sitting in judgment.

"Yeah, I had a drink that night, I won't lie. But drink's the only way to keep a man sane out here," he said.

"You want me to kill. It is what you trained me to do and it's what I'm paid for. It doesn't mean I have to like it. I'm now so immune to it all I've stopped caring. In the end it's blokes like me that are expected to get our hands dirty."

As he spoke he looked intently in the Major's eyes.

"You turned me into a killer sir ... so don't expect me to behave like a gentleman," he added, before sitting back down.

For a moment there was an uncomfortable silence in the room and Blackwood couldn't decide from the expression on his face whether Major Howard was feeling awkward or seething with anger.

Captain Larkin leaned over and whispered in the Major's ear, who glanced at him, nodded and then said something to Lieutenant Bloom sitting on his right.

The three men conferred for a minute or so before Corporal Whitehead was beckoned. The junior officer approached the table where Lieutenant Bloom spoke into his ear as the Corporal leaned forward making notes on a piece of paper.

When he'd finished he turned around and said:

"Private 44278 Edward Bousefield, Nottinghamshire and Derbyshire Regiment, you stand accused when on Active Service that on the first of July, 1916 you did willfully, and in direct contravention of Army Service Regulations, consume alcohol 'in the field' on more than one occasion and strike a superior officer, namely Lieutenant Munroe, of the Nottinghamshire and Derbyshire Regiment.

"Stand up private," he added.

Bousefield stood up, his hands pushing up from the table in front of him. His palms were clammy and damp handprints were visible.

Major Howard then spoke: "After listening to the testimony of witnesses and in considering all the evidence before us, the unanimous verdict of this court is that Private Edward Bousefield is guilty of all charges."

Aside from swallowing hard, Bousefield remained impassive as he focused his eyes on the Major who was condemning him.

"The severity of the sentence must reflect the gravity of the charges you have been convicted of. In this case, the presiding panel's judgment recommends the death penalty is imposed.

"Private Edward Bousefield, you are condemned to death and will be executed by firing squad. Take him away," the Major said calmly, as two armed soldiers appeared at Bousefield's side and led him out of the room.

He wasn't even through the door before he heard Lieutenants Blackwood and Bloom sharing a conversation which ended with one of the officers laughing heartily.

Bousefield was escorted through the building and out through a door which led into a side street.

There, he climbed into the back of a horse drawn wagon and sat with his two escorts as the driver moved them on.

The journey was silent until one of the two soldiers, who knew Bousefield, fidgeted slightly before saying: "Sorry Eddie, really I am."

He didn't reply. Instead Bousefield sat upright, his body swaying in time to the movement and looked out across a vista of battered buildings and scarred streets.

May 2016

"Like I said, my old man was never the same again. How could you be after living through stuff like that?" Arthur asked, as they sat in his lounge.

He was talking after Tom had continued to read more extracts aloud from the diary. One of them had left the old man shaking his head.

'11*th* of July 1916. I made my way up to the front today with the Rev Hitchcock. Conditions were appalling and how men are expected to live amongst that, never mind risk their lives, is something both of us struggled to comprehend.

Whilst we were there we were able to hold impromptu services for some of the men. I hope it offered them some comfort knowing the word of God was with them in their darkest hour.

As we made our way back with some of the wounded we were shelled incessantly and one of the ambulances took a direct hit. I cannot begin to describe the sight before me. I spent the evening attempting to clean and remove blood and fragments of men that covered my uniform.'

"Have I shown you a picture of my old man? I've got one here somewhere," Arthur said, and he began rummaging through the box where he kept the diary and his medals.

"Here you go, he sent this to me mam," Arthur added, handing Tom a small, black and white photograph.

Taking it from him, Tom looked at the man whose thoughts and recollections he'd spent so much time reading.

In the photograph, Roebuck was standing, dressed in his military uniform. Unusually, the picture appeared to have been taken outside, as he saw what looked like a First World War ambulance in the background.

He was a thin man, clean shaven and wearing spectacles. Peering at his face closely, before looking up at Arthur, Tom said: "You can tell you're related, there's a similarity."

Arthur made some comment as Tom turned the photograph over and noticed Roebuck's familiar, flowing handwriting.

'To my dearest Mavis, you are forever in my heart. Lionel, France, May 1916.'

"How old was your dad when he went out there?" asked Tom.

"Ooh, you've got me there lad, hang on a minute," Arthur said and he closed his eyes, deep in thought.

After a moment he opened his eyes and said: "Eighteen ninety-one my dad was born so he'd have been 24 when he went to France. He'd only been a curate for a few months when the war started.

"He and mam had got married when they were both 19, they were very young but it's what you did back then," Arthur continued.

"I think she thought she was going to be set up with a comfortable life as a vicar's wife in a town or village somewhere. The war changed that though and she was left at home with my brother and sister."

"I didn't know you had siblings," Tom remarked.

"Aye, there was John, he was the eldest, and Margaret. They were two years apart and born a long time before I was ... they always said I was their little miracle. More of an accident I think," Arthur said, smiling.

"I take it they're no longer alive then?" Tom asked.

"Oh no lad, John died over ten years ago now. Margaret though, bless her, it was tragic what happened to her," the old man said.

"Really? Do you mind me asking?"

"Twenty third of September 1941, a Tuesday it was," Arthur said, his voice taking on a different, almost melancholy tone.

"She'd been up at the big manor house outside our village, mam got her a job up there as a kitchen maid because the family were regular worshippers at dad's church. Wealthy lot they were."

219

Tom sat listening as Arthur sipped his beer and thought how easily the old man could draw you in with his story telling.

"I was only a kid, eight or nine I think I was, but I can remember going up there to play in the gardens every now and then waiting for Maggie to finish," he said.

"She'd always bring something from the kitchen out with her, usually leftovers like cold meat or a piece of cake, and we'd eat it on the way home.

"A lovely lass was Maggie, such a pretty face. Big eyes and a wide smile, she could light up a room. I can still see her now," Arthur said, gazing through Tom as he spoke.

"Well, this particular day she came home and she was crying, I can remember that. There was then a terrible row with my dad shouting, something I hardly ever heard him do. I recall being sent to my room but I could still hear it going on. Right scared me it did," he said.

"Anyhow, next morning Maggie was gone. And that was that, last time I ever saw my sister," he said.

Tom never expected that. "What!? ... what do you mean, what happened?"

"She simply disappeared and my parents never spoke of her again. So much for forgiveness eh?" Arthur added.

Tom look confused but Arthur added: "There was no mystery lad, well, not that kind anyway. Turns out Maggie had taken a shine to one of the sons at the house where she was working. He was only a bit older than she was and big things were expected of him.

"Well, I guess you can imagine the rest. When she got pregnant she came home and told mam and that was it. Sent packing she was without so much as a goodbye. Terrible it was, she were only a kid herself," Arthur said.

"Oh God that's awful Arthur," Tom said.

"Aye, well that was how it was back then. It wouldn't do for a vicar's daughter to have a baby out of wedlock and aged just 15, never mind how it would have looked for a well to do son of a rich family knocking up one of the maids," he said.

"They must have sorted something out with the family for her to go so quickly. There were rumours of course but I think they probably gave her some money to disappear."

"Did you ever find out where she went and what happened to her?" Tom asked.

"I remember my mam crying a lot. Dad didn't say much. Our John tried to track her down a few years later but then the war came and as I grew up she just became out of sight, out of mind. Tragic really," he said, sounding sad.

"So you have no idea what happened to her?" Tom asked, shocked by what he'd heard.

"No, not at all. I know the son was killed in Italy in 1944 but whatever happened to our Maggie I'll never know," Arthur said.

"When dad died John especially tried to convince mam that we should find her. But this was back in the 1970s, things were a lot different to how they are now, it wasn't that easy," he said.

"I think he was hoping mam would reveal more before she died but her death ended any hopes of that. And then I guess life just got in the way and before I knew it, John had died and I was left with just a childhood memory of my big sister."

"Arthur, that's a really sad story, it really is," Tom said sympathetically.

"You know, we could still try and find out you know? There's lots you can do now using the internet," he added.

"Oh, I don't know lad, best to let sleeping dogs lie I reckon. Anyway, she'll be long gone now bless her," Arthur said.

He paused before adding: "No, I just hope she had a happy life and was loved."

Both men sat silent for a moment before Tom said: "Well, look, give it some thought. As I said, it's never too late to start looking. I can help you if you'd like."

"Thanks lad, but you've done enough. And anyway, isn't it about time you were getting off home? Go and see those girls of yours," Arthur said.

Half an hour later and he was home. Emma seemed genuinely interested in Arthur's progress and concerned enough about him to suggest he come round for Sunday dinner.

"Thanks Em, he'd like that, I know he would," Tom replied, scooping up Daisy from where she lay on her play mat, making her giggle as she was lifted high in the air.

He went on to recount the story about Arthur's sister, knowing she'd find that fascinating.

"Do you think he would like to find out what happened to her? I know she's likely to have died but there are probably nephews and nieces out there he's not even aware of," Emma said.

"He seemed pretty adamant but I can have another go," Tom replied.

"I think it's really sad. That poor girl, it must be awful to be cut adrift by your family like that," Emma added.

Later, as he lay in bed, he wondered how easy it would be to search for a woman who disappeared more than 75 years ago. He resolved to make some tentative searches online. He wouldn't say anything to Arthur; the chances of finding out anything were slim anyway.

Chapter fourteen

August 1916

The six men stood to attention as they listened to instructions. They were standing in the shade of a small copse on the edge of a field a few miles from the front line, close to the town where battalion headquarters was now located.

"When your name is called out you will step two paces forward, stand to attention and salute. The senior officer will then pin the medal on the left hand side of your tunic," one of two men said, speaking loudly.

"You should only speak if invited to do so. Once you have received your medal you should salute again before stepping back into the line. Is that clear?"

The six men responded with a firm: "Yes sir."

The second man then addressed them saying: "This is a proud day for you all and for the Sherwood Foresters."

He paused, smiled and added: "I'm also delighted to inform you that the General himself will be attending this morning's ceremony."

The faces of five of the six men took on a collective look of fear, excitement and astonishment. After being dismissed the men walked away together, excitement evident in their voices.

"Bloody hell, General Haig! What the hell's he doing coming to see us get a medal," one of them asked.

"Because he can't believe you're getting one Freddie and wants to see it with his own eyes," another replied, causing some of them to laugh.

"I'm right chuffed, wait 'til I write my mum that General Haig has seen her son getting his gong," one of them said.

"How about you George? You excited?" he said, turning to the private who had sat himself down under a large oak tree.

Amos simply shrugged and said nothing.

The soldier stepped closer, looking down and said: "Come on George, this is a big deal. It's the bloody General for God's sake."

"I couldn't give a shit," Amos said quietly, as he stood up and walked away.

Two miles away, the man stopped to wait for a gate to open. One of two armed soldiers unlocked a padlock before allowing him to enter. As he walked he heard the gate being locked behind him.

What had once been part of a bustling rail depot was now a military prison. As he strode through the yard he saw a group of shirt sleeved soldiers walking slowly in a line, each carrying a heavy bag of rocks on their backs.

They were watched by two other soldiers who stood casually by in the shade, both holding rifles.

Elsewhere, two men were sat on crates polishing two metal dustbins, which were now gleaming in the sunlight.

He approached another armed soldier standing guard at the entrance to a grey, concrete building.

The soldier stood to attention and saluted as the man spoke, returning the salute.

"The Reverend Lionel Roebuck, 11th Battalion Sherwood Foresters, here to see Private Bousefield."

"Sir," the soldier snapped.

He stepped to one side and unlocked the door allowing Roebuck to enter.

"It's a hot one today padre," he said as Roebuck walked through.

"Yes it is, private. At least you've got some shade where you are," he replied, glancing at the men in the yard, before he smiled and turned away.

He'd hoped it would be cool inside but it wasn't. Probably down to the corrugated roof he thought to himself as he headed towards a man sitting at a desk.

"Morning Charlie, how are things?" Roebuck asked.

The man looked up and smiled.

"Hello padre, this is a nice surprise. We've not had any visitors since you last dropped in," he replied enthusiastically.

"So, which poor sod you here to see today then?" he asked.

Roebuck frowned at him before replying: "We're all God's children Charlie, let's not forget that."

"Yes, padre, of course. My apologies," the soldier said.

"I'm here to see Private Bousefield," Roebuck said.

"Ah, I see. Thought there had to be a reason for you being here again so soon. So, when's the day? Have you heard? We don't get told until they turn up to take them," Charlie said.

"I'm sorry Charlie, I've not been told."

"Ok, well, he's through there," he said, gesturing towards another door, "second room on your right, Billy will let you in."

Roebuck thanked him and headed through the door to find a soldier waiting on the other side. Moments later he'd unlocked a door and the chaplain went inside.

There, sitting on the floor against the wall with his hands on his knees, was Eddie Bousefield.

"Hello Eddie, I'm Reverend Roebuck, your battalion chaplain. How are you?" he asked.

A wry smile appeared on Bousefield's face as he looked the chaplain up and down before his head bowed and he went back to staring at the floor.

Roebuck stood there awkwardly, there was no chair to sit on and only a blanket and makeshift pillow on the floor, next to a slop bucket. The room smelled of faeces.

"We ... we can pray together if you are a man of faith, or simply talk. I can help you write any personal correspondence if you so wish," he said.

Bousefield didn't move, nor did he speak.

The chaplain had been in similar situations before but he always found them uncomfortable.

"Look, is there anything I can do for you Eddie? Do you need anything? Sometimes I can arrange for things," he qualified.

At that Bousefield looked up and grinned.

"You can get me a drink padre," he said. "Oh, and how about a nice French bird? Could you sort that out? I could do with some cunt to take my mind off being shot," he added, almost laughing.

Roebuck wasn't shocked. He'd heard worse.

"Wine and women are not my forte I'm afraid Eddie. I was thinking more a bar of chocolate, or cigarettes. And the word of God of course," he replied.

Bousefield laughed again: "My name's Eddie padre ... not Jesus Christ! I don't think your God's going to be desperate to bring me back from the fucking dead. A fag'd be good though."

"I'll see what I can arrange Eddie. In the meantime, I'm going to pray for your soul," the chaplain added.

Back in the field several companies of men had assembled and were standing upright, forming a square in the middle of which, six others stood to attention. Alongside were two junior officers.

Suddenly, a deep voice barked: "Officers on parade ... atten ... shun!"

The sound of dozens of men stamping their feet firmly into the grass could be heard as a group of five middle aged men, all wearing officers' uniforms, appeared and walked into the centre of the square.

Moments later three men on horseback rode slowly through the ranks until they brought their horses to a halt alongside the group.

The lead horse was white with flecks of grey visible and its rider sat upright, the unmistakeable figure of General Douglas Haig, Commander in Chief of the British Armies in France. One of the officers on the ground approached him and he leaned forward to speak.

The moment was brief and Haig was back sitting upright, manoeuvring his horse around so he was facing the six men head on.

Two of the officers on the ground then approached the six as the deep voice was heard again.

"Three cheers for General Haig … hip, hip,"

"Hooray," replied scores of men who lifted their helmets as they repeated it twice more.

Haig raised his right hand and acknowledged all four sides.

The two officers standing in front were then joined by a third man carrying what appeared to be some sort of tray. On it were six medals glinting in the midday sun.

The loud voice was heard again: "John Rigby, Private, 11th Battalion Nottinghamshire and Derbyshire Regiment, the Sherwood Foresters. For gallantry and devotion to duty under fire, the Military Medal."

A tall, slim man stepped forward and saluted as the medal was pinned on his tunic by a grey haired, clean shaven officer. The two men shared a brief word before the soldier saluted and stepped back in line.

The same process was repeated another four times as another Military Medal and three Distinguished Conduct medals were awarded. All the time General Haig sat watching from his mount, which kept remarkably still.

The grey haired officer stepped to his right and was standing in front of the final man in the line.

"George Amos, Private, 11th Battalion Nottinghamshire and Derbyshire Regiment, the Sherwood Foresters. For conspicuous gallantry and devotion in voluntarily going out 100 yards in front of the line and bringing in a wounded man, the Distinguished Conduct Medal."

For a split second Amos didn't move and looked ahead at the officer who was smiling and then appeared puzzled.

Eventually, he stepped forward and saluted. The officer approached him and Amos felt hands on his chest as the medal was pinned on.

"Very well deserved Private Amos," the officer said quietly, smiling at Amos.

Amos said nothing, saluted and stepped back into the line.

After the final man had been decorated, General Haig rode forward until Amos could hear his horse breathing hard through its nostrils and heard it chomping on the bit of its bridle.

"You men epitomise the spirit and professionalism of the British Army," he bellowed. "I salute you all. God save the King," and with a yank of his reins Haig steered his horse away and trotted off to the sounds of men cheering.

In a windowless room Eddie Bousefield lit a cigarette and blew smoke up towards the ceiling. On the floor next to him was the empty wrapper from a bar of chocolate and a small, leather bound Bible.

May 2016

He thought about Arthur's reaction and had imagined him being both thrilled and dismayed. He'd even found himself rehearsing his explanation for why he'd gone off and done it, if it was the latter.

But that was looking too far ahead. He hadn't found anything yet; more to the point he'd hardly started looking. All he had to go on was Margaret's name, her approximate age and the fact she was due to give birth around the spring of 1942. It wasn't a lot.

Online searches got him started, just as they had when he was trying to track down Captain Harris. But it wasn't easy.

It took him a while, and was costing him money, but he managed to discover there were seven women by the name of Margaret Roebuck who had given birth in England and Wales between April and May 1942.

Then what? How was he supposed to know which of them was Arthur's sister? If indeed any of them were? The thought suddenly occurred to him that she may have changed her name. If she'd done that he may as well give up now.

No, he thought. There was little point worrying about that. So he ploughed on.

He ended up registering on several websites and then paid to download all seven birth certificates. The first five Margaret Roebucks were married. He wondered whether she had found someone in the time she had left. He doubted it.

Then he read the sixth.

It was a birth certificate from 'the sub district of Whitby, in the county of Yorkshire, East Riding.'

Tom zoomed in, the handwriting was difficult to decipher, but there it was.

'When and where: 8th of May, 1942; name, John Arthur Roebuck; sex, male; name and surname of father, blank; name and maiden name of mother, Margaret Helen Roebuck.'

The only other column that had been completed was the address field: '41 Cliff Terrace, Whitby.'

The temptation was there to tell Arthur now, that he was certain this had to be his sister. The baby's name had sealed it. She'd named her son after her two brothers. How poignant that was Tom thought.

Instead, he decided to wait and find out more. Having an address now was a huge help and, after a couple of days of online searching, some of which Emma had done while he was at work, he began piecing together what he could about Margaret Roebuck's life.

Why she'd moved to Whitby he couldn't answer, though he hoped Arthur may have some idea.

It emerged that the seaside address was currently a guest house. And it didn't take him long to discover that there had been a bed and breakfast operating from there since the late 1930s.

He searched death records next but frustratingly, of the 17 Margaret Roebucks who had died between 1938 and the present day, there was no one matching her approximate date of birth, which Tom guessed to be around the early 1920s.

That had to mean she'd got married. He began searching marriage records but initial results threw up more than 83 Margaret Roebucks and it meant going through each one individually.

Thanks to paying another online subscription he was able to view the details easily enough and scan through them quickly.

He wasn't sure how many he'd gone through before he found it.

It was a certificate from the registration district of Whitby, dated 1945. The marriage had been 'solemnized' at the town's register office on 21st February. His eyes were drawn immediately to 'Margaret Helen Roebuck, aged 18, spinster, whose address in the 'residence at the time of marriage' box was the same as the birth certificate.

In the column for father's name and surname was written 'Lionel Martin Christopher Roebuck' and his profession given as 'clergyman.'

Tom knew it was her and found himself smiling. It turned out she'd married a man more than twice her age.

He was pleased with his efforts. He was 100 per cent sure this was Arthur's sister and he now knew where she'd lived after being exiled by her parents, the name of her child and husband. It meant there would be plenty more lines to pursue.

It was another late night but he didn't want to stop yet. He yawned, got up from his chair and walked into the kitchen. Flicking on the light he made himself a tea, grabbed a couple of biscuits and sat back down in front of his laptop.

Arthur had been thrilled with the invitation to join them for Sunday dinner. Tom had arranged to pick him at 12.30pm and he found the old man dressed in a shirt and tie, standing at the window with his coat on when he pulled up outside.

"Looking smart Arthur," Tom said, opening the passenger door.

"We always used to put our Sunday best on, I thought I'd best make an effort seeing as you're going to all this trouble," he replied, awkwardly getting himself in the car.

"It's no trouble Arthur," Tom said. "You're more than welcome," he added, starting the engine.

Over dinner Arthur regaled them both with stories of his youth while heaping praise on the food, Emma's looks, Daisy, and their friendship.

"Just shows you're never too old to make new friends," he said, when they'd finished eating.

"We always used to have Sunday dinner as a family together, my dad was adamant about that. He was a stickler for keeping Sundays special. He'd have hated all these shops opening nowadays," Arthur said.

Tom glanced at Emma. She knew he'd been waiting until today to tell the old man what he'd found out about his sister. Tom had been desperate to tell him before but now, on the verge of doing so, he looked nervous.

Emma sensed it and stepped in.

"That must have been difficult Arthur, knowing the whole family wasn't together," she said casually.

Tom winced, giving her a look which told her he wasn't happy with that.

"Ah, he's told you then?" Arthur replied, looking at his friend.

"No matter, I'm not ashamed of it. Like I said, I was only a boy when it happened, I didn't have a say in it," he added.

"It would have eaten away at me not knowing," Emma said.

Again, Tom looked at her. Could she be less subtle?

"Times were different back then," Arthur said. "Having a baby at that age, out of wedlock ... well, it was frowned upon."

"You must have really missed her?" said Emma.

"I did at first, she was my big sister. Looked out for me a lot she did, more than me mam I suppose," he answered.

"But you know, they say out of sight, out of mind ... and it's true. Well it was for me anyway. I remember crying a lot when she first went ... but I got used to it, I had to. We all did.

"What else could I do? I grew up and got on with my life. I expect you think my dad was a bad man for doing what he did?"

"No, Arthur not at all ...," Tom chipped in, though it was Emma who was giving him a look now.

"Well he wasn't," the old man added.

"He was a good man who was devoted to his family and to the church. That may sound odd but he believed in right and wrong and living your life according to the ways of the Bible. He would have been devastated by what my sister did," he said.

"But she was only a girl Arthur, she needed her family around her," protested Emma.

Tom was worried now; this was not how he wanted the conversation starting. Emma had no time for religion and believed family came first, no matter what.

Thankfully, Arthur seemed in no mood for a disagreement.

"I agree with you love, honestly I do," he said.

"Do I think he regretted what happened? I reckon he did. But he was a proud man and once it had happened, well there was no going back really."

There was an awkward silence for a moment as no one spoke. Emma looked at Tom and gestured for him to say something.

"Erm, Arthur, can I get you a top up?" he said. Emma rolled her eyes and looked away.

"Aye, you know me lad, I won't say no."

He got up and went into the kitchen, Emma following behind him carrying plates.

"I thought you were going to tell him?" she said, whispering.

"I was until you started giving him a hard time," he snapped back.

She looked stunned. "What? I was bringing the conversation around so you could bring it up! But I can't fake my reaction, it was disgusting what happened to that poor girl," she said, dumping the dirty plates on the kitchen worktop.

"Well, I can't tell him now," Tom said, turning his back and opening the fridge to retrieve another beer.

"Of course you can, you've got to tell him," Emma added.

"Tell me what?" said a voice and they turned to see Arthur walking into the kitchen holding three empty glasses.

"I thought you could do with a hand with the washing up," he added.

Tom squirmed but regained his composure quickly.

"Let me pour you another beer Arthur and forget the washing up we'll do that later," he said, gently ushering the old man back into the dining room.

With Emma following them he said: "Listen, I've got to tell you something Arthur, but you might want to sit down first."

The old man looked puzzled and appeared a little wary.

"Everything's alright isn't it?" he asked.

"Yes, yes, everything's fine," Tom said, realising his friend was now worried. He didn't want it to be like this and he was trying to work out how he'd got himself into this mess.

They were going to sit back down at the table but Emma suggested they carry on into the lounge and sit comfortably. When Arthur was seated she saw Tom sitting on the edge of his chair leaning forward. He was worried.

"Right, err ... Arthur," he began. "Listen, I know it must have been difficult to tell me about your sister ..."

"No bother lad, water under the bridge," he interrupted.

"I know, but listen Arthur," he added. "Remember I said I could help you find out about her ... you know, what happened ..."

The old man lifted his arm and waved his hand: "Oh no, like I said, it was a long time ago. It's too late now. We'll never know."

Tom just needed to get it out now.

"Arthur, I've found her," he said, regretting immediately the way he just blurted it out.

Arthur looked at him and then at Emma.

"Found her? What are you talking about lad?" he asked.

"Your sister, Arthur. I've found Margaret."

Chapter fifteen

August 1916

He was surprised he slept at all, let alone so well. For a fleeting moment it was as if he'd forgotten, a by-product of his conscious self not being fully awake.

But it was all too brief because he opened his eyes and became aware of his surroundings. And with that it thundered into his head, dominating his thoughts, obliterating anything else that may have lingered.

It had to be morning; he could hear the dawn chorus and distant rumble of shells at the front. He lay on his back staring at the ceiling, though he wasn't looking at that.

Instead, he was with his sister Katie, she had her arm around him and he was crying. Tears were streaming down his face as she held him tight and he held on to her as if letting go would bring the end of the world.

He couldn't see, her hand was pressed gently against the back of his head, his face nestling into her chest. But he could hear. And it made the terror worse being able to do so.

They'd been playing when he arrived home. The first thing he recalled was the sound of the door slamming and his father's raised voice. He'd been drinking of course, even at his age he recognised what drunk sounded like.

He saw his mother; small, timid and petrified of saying or doing the wrong thing. No matter what she did or what she said, she couldn't prevent it. Maybe she'd reconciled herself to that and instead now tried to mitigate its ferocity.

There was a sequence to it which was grimly familiar; the relative normality until his father got home, the feeling of dread that consumed them all as the moment approached, the fear that came before it happened, the shouts, her screams, his brutality, the sickening violence.

Katie would sing to him, quietly, nervously, a forlorn attempt to shield her brother from the sights and sounds of his father's cruelty. It didn't work.

His character was forged by those events, his life defined by the behaviour he witnessed day after day from the one man who should have been willing to die to protect his family from harm.

But he had died, and deservedly so. Even now he was aware of his fists clenching as he recalled it. He'd been older then; he no longer cried nor sat in his sister's arms. Instead, he stood and watched. Only this time he vowed it would be the last.

He thought there might come a moment of doubt, when he'd baulk at doing what he knew had to be done. But it hadn't come. And that only convinced him he was right.

He'd waited until he was asleep. He wasn't so naïve that he thought he could handle his father when he was awake. No, he'd planned this meticulously. When death came to visit his father, as it would do, he'd have no choice but to acquiesce to its demand.

Even now he could hear the snores, loud and deep, shuddering through the small, pokey, terraced house he had been born in. He wondered if his father had been different then or whether he'd always had a propensity for violence that fatherhood had failed to quell.

Pushing open the bedroom door he saw the huge figure of his dad lying in bed, one arm hanging limply over the side. His mother was downstairs, he could hear her even now scuttling about in the kitchen, her face bloodied and bruised.

Was he nervous? Scared? A little, but he also felt an inner calm. Walking into the room he stood at the side of the bed watching his father's chest rise and fall.

"Father? Father, it's me Eddie ..." he said, speaking normally. There was no response and, as the snores continued, he turned and closed the door.

Lifting a pillow from the other side of the bed he took one last look at his father's face. His eyes had adjusted to the dark and he could see him clearly, his open mouth, his unshaven face.

Walking closer he held the pillow in both hands, paused momentarily and then shoved it down hard over his father's face. For a moment nothing happened but then, eventually, his body started to move. He responded by pressing down harder and then climbed on the bed and sat astride his father.

A sober, conscious man of his size would have had little difficulty in throwing a teenage boy off. But Nev Bousefield wasn't sober. So he flailed his arms about vainly in an attempt to remove whatever it was preventing him from breathing.

The longer it went on the more desperate he became but Eddie was surprised how easy it had been. When his father's body finally went limp he remained in place, pressing the pillow down, as though just to make doubly sure it had done its job.

Finally, he lifted it away and stared at his father's face. His eyes were wide open, a look of shock and terror etched into his features. He thought how fitting it was that his last conscious moments on earth had been flooded with fear.

He replaced the pillow and moved towards the door, opening slightly and listening for any sign that his mother and sister had heard any noise. Confident they hadn't, he opened the door and climbed into bed.

Downstairs he could still hear his mother and sister talking quietly, lest they do anything to rouse his father from his drunken slumber.

But he smiled, knowing nothing now would rouse Nev Bousefield. And for the first time in his life he wasn't afraid any more. And he vowed to never feel fear again.

He thought that would change things, that his life … his mother and sister's lives, would be different. He was wrong.

Eight weeks later his mother was dead. They found her body in the river two days after she walked out of the door and didn't return. After years of living under his fist, it appeared she couldn't live without her Nev.

His sister seemed intent on the following the same depressing path as their mother. She hooked up with a string of men, each one strikingly similar to her father. He tried to dissuade her but she wasn't listening.

So, when he arrived home one night to find her cowering on the floor with a man standing over her, his fists clenched, teeth snarling, the red mist descended. All he saw was his father's face as he beat the man to within an inch of his life.

If it wasn't for passers-by hearing his sister's screams and dragging him away, he would have killed a second man before he was 18. The magistrate gave him a choice - jail, or the army.

Five years on and he'd killed more men than he could remember. He was good at it, he enjoyed it. Death was so familiar, so commonplace, it held no fear. He hadn't felt fear since standing over his father with a pillow.

He heard the key turn and watched as the door swung open, two armed soldiers entering the room.

"Stand up Eddie, it's time," one said.

He thought they looked nervous, on edge. One of them was holding his rifle with both hands, pointing it at him.

He stood slowly and stretched before bending down to pick up his boots. Leaning against the wall for support he lifted one leg and then another as he pulled them on.

"Eddie, come on, don't drag this out," the first soldier said.

He looked at them both and smiled.

"I need a piss first," he said, and stood in front of the bucket in the corner of the room undoing his trousers.

The two men glanced at each other as Bousefield urinated in front of them.

"Right," he said, tucking his shirt in as he fastened his trousers, "lead the way boys."

The three men walked out of the room and through the building until they came to a door which seemed to open by itself. As they walked through he noticed another guard holding it open.

They were outside now. The sun had not quite risen and, though he'd never admit it, he secretly hoped to live long enough to see it one last time. His senses were alive and he absorbed every noise, every smell, every sight that he could.

They walked across a yard towards a group of soldiers standing at the far end. As he got nearer he saw there was a post coming out of the ground and was ushered towards it.

He stood with his back next to it, his arms pulled tight behind him, feeling his hands being bound.

Ahead of him he saw six soldiers from the 8th King's Own Light Infantry, all with rifles, standing in a line looking down at him. He saw their faces, they appeared nervous, unsure, fearful even.

An officer stood to their right, while three others approached from a building inside the yard. As they got nearer he recognised one of them.

Two of the men stopped next to the firing squad but the third, the man he recognised, continued towards him. He was holding something in each hand.

"Hello Eddie, have they treated you ok? Is the rope too tight on your hands?" he asked.

Bousefield looked at him; there was sweat on the man's brow. "I'm fine padre," he said smiling. "Nice morning for it."

Roebuck's eyes betrayed what he was thinking but he didn't respond. Instead, he stepped closer saying: "I'm going to pray for you Eddie, whether you want me to or not."

"You do what you need to padre," Bousefield replied.

The chaplain looked him in the eye and, holding something up in his right hand, added: "I have to ask you Eddie ... do you want to wear ...," his voice faltered.

"Forget it padre. I'm not wearing a fucking hood. I want to look those fuckers in the eye," and he gestured towards the row of soldiers.

Roebuck nodded, stuffing the hood into his trouser pocket.

"Are we ready to proceed Lieutenant?" boomed a voice, one of the two officers who had walked with the chaplain.

"Yes sir," a voice replied.

Roebuck looked at Bousefield. "It's ok to be afraid Eddie but you're not alone. God is with you," he said.

"Death doesn't scare me padre," Bousefield replied icily.

"Stand aside Mr Roebuck, we're ready to proceed," a voice shouted.

The chaplain turned around quickly, "Yes, yes … just give me one more moment, please?"

The officer looked across at one of the older, more senior men who nodded his head.

Roebuck stepped closer to Bousefield, their faces almost touching.

His eyes glancing towards the firing squad, he said: "Forgive them Eddie, they're more scared than you are," before stepping backwards.

Holding a bible in his right hand he said loudly: "Almighty God, accept into your care the soul of Edward Bousefield, in the name of the Father, the Son and the Holy Spirit."

As the officer ordered the six riflemen to take aim, Bousefield saw the sun peeking over the horizon as it rose to signal a new day. He looked at the faces of the men who were to end his life and saw the chaplain was right, they were scared.

"You fuckers had better shoot straight, not like the rest of your fucking useless regiment," he shouted. "If only your lot had shown some balls on July first ... fucking cowards," he said disdainfully.

Then he saw their expressions change, their eyes narrow, and anger flush through their cheeks. And he smiled, because he knew it was easier to kill when rage replaced the fear.

He looked up, the sky was a vivid blood orange. He didn't hear the instructions for the men to take aim.

Roebuck swallowed hard and forced himself to look. And he saw Eddie Bousefield smiling broadly as a volley of shots rang out.

May 2016

He wiped away another tear, blowing his nose into a handkerchief he took out of his trouser pocket.

"Oh dear," he sighed, "I didn't expect this."

"It's ok Arthur, you don't need to apologise. I'm the one who should be saying sorry, I didn't mean to upset you," Tom said.

At the first sign of him getting emotional Emma had gone over to comfort him and was now kneeling next to the armchair with her hand on Arthur's shoulder.

"It's just such a shock that's all," the old man muttered.

"Hearing all this brings back a lot of memories. And regrets ... if only I'd knew where she was," he added, before he choked up again.

Tom felt embarrassed and a little ashamed. Looking at his friend's face, sadness writ large across it, he realised he'd never considered the impact that finding out about Margaret would have on Arthur.

He was angry at himself for being so selfish.

"Are you … you know, sure it's our Maggie?" Arthur asked, wiping his nose again.

Tom shifted uncomfortably in his seat. "Yes, yes, I am Arthur. It can't just be a coincidence. The dates stack up. It has to be her."

A few minutes before he'd gone through everything he knew. Arthur had sat there looking puzzled at first but that had been quickly replaced by bemusement and then shock.

"We know that when Margaret left she travelled to Yorkshire, Whitby to be precise," Tom began.

"Whitby? We went there when I was a young lad … all of us on the train. First time I ever saw the sea," Arthur interrupted.

"That's maybe why she chose to go there," Tom replied, before continuing.

"I think she went to live in a bed and breakfast in the town which was bought outright by somebody that same year."

Arthur frowned and said: "She could never afford that, where would Maggie get the money from to do that? And she was just a kid."

Before Tom could reply he answered his own question, "that'll be what they did. They paid her to keep quiet and disappear … I'll be blowed."

Tom looked at Emma who gave him an encouraging smile and nodded for him to carry on.

"On the eighth of May 1942, we know Margaret gave birth to a little boy," he said, pausing to allow Arthur to absorb that news.

"A boy? Really? Oh my word ... a little boy eh," Arthur said, struggling to speak.

"That's not all Arthur," Tom said, treading cautiously as he delivered the information.

"She must have been really fond of her brothers because she named her son after you both ... John Arthur Roebuck," he added.

On hearing that Arthur put his head in his hands and sobbed as Emma stood and put her arm around his shoulder. Tom went into the kitchen and made tea, giving the old man a few minutes to come to terms with what he was hearing.

After a few minutes he had composed himself and the three of them sat drinking tea with Tom again careful not to divulge too much at once.

Instead, he let Arthur talk through what he'd just heard.

"Must have been bloody tough for her bringing up a little 'un on her own all that way from home," he said.

"She was only a small thing, I remember that about her, but she wasn't afraid of graft. She was brought up right about that ... we all were," he added, raising his voice.

Tom wanted Arthur to set the pace of the conversation; he could only imagine how he was feeling on hearing this.

It was Emma who spoke next: "Arthur, this is a lot for you to take in and we know it must be a real shock for you but we can leave it there for now if you'd prefer," she said.

The old man lifted his head and looked at her perched on the armrest of his chair. "You mean there's more? You can tell me more about what happened to our Maggie?" he asked.

Emma glanced briefly at Tom, surprised that Arthur hadn't seemed to realise that.

"Err, yes ... I mean, yes, there is more. A lot more," she said, looking at her husband, who stepped in.

"I've managed to find out quite a bit more Arthur but we don't like seeing you upset. What Emma means is we can continue or do it another day when you're feeling better," he said.

"I'm fine lad," he replied, indignantly.

"It's just such a bloody shock that's all. But I need to know, I have to know what happened to our Maggie," Arthur said.

"Ok," Tom said, "what we believe is that she gave birth to her son while she was living at the guest house. Now, we don't know what happened to the little boy because unfortunately, despite searching, we can't find any records for a John Arthur Roebuck after that."

"What? ... what do you mean?" Arthur asked. "Has he disappeared too? How can that happen?"

Tom raised his hand as he attempted to explain.

"No, no ... Arthur, listen. I'm only able to search records such as birth certificates, marriages, deaths etc.

250

I've not found anyone of that name either getting married in the last fifty or so years or ... or dying," he added.

Arthur looked puzzled, he didn't understand.

"What I mean is, we simply don't know at this stage based on the information we have, whether he's alive or not. There are lots of reasons why a name may not show up, he might never have married, changed his name or moved abroad somewhere," Tom explained.

"So that's it then?" said Arthur, sounding despondent.

"No, not at all," Tom replied. "I haven't told you everything yet."

Arthur gazed across at him but didn't speak. Tom took that as a sign to continue.

"We believe Margaret was still living in the guest house until at least 1945 because that's when she got married," he said.

Arthur's eyes lit up at that and he leaned forward listening intently.

"Marriage records show Margaret got married in February 1945. She married a man who was a lot older than she was," Tom said.

"Our Maggie, a married woman ... good for her," Arthur muttered.

Tom continued: "We think she must have carried on living in the guest house until the late 1950s. What happened after that though I'm not sure because it was sold in 1959 and we don't know where she went afterwards.

"Now, sadly, it appears her husband died in 1961 a few months before his 63rd birthday. I'm not sure how or what happened. Margaret would only have been 38 at the time."

"Aye, that's right," Arthur said, nodding in agreement.

"I don't think they had children, I've looked and can't find any records," Tom added.

"However ...," he said, pausing to catch his breath and looking up at Emma to catch her eye.

"We can't find any record of Margaret remarrying or ... of her dying," he said. Before Arthur could speak Tom added: "And that's because she hasn't Arthur ... died I mean."

The old man's mouth was open, his face a mixture of shock and surprise.

"Your sister's still alive Arthur," Tom said, a wide grin appearing on his face.

For a minute Arthur was too flabbergasted to speak as he attempted to process what he was being told.

Finally, he looked up at both Emma and then across at Tom before saying: "Is it true? ... are you sure ... my Maggie? ... still alive?"

"Yes," Tom said gleefully. "I'm one hundred per cent sure Arthur. How do I know? Because Emma and I know exactly where she is. She's 89 now and she's living in a residential home in Scarborough.

"Arthur ... we can take you to see her," Tom added, as he saw more tears running down his friend's face.

Chapter sixteen

August 1916

It had ceased to be a wood some time ago. Now, it was an apocalyptic landscape of shattered stumps and jagged splinters, which appeared to scream silently in pain.

Rising out of the earth, charred black and pock marked with craters, they were a marker, a disfigured signpost to the obliterated bodies that still lay among them.

In the daylight, when the summer sun burned fiercely, it held no fear for the men now living in it; their biggest concern was doing anything they could to mask the putrid, rotten stench that hung in the air, the final, cruel indignity of the dead.

Some managed to make crude face cloths which they'd rub with a bar of soap before tying them around the backs of their heads. Others took to wearing gas masks, despite struggling to see or breathe properly while they did.

But at night, Mametz Wood, or what was left of it, became an eerie, fearful place which chilled the blood of the men now ordered to remain there.

A hazy, moonlit sky gave the wood an almost supernatural appearance and for five men lying in a crudely dug trench, the sight and smells of the ground around them was only adding to their unease.

Despite being shelled throughout the day and forced to duck for cover from snipers, they'd managed to reinforce support trenches leading back to the rear and complete more repair work to reopen communication lines to the front.

Now they were exhausted and simply wanted to sleep. But they knew that was unlikely to happen. The last three nights had seen ferocious counter attacks repulsed at a heavy cost and they knew another was inevitable.

None of them spoke and there was little sound and movement as Amos sat peering into the night sky. He had a vacant, haunted look upon his face, one he shared with the men sat alongside.

He no longer thought of home; of days gone by; of happier memories. Nor did he think of making it to the end of the war and surviving. He didn't know anyone who thought like that any longer.

Instead, he thought in seconds and moments, expecting and anticipating his death at any moment. It made for a harsh, surreal existence, in which nothing mattered except looking out for the man next to you.

Three of the five were new recruits brought in to replenish the depleted ranks from the carnage of July first. When the first attack had come they'd been as terrified as Amos was on that fateful day.

Watching the enemy draw closer it hadn't even occurred to him that he'd never fired his rifle in anger before; there simply hadn't been the time or the opportunity. But he had now.

The first time he killed a man had been ludicrously easy; point, aim, fire. He saw the result - a running man lifted off the ground, his chest ripped open before reeling backwards and falling.

There was no time to process the consequences; there were more men to kill. Amos simply did what they'd trained him to do. And the more he did, the easier it became. He learned to love his weapon, marvelling at the design and engineering that had produced such a smooth, simple, elegant instrument to deliver death.

The second attack had seen German infantry come perilously close to the British lines and he could see their faces. Some were boys, younger than him, looking just as terrified.

Others were older; they appeared determined, battle hardened, a look of furious intent on their faces. He aimed for them first and watched them crumple in bloodied heaps.

When they turned and ran, retreating back to their lines, he shared the elation of the men around him. Cheers and defiant jeers could be heard as men scrambled out of their trenches to get a better aim at the backs of fleeing German soldiers.

When it was over he slid back down into the earth, breathing hard. There were one or two who continued firing, picking off the wounded as they attempted to crawl back. He couldn't do that. The memory of being one of those men was still too raw.

Looking up into the night sky he saw a stillness that awed him. There was a tranquility and solitude up there he'd never experience. For a moment he imagined himself floating upwards and for the first time since he could remember, he felt an inner peace, even calm.

The scream of a shell pierced the silence, followed by a huge blast as it slammed into the ground nearby. Multiple screams accompanied it as enemy guns opened up on the British lines.

"Here they commeeeeee," shouted a voice.

The five men didn't panic, they'd done this enough times now. Instead, they quickly went through the routine of making their weapons ready. Following the last attack a Lewis machine gun had been positioned in Amos' trench and two of the men were now on it, one of them holding the handle, his finger poised over the trigger while his companion fixed a cylindrical magazine in place.

"Get ready Sherwoods," barked a voice, shouting to make himself heard over the noise of the shells.

Amos had turned on to his front and now scrambled up to the lip of the trench where he brought his rifle up and lay in a firing position. Ahead of him was a jagged horizon silhouetted by blasts and Very lights which affected his vision.

He tried to force his eyes to adapt so he could see more clearly but had to shut them quickly as a shell landed nearby, thundering earth and debris into the air which showered down on him and the others.

Amidst the din he was now aware of a new noise, this time human. It sounded like the distant roar of a crowd but it was getting closer. He adjusted his eyes and could see it now; ahead of him were shapes, clearly men. They were running, screaming and shouting.

"Sherwoods ... at 200 yards ....," a voice was heard.

Amos and the others lay silent, took aim and waited. The noise intensified as behind him the British guns opened up in retaliation. His mind was clear; there were no distractions, no thoughts of anything else other than killing those before they killed him.

The ground ahead was now a mass of charging men; some stumbled and fell because of the awkward terrain. Then shells began landing among them and Amos watched as groups of men were blown to pieces.

He didn't flinch, didn't waiver, he simply lay waiting, his eyes fixed upon his first target. Chosen randomly, the man was running hard, holding his rifle in his right hand.

As they got nearer their voices got louder and Amos felt the familiar adrenalin surge that dissolved any fear he may have been feeling.

"Sherwoods ... FIRE!"

Amos squeezed the trigger and watched as his target spun round before falling. Several others did the same as British soldiers poured fire on the advancing enemy.

It was now simply a methodical exercise to be undertaken as he moved from one target to the next, calmly but quickly firing his rifle.

To his left he could hear the Lewis gun spewing out bullets as it traversed the landscape ahead, scything down the enemy. He was also aware of men around him shouting now, stirred by a cocktail of adrenalin, fear and excitement.

He reached for a new ammunition clip to replace the empty one he'd hurriedly discarded, and continued firing. But there were more of them this time and they kept coming.

"They're not stopping, they're getting closer," said a desperate voice to his left, it was one of the men on the Lewis gun.

His companion, the man firing the trigger, was shouting now as he did so: "Come on then, come on you Fritz bastards, fucking have this you bastards!"

Suddenly, another voice was heard: "They're coming through ... watch them, watch them!!"

Amos had emptied a second clip and was loading another when to his right he saw advancing German soldiers reach the British lines. As they did so, several of them were cut down by a machine gun but he saw one or two leap down into the trench out of sight.

Others were now only yards away and he glanced to his left as one of the men on the Lewis gun fell backwards, a gaping, bloody hole in the side of his face.

For the first time Amos panicked as he realised what was about to happen and he hurried to fix his bayonet.

He should have done it beforehand but, like so many others, found the weight of the blade affected his ability to aim effectively.

He regretted that now as precious seconds were spent attaching the bayonet. When he'd done he looked up just in time to see three German soldiers appear above him.

One was thrown backwards as a bullet blasted a hole in his chest but the other two leapt into the trench.

In the melee Amos saw one of them standing over a soldier lying exposed on his back, about to thrust his bayoneted rifle into him. The German's helmet suddenly flew into the air as his head was smashed by a rifle butt. As he fell the British soldier turned his rifle and plunged a bayonet into his back.

The second German fired a shot and another of Amos' companions went down clutching his stomach. As he turned towards Amos the two men looked at each other, only for a startled expression to appear on the man's face as the tip of a bayonet burst out of his chest.

The confused German looked down at the bloody spike protruding out of him before it quickly disappeared. A moment later his head exploded as the same rifle fired into the base of his skull from behind.

Amos, covered with blood and brain fragments, spun round to see more enemy soldiers jumping into the British trenches. He shot three or four at close range and bayoneted another who had lunged at him and missed.

Along the British line of the shattered wood, bloody hand to hand combat ensued as men fought using whatever weapons they could find.

There were now only two of them left standing in their trench and he found himself standing back to back with a man who, until yesterday, he'd hardly heard speak and only knew as Jacobs.

He was aware of him shouting, cursing, a constant stream of profanities coming out of his mouth as he fought to stay alive.

More of the enemy jumped into their trench but one immediately fell, hit by a random bullet.

Amos lunged at another and felt his bayonet plunge into the man's stomach. He twisted it quickly before withdrawing it and watched the man slump to the ground, a look of shock upon his face.

He had no idea how long it had lasted but he could tell the offensive was petering out. Some of the Germans had already begun retreating while others made vain attempts in isolation.

Amos turned to look at Jacobs but as he did so caught sight of a German soldier wielding some sort of club over his head. Jacobs saw him and swung his rifle around smashing the butt into his jaw.

The soldier fell to the ground where a frenzied Jacobs now stood over him yelling and screaming as he repeatedly smashed the end of his gun into the man's face.

"You fucking ... filthy Fritz ... die you bastard ... fucking ... die," and he brought the butt down with real ferocity as he spoke.

Amos looked at the man, his face and head brutally smashed open, exposing the inside of his skull. Jacobs wasn't finished. Furiously, he swung his rifle round and then repeatedly plunged his bayonet into the man's torso, seven, eight, nine times, until he finally stopped and slumped to the ground.

The shooting dissipated, as did the noise. The attack was over.

Amos peered over the trench to see a mass of bodies, some of them moving, most of them still. In the distance he could make out the figures of some enemy soldiers who had made it back to their lines.

He turned to see Jacobs sitting on the ground with his bloodied hands resting on his knees. Around him were the bodies of at least a dozen men, three of them British.

Amos saw one of them lying underneath the body of a German who had a gaping hole in his back. He pushed him off using his boot only to discover the Tommy was dead; his throat ripped open, his eyes staring wide and lifeless.

There were groans from two of three of the others but Jacobs heard them, grabbed his rifle, removing the bayonet, and crawled around plunging the blade into the body of every German. Amos said nothing.

He slumped to the ground, a wave of fatigue and nausea enveloping him. He looked up and stared at the stars and imagined himself floating away to a distant constellation.

May 2016

The drive took longer than he'd hoped but Arthur seemed to be enjoying it. The weather was good, as was the scenery, as they headed towards the coast.

Tom had a fairly good idea where he was going but his satnav helped him with the final leg.

Arthur was in good spirits which made for an entertaining journey. He'd had time to process the bombshell that had landed on him and, after a few questions about how he managed to find his Margaret, couldn't wait to finally meet her.

Tom thought his friend would be a little apprehensive but if he was there was no sign of any nerves.

They could see the sea now as they approached the town and that made Arthur even more excited.

"Hey, look there it is, been a while since I've seen the sea," he remarked.

Tom pulled up at some traffic lights on the outskirts, following a sign directing them into the town centre.

"Good job you know where you're going lad, I'd never have found my way up here," Arthur said.

Tom smiled before turning right and heading up a hill.

"It should be at the top of this road Arthur," he said.

A few seconds later they reached the brow of the hill and saw a large, relatively new building set back from the road. From the outside it looked like a modern flats complex, apart from the giveaway sign at the entrance to a car park which read – 'Sycamore Lodge Nursing Home, part of the Artemis Health Group.'

Tom turned his car in and pulled into a parking space close to the entrance.

"Well, here we are Arthur, are you ready to do this?" he asked, looking at his friend as he unclipped his seatbelt.

The old man looked ahead of him towards the building before replying: "Aye, I've waited a long time for this lad and it's a day I never thought I'd see."

Turning to Tom he looked at him and said simply: "Let's go and meet my sister."

The doors to the entrance opened automatically and led into a bright, warm reception area where a friendly faced woman was sitting behind a computer. The sun was streaming through the windows and she looked up as the two men approached.

"Good morning, welcome to Sycamore Lodge, can I help you?" she said.

"Hi," said Tom. "Er, I rang a couple of days ago; we're here to see Margaret Amos? This is her brother Arthur," he said, glancing at the old man and smiling.

The woman looked at her computer screen before saying: "Ah, yes, Mr Harris isn't it?" Tom nodded.

They were asked to take a seat and wait. A couple of minutes later a door opened and a woman in a nurse's uniform approached. She too was smiling broadly.

"Mr Harris?" she said, holding her arm out to shake Tom's hand. "And you must be Arthur?" she said.

After inviting the two men to sit back down she took a seat next to them.

"My name's Claire, I'm one of the senior nursing managers here at Sycamore. It's lovely to meet you and what a wonderful story this is," she said excitedly.

For the next few minutes she asked a number of questions which Arthur was only too happy to answer. Tom, though, detected it was probably a subtle way of checking the voracity of their story.

"Well, I think it's simply marvellous," she said gushingly.

"Margaret has been with us for about four years now. Unfortunately, she doesn't really get any visitors so this will be a real fillip for her," Claire added.

"Don't her family come and visit then?" asked Arthur, sounding surprised.

"Sadly, Margaret doesn't have any family, not that we know of anyway. Until Mr Harris called us we had no idea of any relatives," Claire replied.

"She ... she had a son, we know that much," said Tom.

The nurse looked puzzled before replying: "I didn't know that. Really? No, I'm afraid she doesn't get any visitors but she is a lovely lady and is very popular with the staff and other residents here.

"Now, before we go through, as you know Margaret is almost ninety. She's very frail and hard of hearing and can be a little forgetful."

"Does she know we're coming?" asked Tom.

"Yes, we sat down and spoke to her about it yesterday. I also told her again this morning. We had to broach the subject softly as we didn't want it to come as a big shock," Claire said.

"Aye, I know what you mean. You should have seen my reaction!" Arthur chipped in.

Claire smiled before saying: "Anyway, you've come a long way and I expect you can't wait to see her so shall we go through?"

Arthur stood up smiling and said: "Aye, lead the way lass."

They walked through a door where Claire called a lift. The doors opened and the three of them walked inside where she pressed the button for the third floor.

She talked to them both about the quality of care at the home, at pains to stress that all the residents were treated with dignity and not simply as patients.

The doors opened and they walked out on to the floor. Tom saw there were a number of doors leading off elsewhere. Ahead was a large communal room in which elderly people sat in high backed, soft chairs, some of them watching television, others who appeared to be dozing or asleep.

Claire stopped at one of the doors and, tapping on it loudly before opening and walking in, said: "Here we are this is Margaret's room."

Tom let Arthur go in first behind Claire and detected the first sign of nerves in his friend.

Inside, the room was flooded with sunlight from a large window overlooking what appeared to be a park. He followed Arthur and Claire and then saw an elderly woman's legs, wearing a pair of slippers, perched up on a foot stool.

"Margaret?" he heard Claire say, "Margaret, there's someone here to see you."

She stepped aside and allowed Arthur to move closer. As he did so Tom stepped forward and saw her for the first time.

She was sitting in a chair dressed in a blue tartan skirt and lavender sweater. Her hair was a mass of pure white curls, her face thin and covered in deep wrinkles. She was wearing glasses and sat with her hands resting on the high arms of the chair.

Arthur moved around to be closer to her and said tentatively: "Maggie? ... Maggie, it's me Arthur. Can you hear me?"

The elderly woman lifted her head and looked at Arthur. For a moment she appeared quizzical, confused, but suddenly her eyes lit up and she lifted her right arm, holding her hand out towards him.

Arthur took hold of her thin, bony fingers and clasped them softly in his hands.

"Arthur?" she whispered softly. The old man nodded, "Yes, it's me Maggie, I'm here," he said.

She let her arm fall back and, smiling, Tom heard her say: "My Arthur ... my little brother."

He looked across at Arthur, tears streaming down his face.

Tom felt slightly uncomfortable, as though he was intruding and Claire must have spotted it because she touched his arm, saying: "Shall we give them some privacy?"

"What? Oh, yes … yes of course," he replied and the two of them walked out of the room.

He followed her and they talked as they made their way through to a dining area where two members of staff were serving tea and biscuits to some of the residents.

Claire requested four cups of tea and a plate of biscuits and Tom helped carry them back to Margaret's room. Inside they found Arthur sitting next to her stroking her hand.

He was talking to her and Tom thought he heard him mention his elder brother but then the old man noticed they'd returned and the conversation ended.

"Come here lad," he said, beckoning him over towards them. "Maggie," he said, looking into the old woman's eyes, "this is the lad who found you. Without Tom I'd never have known you were here."

Tom looked at the old woman's face as she tilted her head slightly to look at him. He smiled and thought he saw her smile back.

Her mouth opened and she said something though he couldn't work out what. Arthur though seemed to know straight away. How was that possible he thought?

"She says you're a grand lad, ain't that right Maggie?" Arthur said with a huge grin on his face.

The more time he spent in the room, the more he got a sense of how lucid Margaret, or Maggie as Arthur preferred to call her, was. It seemed to fluctuate. Some moments she appeared to be having a conversation with her brother, though she spoke so softly Tom could hardly hear a word.

Then, moments later she seemed confused, unaware of her surroundings and looking quizzically at the people in the room.

Arthur didn't seem to notice that side of her, or if he did, was choosing to ignore it.

After a while Claire left the three of them to it and Tom felt privileged to witness such a remarkable family reunion. Arthur seemed content simply to spend time with Maggie, repeatedly telling her how wonderful it was that they'd found each after so long.

So it came as a real surprise to Tom when suddenly, out of nowhere, Arthur asked his sister about events more than seventy years ago.

"Maggie," he said, taking her hand again, "What really happened all those years ago. Mam and dad never really spoke of it. Our John told me bits when I was older but I didn't know much."

Margaret gazed at her brother, her eyes looking tired.

Arthur continued: "Dad could be harsh couldn't he? I guess he didn't approve eh? I just wish I'd known where you were."

Tom could see his friend was beginning to get upset and he saw Maggie put her other hand over his, clutching him tightly.

"It's alright Arthur ..." she whispered.

He was sobbing quietly now and Tom stood up and put a consoling arm on his shoulder.

"It's a lot for you both to take in," he said, looking at Maggie.

Arthur wiped his eyes and coughed to clear his throat and, as Tom sat back down and was about to suggest more tea, said: "Your baby Maggie ... what happened to your baby? A little boy wasn't he?"

She looked startled by the question and it clearly distressed her as she began whimpering and crying softly.

Arthur was mortified, "Oh Maggie, I'm so sorry, it doesn't matter. I shouldn't have asked, don't upset yourself, please."

He stood up and leaned forward, attempting to comfort her with a careful hug as she remained in her chair.

It had the desired effect and Arthur sat back down as Margaret regained her composure, wiping her nose with a tissue.

And then she spoke, and for the first time Tom was able to hear her.

"He was lovely Arthur ... big blue eyes ... such a beautiful boy," she said quietly.

An awkward silence followed with Arthur clearly unsure whether to ask anything else, lest she should get upset again.

"I gave him away Arthur ... my little boy," she said, before her voice tailed off.

Arthur looked confused and concerned for his sister, it was clear he didn't want to see her distressed.

"It's ok Maggie, it was a long time ago," was all he could think of to say.

"I couldn't keep him ... I couldn't do it," Tom heard her say.

"Shhh ... Maggie, it's ok, you've nothing to apologise for," Arthur added.

She motioned him to come closer and he stood up again and leaned forward awkwardly, resting his hand against the back of the chair to support himself.

Whispering into his ear Arthur listened before planting a kiss on her forehead, sitting back down and smiling. There was a knock on the door and Tom turned to see Claire walk in smiling.

"How are you getting on?" she asked, before adding: "Margaret usually has a sleep just before her lunch. Would you like to stay and have something to eat here and see her again later?"

Tom looked at Arthur who, for a moment looked unsure, but then stood up and said: "Aye, we could do with a bite to eat."

Turning to his sister he said: "Don't you get going anywhere Maggie, I'll be back again soon."

Tom and Maggie shared a smile as he followed Arthur out of the room. Eating lunch in the dining room the old man looked up from his plate:

"Forced to give up her baby ... I can't imagine what that does to you."

"Must have been really tough for her," Tom replied sympathetically.

"She's had to live with that for a lifetime," Arthur added.

"It scars you I suppose. No wonder she can still remember it all; she even remembers the names of the couple who took her little boy."

Chapter seventeen

August 1916

They were relieved in the early hours of the morning, though they had to wait for the dead and wounded to be taken back down the lines first.

In single file they wearily stumbled their way through the communication trenches, some of them hobbling, others almost dragging themselves along, their eyes hollow, colour drained from their faces.

The guns had been silent for more than two hours now. They hadn't attacked again, though Amos and the other survivors had been forced to endure a brutal artillery bombardment which rained down on their positions.

Fritz's revenge for failing to retake the wood was the reason given by those who sat through every lethal, miserable moment of it.

Cloud had moved in and the dawning day was a grey one. It had begun to drizzle and, though it hadn't rained for some time, it was already making the surface of the trenches greasy and slippery under foot.

By the time Amos found himself out of the lines and was trudging slowly along a country road with several other men, it was raining heavily. As they walked they passed fresh troops heading the other way and had to step into a muddy field as lorries carrying the wounded drove by.

He had no idea how long or how far they walked but by the end every step was painful. Amos didn't know where they were going or who was in command; he simply followed the others in front of him.

Eventually, they approached what looked like farm buildings, around which were tents and supply wagons.

Up ahead he heard a voice barking instructions telling the soldiers where they could find something to eat.

A few minutes later he was sat inside a barn along with scores of other men eating hot, watery soup with fatty chunks of pink meat floating in it. He'd hoped there would be somewhere to wash beforehand, the rain hadn't removed all the blood and brain tissue from his tunic, but there was nothing.

He forced himself to eat knowing he'd regret it later if he didn't. After he'd finished he wanted to lie down and sleep but was distracted by a voice: "Private Amos?"

Amos turned to see the familiar figure of the battalion's chaplain.

Saluting limply he said: "Hello padre, fancy seeing you here."

Roebuck came closer. He was shocked by Amos' appearance but tried not to show it.

"How are you Amos? Have you just come down from Mametz? I hear it's bad up there," Roebuck said.

"It's no worse than anywhere else," Amos replied.

"I've just come from visiting some of the wounded," Roebuck said. "looks like you had a lucky escape up there."

He winced as soon as he said it, regretting the comment instantly.

"Didn't you know padre? I'm the battalion's lucky fucking charm," Amos said and he began to walk away.

"Amos? ... Amos, I'm sorry, that was crass," Roebuck said. "I didn't mean it to come out like that. I'm just relieved to see you're ok that's all."

Amos stopped, turned and gave the chaplain a withering look.

"Yes, I'm ok padre. I'm covered in blood and brains, I've made more women widows and more children fatherless and I stood and watched while wounded men were stabbed to death while I did nothing," he said.

"And do you know what? I didn't give a shit ... we all fucking deserve it; every single one of us. I just hope my time comes soon. I wish it had been last night. When the guns open up I pray for a shell to land right next to me and blow me to Kingdom Come. It's all I live for ... hoping and waiting to die."

Roebuck was caught off guard. He'd seen men react similarly when coming out of battle but he knew this was different. He knew Amos was driven not merely from an expectation that he would die but from the anger he still felt over the death of Eddie Bousefield.

"George, listen to me," Roebuck said.

"I did everything I could to help Private Bousefield but the court martial found him guilty. There was nothing I could do."

Amos stared at him contemptuously before turning and walking away.

"George? George, please ...," Roebuck said shouting after him. But Amos kept walking, the anger fuelling his exhausted body. Roebuck made to follow but stopped when Amos left the barn and walked away in the pouring rain.

He watched him until he disappeared, melding into a throng of khaki clad men huddled together sheltering from the rain. And then, despite it being uncomfortable, he thought back to earlier conversations and events.

"Come on padre, there must be something you can do? They're going to execute him. It's wrong, bloody wrong."

Amos was animated and couldn't keep still. He'd appeared at a prayer meeting Roebuck had held and hung back at the end as the others dispersed.

"George, I'm not sure there is much that I can do. As I understand it, Private Bousefield has been found guilty following a hearing. You were a witness were you not?"

Amos was frustrated, partly for his own performance at the hearing, and now for his lack of ability to get anyone to help him.

"Yes, yes I was, but they'd made their minds up before it even started. Eddie never stood a chance," he said, the desperation in his voice now audible.

"Look," Roebuck said, sounding as sympathetic as he could, "maybe the hearing came to the correct conclusion. We don't know all the facts."

"What? You're kidding right? Look, padre, Eddie and I both went back out there to find Captain Harris. If it wasn't for him I'd most probably be dead! It was Eddie who carried the Captain back most of the way," Amos explained, raising his voice.

"So how can it be that he's getting shot while I got given a fucking medal?"

Roebuck was silent for a moment and felt Amos staring at him intently while he thought. He had no doubt the young soldier was telling the truth and he'd always been uncomfortable with the death penalty being given to soldiers for anything less than capital crimes.

When he finally spoke he did so calmly and in a way which he hoped would placate him.

"I'll tell you what Private Amos, I will speak with Major Howard, I've always found him to be a very reasonable man. I'm sure once the Major knows about your testimony he may want to reconsider."

Amos relaxed and looked a little relieved.

"You'll do that? You'll tell them padre? You'll tell them Eddie's a hero, that they can't kill him?" Amos added.

Roebuck smiled as he began putting his bible away in a satchel he carried with him. "Let's not get carried away Private, I've said I'll speak with the Major. Let's take it one step at a time."

A tap on the shoulder interrupted his thoughts and Roebuck turned to see a soldier holding out a mug of hot tea as the rain continued to hammer down. Thanking him, the chaplain took a sip and then found his thoughts drifting again.

"Ah, padre, how lovely to see you, will you join me?" Major Howard asked, pouring himself tea as Roebuck was shown into his headquarters.

"Er, no, thank you Major, I'm fine," he replied.

"So, what can I do for you padre? This isn't about the men being given more time for worship is it? You know I believe strongly in the importance of faith but I simply can't afford to give them more time, not at the moment. I'm sure you understand," the Major said and he sat down, sipping his tea.

"No, Major, it's not that. You know I remain hugely grateful for the support you and others have shown to me and my fellow chaplains," Roebuck replied.

"Good, good, so what is it?" the officer asked.

Roebuck was nervous and looked ill at ease. He could sense the Major had picked up on that.

"Major, it's about the court martial of Private Bousefield."

Howard looked up from his tea; a slight look of surprise appearing briefly on his face.

"I believe the proceedings for that hearing have concluded and a sentence has been passed," Howard said casually.

Roebuck shifted awkwardly on his feet.

"Why yes …yes, I believe they have. Though it has come to my attention that the tribunal may not have been appraised of all the facts," he added.

The Major looked intrigued, albeit a little wary at the chaplain's intervention.

"Go on padre," he said, inviting Roebuck to continue.

Emboldened by the Major's reply, Roebuck grew in confidence.

"I have spoken with Private George Amos; he is very concerned and upset at what he believes to be the truth about Private Bousefield's role in the rescue of Captain Harris not being, how can I put it? ... not fully recognised or understood," Roebuck said tactfully.

The Major stood and approached the chaplain.

"Padre, if we are to win this war, the men will need faith; faith in God and the belief that right is on our side. You are here to help them either discover, or to keep, their faith. Whatever else happens is no concern of yours. Now, if you'll excuse me ...," Howard added and he turned and sat back down.

Roebuck stood quiet for a moment before turning and walking away. As he was about to leave he paused, looked at the Major and said: "You know Major it was Captain Harris who also told me men need hope ... not simply hope that they will come through this ... but the hope that gives men renewed spirit and a belief that the future will be a better one.

"Without hope Major, the outlook becomes bleak and life hardly worth living. Give Eddie Bousefield and George Amos hope ... we owe them that," he added, before he stepped outside and walked away.

Now, as he stood leaning against a pillar inside the barn, surrounded by exhausted, bedraggled men,

Roebuck knew George Amos was a man without hope. And he prayed for him because he knew how dangerous that was.

June 2016

He needed to speak with his dad, desperately. He'd considered calling him when he'd dropped Arthur off but didn't. He told himself it would be too late but he knew that wasn't the sole reason.

How was he supposed to even broach the subject? He couldn't just bring it up in conversation could he?

"Hey dad, it's me. Yes, the girls are fine thanks. How are you and mum? Oh, by the way, were you adopted?" It was ludicrous.

He had fond memories of his grandmother growing up. Sadly, his grandfather had died when he was only five and memories of him were few.

He hadn't said anything to Arthur. After replaying much of his meeting with Maggie in the car on the way home, the excitement had caught up with the old man and he'd fallen asleep, snoring for the remainder of the journey.

It meant the silent drive home in the dark was spent searching his childhood memories for clues about something he told himself couldn't possibly be true. So, why was it making him feel uncomfortable?

He thought back to the conversation he and Arthur had over lunch and which had changed his mood for the rest of the day.

"Funnily enough, their names were Harris too," Arthur had said casually. "Andrew and Catherine; Maggie remembers so clearly because he was her doctor. You can't imagine that being allowed nowadays can you?"

Tom was stunned, did a double take and asked Arthur to repeat himself. He did so but appeared too caught up in his own emotions to notice the lock of shock on his friend's face.

After that the rest of the day had been a blur. They spent more time sitting with Maggie, Tom taking more photos on his phone before Claire tactfully drew the visit to a close.

Arthur got tearful as they were leaving but promised his sister he'd visit again as soon as he could.

Now, as his friend slept, he repeatedly went over everything he knew, trying to make sense of it. He started with the facts. Margaret Roebuck had given birth to a little boy, John Arthur, in May 1942. He wasn't sure when, but at some point afterwards she had given the baby up.

He wasn't sure if that meant official adoption or some other kind of arrangement.

According to Arthur, Maggie told him the names of the couple who had taken her baby.

He then started thinking about his dad, John. He was a similar age to what Maggie's son would be now. So? What did that prove he asked himself?

But it was his dad's parents he couldn't stop thinking about ... Andrew and Cathy Harris. Or, Dr Harris as his grandfather was known, by all accounts a popular, respected village GP.

He had come across more than one or two coincidences in recent weeks but this was something else.

As he drove, he tried to picture his grandfather, though his memory was hazy and he found himself recalling photographs rather than the man. Thin faced with a friendly smile was what he recalled.

Growing up he learned more about him, mainly thanks to his dad and grandmother. He knew Andrew Harris had spent more than 30 years running a doctor's surgery in a North Yorkshire village.

Before that he'd trained at a hospital in Leeds where he met his future wife who was working as a nurse.

During the Second World War Andrew joined the Royal Army Medical Corps, serving in Italy and later France.

He and Catherine had married in 1939. They'd only had the one child, Tom's dad. He knew his father's birthday was 20 June 1942 and that he didn't have a middle name. Nonetheless, the more he thought about it, the more he became convinced his dad was Maggie Roebuck's son.

His thoughts turned to his grandmother; a diminutive, slender woman, she was the archetypal grandparent. Kind, generous, absolutely committed to the happiness of her family.

He recalled visiting her as a child, looking forward to the unlimited chocolate biscuits she always seemed to have; the big garden with plenty of places to play and hide; her sleeping in the spare room on Christmas Eve and then up at the crack of dawn peeling potatoes.

She'd died when he was 17 but even now he felt a warm glow when thinking of her. She was everything he'd want a grandmother to be and he hoped Daisy would think of his own mother in the same way.

There were no clues in his memories, nothing to suggest a past that was not as it appeared to be. He thought again of his dad but he couldn't recall him saying or doing anything which even hinted that his mum and dad were not his birth parents.

In the absence of any facts, he allowed his mind to wander. What if his dad was Maggie's adopted son? That would make Arthur his great uncle. Tom smiled at that.

But what if his dad didn't know? What if he had no idea that his own mother had given him away because she had been disowned by her family?

Suddenly, he wasn't so desperate to speak to him.

He needed to get home now and talk to Emma. He had to tell someone and she would know what to do. It was one of the things he loved about her, how she would keep her head and always look for a solution, no matter what.

They arrived back at Arthur's and he saw the old man inside, declining his offer of a night cap telling him he ought to be getting back.

It was late when he finally walked through the front door and the house was in darkness. He'd texted Emma earlier to let her know and was hoping she would have stayed up.

Kicking off his shoes he headed straight upstairs, putting his head around the door of Daisy's room, looking at his daughter's face in the soft glow of the night light.

Climbing into bed next to Emma, he heard her moan quietly as he snuggled up against her. And then he lay there thinking; going over it again and again, searching for something, anything that would give him the answer.

He woke early, desperate to fill Emma in on the trip to Scarborough. It was almost amusing to watch her reaction knowing he'd felt exactly the same way yesterday.

But once the shock was out of the way, she'd begun looking for solutions, just as he knew she would.

The first thing he had to do, she said, was get hold of his dad's birth certificate. That would help clarify things. It wouldn't prove anything categorically but he needed to see it.

Secondly, she suggested telling his parents he wanted to compile his family tree, using Daisy as the pretext. That was reason enough to ask them questions and, she figured, he'd soon know if there was any sign of reluctance or worry from his dad when he mentioned it.

He dropped his mum a text later that morning asking after them both and suggested the three of them go and visit. He could sense the delight in her immediate reply.

They arrived in time for lunch on Saturday. He saw his mum's face peering out of the window when they pulled up and she came running excitedly out of the door to greet them.

She was gushing over Daisy, who his parents hadn't seen for a couple of months now, and making a real fuss over Emma as they walked into the house, Tom carrying his daughter inside.

His father was coming down the stairs as they walked into the hall and he enthusiastically hugged his son and kissed Emma before joining his wife in gazing adoringly at their granddaughter.

They had lunch after Daisy had been fed and was having a nap. His dad was still wearing his golfing gear having played earlier that morning.

"My game's not improving son, even now I'm retired and am playing more often" he said, after Tom asked him how he'd got on.

They spent lunch catching up on family matters but Tom avoided completely the whole story about Arthur. In the circumstances he thought it best not to mention it.

After lunch Emma suggested she and Tom's mum take Daisy for a walk, giving 'the men some time on their own.' They'd planned that on the journey up to give him time to speak with his dad.

Once they'd gone he and his dad talked as they cleared the table. Tom was nervous and felt a little on edge. It was not a conversation he was looking forward to.

"So, what else have you been up to son? You still haven't told me everything about that French trip you went on and finding that grave with your name on it. That must have been very strange," his dad said.

"Yeah, it was dad, a real eye opener. And so many cemeteries, I never realised the scale of it before," he replied.

"I was lucky enough to meet a few veterans when I was at work and there used to be an old boy at the golf club some years back. Remarkable men they were," his dad said.

Tom saw his opportunity.

"It got me thinking dad, seeing all those graves. You should know about your family history right? I'm sure there are lots of people who don't even know their relatives fought and died in the war."

"Yes, you're probably right," his dad replied.

"So, I was thinking it would be good to do the Harris family tree. You know, trace back down the line and piece together the family history. It would be something for Daisy when she's older," he said, convinced he sounded nervous.

If his dad was in any way suspicious, he didn't show it.

Instead, he said: "Sounds a great idea, I could help you with that."

Tom smiled, thanked his dad and then asked: "Can I see yours and mum's birth certificates? They're usually a good starter for ten."

His dad looked at him and for a fleeting moment Tom thought he detected a trace of worry in his face.

"I wouldn't know where they are son; you'd have to ask your mother. Though, I'm not sure what else they can tell you that we can't," he replied.

"Oh, I know, I mean, you're right, of course, but I'm … I'm just interested really. I don't think I've ever seen them," he added.

He'd always been a terrible liar and he felt his dad staring at him intensely. The two of them were sitting in the kitchen and he could hear the clock on the wall ticking loudly.

Finally, his dad leaned forward and said quietly: "You know don't you Tom?"

He wasn't expecting that. The question took him completely by surprise and he didn't know how to answer.

His father filled the void.

"So, when did you find out? Or have you known for a while?"

He hadn't been prepared for this and was shocked at how astute his dad was and how calm he appeared.

"Err, dad, I'm not sure … I mean, what do you mean?" he asked, desperately trying to buy himself some time and wanting to confirm his dad was actually referring to what he thought he was.

"I mean how long have you known I was adopted Tom?"

Chapter eighteen

August 1916

When the call for volunteers came he simply stepped forward, saying quietly: "I'll go," before continuing to clean his rifle.

He was the first to offer so didn't notice the reluctance on the faces of the others, some of whom averted their gaze from the Second Lieutenant walking down the trench, hoping not to make eye contact.

Eventually, thanks to the cajoling and encouragement of other officers, six more men were found and they were asked to assemble for a briefing.

The expression on Amos' face was unlike any of the others. Whilst they appeared nervous and apprehensive about what might lay ahead, he simply looked bored.

The junior officer who called them together seemed younger than all of them. Amos didn't recognise him.

"Thank you men for volunteering, I'm Second Lieutenant Benton and I've been asked to lead a patrol from the 26th trench. Our objective is to make contact with the 30th Brigade on the right of our line," he said.

None of them spoke but they didn't need to. Their expressions said more than enough.

"Now, we understand from an earlier patrol that the farm up ahead is strongly defended by enemy forces. It is imperative we proceed with stealth and caution to avoid being detected," Benton added.

"I'll lead the patrol out and ...," Benton paused as he scanned the faces of the men in front of him.

"You Private, what's your name?"

Amos saw the officer staring straight at him.

"Amos sir," he answered.

"Right, Amos, you'll bring up the rear. Now, we don't want to do anything to alert Fritz while we're out there. We leave at 2am so get some rest beforehand. Oh, and by the way, I've arranged for extra breakfast rations for you on our return," he added, before walking away.

There were mutterings among the men when he'd gone, most of them speculating what the point of the mission was and how dangerous it would be.

"Why can't 30 Brigade come and find us?" said one, "why do we need to go out to them?"

"If you ask me it's another pointless fucking patrol. We know they're there, surely they know where we are. Complete waste of time," another man replied.

"Maybe the Second Lieutenant wants to earn his spurs, maybe he's missed out on all the fun we've had so far."

A couple of them laughed at that comment. Amos didn't. He'd turned and walked away when the officer had left and was now sitting with his back against the wall of the trench.

There was a chill in the autumn air making it difficult to stay warm but he managed to huddle himself under a sheet, using his kitbag as a hard pillow, and closed his eyes. Not so long ago he'd have struggled to sleep at all like this and there had been several days when he was exhausted because of it.

But he was different now. Back then he was afraid and scared of dying. Now that fear was gone; replaced by an acceptance that death was inevitable and would come soon. Within seconds he was asleep.

He awoke just as quickly, hearing a voice standing over him calling his name. Minutes later he was ready; standing alongside anxious faces as the Second Lieutenant looked them over.

"Right men, let's do this. Remember, stay silent, no sudden movements and follow my direction. Good luck," Benton said.

He turned and was the first to clamber over the top of the trench, disappearing from view as he crawled on his stomach.

The others followed him one by one until finally Amos did the same, lying flat and creeping forward. It was a moonless night and the lack of visibility both helped and hampered them.

Progress was slow as the patrol crawled forwards, each man following the lead of the one in front.

Amos couldn't help but think of the last time he'd done this. At first he did so without emotion, until his thoughts inevitably turned to Eddie and then Captain Harris.

As he inched himself along on his belly, his face just able to make out the soles of the boots belonging to the man ahead of him, he felt the anger rising within. Only when the patrol suddenly changed direction and Amos found himself turning to his right, did he begin to calm down.

Like the others, he had no idea where they were going or what they were supposed to do when they got there. But unlike the others he didn't care.

Suddenly, the patrol came to a halt and Amos was the last to realise as his face almost came into contact with a soldier's boot.

He lay there in silence, along with the others, unsure of what it was that had caused them to stop.

Over to his left he thought he heard movement. He turned to face it and strained to hear. Nothing.

Then, up ahead, beyond the patrol, the sound of voices. German voices. Amos tensed, feeling the adrenalin flood through him as his senses heightened and his heart rate increased.

He heard them again, there were several, and they were animated. Despite feeling utterly exposed where he lay, he knew that to remain completely still was the best thing to do right now.

Another noise to his left, he could still hear it. Movement; something was out there. He could sense it getting nearer. Very slowly he brought his rifle in front of him, into a position where he could easily fire if needed.

His eyes strained to peer into the blackness beyond in an effort to pick out any moving shapes. For a moment he thought he'd done so and was about to bring his rifle up when suddenly the patrol started moving, quickly, urgently.

Amos wanted to shout out 'no,' to say 'keep still' but it was too late. The men ahead were moving but their speed was making noise, a lot of noise.

He was caught now between monitoring the movement to his left and staying with the patrol. He hadn't time to decide when a voice in the near distance cried out: "Englisch soldaten vor ihnen, sie schießen."

It was followed by two flares which shot into the night sky illuminating the landscape. Amos caught a glimpse of the men in his patrol hurriedly crawling away from the direction of the voices ahead.

In the split second before the light from the flares disappeared, shots rang out and suddenly the ground was engulfed in gunfire.

More flares were fired puncturing the darkness with splashes of light as tracers from rifle bullets and machine guns created a deadly, colourful spectacle.

The shooting appeared to intensify around where he and the rest of the patrol were. Movement to the left again, he saw figures this time and they were coming towards him.

Silhouetted against the flashes he recognised them as German soldiers and realised immediately what had happened. Two patrols on opposite sides had stumbled across each other in the middle of No Man's Land.

He remained where he was, raising his rifle in the prone position and fired a volley of shots in the direction of the approaching German troops. He saw two fall, rapidly followed by others who were now taking cover.

He heard a scream, glancing to his right he saw the man who had been in front of him in the patrol, reel backwards, clearly hit.

The rest of the patrol was either attempting to shoot back or scramble for cover. He reloaded and emptied another magazine in the direction of the German patrol before crawling forwards as fast as he could towards the pinned down British soldiers.

He passed the first who was lying dead, his chest and lower body hit by several bullets. Another was on his knees firing his rifle while Amos saw two others lying flat and shooting, while a man next to them was face down and still.

As he got closer he used the body of one dead man as cover and raised his rifle a third time, this time waiting until a flare exploded to give him a better chance of finding a target.

Up ahead he could make out the figures of men in the German lines and aimed for them, firing all five rounds as rapidly as he could. When the clip was empty he shouted out: "Come on, we need to go, now!"

Two of the men turned and, needing no encouragement, began crawling back towards him.

"Where's Benton?" Amos shouted, as bullets continued to whizz past.

"He's dead, shot in the neck," one of the men replied, as he scrambled across the ground.

By now the British lines were also shooting but it meant Amos and the others were literally caught in the cross fire.

"Go … go!!!" he shouted to one of the men in the patrol, who had stopped next to him and appeared to be reloading his rifle.

The man glanced at Amos briefly before he turned and joined the others crawling as fast and flat as they could back towards their own trenches.

Amos once again found himself at the back and as he crawled back he suddenly thought of home. He didn't know why, he couldn't explain it but his mother's face appeared vividly in his head.

He came to a stop, lying flat on the ground, as though moving again would obliterate the image from his mind. Suddenly, he knew what it meant.

And then George Amos rose to his feet, dropped his rifle and began walking back towards the British lines.

Despite the darkness he saw the distinctive figures of British troops firing over the top of their trenches, tracers whizzing past him in both directions. He had to step over the bodies of the remainder of the patrol who were still crawling desperately along on their stomachs.

One of them lifted his head and shouted something, though Amos wasn't listening.

He wondered what it would feel like when it happened, whether it would be instant or whether he'd die a slow, agonising death. He got nearer to the trenches and was close enough to see one or two soldiers hesitate and stop their firing.

Closer still now, it had to happen soon, he was sure of it.

And then voices: "Get down! Get down you bloody idiot, are you mad?"

"Run, come on mate, you can make it, run!"

But Amos didn't run and simply carried on walking. He slowed down over the last few yards, his confusion at still being alive turning to anger. Only a few feet to go now, there were several British troops urging him on while others fired either side of him.

And then he was there. He'd made it. He stood at the top of the trench looking down at the faces of the men below him, their expressions one of sheer astonishment. He saw some were shouting but again he didn't hear.

Instead, his body suddenly spun wildly as his right shoulder exploded and he fell like a stone into the trench.

June 2016

"I was twelve when my parents told me. We were on holiday at the time and I remember them sitting me down with an ice cream, saying they had something important to tell me."

He sat listening to his father while still trying to figure out what it was that he'd done or said that had convinced his dad that he knew.

"Was I shocked? Yes, I suppose I was, as far as I was concerned they were my mum and dad and it didn't make any sense what I was being told," he continued, sitting cross legged in an armchair.

"What did they tell you?" Tom asked, astonished at how calm his father seemed to be talking about this.

His father smiled as he answered: "Well, they told me sometimes mothers find it difficult to look after their babies and that they need to put them in the care of people who will love and care for them as if they were their own.

"It was only later of course that I learned that my mum couldn't have children. Although my dad was a doctor there was little they knew or understood about infertility back then," he said.

"So they adopted you?" Tom asked, interrupting.

"Yes, but adoption in the 1940s was much different to what it is today. Only the well-off could really afford to do it unless, of course, you were lucky enough to work in a profession where you came into contact with expectant mothers."

"Granddad worked in a hospital didn't he?" said Tom.

"Yes, and if it wasn't for that, they'd never have been able to adopt," his father added.

Tom had so many questions that he didn't know what to ask next. Instead, his father carried on speaking.

"Dad trained at St James' Hospital in Leeds and after qualifying moved to a small village in West Yorkshire where he became the GP. As a doctor he would have seen his fair share of pregnant women, not all them happy about the prospect," his father said.

"Is that what happened then? Did your birth mother ... you know, not want you?" Tom asked.

"I'm not sure I'd put it like that. She was a young woman, a girl even, only around 15 or 16 at the time. She was confused, frightened, her family had disowned her," his father replied.

"So ... so you know who your real mum is then?"

"Yes, I do, her name was Margaret Roebuck. My parents were very open with me and told me much more as I got older. They even offered to help me find her when I turned eighteen but I wasn't interested at the time," he said.

"I had a change of heart in my early twenties but by then she was no longer living at the same address. Turns out she'd moved away. I was bitterly disappointed at the time but you know I've always believed things happen for a reason Tom.

"I don't have any regrets, I had a wonderful childhood and my mother and father were the best parents anyone could ever hope for."

Suddenly, Tom realised his father had never met his real mother and would be oblivious to her still being alive. His mind was racing and it dawned on him that Maggie was also his grandmother.

"Tom, are you ok? I'm sorry, this is probably a real shock for you and here I am rattling on. What gave it away? I mean, there must have been something that raised your suspicions?" his father asked.

He wasn't sure how to answer, how could he even begin to tell the story? It was too incredible.

He leaned forward and said: "Dad, there's something I've not told you, it's ... it's a little hard to believe and, if I'm honest, I'm struggling with it myself."

His father looked anxious. "What is it son, is everything all right?"

"Dad, when I was in France and I saw the headstone with my name on it ... well, it's probably easier if I just start from the beginning," he said.

His dad's face remained anxious but he sat back and let his son do the talking.

He tried to do it quickly and in order, ensuring he didn't miss anything out, but saw his dad looking quizzical when he began talking about his unlikely friendship with a man in his eighties.

The he slowed down as he approached the critical point in his story. He felt he'd been here before when telling Arthur that Maggie was still alive. This was different though; this was his dad and Maggie was his dad's mother.

He was determined to do it properly, sensitively. He wondered how his dad would react when he knew.

Five minutes later he found out.

It occurred to him that he'd never seen his father look bewildered, lost. But that's what he looked now and Tom hated the thought that he was responsible for that.

"Dad? Dad, are you ok?" he asked.

Just then the front door opened and he heard his mum's voice: "We're home, is the kettle on?"

A few seconds later she walked through into the lounge holding Daisy, with Emma following behind. From the expression on her husband's face she sensed something was wrong and it looked serious.

"John? ... what is it? What's wrong?" she said, turning to Tom and asking the same question.

He gave Emma a knowing glance and she worked it out straight away, excusing herself by saying Daisy needed changing before leaving the room.

His dad still hadn't spoken and, aware that his mother was looking at him expecting an answer, he said awkwardly: "Err, mum ... dad and I have been talking ... I had ... there was something I needed to tell him."

"Tell him what? John what is Tom talking about?" she said, becoming increasingly frustrated.

"Lucy, you'd better sit down," his father said, speaking quietly.

She took a seat on the sofa, in between the two of them, and looked at her husband as he continued: "Lucy, Tom knows ... about my real mother."

It was Tom's turn to be shocked now and before his mother could respond he blurted out: "Wait a minute ... mum knows?"

His dad nodded and Tom turned to face his mother: "How long have you known mum?"

It was his dad who spoke again and this time he was his more composed self.

"Tom, the important thing now is that we all know. I told your mother about it shortly after we met. It was my decision and mine alone to keep it from you but I did that for the very best of intentions," he said.

"If I'd had any inkling that my mother was still alive, then of course I'd have told you, I hope you believe that."

This time Tom's mother spoke before he could answer.

"Alive? What ... are you sure? How do you know that?" she asked, looking shocked and puzzled.

Between them Tom and his dad brought her up to speed on what had happened. By the end Emma had returned to the room, Tom explaining that she too was aware.

For a while the four of them sat in silence, as though attempting to process what had happened. Daisy provided a useful distraction, lying on the floor making noises and playing.

His mother finally broke the silence.

"The whole thing ... well, it's just incredible. I can't believe it," she said.

Turning to her husband she smiled and added: "John, you've got to meet her. Your mother. How wonderful is that?"

For the first time since they'd begun talking his father also smiled. Looking at his son he said: "If I was a religious man I'd swear it was a sign."

That seemed to signal that the mood was now one of jubilation rather than an awkward family secret which no one was comfortable speaking about.

His mother set about making tea while his dad wanted to find out as much as he could about Maggie and her brother Arthur.

Later that afternoon as Tom and Emma were preparing to head home, his dad hugged him at the front door, saying simply: "Thank you son, you have no idea how happy you've made me today."

Tom smiled and added: "It's been a heck of an afternoon dad but I can't wait for you to meet Maggie. I'll get it sorted in the next couple of days and let you know."

His parents watched as they drove off, the sun had broken through and it was now a glorious summer afternoon. They were back home within a couple of hours.

He'd only been through the door a few minutes when his mobile rang. The number looked familiar but he couldn't place it.

"Hello."

"Oh, hello, could I speak with Mr Harris please?" asked a female voice.

"Yes, Tom Harris speaking," he replied.

"Mr Harris, it's Claire Aspinall from Sycamore Lodge Nursing Home."

His brief silence convinced her he needed a prompt: "We're in Scarborough Mr Harris, you came to see Mrs Amos?"

"Oh, right, of course, I'm sorry. It's been a long day. Funnily enough, I was going to give you a call. I've found another relative of Margaret's, I was hoping to arrange another visit," Harris replied.

Her voice sounded different.

"Mr Harris, that's why I'm calling, I'm afraid I have some bad news. Mrs Amos passed away peacefully last night."

Chapter nineteen

September 1916

The light flooded in as his eyes slowly opened and he heard voices around him. Above him was an ornate ceiling with a large chandelier hanging from it. There were also a number of hanging lights and it must have been dark outside as they were lit.

His nostrils detected a pungent, chemical odour and for a brief moment he wondered why the ability to smell disappeared during sleep.

More voices, some close, others nearby. And groans, quiet yet audible.

He attempted to turn his head in an effort to look around; it felt heavy. Suddenly a voice.

"Ah Private Amos, nice to have you back with us. How are you feeling?" asked a voice as a man's face loomed large above him.

He was portly, had a greying moustache and wore spectacles. He spoke with a broad Scottish accent.

Amos didn't speak. Instead, he stared briefly at the man before turning his eyes away.

"You're a lucky man Private Amos, the angels were clearly looking out for you," the man added before he turned and walked away.

Amos turned his head, it was painful to do so, and he grimaced as his eyes focused upon row after row of beds, dozens of them, squeezed together in what looked to be some kind of large hall.

Some of the patients were sitting up; others were gathered in small groups at the end of a bed chatting, while several others simply lay still. He counted at least five nurses going to and fro and then saw the back of the man who had just spoken to him.

"Hey ... hey!" Amos managed to cry out, his voice faltering at the end.

The man turned to face him, holding the wrist of a patient lying still in a nearby bed. There was a nurse standing next to him and he looked at her before saying: "Change the dressing nurse and keep an eye on his temperature."

Then he headed back to where Amos was lying.

"Yes Amos, what is it?" he asked.

"Where? ... where am I?" he managed to say, his voice decidedly croaky.

Walking closer until he was stood at the bottom of Amos' bed, the man replied: "You're in a base hospital in Boulogne on the French coast. Number seven stationary hospital to be precise. You've been here for three days now."

He saw a look of surprise on Amos' face but continued talking.

"My name is Charles Baxter, I'm one of the doctors here. Do you ... remember what happened?" he asked, and the expression on his face changed.

Amos stared at him before averting his gaze and looking around the room. He went to turn on his left side but winced with pain.

"Best to stay lying on your back," Baxter suggested.

"Your left shoulder was in a bit of mess when you arrived here I'm afraid. They'd patched you up best they could but it looked like you'd lose your arm," he added.

At that Amos turned his head and looked at Baxter.

"Don't worry Amos, your arm's still there," he said smiling. "But I'm afraid it will never work quite as well as it used to. Too much nerve damage in your shoulder you see."

Amos instinctively peered down to his left shoulder and stared at the bandages that were wrapped around it.

Baxter said: "The good news is your war's over. You're going home Amos, you've done your bit."

"What? NO!" Amos said suddenly, "I can't ... I have to go back ... you don't understand," and he began trying to get out of bed.

"Private Amos, stay where you are, you are not ... nurse! ... NURSE! Give me a hand here," he said gesturing to a young nurse nearby.

She hurried over and the two of them managed to prevent Amos from getting out of bed.

"You need to rest Amos, you're in no fit state to be going anywhere just yet," Baxter added, as the nurse, a pretty looking girl not much older than Amos, smiled sympathetically.

"Now, Nurse Parker here will look after you. Try not to put any pressure on your left side for the next 48 hours. We'll have a look at you then and, if you're doing well enough, you can be on one of the hospital ships and heading home by the end of the week," the doctor said.

Amos didn't speak. Baxter was about to walk away when he paused and said: "Look Amos, for the majority of men there are two ways out of this hospital. You either die, or you recover enough to go back out there and take your chances again.

"But you're one of the lucky ones. You're going home. Ok, your arm's not what it was but you've got all your limbs. You've survived unscathed. There are thousands who'd gladly swap places with you," he said, before walking away.

Amos lay staring at the ceiling.

"Can I? ... can I get you anything? Some tea or something to eat maybe?" said the nurse who was still standing by the bed.

Amos looked at her. She had a friendly face but appeared nervous, he could see in her eyes she looked anxious.

His silence made her uncomfortable but she smiled warmly and said: "My name's Winifred ... but my friends call me Win. I'm from Dartmouth. Where are you from?"

Amos' eyes moved away and he stared up at the ceiling. He said nothing.

"Well, if I can … get you anything Private Amos … do let me or one of the other nurses know," she said.

She'd hardly finished speaking before a piercing scream filled the room; it was coming from one of the beds at the far end.

Amos turned his head quickly in the direction of the sound, causing a sharp pain to burn in his left shoulder. As he looked the cries and wails continued and he saw two or three nurses gathered around a bed.

Some of the more able patients were sitting up while one or two others made their way over to where a man lay screaming.

It took a few minutes to calm him down after which the nurses resumed their duties and one by one the other patients turned away. Amos thought he could hear the man sobbing quietly.

He saw Nurse Parker walk past his bed. "Hey nurse?" he said, beckoning her over.

"What's wrong with him?" he asked.

The nurse turned her head and looked back in the direction where the sobbing patient lay.

"He's just woken up and realised he doesn't have any legs. Most of them react that way … though there are some who don't show a flicker of emotion. It's the shock I suppose," she said.

Amos stared again before looking into the eyes of the woman in front of him. He paused, looking for the right words to say: "I'm … I'm sorry … I mean … I'm George."

In the coming days she was the only person he felt comfortable talking to.

Other patients tried to make conversation, to share their experiences, form friendships. But they soon gave up; some affronted by his coldness, others seemingly content to accept his unwillingness to engage.

But with her it was different. For the first time in weeks he felt able to relax, to be himself. He almost felt normal again. Though he knew he never could be.

He wondered why that was; why talking to her made him feel different, happy almost. Yet he didn't dwell on it; he was simply grateful.

At first their conversations were short, held at his bedside as Win changed dressings, monitored his progress or brought him a meal.

But as he improved and got stronger he was able to get up and walk about, sometimes even venturing outside where he'd inhale the sea air with real gusto, imagining it cleansing his system of the stench and fumes from the Front.

That's where she found him sitting outside one morning, gazing at the ocean, visible from the terrace of what was now a hospital but was once a grand seaside hotel.

"Good morning George, it's good to see you up and about again. What a beautiful day," she said, her head dress ruffling in the breeze.

"Come and join me, take a seat Nurse Parker," Amos said, smiling.

She sat down, resting her hands on her knees, keeping a discreet distance between the two of them.

"So, how are you feeling today?" she asked, the expression on her face one of genuine concern and interest.

Amos was silent for a moment, his eyes looking out across to the sea, before he replied: "You know Win, I was eighteen when I first saw the sea. And that was in a troopship heading over to France."

She listened intently, wondering where he was going with this, as Amos continued to stare at the ocean.

"It's amazing isn't it? The sea, I mean. I could sit here gazing at it forever ... why is that? What makes the sea so ... mesmerising?" he asked, finally turning to look at her.

"Because you look at it and you see life, freedom; it's why it makes you feel so alive, it does me anyhow," she answered almost immediately.

Amos seized upon that, turning towards Win, instinctively taking her hand.

"You're right, that's exactly it! It has that effect doesn't it ... it's like it's calling you ... inviting you to lose yourself in its expanse. I love it," he said.

For a moment the two of them sat there looking out across the water, the sound of a steamer could be heard in the distance and seagulls hovered and shrieked overhead.

"George ... Dr Baxter's really happy with your progress and believes you're now well enough to travel. You'll be going home tomorrow," Win said.

Amos said nothing but his eyes betrayed what he was thinking.

"What is it? Why don't you want to go home?" she asked.

He began to look restless and his right leg began moving up and down rapidly. She wasn't sure Amos was even aware he was doing it.

"You can … you know, you can talk to me George. I'm a good listener," she added, smiling.

Amos turned to look at her and she thought he looked lost and in pain.

"Do you know what happened to me Win? How I was wounded?" he asked quietly.

"Machine gun fire wasn't it? You were shot in the shoulder … that's all I know," she added, suddenly looking puzzled.

"That's true I guess," Amos replied. "But I got hit from behind. I was walking away," he added.

Win looked confused but he carried on talking before she could speak.

"It was a night patrol. We were caught in the open and then they came at us. We repelled the first waves but they kept coming, the stupid bastards. Why do they do that? Why do we do that?" he asked.

Again, he carried on before she could reply.

"I'd had enough of killing them so I just got up and walked back to our line. I have no idea why I lived. Most of the others were killed, so why wasn't I?"

"You mustn't think like that, you need to be thankful you're still alive," Win said.

Amos was thrown by her intervention, as though he hadn't been expecting her to speak.

"What? No, you don't understand … that's not what I mean. I mean it's inevitable … we're all going to die out here. That's clear to me now. I simply want to choose my time, I'm tired of waiting for it to happen," he said.

She tried again: "George, I know it's difficult … but really you …"

"I'm bored with it Win. I sat and watched a man bludgeon a Fritz to death with the butt of his rifle. He smashed his head and face in and I was splattered with his brains," he said matter of factly.

"It was the most normal thing in the world and it bored me," he said, his quiet tone now worrying the nurse.

"And then when the patrol went bad I turned around and walked back to our lines. I figured if I made it back they could arrest me and I'd be shot like Eddie … or Fritz had a free shot. Just my luck he can't bloody shoot straight," he added.

"Who's Eddie?" asked Win, trying desperately to get him to engage with her.

"Eddie saved my life," Amos replied. "He deserved to get a medal, not me … but instead the bastards killed him. And now all his family will ever know is that Eddie Bousefield was shot at dawn."

She was struggling to understand, she had no idea who Eddie was or what he was talking about. But she wanted to help him; she had to help him. So she tried changing the course of the conversation.

"You got a medal? What for?" she asked.

Amos stood up, took a step forward and, with his back to her, said: "It doesn't matter what for because it made sod all difference to anything. All it did was get Eddie killed."

He turned to look at her and she saw a different expression on his face now, one of contempt.

"They made me out to be the hero ... can you believe that? That's probably the reason they didn't shoot me for deserting my post and walking back ... wouldn't do to shoot heroes would it?" he said scathingly.

"Well, they can shove their medal, I don't want it; I just want to go back and die."

Win stood now too and moved to put her arm on his shoulder.

"George, come on now, please don't talk like that. You don't mean that," she said.

"Don't I? Don't I Win?" he said, pushing her away and raising his voice enough for others walking nearby to turn their heads towards them.

"The first chance I get I'm going to walk straight out into No Man's Land and this time hope Fritz blows my bloody head clean off. Or better still get obliterated by a whizz bang or a Jack Johnson."

She was silent for a moment, as though weighing up what to say next.

Finally she spoke.

"You could do that I suppose," she said casually.

"Or you could find a reason to live. Like finding this Eddie's family and telling them the truth."

June 2016

He counted nine, including himself, in the crematorium chapel. He and Emma stood either side of Arthur while his mum sat clutching his dad's hand.

The only other mourners were two staff from the nursing home, including Claire, a former neighbour of Maggie's before she moved into the home, and an usher from the undertakers.

It didn't amount to much for almost 100 years on the earth he thought to himself as they began singing *Bread of Heaven,* his dad singing with real gusto above everybody else.

He glanced across at his dad, tears rolling down his face as he bellowed out the hymn.

Even now ten days on, he could think of nothing more cruel than finding your own mother after a search of more than 70 years, only to have that joy snatched away in an instant.

He thought it had been difficult telling Arthur and his dad that Maggie was alive; having to tell them she'd died was excruciating.

They were stunned, both had broken down and cried, yet for all his fears, they'd been remarkably resolute. He figured that came with age and, in his Arthur's case, his faith.

After the hymn his dad got up and spoke eloquently about his own loss and the belief that he'd finally meet his mother one day in eternity. Arthur struggled. He'd been determined to stand up and say something but when the moment came the words deserted him.

In the end Emma stepped up and helped him back to his seat, lest the old man was left standing there bereft.

The service ended with the curtains discreetly closing around the coffin as the strains of Matt Monroe's *The Impossible Dream* played over the chapel's sound system.

Thirty minutes later they were back at the nursing home which had kindly offered to put on food so mourners could get together along with some of the more able residents who had known Maggie but were too frail to attend.

After a while the atmosphere and the mood lifted and Tom took real pleasure watching his dad and Arthur talk, getting to know each other.

"Mr Harris?" said a voice and he turned to find Claire, the senior nursing manager, standing next to him holding a small plate with a half eaten cake on it.

"It was a lovely service Mr Harris even though I know how difficult it must have been, especially for your father and Mr Roebuck," she said sympathetically.

"Thanks, that's very kind. Yes, it's been a surreal few days really," he replied.

"I really feel for my dad because at least Arthur got to spend some time with Maggie but, you know, he's pretty strong and at least he can now get to know the uncle he never knew he had," he said, turning to look at his dad and Arthur immersed in conversation.

Claire smiled before commenting how she hoped that would provide some comfort to both of them.

"Look," she added, "I haven't mentioned this to Mr Roebuck or your father, but there are a few things of Margaret's upstairs in her room. Clearly, they ought to go to her family but I thought it'd be easier to mention to you first?"

"What? Oh, yes, of course. If you need them moving I can..."

"Oh no, no, I didn't mean that," Claire said. "To be honest, there's not a lot bless her. But there are some personal things which your father or Mr Roebuck may like to go through and keep. Why don't I get them all put together and you can take them away with you when you leave?" she suggested.

Later he picked up a cardboard box from reception while Emma got Arthur into the car ready for the long drive home. He made his parents aware of it as they said their goodbyes but his dad told him to take it with him and let Arthur look through it first.

"I've told Arthur your mum and I will come down and visit him next weekend so we can have a look through anything then," he said, before hugging his son.

"Take care of yourself, drive safe and give my granddaughter a big kiss," he added.

It was getting dark as they drove home and it wasn't long before Arthur fell asleep in the back. Tom didn't tell him about the box.

When they finally got back he helped the old man inside while Emma stayed in the car. She was desperate to pick Daisy up from a friend who had been looking after her, so he didn't have long.

"Get a good night's kip Arthur, it's been a long, emotional day," he said, helping him through the front door.

"Aye, you get off lad, I'll be fine. You've done more than enough," he replied.

Daisy was fast asleep when they collected her and Emma transferred her straight to bed while Tom took a bottle of white wine from the fridge and poured two glasses.

"Oh, no, not for me Tom, I'm knackered, I'm having a bath and then going straight to bed," Emma said as she walked into the kitchen. Kissing him on the forehead she added: "Don't be late coming up, it's been a long day."

"I won't, I just want to unwind and have a drink," he replied.

Ten minutes later he sat with the box in front of him sipping his wine. He leaned forward, opened the lid and looked inside.

Reaching inside he lifted out a bible. The black leather was worn and faded giving it an old, weathered appearance. It also gave off the distinctive scent of an ageing book.

Opening the cover he saw there was a handwritten inscription in the right hand corner. *Our beloved Margaret, may God bless you always, love mother and father, Christmas 1935.*

He set the book to one side and looked inside the box again, picking out a yellow and red wallet-style envelope with the words *Your Kodak Prints* written on the front.

He lifted the flap to reveal several photographs inside. He began flicking through them, a mixture of colour and black and white. He reckoned they were at least forty years old, some clearly a lot older.

Most of the black and white prints were of the same two people, he assumed Maggie and her husband. There were holiday snaps, one of a woman in her mid thirties laughing as she sat in a deckchair; another showing a middle aged man eating an ice cream, the sea visible in the background.

There were Christmas photos showing the two of them, sometimes pictured with other people, along with obvious sight-seeing snaps. None of the colour photographs showed the man and that puzzled Tom until he remembered her husband had died in the early Sixties.

He looked through various images of Maggie, aging before his eyes, a woman frozen in time in 70s and 80s clothing. He went back to the black and white pictures and looked at her again, closely this time.

She was an attractive woman, slim and dressed fashionably for the day. But as he skipped through the prints she turned middle aged, her hair greying before turning white, glasses now appearing on her face.

In the final picture she was sitting in an armchair holding on to a balloon with a large number 70 on the side. There were birthday cards visible on a mantelpiece and two smiling women leaning over the back of the chair. Maggie was smiling broadly and Tom immediately spotted the family resemblance with Arthur.

He carefully put the photographs back into the wallet and set them down next to the bible before reaching into the box again. This time he pulled out a bundle of envelopes; most were handwritten and clearly dated back several years.

He thought about opening one to read but was more intrigued about the final item in the box. It was an upright, rectangular tin with a brown lid, on which the words *Rowntree's Cocoa* were embossed.

The side of the tin was pale cream and brown with the same words written on it. Above the writing was the image of a cup and saucer while below was a picture of a young girl with long, flowing hair, holding a tray with a jug.

The lid was stiff and difficult to open but he prised it off. Inside were more envelopes along with some heavier items he could feel and hear moving around at the bottom of the tin as he cradled it in his lap.

There were around a dozen or so letters fastened together with an elastic band.

He scanned through them, noting they were all addressed to *John and Arthur Roebuck*. The postmarks had faded but all seemed to date from the 1940s.

On each of them the address had two lines struck through it while the words *return to sender* had been written in large letters.

Tom opened one of the letters and read.

To my beloved brothers. I do so hope this letter finds you well. Please know that I miss you both terribly but I am fine and in good health. I am enjoying living by the sea where the air is so clean.

I have become a regular worshipper at a beautiful church on a cliff top above the town. They have welcomed me into their congregation with open arms and it is both a comfort and solace for me to be close to God.

I do so hope mother and father are well. I love and miss them both also. I dream of the day when both of you can come and visit me, I very much pray that day is soon.

All my love to you both

Maggie

He refolded the letter putting it back in the envelope and knew that Arthur and his late brother had never seen these letters or even been aware of their existence. Tom felt a flash of anger surge through him, directed at the chaplain whose wartime diary had helped him learn so much.

He opened another larger envelope, this time separate from the bundle of letters to her brothers. Inside was a black and white photograph of a baby. It was clearly a boy, sitting on a cloth in what appeared to be a professional studio photograph.

He turned the photo over and his eyes widened as he read, *John Arthur on his first birthday, May 1943.*

Then he read the letter that was with it.

Dear Margaret

I will never forget the great personal sacrifice you made in allowing us to adopt baby John and bring him up as our own.

My husband and I remain forever humbled by your generosity of spirit and selflessness. To know that we are now parents has brought more joy into our lives than you can imagine and I hope it gives you some comfort knowing how precious John is to us.

Rest assured that we will love and cherish him forever and, when he is old enough, tell him about the remarkable woman who brought him into the world.

Devotedly yours

Lucy Harris.

"Jesus," whispered Tom to himself as he read the letter from ... one of his grandmothers to the other? How strange was that he thought, staring at a photograph of his own father as a baby boy.

Another envelope caught his eye, this time addressed to a *George Amos.*

Tom took a final gulp of wine to finish his glass before lifting the flap and withdrawing the letter. It was two pages, folded in half and written in scrawny, black ink. There was a Manchester address at the top of the page and it was dated *12ᵗʰ December 1916.*

He leaned back and read.

Dear George

Letter writing does not come easy to me and I'm not good at finding the right words to say. However, I had to write following your sudden and unexpected visit a week ago.

Being able to meet and speak with someone who knew Eddie and served with him at the Front is something I never thought would be possible. That would have been comfort enough as I struggle to come to terms with his shameful death.

I know how difficult it must have been for you to talk about what happened but I am so grateful for you taking the time to find me and come and explain what really happened over there.

I cannot begin to describe the shame one feels when told that your loved one has died in the way that Eddie did. But thanks to you I now know the truth, that he was a hero and his death is a stain on the British Army.

I am unable to describe the relief and pride that now soothes my grief.

Finally George, please know that I was extremely humbled by your insistence that I take your Distinguished Conduct Medal and keep it on behalf of Eddie. That you feel he deserved this for the bravery you both showed in rescuing poor Captain Harris means so much to me.

However, I cannot accept it and hope you understand why. I will keep it here safely for you as I am reluctant to send something so precious in the post. It is here for you George when you are ready to collect it as I hope one day you will.

God bless you George Amos, my prayers and thoughts will be with you always.

Yours faithfully
Katie Bousefield

Tom did a double take and read it for a second time before going through more of the correspondence.

"Oh my God" he muttered to himself as he read through more letters. And slowly, all of the pieces began to fall into place

Chapter twenty

October 1916

He chose to stand outside on the deck for much of the crossing, leaning against a rail despite a stiff breeze that made it feel much cooler than it was.

When they docked, the walking wounded disembarked down a ramp while at the other end of the ship those on stretchers were lifted off and transferred into waiting ambulances.

The quayside was a hive of activity but Amos was directed to line up in a queue alongside several other soldiers who, like him, were to be medically discharged.

As he waited in line they shuffled forwards, heading towards a table where two men sat in uniform. Finally, it was Amos' turn and he stepped forward and stood in front of them, both of whom were looking down writing.

Without looking up, the one on his right, a sergeant, said: "Name, rank, serial number and regiment."

"George Amos, private, 16407, Sherwood Foresters," Amos replied, irritated that neither man had yet to look at him.

"Z22 form Private," the second man said, finally lifting his head to look at Amos as he held out his right hand.

Amos retrieved Army Form Z22 that had been given to him before he'd left the hospital, from his right tunic pocket and handed it over to the waiting corporal. It stated he was now medically unfit for service and allowed him to make a claim for any disability arising from his service.

The corporal took it, unfolded the paper and then scanned the document before looking up and saying: "Do you have your Z18 as well? We can't process you without it."

Amos nodded before replying: "Yes sir," as he handed over another form, this one a certificate of employment showing what he had done in the army.

The two men sat scribbling before the corporal stamped both forms and put them in a tray to his right. The sergeant then handed Amos more papers.

"This is your Z44 plain clothes form and your dispersal certificate," he said, now looking at Amos.

"Remember you are responsible for all military equipment until you reach the dispersal centre. If you lose anything, your pay will be deducted, do you understand Private?"

Amos nodded for a second time.

"Right, follow the others," he said, gesturing to a group of men on his left. "You'll be transferred to the dispersal centre where you can leave your equipment and be given a railway ticket home. Next!"

Amos moved off to his left, his right arm aching from carrying his kit bag. Already he was acutely aware of what it meant to only now have one good arm.

An hour later he was with several other men at a military camp where he handed over his equipment, was told to exchange any foreign currency and given a railway warrant for a ticket to his home station.

Later that day he boarded a train bound for London wearing a civilian suit. In the inside pocket was an advance of his pay, a ration book and a voucher for handing in his greatcoat.

Luckily, he found a carriage on his own. He wanted to avoid making small talk with others. He slid the door closed, put his bag on the overhead rack and sat down looking out of the window as steam enveloped the platform and the train moved off.

As it did Amos reached into his right trouser pocket and took out a small, cylindrical cardboard box and opened it as the train gathered speed.

Inside was a small silver lapel badge in the centre of which was a voided cipher of King George V and Crown. Around the rim were the words: *For King and Empire* and *Services Rendered*. Amos turned it over and saw there was a number on the back ... 2183.

He turned it over repeatedly in his hands. He knew it was supposed to be worn on his right lapel but he looked at it one last time before putting it back in the box and into his pocket.

He'd never been to London before and was shocked by the sight of so many people when the train pulled into Charing Cross Station. He got off and spent a few minutes simply looking around, gazing up at the station and beyond.

He saw a sign for a café and walked inside ordering tea and a cheese sandwich. Sitting at a table in the window he spent time simply people watching. Two women caught his eye; they were clearly together and were talking as they walked along the platform.

One of them glanced in his direction and looked again as she saw Amos drinking his tea. She turned and said something to the other woman and a moment later both of them had walked into the café.

Amos expected them to take a seat but was taken by surprise when they approached him. Neither looked happy.

"How old are you then?" said the first, a young blonde woman speaking with a strong cockney accent.

"Looks older than your Albert that's for sure," the other woman said, not waiting for Amos to reply.

"Too right," said the first glaring at Amos, "though I wouldn't know any more seeing as my Albert's dead. Killed at Neuve Chappel he was.

"So what's your excuse then? Or are you just happy to let others do the fighting while you sit it out?" she added, spitting out the final words with venom.

Amos didn't reply and instead picked up his sandwich and took a large bite.

"Ere ladies, leave it out, I don't want you scaring my customers away," the elderly café owner said, trying to intervene.

"Don't worry, we're going. We don't like mixing with cowards," the first woman snapped.

"Shame on you, letting others do the dying. Ere, you deserve this," she said, suddenly producing a white feather from her bag and slamming it on to Amos' table, the force spilling tea from his cup.

With that they both walked out of the café. Other customers who had remained silent now got up and left, staring at Amos as they did so.

The owner approached him looking awkward. "Ere, listen mate … I think it best once you've finished up to be on your way eh? I can't afford for customers to stay away."

Amos remained silent, picked up his sandwich and stood to leave. As he did the owner called after him.

"You know, I don't like to judge, but you should think about doing yer bit. The country needs boys like you if we're going to beat the Hun," he said.

Amos didn't even turn around as he opened the door and walked back out on to the platform.

He looked for a sign directing him to the ticket office and headed over to the booth at where an elderly, bespectacled man with a large greying moustache sat. He purchased a standard ticket for Manchester and headed to platform three where he sat waiting for the train.

He didn't notice the same two women standing a little further away on the platform; but they spotted him.

"There is he again Irene, he's got some brass I'll give him that," one of them said, speaking loudly enough so others heard and turned to look in Amos' direction.

"Want another one of these do ya?" the second woman shouted, producing another white feather from her bag.

Within seconds a small group had gathered around the women who were walking towards him. Their voices were animated as they talked among themselves before turning on Amos as they stood around him menacingly.

"You bloody coward," "Sling yer hook, you're not welcome," "You won't find the Hun up north."

"They should lock up cowards like him or force them to go," a middle aged man was heard to say. "What's your excuse?" another voice was heard to say.

It never even crossed his mind that not so long ago he would have found this intimidating. But he wasn't the same George Amos any more.

He didn't speak as he stood up and tried to move away, but the small crowd had been swelled by others, including those simply curious as to what was going on, and they refused to let him through.

"Explain yourself?" shouted one, "You're not getting away that easily," said another, while the same middle aged man as before demanded Amos should be forcibly marched to the recruiting centre.

He suddenly found himself being jostled and harangued before a whistle could be heard and a man's voice, an authoritative voice, was heard to say: "What's going on here, step aside."

The crowd parted and Amos found himself staring at a tall, stocky policeman.

The brief silence was broken when one of the crowd accused Amos of being a coward or a deserter and demanding the officer arrest him.

The policeman approached Amos and, with the crowd circling around him, said: "Well lad, what's your story? Who are you and where you off to?"

Despite his size the officer looked wary; there was a look on Amos' face that made him apprehensive, cautious. His right hand felt for his truncheon and he instinctively held on to its handle, trying to do so without being noticed.

"Come on lad, I've asked you a question. Or would you rather accompany me down to the station?" he asked.

Amos finally spoke.

"I've done nothing wrong constable, I'm simply waiting for a train," he said, speaking quietly.

The officer looked taken aback by how calm Amos appeared to be.

"Well, you're causing a breach of the peace lad for starters and I also notice you're not in uniform, so how about we go and have a chat down the station," he replied.

Amos looked down, breathed deeply and bristled. He was aware of all eyes on him and felt the atmosphere shift as though his demeanour had now made the crowd cautious.

"Watch him officer, I don't trust him," a voice was heard to say as Amos reached into his right trouser pocket.

He fiddled with the small box inside and felt for the badge, taking it out and throwing it on to the platform.

"There you go; is that what you want to see?" he asked.

One of the crowd, a young woman, bent down and picked up the small silver badge, handing it to the policeman.

The officer looked at it and appeared confused.

"Why, this is a silver war badge ... why aren't you wearing it?" he asked, before addressing the crowd who appeared similarly puzzled.

"This man has done his duty," he said loudly, holding the badge up with his hand. "This badge is for services rendered to King and Empire ... this man is no longer able medically to continue active service."

There were hushed voices among the crowd and embarrassed looks on their faces until one of them suddenly began clapping ... which led others to follow. Moments later the whole crowd was applauding.

Amos had to get away; he picked up his bag, slung it over his right shoulder and saw the crowd part as he began to walk away.

"Here you go lad, you'll be wanting this," the police officer said as he handed Amos his silver badge. Amos took it without looking at him and pushed his way through.

"Good on yer lad," "well done," he heard voices say, "no harm done mate eh? We had to ask," said another.

He walked faster, desperate to get away. He hated them and a huge part of him wanted to hurt them. He wished he still had his rifle and imagined himself turning round and firing into the crowd.

He saw bodies begin to fall as the others tried to flee, gripped by terror and panic. He wondered how many he'd be able to kill before some managed to get away. He saw himself reloading, once, twice, three times, firing as they fled.

It would be so easy and they deserved it; every one of them. They would never understand what it was like but he would show them; they would know what real fear was, what it was like to see human bodies ripped open, their guts spilling out on to the platform, heads exploding in front of their eyes.

He felt his heart racing thinking about it, the adrenalin rush he felt before going over the top and the thrill that bizarrely, they all felt; the excitement that punctured the fear.

He'd never know it but other commuters standing on the platform saw a man there in body only; his mind was clearly elsewhere as he stood prowling, panther-like, to and fro, the fist of his right hand clenched tight, his left arm hanging limply.

A natural sense of caution led them to back away, keeping their distance, as the sound of a train could be heard approaching. A guard's whistle signalled its arrival but Amos only heard the signal to attack and he let out a piercing scream from the depths of his insides before falling to his knees sobbing.

June 2016

He must have re-read it several times to the point where he could now probably recite it if asked.

Of all the letters and correspondence in the box, this was the one; the one which nagged away at him. Why had she kept this? What could it possibly mean?

And then he had a thought and he ran with it; but then dismissed it for being too incredible. Yet, the more he thought about it, all kinds of theories popped into his head.

Feeling intrusive, he wondered how many other people had known about the letter and its contents.

He tried to think of some way to find out what it meant, corroborate it, something that would prove with absolute certainty that he was calling this right. But he knew that could never happen. That chance had gone when Margaret Amos had drawn her last breath.

So now he was left with an unsolved jigsaw, a few pieces of the puzzle frustratingly missing and unlikely ever to be found.

After everything that had happened it was all the more remarkable that he never told anybody.

Not at first anyway, not even Emma. She'd asked him about the box and he'd told her almost everything he'd discovered. But not this.

He had no idea why; it's not as if she would be bothered by it, why would she? Or anyone else for that matter. In the great scheme of things it was simply just another piece of Maggie Roebuck's life jigsaw.

So why the reticence? Because it's just a theory, he told himself. And without any proof it was probably wiser not to mention it. Then why remove the letter from the box? Because that's what he had done, something else, if asked, he wouldn't be able to explain with any real conviction.

It was at the back of his mind in the days that followed and now, as he drove home from Arthur's where the two of them, joined by his dad, had gone through its contents, he felt guilty at having kept it from them.

Yet he was also excited; excited at the prospect, albeit remote, that maybe there was a way of finding out what it meant. It had come to him while watching Arthur and his dad go through Margaret's letters and personal belongings.

He'd seized upon a throwaway comment Arthur had made about Margaret's exile from the family home.

What was it? "Me mam always rued the day our Maggie started working for the Willoughbys."

Why hadn't it occurred to him sooner? It was staring him in the face. No matter, he had it now. It was a chance, a faint chance admittedly, but he had to pursue it.

Upstairs at home, he reached behind the shelf inside his wardrobe and felt for the letter. Sitting down on the bed he opened it. It was in remarkably good condition for a letter that had been written in 1942.

There was no address or name on it but the author was Colonel Thomas H Willoughby. Tom read it for the umpteenth time.

He knew then what he had to do. It was a long shot and it might lead him nowhere but he had to try and find out.

The following days meant more online detective work late into the night, trawling websites for Census information, births and deaths, anything that could help him. It gave him leads to follow and even a couple of names but that's where the trail ran cold.

He had little choice but to speak with Arthur, though he'd tread carefully so he didn't give him reason to question why he was asking.

He needn't have worried. As ever his old friend was simply happy to talk. Despite his sister's death the events of the last few weeks seemed to have re-energised him and he was happy to answer Tom's questions about his childhood.

He felt guilty knowing he had an ulterior motive but such was Arthur's ability to tell a story that he was simply fascinated to listen.

He couldn't take the risk of lying to Emma again, not after his first meeting with Arthur, so he sat her down and told her everything. He was surprised how excited she seemed by the prospect of him finding out what the letter meant and why Maggie had kept it.

That gave him the green light he needed for a day trip north and so, with Emma's blessing, he made arrangements to drive up to Arthur's home village.

It was gloomy when he set off but the further north he drove the cloud broke and the sun shone, making for a warm, spring day.

Swinging north-west he avoided driving through Leeds but then had to concentrate as his satnav steered him off the main roads and into the West Yorkshire countryside.

Shortly after noon he saw the first sign for the village and five minutes later found himself driving into it, passing a pub on his left and then a small shop with a newspaper sandwich board outside.

Carrying on he saw a school on the right hand side, an old Victorian style building with tall windows, adorned with colourful posters and paintings. The houses were a mix of detached, semis and rows of cottages, three or four at a time.

At the end of the village was another pub, the Prince of Wales, and he pulled into the car park before going inside. It was a typical country pub with low beamed ceilings, small windows and a separate bar and lounge area.

Tom walked into the bar where, apart from a couple sitting at a table near the window, the only other customer was an elderly man sitting on a stool cradling a pint of beer.

"How do, what can I get you?" said a voice belonging to a large built man with thinning hair and a red face who was behind the bar waiting to serve him.

He ordered a pint of local ale, asked if there was any food available and requested ham, eggs and chips.

"It's a nice pint this," he said, "lovely village too."

"Aye, we've no complaints," the barman replied. "Your first time here then?"

"Yes, it is. I recently found out my grandmother grew up here so decided to come and visit," Tom said.

Before the barman could reply Tom added: "Her dad was the vicar at St James' church after the First World War so I'd like to go and see it. I'm trying to find out more about my family's history."

"The church is down the main road and turn right, you can see the bell tower from the car park," the barman said.

"Ere, you should talk to Sam," he said, turning to the elderly man at the end of the bar, "he's lived here all his life ain't that right Sam?"

Tom glanced at the man who turned to face him after hearing the barman mention his name.

"How do ... what's up?" he asked.

"This lad's family is from around here," the barman explained. "He's here to see where they grew up. I told him he'd do worse than speak to you," he added, before he disappeared into the back, emerging moments later with Tom's food.

"How do, I'm Sam Barnes, I've lived here for 70 odd years," the old man said, extending his hand which Tom shook.

"Nice to meet you, I'm Tom Harris. My grandmother Maggie Roebuck grew up here, her dad was a vicar, Lionel Roebuck?" Tom said.

He looked at the old man's face, his craggy features locked deep in thought.

"I remember Reverend Roebuck, I think he married my parents and baptised me. I can't remember a Maggie though," Sam said.

"She left the village in the early 1940s, before you were born I'd imagine," Tom said. "She did have two brothers though, Arthur and John?"

"No, sorry lad, they don't ring a bell," he added before taking a long swig of his beer.

Tom tried to hide his disappointment as he ate before asking: "I know my grandmother worked for a family at a large house in the village, the Willoughby family. Do you know anything about them?"

This time the old man answered quickly.

"The Willoughbys? Oh aye, everyone knew them. They had the big manor house at the top of Keeper's Lane. Employed half the village at one time or another," he said.

"What happened to them? Do they still live in the village?" asked Tom.

"No, they moved out in the 50s. The old colonel lost both his boys in the war and when he died it remained empty for years. Shame really, it's a lovely building. Fancy apartments now, someone made a packet when they sold them ... they weren't cheap," Sam replied.

"Oh, that's a pity, I know it was a long shot but I was hoping the family may still live around here," Tom said, again trying to hide his disappointment.

"No lad, the Willoughbys have long gone," Sam added. "There's still one or two in the village who would remember them though I reckon. Daphne would, her mam was head cook there in between the wars."

"Whose Daphne?" Tom asked.

"Daphne Walters, lives on Cow Lane. Salt of the earth is Daphne," Sam said.

"Do you think she'd mind talking to me? I wouldn't want to impose," Tom asked.

Sam laughed and replied: "Once you set Daphne off you'll do well to stop her. You won't shut her up once she gets going."

"Hey, that's fine. It's what I'm here for," he said. "Listen, I really don't want to put you out, but if she's around would you mind introducing me?"

Sam finished the rest of his beer, put his glass down on the bar and said: "No, not at all lad. Though I wouldn't mind another pint first."

Twenty minutes later the two men pulled up outside a row of cottages.

"That's Daphne's there, the middle one. Likes her garden does Daphne," Sam said.

"Listen, are you sure she won't mind me just turning up on her doorstep? I don't want to worry her," Tom said.

"Nae, don't be daft lad. Come on, you'll be reet," the old man said as he opened the passenger door and got out.

Moments later they were standing in front of a pastel blue wooden door, some of its paint beginning to flake off and a mature clematis growing around the frame.

Sam rapped on the door which was opened by a small, elderly woman with grey curly hair and glasses. She was wearing a blue checked skirt, slippers and a green knitted cardigan.

"Sam Barnes, what brings you here?" she said.

"How do Daphne, this is Tom, he's looking into his family history and has come visiting. His grandmother was Lionel Roebuck's daughter, you know the old vicar from way back," Sam said.

"Is that right?" she said, looking at the stranger weighing him up. He was about to speak but Sam continued.

"Aye, and she worked for the Willoughbys up at the manor house. I told him your mam worked up there too."

"I'm just trying to find out more about her life," Tom said, interrupting the old man.

She looked at him for a moment before saying: "Aye, my mam worked up there for more than twenty years. The Colonel always said she was the best cook he'd ever come across."

Tom smiled and added: "I, I really don't want to impose Mrs Walters, but I'd love to find out more."

"Well, for a start it's Ms Walters and yes, I can tell you all about the Willoughbys. Come on in," she said, stepping back and opening the door.

Sam left them to it and Tom followed the woman inside.

Chapter twenty one

October 1916

It was raining heavily and he was soaked through but didn't care. He'd known much worse than this. He'd been walking for more than an hour since getting off the train but it was nothing compared to marching for hours at a time.

Speaking briefly to two people, simply to ask directions, he continued on his way. He had an idea where she lived but beyond that, well ... he'd not thought beyond that.

Walking along a main road he felt his stomach growl and realised he hadn't eaten since the sandwich back at Charing Cross. Looking up through the driving rain he saw the lights of a pub on a street corner.

It was shortly after opening time but it was already filling up and he had to squeeze himself through to the bar where he dropped his bag to the floor and stood drenched waiting to be served.

He was surprised by how much weight the small silver badge on his lapel carried. He'd noticed it getting off the train when he'd heard shouts of 'well done lad' and 'thank you' from fellow commuters.

Now, it was evident again when the landlord gave him a free pint and then others offered to buy him a drink.

Two or three gathered around and began asking questions, where he'd served, what it was like, which regiment he was with.

"Give him a chance, the boy's just come in. Let him enjoy his pint," the landlord said, at which the questions stopped.

"It's ok, honestly," Amos said and he smiled at the landlord before turning round to face the three or four men who had been asking.

"I was with the Sherwood Foresters, 11th battalion. We got beaten up pretty badly on July first," he added.

There were mutterings from the men who were now joined by others who had overheard, suddenly interested in hearing news from the Front.

Amos spent more than an hour in their company, answering their questions and drinking with them. Then one of them asked what had brought him up to Manchester.

"I'm looking for someone; the family of ... of a friend of mine. Eddie Bousefield. He was killed. I want to tell them about him, tell them what really happened," Amos said.

"You knew Eddie?" said a surprised voice from the back of the group.

Amos watched as a middle aged man squeezed himself through until he was standing next to him.

"I knew Eddie, strong as an ox he was. He knew how to look after himself too that's for sure," the man said, clutching a half drunk pint of dark beer.

"He was no fucking coward I know that," snapped another. "Some say he was shot by our lot? Is that true? Do you know what happened?" the man asked.

"Yes he was. And I do know," Amos replied before looking down, lost in thought.

For a moment no one spoke leaving Amos staring at the floor, his eyes narrowing as his mind drifted. Just as suddenly he snapped out of it and was back, looking up at the faces around him.

"Do you know where I can find them? Eddie's family?" he asked.

"Just a sister left now, both his parents are dead. Her name's Katie. Last I heard she was living in Preston Street, it's not far from here," one of the men said.

Ten minutes later Amos was back in the rain following the directions he'd been given, looking for Katie Bousefield's house.

The streets were dark and grimy, the wet weather giving them a bleak, grey appearance. Above the rows of terraced houses Amos could make out the outline of huge factories in the near distance, their chimneys spewing out smoke, making the sky even darker.

Not surprisingly the streets were deserted though Amos could see a figure approaching, head down walking quickly through the rain. As it got closer he tried to make out whether it was a man or a woman but before he could tell they stopped and turned into one of the houses.

He was in Preston Street now though he had no idea whether Katie still lived here or if she did, where. He had no choice but to knock randomly on doors.

"Who's there, what do you want?" a woman's voice yelled through the door of the first house he tried.

"I'm … I'm looking for someone, Katie Bousefield? I'm a friend of her brother's Eddie," Amos shouted in reply.

"Never heard of her," the voice came back.

He walked a little further, crossed the road and knocked on a second door. This time it opened slightly and a younger woman peered at him through the narrow gap.

"Yes? What do you want?" she asked.

Amos repeated himself and, though she didn't reply, he saw something in her face which told him she knew something.

"Are you Katie? Please, I want to talk to you, I knew Eddie, I was with him when …," his voice tailed off, suddenly unable to think of what else to say.

The door opened and the woman, slim and wearing an apron over her dress, said: "No, I'm not Katie. But I know her. She's a pal of mine."

Standing there in the pouring rain, Amos looked up, his clothes drenched and water running down his face.

"Please," he said. "I really need to speak to her."

"You'd better come in," she said, "you'll catch your death if you stay out there any longer."

Her name was Lily, she was in her early twenties but was already widowed. Her husband Stan had been killed in Gallipoli the year before. Now, she was working at a factory in Manchester producing war materials - rubber goods - and it was there she knew Katie Bousefield.

"So, Katie works there too at this ..."

"Macintoshes," Lily said, finishing the sentence.

"And she's there now?" he asked.

"Yes, she's on afternoons. She won't finish 'til ten," she replied. Noticing the look of disappointment on Amos' face she added: "You can wait here if you like and dry off a bit. That's all though ... I'm not that kind of girl."

Amos felt awkward and struggled to find something to say. "Ok, thanks," was all he could muster.

Lily disappeared and returned a few minutes later with a faded blue shirt and a pair of grey trousers.

"Here, you can change into these and put your clothes in front of the fire. He was about the same build as you, though you're probably a little taller. I was going to make some tea. Do you want some?"

"Yes, tea would be good. Thanks," he said.

Lily looked at him and smiled briefly before turning away and walking into the kitchen. When she walked back in she saw him struggling to put the shirt on, his arm handicapping his ability to do it easily.

She wanted to help but thought better of it and waited until he'd managed to do it himself.

The pair then sat drinking tea in front of the fire, an awkward silence punctured occasionally by one of them trying to make conversation.

"You're invalided out then ... you've made it through," Lily said.

Amos glanced at her but looked back at the fire. "Yes. Though I often wish I hadn't."

"You shouldn't think like that," she said matter of factly. "There's plenty of boys who aren't ever coming home, my Stan being one of em."

Amos cringed inwardly, berating himself for his insensitivity.

"I'm ... I'm sorry, I didn't mean ... were you married long?" he asked, changing the subject.

"He proposed to me a week before he left for Southampton and we got married the day before. We thought he was going to France. I don't even know where Turkey is," she said.

"They said he was shot and died instantly during an attack. I got a nice letter. They told me he didn't suffer and he has been buried," she added.

Amos thought of all the men he'd seen die and had yet to know one who hadn't suffered. He wondered whether Stan had been ripped apart by machine gun bullets or his body obliterated by an artillery shell.

Was his body left lying out in the open for days on end, blackened by the sun and infested with flies feasting on his rotten flesh? What did it matter either way Amos thought, he's still dead.

He needed to leave, he suddenly felt incredibly uncomfortable. He was sitting in a dead man's clothes, in his home, talking to his young widow. He felt guilty, not because of that but because he had nothing he wanted to say to her.

There were no comforting words, he didn't have any. She was simply one more grieving woman, forced to confront the unthinkable. He could see she had been attractive once but not now. Grief had changed her; it would shape her life thereafter as it would his and countless more.

"I, I should go ...," he said, standing up, deliberately avoiding eye contact.

Lily didn't question him or protest, he wondered whether she felt just as uncomfortable.

"Your clothes are still wet but you can put them in your bag. You can keep Stan's things ... though it's still raining so you'll be wet again soon anyway," she said.

"Thank you," he said, picking up his bag and stuffing his damp clothes inside. He walked to the door, opened it and then turned back to look her.

"I'm ... ," and that was it. Nothing came out and he stood in silence staring at her, the only noise coming from the rain through the open door.

"It's alright," Lily said. "Katie lives at number three. She'll be home by ten thirty."

He didn't reply, closed the door behind him and stepped back out into the rain. Walking down the street he found the house, it was in darkness. Across the road, on the corner, there was a doorway and he stood inside sheltering from the rain.

He would wait for her to come home; he was used to waiting. He slumped down and sat with his hands on his knees; and then he heard the shells flying and he saw them fall; mud, men and debris thrown into the air.

She was running to get out of the rain and he heard the footsteps approaching before he saw her. Moments later a small figure draped in an overcoat with a hood up stooped in front of number three and opened the door with a key.

And then Amos began to have second thoughts. He couldn't knock now, it was too late. What if she didn't want to speak with him? What did he really think he could achieve by seeing her?

After a few minutes he saw a light in the bedroom and that made his mind up; he'd decide in the morning. Turning on to his side, using his bag as a pillow, he brought his knees up to his chest and closed his eyes.

"Ere, you can't stay there, go on, hop it."

The voice was angry and as Amos opened his eyes he saw a short, squat woman standing over him carrying what appeared to be a large laundry bag.

Recovering his senses, he struggled to his feet: "I'm sorry, I'll be on my way," he said.

"You do that, we don't want vagrants loitering around here," she said.

Amos gathered his things and stepped out of the doorway, the sky was blue, it was a cool day and the road was glistening from the rain that had fallen overnight.

"What ... what time is it?" he asked the woman who was eyeing him suspiciously.

"Time you were gone from here, or do you want me to call my Fred?" she replied testily.

He didn't reply but walked away, crossing the road; all the time conscious she was staring at him. He didn't want her to know why he was here or who he was going to see so he kept walking.

As he got to the end of the road he turned and saw her walk away, heading in the opposite direction.

He retraced his steps back, the street was empty and it felt relatively early. For the first time in a while he felt nervous and the adrenaline and increased heart rate triggered the usual memories.

Ignoring them, he stopped outside number three and knocked on the door.

Seconds later it opened and he stood looking at her. Her dark hair was tied in a bun which sat neatly on the top of her head, exposing her pale face, high cheekbones and a slim nose. She had brown eyes and Amos' first thought was how pretty she was.

"Hello, can I help you?" she said.

"Katie? Are you Katie Bousefield?" he said awkwardly.

Her eyes narrowed and she appeared a little nervous.

"Who wants to know?" she asked suspiciously.

"My name's George ... George Amos. I was in the Foresters ... I served with Eddie," he said and in an instant he saw her face change.

June 2016

"Here it is," she said, retrieving a black and white photograph from an album, "this must have been taken around 1940."

Tom took the picture from her as Daphne then stood over him to explain what he was looking at.

"This is all the staff with Colonel Willoughby pictured in front of the house. That's me mam, Jane Walters, there on the right," she said, pointing a bony finger to a plump looking woman who sat rigidly with three other women either side of her.

Her finger hovered over the picture before it settled again on what appeared to be a teenage girl.

"And that there is Maggie Roebuck; I know that because me mam told me about her years later when she used to tell me stories about working for the Willoughbys. She knew much more than she let on did me mam," Daphne said.

Tom was intrigued, both by the photograph and Daphne's recollections. He forced himself not to interrupt and ask questions as she continued.

"Mam reckons the house was cursed after the Great War, she said the Colonel was never the same again, what with losing his brother and all," she said.

She noticed him glance up at her quizzically at that point and elaborated.

"More than half the people in that picture were dead before the end of the Second World War. Of the five male staff, three were killed serving while that fella on the end there," and again she pointed this time to a man standing upright holding what appeared to be a garden rake.

"That man's George Amos, he was the head gardener. Strange bloke according to me mam, never really mixed with the other staff," she said.

Tom was stunned, feeling the hairs on the back of his neck stand.

"What ... what did you say?" he managed to blurt out.

He made no attempt to hide his reaction and it puzzled Daphne who could see the shock in his face.

"I said that's George Amos ... why?" she added.

"Err, nothing ... I mean, don't worry. Carry on," Tom replied.

"You say Maggie was your grandmother?" Daphne asked, seemingly content to move on.

"Yes, yes she was," he answered.

"There were stories about her you know, rumours and the like," Daphne said, sounding a little cautious all of a sudden.

Tom shuffled to the side of the armchair so it was easier to look up at her.

"If you're talking about her getting pregnant by one of the Colonel's sons and having to leave the village, then yes, I know about that," he replied.

"Oh, so you know that then?" she said, the surprise evident in her voice. "It was kept very hush hush at the time, I know that from me mam."

"My great uncle Arthur told me. He said Maggie was disowned by her parents when she came home pregnant and they sent her away," Tom said.

Daphne moved away from his side and sat on the sofa opposite. Looking across at him she said: "It would have been a real scandal at the time, for the Colonel, his son and for her father. They did well to keep it quiet"

"What do you know about the Willoughby family?" he asked. "I mean, the son, the father of her baby?"

"Well," she said, staring at him intently now, "I only know what my mam told me. The Colonel trusted her and she never betrayed him. It was years later when she confided in me."

Tom was intrigued and his expression clearly spoke for him as Daphne continued.

"The Colonel had two boys, James and Simon. Their mother died giving birth to Simon. James was the eldest and the more talented of the two. He went to one of them posh public schools down south and he hardly ever came home after, except for holidays and the like," she said.

"But Simon was different; a lot quieter, not into sport like his brother. When the war came James joined the RAF. He was shot down and killed in late 1940 I think," Daphne said.

"Simon didn't join up until much later though. Some said his dad really had to push him into it. Anyway, he went into the Army but was killed in Italy in 1944. That proper finished the Colonel. Like I said, he was never the same after the death of his boys."

Tom shuffled again in his chair; he wondered what this had to do with anything.

"I don't understand Ms Walters, I mean what does this that have to do with ..."

"Call me Daphne, everybody else does," she said smiling. "What I'm saying is that the real surprise wasn't that your grandmother got pregnant but who she got pregnant with."

He was confused now.

"Well, yes, I get it would have been pretty scandalous for someone in his position getting a kitchen maid knocked up," he said.

"Oh no, I didn't mean that dear. No, I meant because, according to my mam, he wasn't into girls at all. Simon Willoughby was homosexual."

For the second time in a matter of minutes Tom was left reeling.

"What? How? ... how do you know that?" he asked.

"As I said, the Colonel loved me mam," Daphne said. "She served him faithfully for more than 30 years and was with him until he died. He confided in her and she knew a lot of things about what went on in that house.

"It can't have been easy for the boy; times were very different back then. And I'm not sure when the Colonel found out but me mam says it was one of the reasons he pushed for him to join up and go in the Army. He wanted him to prove himself as a man," she added.

"That's why he could never forgive himself when his boy was killed."

Tom didn't speak, he was busy trying to process what he'd learned in the last few minutes. Not only was a George Amos working at the same house as Maggie Roebuck but the boy who had got her pregnant was secretly gay.

"No, the real story about Maggie Roebuck ... well, it's something my mam swore me to secrecy about," Daphne said.

Tom was even more confused: "What? I don't understand ... please Mrs Walters, Daphne, what is it you know?"

She thought for a moment looking at him before saying: "Well, I've lived with it long enough I 'spose ... and everyone involved has long gone now."

He was on the edge of his seat. "What is it?"

He was glad to have been sitting down as the revelation left him stunned. He'd never seen that coming. He didn't need to ask how or why. Whether it was relief at finally sharing her secret or simply someone who couldn't resist spilling the beans, Mrs Walters seemed more than happy to talk.

When she'd done he found himself sitting there in stunned silence. Then he heard the chimes of the clock on her mantelpiece and realised he needed to go.

"Listen, Daphne, it's been fascinating talking to you but I've got to get going, I've got a long drive home."

"Not at all, happy I could help," she added as Tom got to his feet and began inching his way to the door.

His head was spinning as he drove away because now he was getting closer to the truth.

Driving past the Prince of Wales he turned right and saw the church up ahead. He pulled up outside the churchyard, parking under a huge oak tree and got out.

It wasn't unlike the church he'd been to in Norfolk where he'd found Captain Harris' photo on the wall alongside a memorial and the letter from Lionel Roebuck. Now he found himself outside the church where the same man had been vicar.

It was mid-afternoon now and the sun was shining as he sat on a bench surrounded by old gravestones.

Reaching into his pocket he retrieved the envelope, opened it and looked again at the letter written by Colonel Willoughby more than 70 years ago.

He read it again but now, for the first time, he understood what it meant.

January 1942

Loyalty is an extremely important characteristic to me. I'd ask you to remember that and think how I took you in and gave you a job and put a roof over your head.

In that time you have proved yourself a very able employee, both in terms of your ability and, for your discretion on certain matters. So, I'm sure you can imagine my dismay that you would now attempt to use this against me.

I have had time to consider your offer, though I'd prefer to call it by another name. I sincerely hope you understand what you are doing and have thought through fully, the implications of your actions?

Reluctantly, I agree to your terms. Therein, I will make funds available to you on the proviso that you move away from here and do not contact anyone in my employment or connected with my family ever again.

This will represent a one off payment of which there shall be no repeat.

In return, I expect you to take a vow of silence and never speak of the events you witnessed at Willoughby Hall. This arrangement I'm sure, is the best for all concerned, not least Miss Roebuck.

Colonel Thomas H Willoughby

Tom put the letter away, stood and looked up at the church before him. He knew he would never uncover the full story of what happened back in this village more than 70 years ago.

But as he walked out of the churchyard and got into his car to drive home, he was now certain he knew who the Colonel had written to.

It was George Amos.

Chapter twenty two

March 1919

When he walked into the room Amos immediately stood. His first inclination was to salute but that would have been ridiculous. Instead, he simply addressed him as sir.

The Colonel was a tall man with broad shoulders. He had slicked back dark hair and a thin moustache. Dressed in a tweed three piece suit he glanced at his watch before returning it to his waistcoat pocket.

"So, the Reverend tells me you served with the Foresters, is that correct?" he said, speaking as he approached Amos.

"Yes sir," Amos replied.

"Damn fine regiment," the Colonel added, "I was a young officer at Vlakfontein in South Africa in 1901. They bayonet charged those bastard Boers. We watched them run for their lives," he said, sitting down in a high backed chair, crossing his legs.

Amos said nothing and continued to stand, holding his flat cap in both hands.

"You look surprised to see me," the Colonel added. Before Amos could reply he continued: "Well, I'm different Amos. I like to know the people who work for me because I expect a great deal of trust and loyalty. Do you understand?"

"Yes sir," Amos said.

"Had any experience of a garden this size?" the Colonel asked.

"Er, nothing this size sir, but I grew up in a village; I know the land, what works, what doesn't. And I'm a quick learner," he said.

There was silence for a moment and the Colonel appeared to make no secret of the fact he was weighing Amos up.

"Fought at The Somme didn't you? The Reverend tells me you have a busted arm. I'm not sure a gardener with one good arm is any good to me," he said.

Amos didn't know whether the Colonel was thinking aloud or whether he was expected to answer. He deliberated for a moment before saying: "Yes sir, I was at The Somme and yes, my left arm's not as good as it used to be.

"But I'm a good worker and would back myself against more able bodied men," he added.

The Colonel stood and came up close to Amos looking him straight in the eyes.

"My brother died at First Ypres. Killed by the Bosch at Nonne Bosschen Wood, can you believe that? They were

355

a menace Amos; they're a war mongering race who needed to be stopped. Any man who played their part in doing that has my respect," he said, turning around and walking back from where he'd appeared.

"You've got the job. My head gardener will sort out the details. There are live in quarters available should you need them, rent will be deducted from your earnings," and with that he opened a door and disappeared.

Amos started a week later, at the same time moving his meagre possessions into a tiny room he'd been allocated above one of the stables.

The head gardener was a man called Hargreaves, an ordinary looking thin man in his 50s. He had never married and had spent most of his adult life working for the Willoughbys. Amos found him quiet but fair.

Despite allowances being made for his arm, he was keen to prove it didn't hinder him and he put extra effort into the tough, physical tasks. He enjoyed being outside and his contact with other people was kept at a minimum, something else which appealed.

Amos was quick to settle into his routine; up at 5am for a 5.30am start. It was the spring of 1919 when he started and he loved the chilly, sunny mornings which later gave way to pleasant, warmer days.

He would eat his lunch sitting with his back against the wall, usually a hunk of bread and cheese one of the kitchen maids had prepared for him. He would gaze at the blue sky, listening to the breeze blow through the trees and the birds singing.

The visions still came; at any given moment they'd flash into his mind, the quiet, tranquil surroundings shattered as his brain was flooded with images of the battlefield. But he was used to them now, expected them even, and he simply endured them until they passed.

He heard screams; these were different, they seemed real, sounded nearer. He turned his head from where the noise came from; convinced it wasn't in his head. And then he heard it again. No, he was right. It was a girl's voice.

Amos stood and walked briskly in the direction of the sound, it was quiet now but he guessed it was coming from one of the outhouses near to the stables. He was sure he could hear a man's voice too.

Getting nearer he saw one of the large wooden doors ajar in the end outhouse and heard noises coming from within. Walking up to the door, he pushed against it gently and put his head through the gap to peer inside.

He knew it was the Colonel, he didn't have to see his face. With his back to the door and his trousers around his ankles, the master of the house was standing behind a young girl. Amos knew it was one of the young kitchen maids, Megan. He could hear her sobbing as the Colonel held her face down.

He had to say something, he could hear the distress in the girl's voice. How old was she? Fourteen at the most? But he knew that by even going in he'd probably lose his job and he hesitated before stepping inside.

"Nothing for you in there Amos, best walk away lad," a voice said.

He turned to see Hargreaves walking towards him holding a shovel. Before Amos could speak he was almost next to him and ushered him away from the door adding: "The Colonel has, what shall we say? Particular tastes.

"But she's a fucking child," Amos snapped, the anger evident in his voice.

Hargreaves stopped, turned to Amos and said: "Aye lad and she's got a job and a roof over her head. So what if the boss gives 'er one occasionally? At the end of the day it's his house, he can do what he damn well wants."

"And that includes raping kids does it?" Amos said.

It was Hargreaves' turn to look angry now. "Keep yer fucking voice down Amos. Now you listen to me lad. You forget what you just saw and never speak of it. Just get on with your job and you'll be looked after. Anything else is none of your business. Now go on, get back to work."

Amos sloped off back into the gardens, picking up a rake which was leaning against the wall. When he was out of sight from Hargreaves he lifted it above his head and repeatedly smashed it into the earth.

He was used to feeling ashamed and guilty for some of the things that he'd done. But this was different, the shame and guilt now came from something he didn't do. Because he took Hargreaves' advice and he kept quiet.

He dealt with it by keeping away from the house and its staff as much as possible, only mixing with them when he needed to.

There was an awkwardness every time he went to the kitchen and the other staff thought him cold and distant for wanting to eat alone most of the time.

Months turned into years and Amos cemented himself as part of the household's trusted employees. A mixture of convenience and fear forced him to turn a blind eye to what the Colonel was doing.

He learned to ignore the look he saw on the man's face whenever one of the young kitchen hands or maids was around. And he'd put himself as far away as possible at the other end of the garden whenever one of them was 'chosen' by the Colonel to join him for 'a little chat.'

Yet, there was another side to the man, one of real benevolence and generosity when it came to his staff. In 1929 Hargreaves fell from a ladder while pruning one of the estate's large maple trees, breaking his back.

He was hospitalised for weeks and what was left of his life was now spent in a wheelchair. Amos knew the Colonel covered all the medical expenses and then insisted he remain living on the estate, even paying him a small pension.

Hargreaves's misfortune saw Amos promoted to head gardener, a role which came with increased pay and better accommodation. But it also meant a closer working relationship with the Colonel, something which he came to tolerate, despite the distaste he continued to feel for the man.

Despite his efforts he felt himself increasingly implicated in the wrongdoing he knew was happening almost every single day. Only once did he consider speaking to somebody else about it, but in the end he couldn't bring himself to do so.

That happened after Amos found one of the young scullery maids sat huddled behind a wall in the garden, face buried in her knees, sobbing.

When she heard him approach she lifted her head, a look of real terror on her face and she began scurrying backwards, using her legs to back away.

"It's ok, I'm not going to hurt you, it's Martha isn't it?" Amos asked, speaking in hushed tones.

The girl didn't speak, her face was a mess. Aside from the redness caused by the crying, Amos saw her right eye was swollen, a bruise beginning to form. She had blonde hair, tied up at the back, and Amos reckoned she was about 15.

She had been working at the house for around six months and he remembered her as a cheerful, happy girl when she first arrived. But in recent weeks her demeanour had changed, she was timid, fearful even.

"Let me help you, let's go and get you cleaned up," Amos said, hoping to encourage and cajole her to respond.

The girl shook her head and was now sitting with her back leaning against the brick wall in between the shrubbery.

"Well, you can't stay here girl, we need to get you back to the house, let Mrs Walters have a look at you. I'm sure she'll have something for that eye," he added.

Eventually, the girl stood gingerly, her body language telling Amos to keep his distance lest she become even more terrified. As she stood he noticed there was blood on her pinny and in between her legs. Walking her back to the house he felt a nausea he'd not felt since France.

The next day and the girl was gone, 'not up to scratch' according to Mrs Walters, Amos heard. He had no idea where she was but privately he was relieved, both for her and himself.

The turnaround in young, female staff continued uninterrupted throughout the 1930s. If anyone ever thought it strange at how often they were replaced, they never voiced their disquiet. Instead, all of them, Amos included, never gave it a second thought anymore.

In 1939 Hargreaves died in his sleep. The Colonel paid for his funeral and his two sons and all the staff were at the service. It was held in the village church and conducted by the Reverend Roebuck.

Amos had seen his former battalion chaplain occasionally over the years, mostly at Christmas and Easter services which the Colonel was insistent everyone should attend. He knew he'd been partly responsible for helping him get a job at the house, recommending him to the Colonel when he'd heard about him living rough in Manchester after the war.

Roebuck always seemed delighted to see him and would attempt to make conversation, even inviting him over to his house to join his family for Sunday lunch. Amos was polite but always declined the offer.

Now, standing in the church he listened again to Roebuck conduct a funeral for the second time and his mind wandered back to the early morning burial of

Captain Harris, lowered into a makeshift grave as artillery shells landed around them.

He recalled the chaplain carrying on, regardless of the danger to himself, and suddenly found a growing respect for a man he had once hated over his part in Eddie's death.

When the service was over Amos joined the half a dozen or so other mourners who filed outside. He then watched as the Colonel and Roebuck emerged, the two men engaged in conversation.

After a few minutes the Colonel shook his hand and walked away. Amos then caught Roebuck heading straight towards him.

"George, it's so good to see you, it's been too long," he said, walking up to him, his right armed extended.

"Hello Padre," Amos replied smiling, shaking his hand. "It's good to see you too."

"Still up at the house then? How long is it now?" Roebuck asked before adding: "Must be more than 20 years, where does the time go eh?"

"Look George, I'm not going to give up inviting you over for Sunday lunch. I know Mavis would be thrilled to see you, she won't mind another mouth to feed," he said.

Amos shuffled awkwardly, "Thanks Padre, it's good of you to ask but you've got your family and I get my meals provided up at the house."

"Nonsense George, it's not a problem. I absolutely insist and anyway, you'll be doing me a big favour," he replied.

Amos looked puzzled and Roebuck smiled adding: "I've just been speaking with the Colonel, he's agreed to give our Maggie a job in the kitchens when she turns 14 next year.

"So come on over, Mavis will feel so much better knowing there's someone up there to look out for her."

June 2016

As the cloud thickened, the sun disappeared and it began raining, all Tom could think about was George Amos.

He was the thread throughout this story, he knew that now. As he drove he recalled the chaplain's diary and remembered reading Roebuck describe how *'Private Amos was responsible for going back out on to the battlefield to bring back the injured Captain Harris.'*

Then he remembered Maggie Roebuck's marriage certificate; she'd married a George Amos, almost twice her age, and he was a gardener. Tom was annoyed with himself for not picking up on this earlier.

He recalled the letter from Katie Bousefield to Amos that he found in the box of personal belongings and then went back over this latest discovery that he was working for the Willoughbys at the same time as Maggie. It was the same man, of that he had no doubt.

It occurred to him Captain Harris had long ceased to be at the heart of this now. He was simply the catalyst for what was becoming an ever more remarkable story.

He was utterly convinced George Amos was the recipient of the Colonel's letter. It was a blackmail letter;

the Colonel was right, there was no other way to describe it. But that only made it all the more incredible.

The traffic was heavier now and the spray was making visibility difficult as he drove down the motorway. But his thoughts were on George Amos, a gardener at a country estate, who was blackmailing his employer, a rich, powerful man.

He thought back to Daphne Walters' revelations - the first that the Colonel's youngest son was secretly gay and the second ... well, that was simply extraordinary.

The more he thought about it the more he realised the story about young Willoughby being the father of Maggie's baby had to be a smokescreen. It was there to conceal the fact he was actually into men but, more importantly, to hide the identity of the real father.

If what Mrs Walters had told him was true then there was no doubt at all in his mind ... Colonel Willoughby was his grandfather.

He had got young Maggie Roebuck pregnant when she was a fourteen year old girl. And somehow, George Amos had found out about that and young Willoughby's homosexuality. And that was what he held over the Colonel.

He tried to consider what else it might be but couldn't think of anything remotely plausible. For a moment he wondered whether George Amos might actually be the father, maybe it was he who made Maggie pregnant.

But then why put the baby up for adoption? And how come he then later married Maggie? No, Tom thought, that didn't make sense.

His first instinct had to be correct. There was no other explanation. It was quite a revelation and it would mean having to tread very carefully with both Arthur and his dad when it came to telling them.

He braked suddenly as a car changed lanes, pulling out into his path; the speed of his windscreen wipers increasing as spray from the road got heavier. Cursing as he eased off on his accelerator, he allowed more distance between him and the car in front.

He wished now that he'd spent more time researching George Amos. Maybe he should ask Arthur if he knew anything more about him. There was no harm in it he thought but he wasn't hopeful. His old friend had not done or said anything to indicate the name was known to him when Tom had told him about Maggie's husband.

Plus, he was only a young boy when his sister had left so his chances of even recalling Amos were slim.

Instead, he resolved to concentrate on finding out more about him. What did he know so far he asked himself? Amos served in the Great War, he was responsible for bringing Captain Harris' body back from No Man's Land.

Without even thinking about it he indicated, glanced in his wing mirror and overtook the car in front, moving into the fast lane.

What else? Roebuck's diary revealed Amos was unhappy about what had happened to another soldier who helped bring Harris back.

The chaplain later had to tell him his friend was facing a court martial and could face execution. Tom dug deep, trying to remember what else there was. The letter from Katie Bousefield ... it proved Amos had visited her to tell the truth about ... what was his name? ... Eddie, Eddie Bousefield.

Tom said the name out loud, looking into his passenger wing mirror this time as he moved back into the middle lane.

Ok, then what? Somehow Amos got himself a job as a gardener for the Willoughbys. How did he do that? Of course, he thought; Roebuck ... it had to be Roebuck. Maybe the two stayed in touch after the war and he put a word in for him with the Colonel?

He was pleased with himself for coming up with what seemed to be a plausible link putting Amos in the same village as Lionel Roebuck; and for working at the same house as his daughter Maggie.

He thought about her again now. She had fallen pregnant in late 1941. Weeks later she was gone, banished from her family home because of the shame of it.

But the blackmail letter ... that was January 1942 wasn't it he asked himself, having to slow down again as the traffic ahead began braking in the wet.

That must have coincided with Maggie's departure from the family home. He went over the letter again .., what had the Colonel said? '*Loyalty is an extremely important characteristic to me ... I'm sure you can imagine my dismay that you would now attempt to use this against me.*'

Tom couldn't help but think this reaffirmed his view about what Amos had over his boss ... it was certainly powerful enough to make the Colonel pay to keep him quiet.

'In return, I expect you to take a vow of silence and never speak of the events you witnessed at Willoughby Hall,' the letter had said.

Yes, this had to be about Willoughby's son, his homosexuality and Maggie's pregnancy. He used that against the Colonel, threatening to expose him unless he gave her money.

That makes sense he told himself as the traffic began flowing again, though the weather was now getting worse.

Yes, he now concluded, George Amos was more than likely an honest man, someone who had risked his life to save a dying officer in the war. He'd then complained bitterly about the treatment of his friend who had gone out there with him

Now, more than 20 years later, he was witnessing another injustice. He would have been unable to stand by and let a vulnerable, pregnant teenage girl be cast adrift knowing the guilty party had got off scot free.

Tom began to like and admire George Amos; a man who it appears had also stood by Maggie Roebuck and then ended up marrying her when she was older.

Once he was back home he would do more digging, find out more about him, maybe track down his war record, where he was buried, that sort of thing.

He yawned, it had been a long day and it was beginning to catch up with him. He glanced in the rear view mirror, there was a lorry behind him now, its headlights were on full and they dazzled him.

He accelerated to move out of its glare before looking again to make sure it was no longer in view. In the split second his eyes were on the mirror he didn't notice the grey saloon car pull out in front of him.

When he did his natural instinct was to react but instead of braking he involuntarily swerved to his right, into the path of the fast lane traffic.

The white van, which had been about to overtake, had nowhere to go; its front end collided with Tom's offside rear door, sending his car into a one hundred and eighty degree spin.

As it turned the passenger side smashed into the central reservation; Tom had no control of his vehicle, though his hands were desperately turning the steering wheel and his right foot was pressed down hard on the brake pedal.

His brain was trying to process what was going on and for a split second he was puzzled as to why he was now looking out into the path of oncoming traffic. Then his body was rocked by the force of the impact as another car smashed into him.

He would have no idea that it set off a chain reaction of collisions and shunts going back hundreds of yards. The last thing he felt was the airbags deploy before everything went black.

Chapter twenty three

June 1941

There was a permanent knot in his stomach knowing she was in the house and there was little he could do to protect her. It wouldn't happen straight away, the Colonel didn't operate like that. But every day that passed only brought the inevitable nearer.

Amos knew Willoughby would wait a few days, weeks even, letting her settle in. He'd be the perfect employer, going into the kitchen occasionally asking after all the staff yet, all the while, his attention fixed firmly upon her.

It now dominated his thoughts and was rousing an anger in him that had not surfaced for more than twenty years. Dark thoughts would return and he'd see himself confronting the Colonel, taking pleasure from the look of horror on his face as he saw Amos standing there with a shotgun pointed at him.

And then his imagination would run with it because Amos knew what it looked like when a man's insides were torn open by gunfire. He'd fire twice, once in his groin, watching him writhe in agony on the floor of his study – it was always his study – before standing over him savouring the pain and fear visible in his eyes.

Then the second shot at point blank range would obliterate the bastard's face.

"Ah, George … busy as ever I see. The garden's looking damn fine as ever," Amos turned to see the Colonel approach; he was out walking his beloved Labrador Bertie.

He couldn't remember when it was the Colonel had begun using his first name. After he'd taken over from Hargreaves maybe?

"Thank you Colonel, nice morning," Amos replied.

He stopped working as Willoughby came over and listened as he made small talk. After a couple of minutes the Colonel said: "Right, I'd best leave you to it," and went on his way.

After a couple of steps he stopped, turned and added: "Oh, erm listen George … don't let anyone come near the stable block after lunch. I've offered to show young Maggie the horses."

Amos saw him smile as he turned and walked away. His instinct was to run up behind him and smash a spade into the back of his head and again his fury was abated at the thought of inflicting pain … today, it was going to be today.

He felt a wave of nausea wash over him and began desperately thinking what he could do to prevent it happening.

Two hours later and he was no closer to finding a solution as he trudged back up from the garden to the house where he let himself in and went through to the scullery.

She had her back to him and was scrubbing a large pan when she heard him walk in. Turning to face him she said: "I've got your lunch ready Mr Amos, it's some of the soup left over from last night's dinner. Mrs Walters says it's one of the best she's ever made."

He looked at her face, she was naturally beautiful and seemed to be permanently smiling. Maggie disappeared into the kitchen and emerged a few moments later with a bowl of steaming soup and a plate of fresh bread.

Amos was silent, he couldn't bear to make eye contact with her and sat with his head bowed eating his lunch.

"It's a lovely day out there Mr Amos. I sometimes wish I could work outdoors, though I reckon my father would have something to say about that", and he detected a slight giggle as she said it.

Looking up briefly from his soup bowl Amos said quietly: "Maggie, I've told you before, call me George."

He saw her smile at him again and his stomach churned as she said: "Ok ... George! Oh, guess what? Colonel Willoughby is going to show me the horses this afternoon, isn't that wonderful? When I was younger I always wished I could have a pony. I'm so excited.

"Mrs Walters says I've got to get all my jobs done first though so I'd better hurry up. Enjoy your lunch," she said, turning towards the door.

"Maggie ... wait," Amos said.

She paused and turned her head, "Yes George?"

He found himself fiddling with his spoon, twirling it around in his hand as he tried to think of something to say, anything that could save her.

"Look, just … just be careful. The Colonel has … well, he has certain ideas on how his staff should behave," he was struggling and he knew it.

"Oh, don't worry George. I love working here and won't do anything to spoil that. I'll be on my best behaviour at all times," she replied.

"No! no … you don't understand," Amos said, irritation evident in his voice.

"Listen, why don't you give the horses a miss today, I'll talk to Colonel Willoughby. I can take you down there one day," he said.

Before she could reply the Colonel's booming voice was heard before he appeared in the kitchen doorway.

"Nonsense George, I like to look after my staff. I've offered to show Maggie around and that's what we're going to do, now are you ready young lady?" he asked, smiling at her in a way that made Amos inwardly fume.

He watched helplessly as the Colonel put his hand on her shoulder and ushered her out of the back door and then sat there staring down at the table. He heard Maggie giggle as the two of them walked towards the stables.

His hands gripped the edge of the table and he sat there seething, unable to think rationally. He had no idea how long he sat there but eventually he made his mind up. He would not let this happen.

Pushing his chair back urgently he stood and was about to walk out of the door when a woman's voice said: "Don't be daft George, leave it be." It was Mrs Walters, the head cook.

Amos turned, the look in her eyes told him she knew.

"What? Do you know about this? What that bastard's doing?" he asked, raising his voice.

"It's nowt to do with us George. You'll only cause trouble for yourself if you go down there. Now, let me make you a brew before you go back to work," she said.

He was consumed with rage and flung his soup bowl and plate across the room, Mrs Walters flinching and putting her arms over her head to protect herself as they smashed against the wall. Then he stormed out of the scullery, slamming the door behind him.

The next hour was spent taking his frustrations out by working in the garden. He couldn't bear to be near the house and kept well away from the stables, though there was no escape from the images in his head.

He deliberately stayed away and it was late into the evening with night drawing in when he began packing his things away. Up ahead he saw movement, it was near the perimeter wall which ran parallel to the main road leading into the village.

He stood still, squinting through the evening gloom to get a better look. Moving closer, he picked up a spade leaning against a wheelbarrow. There were two figures, he could see them now. Taking care not to be seen or heard, he moved quietly.

As he got closer he recognised one of them and his heart rate dropped as the tension dissipated.

It was Simon Willoughby, the Colonel's youngest son. But what was he doing scaling the garden wall and who was that with him?

The two men had clambered over the wall and were now in the garden. Amos was about to shout in their direction when he saw the second man quickly unbuckle his trousers, letting them fall to the floor. He then watched as the young Willoughby sank to his knees in front of him.

Amos had seen men having sex before, on at least two occasions during the war. But this was different. He had no idea Simon was homosexual. The boy was only nineteen and, though he could be quiet and moody, the thought had never occurred to Amos.

He watched as Willoughby stood and turned around, his back to the second man. Amos now recognised his face; it was Norman Barnes, a married father of two who lived in the village. Amos had seen enough, he turned and began walking back towards the house. And then he stopped. He doubted the Colonel knew about his son.

There was a brief flicker of a smile on his face as he turned and walked purposefully back in their direction.

"Master Willoughby? Master Willoughby is everything all right sir," Amos shouted as he got to within full view of the two men. His voice startled them both and the older man looked at him in horror as he fumbled with his trousers, stepping backwards leaving Simon Willoughby exposed naked from the waist down.

374

"What the fuck? ... Amos, what the fuck are you doing ...," Willoughby spluttered, desperately arranging his clothing.

"I heard noises sir, thought it might be folk up to no good," Amos lied.

The older man turned his back on Amos and whispered something to Willoughby who listened before saying: "Err, listen Amos ... I ... I need to talk to you. About what you saw ... about what you think you saw."

Amos looked at him and smiled, replying: "My eyes have always been good Master Willoughby."

At that, the second man whispered something to Willoughby again before scurrying away quickly, climbing back over the wall and disappearing out of sight.

Amos watched him go as Willoughby approached.

"Look George," he said, referring to him by his first name for the first time.

"You've worked for my father for as long as I can remember. He likes you; you've been a very loyal servant over the years."

He was smaller than Amos and he looked up at him as he continued: "George, I want you ..." he paused before adding: "No, I'm sorry ... I mean, I hope you will show me the same degree of loyalty."

Amos was enjoying Willoughby's discomfort and relished the control he now had. He thought for a moment, deliberating not saying anything to increase the younger man's anxiety.

"Back in France I once saw a young Private beaten to within an inch of his life because one of the lads thought he was making eyes at him," he said, speaking quietly.

"His injuries were so bad they had to send him home. He'll never walk again. There was another lad, Queer Pete we used to call him. He got given all the shitty jobs like cleaning out the latrines, doing the night shift on watch, that sort of thing.

"Some of the lads used to force him to suck them off. They reckon he was killed because he deliberately stuck his head up over the parapet one night ... others say he was forced at bayonet to climb the ladder and look out over the top."

Even though it was getting darker Amos could sense the look of fear and unease on Willoughby's face.

"Does your father know?" Amos asked.

"What? No, good God no," Willoughby spluttered. "And he can't find out George ... it would mean ... well ... it would destroy him."

"Goodnight Master Willoughby," Amos said, walking away.

"George! George, can I count on your loyalty? Please George," Willoughby shouted. He couldn't see Amos' face but if he had been able to, he would have seen him smiling.

June 2015

It took more than an hour for them to cut him free. His legs had been crushed by the steering column and, though the airbags had deployed, the front of his car had completely crumpled, trapping him inside.

It was dark when they finally got him out, though the rain had stopped, and he was carefully laid on a stretcher and strapped in before being put in one of a fleet of ambulances, their flashing blue lights illuminating the scene.

The motorway had been closed in both directions and emergency vehicles were using the opposite carriageway to ferry the injured to hospital and get access to and from the crash site.

A dozen vehicles had been involved and, though the majority of injured were walking wounded, there were three who were seriously hurt - Tom was one of them.

His wallet and phone were retrieved by a firefighter from the wreckage and given to a police officer. That led to checks being made to trace relatives.

Within ninety minutes Emma had received a knock at the door from two police officers giving her the news. After frantic calls to family and friends to arrange care for Daisy, she was driven by them to her parents.

From there, she and her father travelled north, arriving at the hospital late into the night to find her husband critically ill in intensive care.

Because of concerns about swelling on the brain Tom had been placed into an induced coma. His left leg was broken, he had a number of lacerations to his face and three broken ribs. But the real worry was the extent of his internal injuries.

He'd been taken into theatre immediately on arrival where surgeons performed a thoracotomy to identify and stem the internal bleeding. That done, they reset his broken leg.

They were unable to do anything surgically for the swelling on his brain but after being taken into intensive care, he was put on a ventilator. That allowed a good flow of oxygen which was crucial to aid his recovery.

He was also given steroids in an attempt to reduce the swelling and other drugs to maintain adequate blood pressure and a normal heart beat. After that, it was simply a case of waiting to see how he responded.

It meant an exhausting, emotional bedside vigil for Emma and the rest of his family who sat helplessly as Tom lay still, his body attached to tubes and drips, the only noise coming from the rhythmic breathing sound of the ventilator.

On day three his parents brought Arthur to the hospital where he shared a tearful hug with Emma. He then offered to sit with him while Tom's mum and dad took her for something to eat and a change of scenery.

When they'd gone the old man found himself sitting next to the bed, tears in eyes, looking at his friend.

"There's a hell of a lot of people rooting for you lad," he said, his voice breaking as he struggled to hold himself together.

Leaning forward, he rested his arms on the bed and said: "You've got to pull through ... Emma and Daisy ... they need you lad ... we all do."

Chapter twenty four

August 1941

He was taking a huge risk, he knew that. But whenever he faltered he thought of Maggie, her ordeal at the hands of Willoughby and now, shockingly, heartbreakingly, the revelation that she was expecting a child.

They'd never talked about what she had to endure, though the look in their eyes when they saw each other told both that they knew.

The first time was the worst. He'd seen her again the next day, despite his efforts to stay away, and that in itself made him feel ashamed.

But he felt a hundred times worse when he looked at her, seeing a little girl lost, terrified and staring back at him with eyes pleading for help.

And then there was three days ago. He'd found her sitting scrunched up on the floor of one of the greenhouses, far away from the house, her arms clutched tightly around her knees.

She was crying quietly and the redness around her eyes showed a hollowness within. Amos knelt beside her, being careful not to touch her.

"Maggie, I'm so sorry, I truly am," he whispered.

Wiping her sleeve across her face she stared at him mournfully and Amos suddenly felt himself looking at her differently.

She didn't speak and, finding the silence awkward, he added: "I, I didn't think the Colonel was at home ... I mean, has .. has something happened today?"

"I'm ... I'm pregnant George. I'm more than five weeks late now ... I, I don't know what to do," she said, burying her head into her arms.

He could do nothing else but shuffle alongside, put an arm around her and then sit holding her as she wept.

Now, he thought of that broken girl as he stood in the darkness, not wanting to be seen as he waited for him to come into view.

He had no idea how long he waited, an hour maybe? But then he heard voices and saw four men emerge from the door of the pub. They exchanged words before one went in the opposite direction and the others walked towards him.

He watched them pass by, talking to each other before they paused, exchanged more words and then said goodbye, going their separate ways. Amos stepped out of the shadows and followed one of them until he got to the doorway of a small cottage.

Before he could open the door Amos quickened his pace to within a few feet and said: "I need to have a word with you Norman."

The man was startled and spun round to find himself confronted by Amos. In the darkness he had no idea who it was.

"Who ... who is this? What ... what do you want?" he said, the fear evident in his voice.

Amos stepped closer so the man could recognise his face.

"Do you remember me now Norman? Or were you too busy fucking Master Willoughby to remember my face?" Amos asked. There was menace in his voice.

"I ... I don't know ... I don't know what you're talking about ... you've got the wrong man, please, ... I" Barnes replied nervously.

"Don't waste my fucking time Norman. The only reason I'm here is because Master Willoughby sent me," he lied.

Barnes look puzzled. "What? He ... he sent you? I ... I don't understand."

"Let's go inside Norman, we need to have a talk," Amos said.

He could see that suggestion worried Barnes even more and, while he needed him to be scared, he didn't want him to do anything rash.

"Calm yourself, I don't want any trouble."

Barnes opened the door and the two of them stepped inside. The cottage was in darkness and Amos knew his wife and children were probably upstairs asleep.

"Master Willoughby doesn't think he can trust you Norman," Amos said, standing against the door.

"What? That's ... that's nonsense, why would I say anything? I've got my own family to think of," he replied.

"With all due respect Norman, he's got more to lose than you," Amos said. "He's concerned you'll ... well, that you may decide to use this against him one day."

Barnes looked aghast: "What? No ... never, I'd never do that. You think I want this getting out? I can't take the risk, I'll be ruined, my family."

Amos didn't reply, he was buying himself time ... time to think what to say next. He hoped and now knew Barnes was terrified but he needed him to have something on Willoughby, otherwise he'd have nothing to use.

Barnes seemed to take his silence as something more sinister.

"Look, I'll ... I'll do anything I can to help Simon ... I mean, Master Willoughby. Surely he knows that?" he added.

Amos seized on that comment.

"Well you tell me Norman, what reassurances can I give to Master Willoughby that your ... discretion ... can be counted upon?"

Barnes thought for a moment, his face a picture of fear and panic.

"I ... I have the letters he sent me. I'll ... I'll destroy them all," he replied.

Inwardly, Amos had to rein himself in, careful not to reveal his excitement at that comment.

"The letters? Yes, Master Willoughby mentioned those. He wants them back. All of them. That way he will know they won't fall into the wrong hands," Amos said.

Barnes got up from the table where he'd been sitting nervously. "Ok, yes, yes, of course. I've got them somewhere safe, I ... I can get them for you," he said.

Amos nodded and Barnes disappeared in another room. He was back a few minutes later holding something wrapped in cloth.

"These ... these are all of them. I ... I would never ... Simon ... he ... he must know I'd never betray him," Barnes said, tears in his eyes as he handed the cloth over to Amos.

"We ... we were supposed to meet on Friday. I ... I assume this now means it's ... it's over?" he asked, his voice breaking as he spoke.

Amos looked at him one final time before turning towards the door, saying: "Yes, Norman, it's over. Master Willoughby's got bigger problems than you to deal with now."

He waited until he was back at the house, inside his room. It was after midnight now but he was too excited to sleep. He got undressed for bed and then lay down and began reading.

July 2016

Fear and panic was etched across the old man's face as he was ushered out of the room by a female nurse who then closed the door.

Inside he could hear voices, speaking quickly, urgently, one of them issuing instructions. The door opened suddenly and another nurse appeared, rushing past Arthur, before a man dressed in a white doctor's coat dashed past him the other way and into the room.

In his haste he left the door open and Arthur stood looking in to see four clinical staff gathered around the bed. One of them was pressing buttons on the electronic machinery from which tubes and wires were attached to his friend.

Another was calling out random numbers, none of which the old man understood as he inched himself forward into the edge of the room.

The man issuing instructions was stood next to Tom and was holding one of his eyelids open as he shone a light into his eye.

"ICP is still rising," said the woman monitoring the digital displays above Tom's bed.

The clinician in charge frowned before replying quickly: "Open the ventricular drain and administer five milligrammes of dexamethasone."

Arthur didn't know it but the female nurse who had rushed past him out of the room, now dashed back in, shutting the door behind her.

He stood there in a daze trying to make sense of what had happened. He'd only been with him for a few minutes when suddenly one of the machines had started beeping loudly. The next thing he knew a concerned looking nurse had appeared who then pressed the emergency button above the bed.

"Arthur? What's going on, what's happening," the old man turned around to see Emma and Tom's parents hastily approaching.

"I ... I don't know love, they're in there with him now ... I was sitting talking to him ... then this ... alarm ... it went off ... they all came dashing in," he replied.

While Tom's father went off in an effort to find out what was going on, Emma paced up and down outside her husband's room, Arthur a helpless spectator sitting on a chair.

A few minutes later the door of Tom's room opened and they watched as he was wheeled out on his bed by the clinical staff and quickly taken down the corridor.

"What's happening? Where are you taking him?" asked Emma desperately.

The man who had been issuing instructions at his bedside approached Emma.

In his 50s, with short dark hair which was beginning to show signs of grey, he wore steel rimmed glasses and had his hands in the pockets of his white medical coat.

"Mrs Harris? My name is Andrew Dell and I'm the neurological consultant responsible for the care of your husband," he said, speaking softly.

"I'm sorry, I can't tell you any more at the moment; we need to take your husband into theatre immediately. His condition has worsened and we need to perform surgery as soon as possible.

"I'll speak to you again when I have more news," he added, before smiling sympathetically and hurriedly walking down the same corridor.

The next two hours were agonising. There was nothing they could do but wait and the four of them sat in a windowless room with soft cream coloured seats, a table littered with old magazines and a jumble of toys for younger children in the corner.

Emma hardly sat still and was continually pacing the room, texting family and friends and at one point breaking down in tears as she spoke to her mum.

Tom's dad made himself useful by fetching hot drinks from the cafeteria on the first floor. He also brought sandwiches but no one felt like eating.

Arthur felt helpless and at times wondered whether he was getting in the way. He didn't want to bother Emma but turned to Tom's father and said: "I don't think I should be here, if you could ring a taxi for me I'll leave you two alone."

But Emma overheard him as she fiddled with her phone and said: "What? No, Arthur please stay ... Tom would want you to be here and so do I."

The old man smiled warmly: "Only if you're sure my love, I don't want to be any bother," and at that she got up and hugged him.

There was a television on the wall of the lounge and Arthur sat gazing at it, watching the rolling news channel it was tuned into.

On the screen flashed the headline *Battle of the Somme Centenary* and a female reporter was seen speaking to the camera from a First World War cemetery.

"Exactly one hundred years ago today on the first of July 1916 almost 20,000 British soldiers were killed and another 40,000 injured on the opening day of the Battle of the Somme. It remains the bloodiest day ever for the British Army," the reporter said, as the screen showed grainy, black and white footage of soldiers going over the top.

"I'm here at the Contalmaison Chateau war cemetery in France where the bodies of almost 250 British soldiers lay, who died in the bloody fighting of the Somme," she added.

The volume wasn't high and Arthur found himself straining to hear as the camera panned out to show the reporter about to interview someone.

"Mrs Harris?" it was the voice of the consultant who appeared in the doorway of the room.

Emma sprang to her feet anxiously, Tom's parents standing next to her, his mother's arm around her shoulder. Arthur rose to his feet as the consultant said: "Why don't we step into this side room where we can talk privately," motioning with his arm towards the direction of a small room nearby.

"Are you all family?" he asked.

"Yes, these are Tom's parents and his great uncle," Emma replied, glancing at Arthur.

The four of them stepped into the room and all eyes were on Mr Dell as he sat them down.

"Now, as you know Edward sustained serious injuries in the accident and it was the bleeding on his brain which has been giving us the most cause for concern," he said, deliberately speaking softly and slowly to ensure they could absorb what he was about to say.

"Brain injuries can be problematic because they invariably lead to swelling. Because of the size of the skull there is no room for the brain to expand. This leads to pressure which can prevent blood from flowing to the brain and lead to oxygen deprivation."

The four were listening intently, holding each other's hand as they sat together. Arthur was struggling to understand what the consultant was saying.

"As you know we have been monitoring Tom very closely for the past few days. One of the reasons we placed him into an induced coma was to help reduce the swelling on his brain," Mr Dell continued.

"However," he said, now appearing a little nervous.

"I'm afraid his condition worsened this afternoon."

The consultant shuffled uneasily in his seat and leaned forward.

"The swelling got progressively worse and we believe that it began to push the brain stem down towards the spinal column."

Emma put her hand up to her mouth and became tearful as Tom's father asked: "What does that mean? Is he alright?"

The consultant continued: "We had to take him into theatre immediately and operate in an effort to reduce the pressure."

Emma was crying now as was Tom's mother, both women locked in an embrace to comfort each other. Arthur began trembling.

"Mrs Harris, we did everything we could to alleviate the pressure on your husband's brain, believe me we did. But unfortunately, the damage was too great and we were unable to prevent the deprivation of blood and oxygen flowing to the brain."

He paused and swallowed hard before adding: "Mrs Harris, I'm so sorry to have to tell you that your husband died a few minutes ago. Please accept my sincere condolences and those on behalf of this hospital."

The scream that emanated from Emma's mouth was something Arthur would remember in vivid detail for the rest of his life. The following minutes and hours were a blur and at times he felt like he was intruding on their grief.

It was a friend of the family who gave him a lift home from the hospital. When he closed the door of his house and was alone for the first time, he walked into the lounge and slumped in his armchair in the dark.

And there Arthur Roebuck sat and wept for his friend.

Chapter twenty five

August 1941

Amos was angry for feeling nervous but he couldn't help it. He wondered why that was and tried to dismiss it as adrenalin and excitement.

He knew the Colonel was home and he knew exactly where he'd be – in his study, where he always was between six and seven o'clock, before Mrs Walters served dinner.

Simon Willoughby was away; he'd deliberately stayed out of Amos' way since being discovered and it was another reason why Amos knew he had to do this now. In his pocket he had one of the letters, the others were safely hidden.

Walking through the house it suddenly occurred to him how big it was. He didn't hurry, he knew he was in control; but he was irritated because he couldn't help feeling nervous.

The door of the study was ajar and he could smell cigarette smoke. As he got closer he could see the

Colonel sitting in a high back leather chair reading a newspaper, smoke rising from behind it.

Amos tapped on the door and the Colonel lowered his paper: "Ah, George, not often we see you indoors ... come in, come in, what can I do for you?"

He entered the room, his mouth felt dry but suddenly the nerves disappeared. He was determined to relish this.

"Colonel, I want to talk to you about Maggie Roebuck," Amos said.

Willoughby appeared puzzled and folded his newspaper before getting to his feet.

"Young Maggie? Why? What's she done?" He asked.

"It's not what she's done; it's what you've been doing to her. And all of those before her," Amos replied.

A flush of red appeared on Willoughby's face but then he bristled and took on another demeanour, one Amos had not seen before.

"Now you just stop right there George. I'd be very careful before you say another word," he said.

"You don't frighten me Colonel and no, I won't stop. You're going to hear this," Amos replied, stepping forward to indicate he wasn't afraid.

"I've turned a blind eye long enough," and at that Willoughby's face was a mixture of shock and anger.

"But you crossed a line with Maggie. I've known her since she was a born, her father trusts me to keep an eye on her," Amos added, before he was suddenly interrupted by a laughing Willoughby.

"So that's what this is about. You fancy the pretty little thing too do you? I don't blame you George, she's young and fresh and you can have a lot of fun with that one. Go on, help yourself, tell her I said it's ok," he said, before adding: "Now, is that all?"

The dark thoughts returned in an instant, flooding Amos' brain. He had to use every ounce of self-control to prevent himself going for Willoughby. He wanted to hurt him, badly. Out of the corner of his eye he spotted an ornate paperweight on the desk and imagined himself beating Willoughby's face to a pulp with it.

"She's pregnant. And it's yours. Yes, that right," Amos said, as the smile disappeared from Willoughby's face, "you've got a 14 year old girl pregnant."

The Colonel quickly regained his composure: "Nonsense, the little tramp's obviously been putting it out across the village, it could be anybody's."

"No, it's yours. You've been raping her for weeks and now she's pregnant," Amos said.

Willoughby looked uneasy and walked towards the window, his back to Amos.

"I've told you George, you need to be careful what you say. That's an outrageous slur ... I won't be intimidated in my own house. Now, if it's true about young Maggie, well, she'll have to go, she can't stay here. I'll make the arrangements," he said.

"It's not going to happen like that," Amos said.

"How do you think her family is going to react when they find out? Her father's the vicar for Christ's sake," Amos continued.

"Like I said, it's not my problem George. Who's going to believe the little tart over me anyway eh? Answer me that?" Willoughby demanded, raising his voice for the first time now.

"You've got some brass, I'll give you that, Amos said. "But this is where it ends. Tell me, do you know what Simon gets up to in his spare time?"

The sudden reference to his son threw Willoughby who looked quizzically at Amos. "Simon? What's he got to do with this?"

"Do you know your son meets up with other men? And he lets them fuck him?" he said, deliberately accentuating the profanity.

"Your son's a homosexual Colonel ... there's laws against that you know," Amos said, savouring the look that appeared on Willoughby's face.

"What on earth? How dare you! You bastard, get out of my house," he said, raging now.

But Amos stood firm. "I'm not going anywhere Colonel," and he took the letter out of his pocket.

"This is a letter from your son. It's got his signature on the bottom," and he held it up for Willoughby to see.

"Let me read an extract for you," Amos added and he held the letter out in front of him.

"How I long to feel you inside me and to taste you as I look into your eyes," Amos said, looking up to catch Willoughby's reaction.

He continued: "I have been with other men before but I have never felt this way ... I am thinking of you constantly, your hands touching me, your ..."

"Enough!" Willoughby yelled and from the expression on his face, Amos could see he looked broken.

"There are plenty more letters like this," Amos said. "And I have them all. Now, do you still want to kick Maggie Roebuck out on the streets or do you want to atone for your sins Colonel?"

Willoughby looked across at Amos and asked quietly: "What is it you want?"

Amos felt supremely confident now. He walked over and sat in Willoughby's leather chair.

"She'll need money, enough to set her up somewhere. And there'll be no more young kitchen hands here at the house. You're going to have to get your fun elsewhere Colonel," Amos said.

Willoughby stood staring out of the window, his back to Amos.

"And in return?" he asked.

"I'll give you your boy's letters and I'll keep quiet about his ... preferences," Amos said.

"How do I know you'll hand over all the letters, that you'll keep your word?" Willoughby asked.

Amos smiled, stood up and said: "You don't. But it all depends on you Colonel ... you see Maggie right, stop molesting young girls and I'll keep my end of the bargain."

Willoughby went quiet and appeared to be thinking.

"I need some time to think," he said.

Amos walked towards the door. "You've got three days. And I want your reply in writing ... I need some extra insurance for when I hand the letters over."

Willoughby looked at him before adding: "If I do agree then it's the end for you too George … you'll have to go, you know that right?"

Amos paused in the doorway, turned his head and said: "Do you think I want to stay here for a minute longer than I have to?"

March 2017

He'd been coming every week, mostly on a Wednesday afternoon after spending the morning at the Legion.

Most of the time he'd get the bus up there and then walk the short distance to the entrance.

Usually, he'd have to sit and rest for a while on a bench just inside the gates; the drive leading up from the road to the crematorium at the top of the hill was long. When the weather was fine it was a beautiful place, high on a hill overlooking the city on one side and the countryside on the other.

But today, it was grey and overcast. There was rain forecast for late afternoon and it wasn't warm; but it never occurred to him not to go. He wouldn't let his friend down, not after everything he'd done for him.

Trudging up the drive he felt a few spots of rain and hoped it would stay away long enough so he could sit with him as he always did. At the top he passed the crematorium, unusually there was no sign of a funeral for a weekday afternoon, and carried on over the hill.

He passed the memorial garden which was still littered with splashes of colour from wreaths mourners had left.

And then he was there.

The headstone had only recently been laid, in view of having to wait for the grave to settle properly and the ground to be firm enough to support it.

There were always fresh flowers. He knew Emma brought Daisy every weekend and they would always leave them in a vase sunk into the ground next to the headstone.

"Hey lad, it's a nippy afternoon but a bit of a rain and wind's not going to keep me away," Arthur said, talking down to the ground.

"I'm a bit later than usual; there was a bit of a do for Jock at the Legion ... he had a win on the lottery, only a few hundred quid, but he wanted to buy everyone a drink and put a spread on for us all," he said.

"I told him that's the first time I'd ever known a Scotsman put his hand in his pocket," and Arthur let out a laugh. But then his face dropped and he looked sombre.

"I thought it'd get easier by now lad but it's not ... my beloved Anne and Maggie, they'd both lived long, full lives. It was sad but then death's part of life isn't it?" he asked no one.

"But you? Well, it makes no bloody sense. My old man could never explain it when people asked him ... though he'd try. All part of the good Lord's plan he'd say. Well, it's a bloody rubbish plan I reckon," Arthur added.

The raindrops were getting more frequent and Arthur drew up the collar of his overcoat and took an umbrella out of his bag.

"Right lad, I'll only be over there as usual, you know if I sit down here I'll never get up," he said, making his way over to a bench a few feet away.

Sitting down he opened his bag, taking out a bottle of ale and a cloth in which he'd carefully wrapped a glass.

Putting the glass between his legs he used a bottle opener on a key ring to open the beer and poured it.

"Cheers lad," he said, before taking a long swig.

He thought back to the days and weeks following Tom's death and how shocked Emma had been when she came to tell him what she'd discovered about his will. She had no idea he'd changed it a few months before his death asking for a burial rather than a cremation.

Arthur knew she was uncomfortable with the idea and she was also upset that he'd never told her.

"He probably thought he'd have plenty of time love," Arthur had said, trying to make her feel better.

The funeral was tough; they always were for younger people he thought. Daisy had been at the service but she was taken away by friends when it came to the burial.

Arthur then recalled standing in the summer sunshine watching Emma, supported by her parents, look close to collapse as her husband's coffin was lowered into the ground.

He finished his beer, wrapped the glass back in the cloth and put it and the empty bottle back in his bag. Then he stood and made his way back to Tom's grave.

"Right lad, I'd best be off. I don't want to get caught in this rain when it comes. Same time next week God willing," he added, before taking one final look at the black granite headstone below:

Edward Thomas Harris
Born 27th November 1986
Died 1st July 2016.
Devoted husband of Emma and beloved son of John
and Lucy Harris. RIP

Chapter twenty six

May 1944

Together they strolled across the beach, the water washing over their feet as the tide gently rolled back and forth. Once they reached the cliffs they began their ascent up wooden steps that had been constructed over the rocks.

At the top they paused to catch their breath before continuing on along the cliff top. The remains of the Abbey loomed large and they could see the graveyard and St Mary's Church perched high above the town.

Halfway along they stopped and Amos put down the picnic basket and opened it, unrolling a blanket which Maggie then sat on.

"I love it up here George, it's so beautiful," she said, her eyes gazing out to sea.

Amos lay on his side, putting the weight on his right arm which cradled his head. He couldn't stop looking at her. At first he was disgusted at himself for thinking of her like that. He was nothing like the Colonel; he never would be.

But this was something else; something deeper, not simply something borne out of lust or physical attraction.

He thought back to when she'd come to him, confused, terrified and alone. He never expected her family to react the way they did. So much for the love, forgiveness and compassion her father preached he thought.

He'd found her sheltering outside the lodgings he'd managed to find on the outskirts of the village, after leaving the Colonel's employ. She was cold, hungry and scared and she sobbed as she relived the moment her father ordered her to go.

The familiar feelings of rage surfaced at the injustice and his first instinct was to confront Roebuck, the thoughts of physical violence never far away. But she needed him and he wouldn't leave her.

Instead, he took her in and that evening he told her everything, breaking down in tears on his knees in front of her as he admitted to knowing what the Colonel would do when she worked for him.

He had no idea whether she stayed because there was nowhere else to go or whether she simply forgave him, because it was never spoken of again.

Instead, he went on and told her about Simon Willoughby and his ultimatum to the Colonel. He remembered the look of shock on her face as he recounted the conversation the two men had in Willoughby's study.

Two days later he received the Colonel's letter of reply,

agreeing to his demands. Within a week they had gone, leaving the village early one morning for the long walk to the neighbouring town which the railway line ran through.

At the station he glimpsed for the first time a look of excitement and happiness on Maggie's face as he asked her where she wanted to go. Anywhere you'd like, he said, we have the money.

She gazed at a map on the station wall and looked deep in thought before saying: "The coast. I've only ever been to the seaside once. I'd love to go back."

Within hours they'd arrived in Whitby, the look of excitement on her face something he'd always remember. They spent their first night in a bed and breakfast overlooking the sea, both of them ignoring the contemptuous looks a pregnant teenage girl and an older man received.

Now, as he lay there looking at her, he sensed she was finally happy again. It had been weeks now since he'd found her sobbing, breaking down at random moments, unable to cope with it.

The worst period had been within days of giving birth. Torn between the love a mother has for her baby, she was wrestling with the disgust and shame she still felt for how her little boy had been conceived.

In the end, it was fortune that intervened; a passing remark from her GP at how his wife was unable to bear children. Together, they talked about it and it was Amos who made the overture, turning up one late evening as Dr Harris was leaving his surgery.

A few weeks later and it happened; Amos remembered the care and dignity they showed to Maggie on the day they collected baby John. From then on she had improved little by little, day after day.

Thinking back, he wondered whether it was now the fact that he began to see her for the young, vibrant woman she was and not a victim or someone to be pitied. He realised his feelings were no longer confined to a protective, paternal instinct.

No, they were ... love? Yes, he was absolutely convinced of it now. He was in love with Maggie Roebuck.

He knew she would never reciprocate; she didn't look at him like that. She was twice his age and she'd never once shown any sign that she had feelings for him beyond those of a friend.

"You've not eaten much, are you not hungry?" Maggie asked, as she picked at her food, the afternoon sun glistening on the sea, bathing the cliff top in dazzling spring sunshine.

"Mmm? What? Oh, no, sorry ... I've not much of an appetite today Maggie," Amos replied.

"That's not like you George Amos, I hope you're not sickening for something?" and for a fleeting moment he thought he saw a glint in her eye. When he looked back on this moment years later he never could find a reason to explain why his mind suddenly jolted back to the war.

He was marching proudly with Bill Dove, the two of them in their new uniforms, chests puffed out as the crowds cheered them on.

And then he was crawling in the dirt, petrified, even now able to feel the weight of Captain Harris on his back.

He saw Eddie Bousefield's face and heard him cursing; and his palms went clammy as he remembered hordes of German infantry rushing towards him.

He remembered the officer pinning a medal on his chest and then recalled throwing it into the sea from this very cliff top; Maggie standing next to him, holding his hand, knowing why he had to do it.

And then he recalled vividly wanting and hoping to die ... and he remembered how desolate that felt. And he vowed to never feel that way again and to savour every single second of being alive.

Bill, Captain Harris, Eddie ... they would always be with him; they were part of who George Amos was now and they forever would be.

He felt his heart beating faster, a surge of adrenalin run through him and his stomach churned ... but in a way that excited rather than scared him.

"Maggie?" he said, reaching out and taking her hand.

She gazed into his eyes and he saw a look that told him he had nothing to fear.

"Maggie, there's something I really need to tell you."

The End

Author's acknowledgements

If the old adage that 'everyone has a book in them' is true, then I guess this is mine. For obvious reasons I refrained from announcing to all and sundry that I'd begun writing a novel. It was much more satisfying being able to declare 'I've written a book' when it was completed.

Because of that there are few people to thank, though that in no way diminishes my heartfelt gratitude to those who helped me get this far.

Firstly, there are the authors who introduced me to this extraordinary time in our history. These gifted storytellers were privileged to meet many of the remarkable men fortunate enough to survive the slaughter on the Somme and, in some cases, the battles that followed.

I was inspired and awed by the work of Lyn MacDonald, Martin Middlebrook, Max Hastings, Barbara Tuchmann, and many, many more.

The genesis for *Shadows of the Somme* was born out of my frequent visits to the battlefields and war cemeteries of Belgium and northern France. It is there, while walking among those endless rows of headstones, that you yearn to know more about the names carved into the stone.

It is for that reason I wrote the story of Captain Harris and George Amos.

My thanks go to my former colleague Jo Hall for her proof reading skills for which I'm hugely grateful.

And of course my beloved wife Jo and my family for their unwavering love and support. I love you.

Printed in Great Britain
by Amazon.co.uk, Ltd.,
Marston Gate.